# Monomania, Mon Amour

A TenGuKru book

ISBN: 9798704222316
Imprint: Independently published

Cover design and artwork by: Adrian Stranik
Struck Dead font from the Cumberland Fontworks

Library of Congress Control Number: 2018675309
Printed in the United States of America

*To my worlds, Charlie, Tallulah-Mae and Reno...*

*... and all the visionaries lost to history's asylums.*

# CONTENTS...

*He that was dead came forth, bound hand and foot with grave clothes; and his face was bound about with a napkin. Jesus saith unto them, Loose him and let him go.*

*John - Chapter 11 Verse 44*

# 1. ARBUCKLE

**1957**
**Sunday December 8th**
07:04

Wan morning sunlight filtered between the thick velvet drapes and fell across the swollen purple face of Diane Stevenoski. Bug-eyed and exhausted with slow death, her teeth held her black tongue out on display as a big dusty fly twitched and jerk-explored its dry tip.

The body knelt in the middle of the room suspended by a web of nylon ropes and pulleys. Piano-wire, tangled in the chandelier, descended from the high ceiling, culminating in a ligature around her neck. She was naked but for a leather garter around her leg and a brassier twisted around her waist. Her heavy abdomen threw an apron of shadow down over her thick thighs.

Leonard Borg scanned the plush royal red of the Presidential Suite of the Roosevelt Hotel and absorbed its opulent desolation, the gigantic mirror; removed from the wall and placed in the middle of the room beneath the dead woman; the overturned furniture; broken ornaments and empty liquor bottles; the movie camera on its tripod and discarded costumes. He moved over to a low table of heavily lacquered tobacco, ignored the empty drug vials and picked up one of three copies of the same black leather-bound book: *La Philosophie De La Boudoir* by the divine Marquis. He flicked the pages and stopped them at random. His small eyes narrowed to pinpoints as he read,

*'Frenchmen! One more effort if you wish to be republicans!'*

The suite was warm, muggy with the smell of sweat and urine. He fanned himself with the slim volume, undid the buttons of

1

his heavy coat and loosened his tie. He stooped to regard the grotesque stupidity of the dead woman's face then her young husband John, the son of Senator Cornelius Stevenoski, breathing heavily as he lay face down on the carpet wearing only his grey socks. Borg looked at John's shiny scrotum crushed between a red silk cushion and his scrawny body. Those balls, he thought, have a lot to answer for.

He knew about their thing! That John and Diane's *thing* is cartoons. He's got a thing for Betty Boop; she goes for big dogs, and judging by the leather dungarees on the floor, Goofy in particular.

The redhead, on the chaise with her bare feet on John's back, was zonked to horse town. Fresh scabs inside her forearm declared it. Her scarlet velvet dress was up around her neck, a brown rubber dildo on her lap. Another identical one lay in her limp hand.

Borg felt a painful twinge up the left side of his distorted jaw. For a moment his vision lost its depth of field, and everything appeared as a flat picture, inches from his face. This, he knew, was a prelude to one of his migraines. It wasn't the hideous-ness of this scene that was about to induce this mind crush: this was Angel City, and he was all about this scene or ones just like it.

No.

It was the colours.

A surreal vista of red—too much red and white and brown.

Like meat and bone and shit—this room, pale flesh and rubber—an abattoir of deviance.

The quicker the fix was in, the quicker he could be out of here.

He knelt reverently before the redhead, pulled the dress down over her grazed knees, touched her face. A fatherly gesture.

With a start, she looked at him with something close to consciousness, but her eyes rolled back again, lost in space.

'Quite a party you've had here, Mr. Stevenoski,' Borg muttered.

John Stevenoski groaned and farted.

Chauffeur Lee haunted the door. It was he who had raised the alarm—called Borg at his Glendale apartment at 05:56—told him they had an 'Arbuckle at the Roosevelt.'

Chauffeur Lee moved towards the window.

Borg stood up, went behind the chaise, and said, 'Leave the curtains alone, Lee. Check that camera for film.'

Chauffeur Lee did as he was told; removed the film from the big Bolex and handed it to Borg. Borg pocketed it and then positioned himself behind the redhead; gripped her chin with one large hand; placed another across her forehead; whispered, 'De beaux rêves, mon amour,' and, with a loud crack, snapped the life out of her. He released her limp corpse, which lurched forward, landing face-first in the middle of John Stevenoski's ass. She twitched twice and shuffled it off.

He'd seen her around. She was one of Jo Jo's girls. Her disappearance would not be problematic. He flexed fingers and glanced blankly at Chauffeur Lee who feigned nonchalance. It wasn't as if the chauffeur hadn't witnessed this process before. Borg clicked his neck with a violent jerk, came around the chaise, and pushed the redhead's body off Stevenoski with his brogued foot.

'Help me get this daffy bastard in the other room.'

Borg grabbed the unconscious man's wrists. Chauffeur Lee grabbed his ankles. They carried him to the nearest bedroom and dropped him on the bed.

Borg's commands came on autopilot, 'Call clean up. And I want to proof-read whatever our blurb boys come up with for the wire—before sundown!'

'What about the other girl?'

'What?'

Chauffeur Lee's feigned nonchalance was just that—feigned. His suppressed panic had obliterated all rational thought amid this cover up. He swiped one of the photos off the floor—one of the glossy eight by tens scattered around—and handed it to Borg. 'There was another girl.'

Borg studied the photo. 'You got a name?'

'That's Peggy Deveroux.'

Borg drew a blank. '*Elaborate.*'

3

'She's a Playboy model.'

The photo was of a black-haired woman—a beauty, no question—in fancy lingerie; a gimp-ball in her mouth and suspended off the ground much like Diane Stevenoski still hanging in deathly repose out in the lounge.

Borg held the photo up. '*This* look like a Playboy spread to you?'

Chauffeur Lee elaborated further about how he picked her up from the airport when she flew in from N.Y. on Tuesday; and about the Rockcliff bungalow where he took her to one of Howard Hughes' old fuck pads; and how he picked her up and brought her here with the redhead last night.

Borg flipped the photo and saw it—a hand-stamped PO BOX number. Material of this ilk—bondage shots—tended to be *'by private special request'*. He handed it back to Chauffeur Lee.

'Trace this PO. I want the peddler's name and address. Make your calls from the lobby.'

Chauffeur Lee disappeared fast.

Borg went into the bedroom where Stevenoski continued to fart and groan. He slipped off a glove, grabbed the bedside phone and made calls... to his LAPD hotline. Told them to get a man over to the Rockcliff address. 'Hold anyone you find there and call me.'

All Hughes' places are wired-for-sound, so he called the Romaine Street Exchange—a second-line repository of any, and all, calls going in and out of Uncle Howard's residences. Borg gave them his ID code and ordered the calls-register to and from the Rockcliff address. They gave him three numbers—two to the same number in New York, one to Miami and another to a local taxi firm... two hours ago.

He called his wire tappers in N.Y. and Miami. Gave them the numbers and told them to call him back with anything that went through them. The Romaine Exchange called back: a Taxicab had dropped Deveroux off at L.A. International an hour ago. Both N.Y. calls were to a number registered to a P. Krane.

Chauffeur Lee returned with the name behind the PO Box— Film Fan Fotos, New York, owned by I & P Krane.

*And* her address via her agent, William Morris. Ditto N.Y.

Bingo.

Within two hours Borg was in the air, flying non-stop from Hughes' private Culver City airfield. He slept fitfully. Touched down at Floyd Bennett, New York, eight hours later—local time, 17:55.

As they landed, 'clean up' radioed him a Manhattan address. He dropped two dexies and got with it.

The staff car waiting on the tarmac took him through bleak Brooklyn neighbourhoods, under the East River and to a four-story walk-up on 46th Street. First, he made a call from the booth across the street.

Her plane had been delayed in Chicago.

Borg's huge frame ascended the final steps and onto the third landing. He found her door. Knocked lightly and listened. Silence prevailed. He skeleton'd the lock and stepped inside.

The dying light filtered languidly through the half-closed shutters. The sound of a saxophone, Borg guessed, from two floors down, enveloped the moment. He didn't much care for that Bebop shit but the bleats and squeaks seemed to punctuate the rumble of 46th Street traffic and the arbitrary nature of his hunt.

Floorboards creaked as he entered an area encompassing a lounge and kitchen—two brown armchairs, a dining table and another two chairs—wooden. Sears catalogue junk... enough houseplants to start a greenery. Even the artist's draftsmen board fitted to the windowsill was fauna-filled.

Over the sink, a calendar, open to the month of November, dates busy with red rings and scribbled notes until the 30th... then nothing. A pin board, covered with postcards from Key West and Nashville; family shit, along with a lobby card of Gregory Peck from *Designing Woman*; a bunch of unpaid bills in the centre of the board stuck with a hairpin. A low coffee table in the lounge—on it a stack of well-thumbed movie magazines.

He went to the window, absorbed the view—her view, her 46th Street, her New York.

5

Odours suggested her—implied her rhythms—how she moved, her tempo, the veracity of her motion. He went to the bedroom where discarded brassieres, corsets, nylon stockings, a shirt and three cheap dresses were strewn across the bed.

He got undressed leaving his suit and heavy coat in an ordered pile on the edge of the bed. He pulled on a pair of her panties—baby blue silk. He was no fag but total absorption was central to his method. He regarded himself in the full-length mirror. He didn't see a huge man with small black watery eyes, oily black hair, a scarred jaw and thin lips - no large muscular stomach and thick legs. He saw surgically plucked eyebrows. He saw her little-girl-lost pout.

He saw her.

He saw her tiny waist and those 'dead men's' curves. That contrast of cream flesh thighs and black stocking tops... and beyond it?

Oblivion.

Naked but for the panties he went to the adjacent bathroom with its cracked black-and-white tiles—a deformed chessboard. He dropped to his knees in front of the pan and examined the spotless porcelain... pristine... not a stain.

The panties tightened as his prick stirred into semi-consciousness.

*Was this girl next to godliness?*

He inhaled deeply. The odours took him through the dimensions... back a week, to her frenzied packing. Her last meal here... He detected coffee, he detected pasta... chicken...

A health nut?

Get inside her...

He went back to the lounge, sat down, watched the door... and waited.

# 2. THE THIRD GIRL

### 21:58

Hollywood had not gone well for Peggy Mae Deveroux. The funk of failure clung to her like a dying ape and, by the time she emerged from the arrivals lounge at Idlewild, it began to stink like one.

Hillie from the agency got the wire last Monday and called her immediately. 'RKO requests a screen test.' They took head shots three years ago and only *now* they're getting back? But hey, '*RKO requests a screen test.*'

Someone was sending those death threats again and they were piling up. She received another one only last week. Getting out of town had never been so appealing! She told Hillie, *yes*, and cancelled shoots for the next two weeks.

She took a direct from N.Y and landed at L.A. International, 5pm, Tuesday. A limousine collected her and dropped her at the entrance of a leafy stucco bungalow on Rockcliff Drive—up in the hills, near the sign. On entry, a phone call greeted her. The voice was cheerful, maternal—told her to make herself at home—to await further calls.

Pages of scenes awaited her, placed in mannered piles on the coffee table, from screenplays she assumed were yet to see celluloid.

She spent the first morning learning the lines. She played with the delivery; riffed on all the exercises she learned at Herbert Berghof; their mantra, *'Don't think of the white bear'*, echoing across the continent.

A maid and a cleaner turned up that afternoon—both Hispanic. They spoke, if pressed, bad English. They 'noo naaarthing...'

More calls telling her to await more calls. She couldn't leave and explore the Promised Land that lay beyond the window for fear of missing the big one.

She sat in the sun on the balcony lounger and tried to envision the stars finally aligning for her beyond the California blue.

7

She was thirty-four now.

Old.

Last chance saloon.

It had been twelve years since the last time she was in Hollywood for that farcical screen-test for Fox. A decade of being the country's hottest pin-up paled against the salvation of movie immortality. If someone had told her back then that it would be this long before she'd get another shot, she would have jumped right in that ocean.

Thursday morning, a delivery boy brought groceries. She asked him to bring a paper tomorrow, more for the conversation this brief exchange garnered than for any genuine desire to know what the world was doing. He said he would and was on his way.

The fridge and the larder were fully stocked. She ate… but not too much. She went over her lines, slept through the afternoon, went over the lines again and received another call - the same voice, checking in that she was comfortable and whether she needed anything. She had everything she needed and nothing she wanted. She held her tongue and said only that she was very much looking forward to the audition.

She called Patty a couple of times – just to hear a familiar voice. She sounded distracted and beleaguered. She called Beatie in Florida. Another visit was well overdue.

By Friday evening, after another day of light snacks, a snooze and Stanislavski, she had gone beyond the point of suspecting some kind of hoax when, finally, she received the call that said 'tomorrow night, ten O'clock, a car will come for you—it's an informal meet and greet, so relax. Just… look incredible.'

And she did…

Double-breasted and clutching his cap, the same chauffeur who had collected her from the airport on Tuesday was already waiting with the limousine passenger door open.

Peggy emerged from the bungalow and out onto the steep, deserted road in a dark green taffeta cocktail dress and court shoes. She had ignored the vast collection in her size that she found hanging in the wardrobes and wore the one she had brought from Saks, especially for this: the day she may just have been born for! It wasn't a Dior, but unless you really knew your stuff, it rung dead. Her hair shone gunmetal under the streetlights. She felt submerged... a dream from 50,000 fathoms. As she approached the silver science-fiction shark of a limousine, she saw the other girl, a redhead, watching her from the back seat. She reminded Peggy of Jane—Jane Prince—another model from Igor and Patty's Film Fan Fotos stable.

Peggy lowered herself onto the cream leather interior of the car and smiled at the girl next to her. The redhead wore a bona fide red velvet Dior pencil dress—with nails painted dark blue.

The driver carefully closed the door, silencing the high squall of chirping crickets, and replaced it with a roaring blast of conditioned air. Nifty as a squirrel; neat steps took him around to the driver's side. He got in, flipped his cap on.

With a sigh and crunching gravel, the car lurched onto the winding road and descended into the balmy Hollywood night.

The redhead turned towards Peggy, folding a leg beneath her, revealing thigh. 'You drinkin'?'

Peggy smiled that smile, 'I don't, no. Thank you.'

The redhead was a traffic stopper, but Peggy had her down: 'LOST LUGGAGE' should have hung over her like a neon sign.

The girl rummaged through the cocktail cabinet in front of her. Glass clattered. The blue nails with the red dress jarred more. They suggested sudden changes of scenery. Fast exits.

Peggy asked her, 'Do you know anything about this soiree? I'm kinda mystified by the whole thing.'

The redhead's nose wrinkled liked she had just been poked in the face but continued her noisy search.

'Soiree?'

'This meet and greet with RKO?'

The redhead finally produced a Remy miniature. 'Oh, I don't know about *that*, honey. Didn't Lucille Ball just buy that studio? You an actress?'

The chandelier of the Roosevelt lobby hung above the noisy crowd like a diamond flying saucer. Peggy stood with the redhead in the foyer while the chauffeur exchanged hissed info with the bellhop. The ceiling was high enough to warrant a surrounding first-floor balcony, but, somehow, the dimly lit ballroom offered only claustrophobia. The bandstand was no more than a plinth on which a ragged quintet massacred Stella by Starlight. The air was a smorgasbord of exotic colognes and Cuban cigars. Over by the fountain, a crowd of unshaven Hungarians—lousy with Martini-fuelled bonhomie—clinked tall glasses. 'A toast! To all the invisible artists of the world's asylums!'

Peggy had envisioned moments like this all her life; now, like a mass epiphany, they all seemed to parade before her like prizes in a television game show. Outside, she had just seen Farley Granger handing his keys to the carhop. Kirk Douglas nodded a vague hello to her in mistaken recognition as he passed her on the way to the men's room. She realised that the heavy-set man in the sharkskin suit, quarrelling with a photographer at a table in the corner, was Robert Mitchum. Wasn't he a friend of Howard Hughes? Could Hughes, the great American hero, be here?

The chauffeur beckoned the two women across the mayhem of the foyer to a gleaming brass elevator. It took them up to the twelfth floor. They followed in silence until, along plush carpeted corridors, they came to a door with no number.

The suite within was huge. Its outer reaches a matrix of shadows. The chauffeur seemed to dissolve into them as a woman, like an over made-up doll, emerged smile first.

'I'm Diane. Please, take a seat and make yourself comfortable.'

The redhead had already done just that; fixed herself a highball, planted herself at the baby grand and padded out a discordant *My Funny Valentine*. Clearly, she knew the drill.

Peggy took an X-Chair by a large window where the curtains were drawn.

Diane moved to a small bar in the corner. 'Peggy, let me fix you a drink... what'll it be?'

Peggy asked for a soda. She matched the woman's voice with the one on the phone that had been calling her at the bungalow all week. The woman's bizarre costume suggested there would be some kind of audition after all. Peggy's eyes had adjusted to

10

the meagre light, and she realised Diane's black and curly hair was a wig. The makeup was cartoonish, and the leather garter on her thigh was tight enough to cut into her leg. The penny dropped and she realised Diane was supposed to be a come-to-life Betty Boop.

Diane set the drink down on the low table in front of her; next to a pile of curled eight by tens; Peggy's bondage shots; the ones she did for Patty and Igor *by special request*... she had never seen *those* pictures in the cold light of day; never beyond the confines of the Krane's studio, but here they were in the hot night of this suite.

*Red stop sign...*

Diane clasped manicured hands and said, 'Oh, Peggy! Our dark angel! Johnny will join us in a moment. We are *such* fans; I can't tell you! Peggy, are you familiar with De Sade?'

Peggy eyed the big 16mm Bolex in the corner. Actors and directors spooled through her mind's eye. De Sade was not among them, and when 'Johnny' appeared suddenly at the bedroom door, she knew he wasn't among them either. His entire body was encased in black plastic. His face was covered with some kind of gas mask. With the long tail behind him he looked like a giant nightmare rat. Only his fat pecker was visible as it hung from an opening in his leather dungarees. He swung it from side to side then bowed low and announced in a muffled growl, 'Come kiss me my killer, for I adore you...'

*Red stop sign...*

The death threats...

Could these whack-jobs be the perps?

She didn't wait for the rest.

That big brass elevator descended painfully and slow. She wished it would just keep on going, straight through the planet and into outta space.

And now, nearly twenty-four hours later, her taxi from the airport ascended the Midtown Tunnel. The RKO ruse chewed into her relentlessly and, like that big brass elevator, failure descended. Failure that began to decompose into fears.

She scrutinised the streets as they approached her apartment block. It was gone eleven now and she felt the night-time air tighten.

'Stop! Pull over.'

The driver answered with an under the breath expletive and jerked the car to a halt.

She peered from the back of the darkened cab; at the area around the entrance doors; cars parked out front... passers-by... She slid down in her seat, furtively scanning the third floor, calculating which apartment windows were hers. She located her blue curtains and watched carefully at the void between them.

Movement.

A trick of the light?

Her vision refocused. And there! A figure stood squarely at the window. Her blood ran hot-needles. She kicked the back of the driver's seat. 'Go! Go go...'

The driver sucked enough breath to say 'Lady—'

'Just drive,' Peggy told him. 'Now!'

Her connection had been delayed in Chicago. She should have—*would have*—been home by now. Feds had already grilled her twice. Young FBI agents waving photos in her face—camera-club nudes of herself that she had not even seen. And then the death threats—warped fantasies of gynaecological dissection. The cops said it was some kid who lived up the block. She never believed it, and now tonight there was somebody waiting in her apartment.

She lammed it at a cheap room on 34th—the edge of Hell's Kitchen. There was a pay phone in the hall.

She made calls.

She got Beattie.

She decided on an exodus south.

Like pronto.

Like, that very morning.

Twilight hours dragged themselves to an anaemic dawn as she perched on a stool at the window. The city twinkled with untold horrors. Eyes were out there searching… eyes of persons unknown. She picked at the grime caked into the window's seals. At the end of a hallway, in the building across the street, was a sign that glowed like radiation—EXIT.

# 3. EXIT

I t was 03:00 now. Borg got dressed, put the panties back on the bed as he found them, and got out of there.

He hit the phone booth across the street again and checked on those numbers she'd used in L.A. He hit pay dirt. Deveroux had called some dyke photographer in Miami. She was going south to top up her tan. Gave up the train times and everything.

Beautiful.

Leonard Borg, however, was not going to Miami. He'd already followed this tramp across the country. He had no intention of chasing her to Florida.

Giant flies and alligator shit?

No siree-bop.

### Monday December 9th
07:07

The voice, nasal export-Hoboken, crackled through horns, *'Atlanta, track nine, track nine. Atlanta, track nine, track nine...'*

Under a bunch of illuminated orbs, Borg stood with his eyes closed tight in an attempt to filter out the aural pandemonium of mid-morning commuters. The screeching and breaking of distant Pullmans, arriving and departing, reverberated around the vast cavern of the Grand Concourse of Pennsylvania Station. Constructions of this immensity unnerved him. They messed with his perception. Twenty-four hours of cross-country chase and stakeout were taking his edges off. Borg popped another two sharpeners and got with it. His kid-gloved hands dug deep in the pockets of his overcoat. He rotated his

13

thumb tenderly over the button of his switchblade. To the noisy hordes of station workers and travelling salesmen Borg was just another passenger waiting for his connection. But he wasn't a passenger, and he had no desire to connect.

He was waiting for her.

He knew she wouldn't make a grand entrance through the sun-drenched main concourse doors and descend the even grander stairs.

No.

She would come in through one of the side tunnels like the rat she was—wearing, he guessed, a scarf to conceal those giveaway black bangs. Or a hat? No, it would be a scarf. Once she was inside it would be goldfish and barrel time.

He had always suspected that there was something supernatural about women like Deveroux—something inherently evil about women who would allow themselves to be photographed like *that*—like the photos at the Roosevelt. In his line of work, he'd seen men's worst excesses committed to celluloid. He'd seen Tijuana snuff extravaganzas. So, in the grand scheme of the stag film game, a few bondage shots were kid's stuff. But nevertheless, it was venal, and it was sick.

'Sir, are you alright?'

Borg opened his eyes with a start. In front of him stood a fresh-faced cop—mere days out of training, he surmised. It took him a moment to reoccupy his body and say, 'I'm fine, thank you, officer,' when in a zepto-second he realised everything had changed. His heart pumped permafrost.

She was here!

*'Miami, track fourteen, track fourteen. Miami, track fourteen, track fourteen...'*

The light she had around her was an antenna presenting danger like a red stop sign, and as she entered the ornate doors of Penn Station in a thick black coat and a red scarf to conceal her giveaway oil-black bangs, she saw that red stop sign again—in Panavision.

14

That man—big—standing ten feet away from her platform turnstile in a camel coat and derby—seemed to jerk and twitch as if badly superimposed onto reality as the pedestrian chaos around him over-cranked into slow motion. She saw to her horror that his gaze seemed to roar across the vast expanse of the station concourse—into her—his face pale and featureless—two small black holes where his eyes should be.

*Hot needles...*

As she backed towards the entrance, the big man suddenly leapt into action and was coming her way—his deformed jaw tight with determination.

Out on the street, a miracle yellow cab screeched to a halt in front of her. She kneed her case into the back seat and flung herself in after it. 'Harlem!'

Borg side-stepped the cop and bustled his way through the crowd towards the stairs. His legs tangled. He stumbled and fell over a kid on a tricycle, taking a teenage girl with him. They all hit the floor with a smack. The kid began wailing and the girl scrambled for the contents of her spilled-out handbag. Borg was back on his feet with a speed uncanny for his bulk and cut through the crowd like a torpedo through the Pacific.

Out into the glare, his sight locked on his target across the bedlam of 8th Avenue. Of all the lousy luck a cab pulled up right in front of her. In the split second it took for panic to propel him into the road, Borg knew he'd made a mistake. Immediate events confirmed it. The wing mirror of a delivery van hit his shoulder and spun him into the path of a truck. And already it seemed like old news...

He blacked out for a second and was startled to find himself looking up at the growling underbelly of the huge machine. The stench of burning rubber and exhaust fumes jammed itself down his throat like a fist. The sequence of the last four seconds began to present themselves like a flicker-book action replay. He'd landed stomach first on the truck's right headlamp as his arm crumpled into the radiator grill—flew onward like a rag doll, momentarily embedded in the back of a sedan, before bouncing back in a shower of crushed glass into the path of the truck as it skidded to a halt—the huge tyres clipping his hip and popping his abdomen like a balloon full of Jell-O.

Her cab lurched forward.
 She dared not look back but eyed the rear-view mirror.
 A Commotion.
 A gathering.
 Horns raised in anger.
 Screams.
 Crowds congregating in the middle of the street.
 An accident.

## PART 1

# 4. A EULOGY FOR BOBBY MILK

**JOURNAL: MAY 1st, 1988**

**47 PITT STREET #6:** I've killed people. Two for sure, maybe three. No big deal. It was a long time ago. Eight years and in a land far, far away... It was my big score. And I hit big. The first was wanton teenage idiocy, during the Brooklyn riots. No rhyme, no reason. Human vandalism, really. To this day I have no idea whether my bullet found its target. But the other two... different gravy. The job was $20,000 for the both. I took the guns they gave me, shot the people they wanted, and they paid up without static. I'd been away a year but flew back to New York the next day.

What they didn't know about... was the other $250,000.

Like I say, that was eight years ago. That money is gone. But the original $20,000? I never touched it. Didn't trust it. Put it away and tried to forget it. I'm down to the last $1,700 of the two-fifty large. It's time to make good on my promise to the big adios. It's time... to check out.

## 1988
## Monday October 3rd
11.44am

I t was rent day.
First Monday of the month.
It was time to go to the bank.

Marco Mascini went to the wardrobe. Didn't need to pull the curtains. The bedroom was blacked out. Had been for years. He took a deep breath and listened. His ears trained specifically on the hallway outside his apartment door. Traffic from the bridge grumbled. This process of falling to his knees, unlocking this wardrobe, unlocking the floor within it, removing the case, and taking whatever cash he needed was performed like a religious rite.

He slit the end of the cellophane-sealed block with his switchblade and slipped out nine Bennys. He put the block back in the bag with his long-neglected journal—or confession—depending on what mood he was in on the rare times he thought about it; put it back in the steel case; spun the combination; placed it carefully in the hole in the bottom of the wardrobe and locked it. He piled the shoe boxes back on top then locked the wardrobe too.

The day had finally come.

He was almost down to that final twenty large. The twenty he swore he would never use.

But it was cold now… surely.

*This last twenty-thousand dollars* they knew about.

The *other* two hundred and fifty thousand he'd been living off all this time… they did not.

But it was all gone now so there wasn't a damn thing anyone could do about it.

It was his big score and he hit big. It bought him nine years but now it was time to come back to the world.

For the first time in nearly a decade he thought of the future. He was given to making wild pacts with himself. One of them was his promise to kill himself when the money ran out.

18

Embracing the straight life was unthinkable. It was the movies that helped him in moments of internal conundrum. So, he would see one tonight.

But soon he would have to die... or find a job.

Kuzma sat like a permanent fixture behind a Perspex screen, almost encased in lotto tickets and cigarette boxes in the convenience store next to the apartment block he also presided over. Marco assumed that the entire building, including the store, was owned by unseen powers, and that Kuzma was the interface between said power and Marco's tiny world. But who knew? Maybe Adrian Kuzma was the ruler of the little he appeared to survey. Kuzma was connected to the Russian mob over in Brighton. So, along with cheap steaks, discount booze and smokes, he also had the hotline to whores and narcotics. He was around fifty, looked like he was in great shape, thinly mustachioed, hair flecked white, alarmingly as if flanked by explosions. He had a penchant for Brioni suits, even when working the counter in this overstuffed convenience store. He did a few hours once a month—every rent day. He liked to touch base with his tenants and convey his availability.

Marco handed over the bills. 'Money, honey.'

Kuzma slipped them in a pocket without counting them. 'All good?'

'Yeah.'

'The boiler still making that noise?'

'Not for a week now. Seems to have rectified itself.'

'Well, if it comes back, you get Patel. It's what he's there for.'

'I will. Yeah.'

On the small black and white in the corner, the sound was turned down, but Ollie North and the Iran-Contra circus still loomed large. The beetle-browed Reaganite stooge held up a book, testifying to something or other.

Marco watched with a jaded eye. 'When's the world just gonna get on and fuck itself?'

Kuzma tunefully sang a line from that R.E.M. song—the one about the end of the world.

Marco's grandparents knew Kuzma's people from when they lived over in Brooklyn—always got along. Remembered the shashlyk cook-outs over at their big apartment in Little Odessa when he was a kid. They had a garden on the roof which, to Marco's childhood eyes, was some kind of sky-born oasis. Kuzma's uncle Rostislav was a main wheel—an avtoritet—in that neighbourhood, around which family, friends, and associates revolved accordingly. Nephew Kuzma had been Marco's gateway back to the world when he had returned from his travels nine years ago. Kuzma was only a fearsome presence if you were aware of his connections. On the surface—beneath which Marco which had no desire to submerge himself—Kuzma conveyed a lot of whatever the Soviet equivalent of joie de vivre was, along with impeccable dress sense. But Marco knew shit could go Stalingrad at the drop of a Tokarev with this seemingly amiable Russki. Soon after moving into the apartment, he witnessed the results of Kuzma's ire first-hand. It was on one of the rent days when he had popped into the shop and found some melon-head from the Gompers projects across the road, giving Kuzma some shit over the price of his milk. Kuzma let him carry on without response and let him vent. The guy was someone you saw around. A local fixture. Noisy. One of those idiots that seemed to need the acknowledgement of strangers, so played up to get it. After the milk incident, Marco only saw the guy one more time... with no teeth and a piece of his lip missing. After that he never saw him at all.

One of the kids Kuzma hired to run the store came in. Kuzma came around the counter to let the kid take his spot.

Marco asked Kuzma, discretely, 'I need to restock.'

Kuzma knew what he meant and inclined his head towards the kid. 'Patsan here will drop by tomorrow.'

Marco surprised himself when 'I might be looking for a job soon,' escaped his lips. 'If you hear anything that might be going...?'

With pale grey eyes, Kuzma appraised Marco's face as if searching for the right part of it to respond to.

'I'll call you.'

'You know I still don't have a phone, right?'
'This I know. '

Cinema Village was on 22nd East 12th and was a particular
favourite of Marco's—not a grenade's throw away from his
apartment. But now, it seemed, video was also killing the
movie star. Until very recently, this had been the place to bask
in the Technicolor glory of triple bills of cinematic nectar. Now,
the place was reduced to showing the same shit as the chain
cinemas up town—and only one movie to boot. This, Marco
thought, was yet another sign of the times—an era when being
a fucking idiot had been re-marketed as attention deficit
syndrome.

Tonight, was De Niro's new one, but even before the curtains
parted, Marco had a bad feeling about it. *Midnight Run* had
been out a couple of months and, as was always the case with
movies he intended to see, he tried to avoid the reviews. But
some unauthorised info had slipped through the net. Back in
the summer, a girl sitting next to him on the train had her
paper open and he couldn't help but notice something about
the new De Niro being directed by the guy who did the *Beverly
Hills Cop* movies. This drew him in, and it was too late before
the words HOLLYWOOD FORMULA and COMEDY seemed to
punch him in the throat. Ever since '76—since *Taxi Driver*—the
usual procedure was to be down front and centre as soon as a
new De Niro opened. But those words HOLLYWOOD FORMULA
and COMEDY had nipped at his heel, and it took until now for
him to bite the bullet and hope...

One hundred and twenty-six minutes later, the house lights
came up, the curtains closed, and Marco knew it was the end of
an era.

Emerging from the subway, Marco hurried back to his
apartment, past the closed department stores and 'grease-fest'
chicken emporiums and along the busy sidewalk for the five-
story 'walk up' on the corner of Pitt and Delancey. The street
descended to the building which stood forlorn and cornered by
Gompers, that grim housing project over the road, and the

21

Williamsburg Bridge—a million tons of unloved steel screaming at Brooklyn. It was an enclave where the brief silences between the squall of police sirens were a cause for alarm. His eyes watered as a gritty wind swirled around him as he turned the corner, away from the mundane intrigues of night-time commerce on East Broadway. The building's spray-canned entrance door was locked, as always. A fresh addition said, *DIE YUPPIE SCUM.*

He let himself in and lurched up the stairs, two at a time, to his apartment on the fourth floor. He carefully unlocked all three vault-grade Yales in turn. He shouldered the door open and stepped inside. It swung closed and locked itself behind him. He stood and let his ears search dark and unseen rooms. Silence reigned.

Happiness is an empty home.

He hit the light.

The apartment was a monument to Americana kitsch—like the 50s never ended but crash-landed like Buddy Holly's Beechcraft Bonanza into this small collection of rooms—a visage of ellipses and stripes, like the set of a life-sized cartoon. Framed photos of 'conked' negro singers, redneck rockabillies, cheesecake swimsuit models and vintage movie posters punctuated the pastel pink polka-dot walls.

Rows and rows of old vinyl records filled the shelves in the lounge, flanking an immaculate Rock-Ola 'Empress' jukebox which dominated the room. He took a quarter off the top, dropped it in the slot and pushed big buttons. Today would have been Eddie Cochran's 50th birthday. He had to play something. Mechanics whirred and flipped into action...

*... this dark, lonely street. Here am I, I walk alone; I have no love of my own.*

He made coffee, slapped honey on bread, and thought about Robert De Niro. *Midnight Run* was Tinseltown bullshit par excellence! From the opening sequence, with its 'sho nuff funky shit' theme and De Niro's Jack Walsh mugging and sending himself up and playing the game... the Hollywood game. *Mean*

22

*Streets*, *Taxi Driver*, *Greetings*, *Bloody Mama*, *Godfather 2*—
these were street movies—Rock-and-Roll generation kids
telling Hollywood to go fuck itself and, by extension, the world.
But with *Midnight Run*, De Niro had cashed in his chips, sold
his soul, pulled a Brando.

Rock-and-Roll was long dead, but movies had sustained him
like a life raft in an ocean of nothingness. Tonight, he was
drowning. It was like an oily black hand seeping up from the
subway, the sewers—its fingers engulfing the city... the
world... and sliding its fist down his throat to crush his heart.

He took the snack out onto the fire escape, set it down and
sparked a half-smoked joint.

The puddle-dashed street below was all but deserted, in stark
contrast to the Sturm und Drang of traffic which crawled and
growled high across the East River—a concerto of
precipitation and flue gas. But Eddie Cochran's baritone croon
from the lounge took edges off the chaos.

*Out of reach, out of sight, will I find her tonight on this dark
lonely street...*

He lived his life like a movie—like an extended 'Are you talking
to me' sequence. He walked and talked like he was watching
himself from the back row of some derelict picture house. He
was God's lonely man who spent hours perfecting that scene
from *Taxi Driver*—studying himself in the bedroom's full-
length mirror, catching himself in storefront windows,
squinting his eyes just enough until he could see Travis Bickle,
Jake La Motta, young Vito Corleone... The magic would only
fade with the rising of the sun when he would attempt to
sleep—an enterprise which would usually result in a few hours
of half-conscious fitfulness in his blacked-out bedroom. But by
the time he regained full consciousness there would be a
showing of something somewhere in the city, and he would set
off from his apartment for another day of monochrome and
panoramic dreams.

He kept every stub. Along with his neglected journal, which he
imagined would be made into a movie one day, these stubs

23

were his diary. All-nighters—triple bills... Lost in the transporting qualities of cinematic worlds, the final reels would roll, the house lights would rise, but his journeys home would be beatific.

```
Movies...
...they made him...
...more.
```

When he wasn't sleeping the days away, he'd spend afternoons standing in the centre of his living room just to see how long he could. He'd project his senses to the city around him and let untethered streams-of-consciousness take him where it would. He'd picture graffiti on other planets... Intergalactic urban discontent...

Space and time and distance obsessed him. He'd blow a morning looking at his big atlas. He would constantly grasp at random estimations of who was the nearest person to him that was listening to... Gene Vincent... who was wearing an item of clothing once owned by Elvis... the last stranger to visit Johnny Ace's tombstone...

Old rock and rollers obsessed him. Not the known biographical stuff anyone could find out. It was the unknowable that gripped him. This was the arena of freedom where fancy took flight. He'd sit opposite the Brevoort Building on 5th Avenue, where Buddy Holly lived out his final months. He'd carefully eye each balcony and tried to envision the young, doomed legend in a domestic context—perhaps staring out of the window, smoking a Lucky and looking at the exact spot that Marco himself would one day occupy—pondering on futures that would never come; of his making love to his Puerto Rican wife; of strange dreams of fireballs on the morning of his departure into the pantheon of mythology...

He would try to calculate, in various systems of measurement, the distance between the folds of his cerebral cortex and various objects in his apartment: the electric 3D Ava Gardner beach shot on the wall; the solid steel Mr. Peanut dispenser in the corner; the five-foot-high Tiki sculpture in the hallway...

He would mentally itemise all his possessions and wonder for how long their basic elements waited in the ground, or the air, or outta space before they were transformed from that material into their current state. How long they would remain in his possession? What would be the longest surviving article in his apartment? Who were the people who would one day own his record collection? His guns? Would they wonder who they had once belonged to? Would his stuff evoke him?

Once, he found himself face down on the rug asleep. He'd lost track of time and had no idea how long he'd stood there riffing on the endless cross-fade of his existential song. Until recently, he believed these rituals and obsessions were part of the self-development that comes with living life without clocks. Now, he began to suspect they were the symptoms of an unprecedented boredom; of his mind turning in to devour itself.

*Maybe this cigarette will help me to forget this dark lonely street...*

Mechanics whirred and flipped again. Silence reigned once more.

De Niro...
Robert... *fucking*... De Niro...

He took a final mouthful of the honeyed toast and washed it down with the cold coffee—a carb and caffeine eulogy. He thought about killing him. Going to Hollywood—finding the motherfucker—and giving him two in the head.

Robert De Niro 1943 – 1988 R.I.P.

# 5. UNDER THE BOARDWALK

**Tuesday October 4th**
6.13am

He'd fallen asleep on the fire escape and awoke to a dark and desolate morning. He reached for the half-finished blunt and ignited it. As he often did, he thought of Bonnie Rachanski—of their first night together when they'd fallen asleep together on this fire escape.

He played with the smoke in his mouth and watched a lumpy mulatto male in a Puffa jacket hanging around under the awning, on the corner opposite the parking bay beneath the bridge. There were three cars in the bay—a new Cutlass Ciera, a rusting hulk of a 60s Impala on bricks and Marco's car which languished in virtual storage under a heavy vinyl sheet.

Trotting with quick steps over the cross-junction, the thief approached the bay and turned, walking backwards at the last moment to scan the area. He let a steel rule slip down from his sleeve into his hand. It was at that precise moment he looked up and saw Marco watching him. The thief froze.

Marco's only reaction was a final suck on the joint and letting it fall from his fingers. The butt hit the fire escape railing below and died in a pathetic flurry of ash and sparks. His Remington 700 was behind the curtain and within easy reach.

Like a signal that spurred him to action, the thief turned, punched the rule into the Cutlass' door sill, tore it open and threw himself under the dash. In seconds, the car stuttered and lurched out onto the street. Marco could see the thief peering up through the rain-splashed windshield as he passed below him with his best *I know where you live* scowl. Marco met it with a grin and went to the head.

He stood, pissed, and stared absently at the framed *In person - Little Richard & His Orchestra* poster before him and wondered

26

if he really would have shot the kid if he'd gone anywhere near *his* car...

He climbed back out onto the fire escape and watched the traffic crawl over the bridge and imagined the scenario of the thief taking his car—boxed in—its progress speaking in inches. He pictured an absurd sequence of events where he would grab the gun and pummel the thief from this kitchen without hitting the car's bodywork, and his subsequent enquires to local screen-fitters to replace the driver's-side window for a black Tatra T 603.

He loved that car. A deformed 50s Cadillac. A Soviet bastardisation of Americana. It looked like a giant beetle getting ready to drop-kick somebody. He had it shipped over from Czechoslovakia. It belonged to a half-Czech/half-Italian model he'd had a marijuana-loaded dalliance with, in Prague. He remembered it one day. Called her. She still had it, so made her an offer she couldn't refuse. The cost of shipping it over was more than the car itself.

He took Bonnie out in it. They'd go driving just to be driving. Yeah, they christened it out in the woods upstate, on the hood, on four occasions... He hadn't driven it since she left.

He should have sold it or put it in storage but joked to himself that it would die without him. So, there it sat, shrouded, only its flattened whitewall tyres visible. Its presence became part of his morning ritual; black coffee, honey on bread and gazing at it from this fire escape.

The doorbell rang and jangled. He was surprised that it still worked. He couldn't remember the last time it rang. Whoever it was had come in the main entrance. He took the.38 from the drawer and hid it behind his back as he checked the spyhole in the door. It was the kid. Patsan? — from Kuzma's store, ballooned and distorted by the fisheye lens. He opened the door as far as the three chains would let him. The kid, olive-skinned and smiley, brought news. 'Mr. Kuzma says you should go see Mr. Kluge over at Coney Island.'

'Coney Island? Why?'

'Said to see him about a job.'

'See Mr.... Kluge? About a job at Coney Island?'

27

'That's what he said…' The kid handed over a small envelope. '… and to give you this.'

Marco knew it contained the weed he asked for and stuffed it in a back pocket. 'Did he say when?'

'Eleven this morning or tomorrow.'

'Same time?'

'Same Time.'

The kid turned on his heel and disappeared down the stairs.

Was he ready for this? A job? From a connected man like Kuzma, it could only mean one thing. It could only be criminal. But surely it wouldn't be anything *too* involved. Surely it would be some kind of sound out. A mettle tester. A dry run to see what he might be capable of. No one, not even Kuzma, knew he'd killed before, so if he passed any initial tests with flying colours, would… *could*… things escalate? And if it really came to it, could he kill again? Here? In the real world?

But no, this would be small-time stuff. Maybe helping to store or move hot contraband. No *way* would this be anything heavy.

He opened the envelope. A tight packet of Cali grass, as expected. He put it in the drawer with the gun. The cooker, the only visible timepiece in the place, said 6.25. The apple was stretching and yawning, and so was Marco. Clouds hung like bags of cement over the city and threatened to drop their rumbling guts. He had hours but, in the aftermath of last night's *Midnight Run* debacle, the concept of walking on the beach in a downpour appealed to him.

He exited Stillwell Avenue Station and headed for the beach. The amusement park was desolate at the best of times, but now, under this morning's concrete coloured sky, it pleaded for a quick and painless death from the wrecking balls.

The threat of heavy rain had not come to pass by the time Marco had trudged all the way to Brighton beach and back. The sun was beginning to scorch the edges of sky-wide grey clouds. He approached the boardwalk at Coney Island and saw a couple of homos under it disconnect from each other and march in opposite directions—one up towards the fair and the other west, away from him.

The Drifters—this was the very boardwalk they sang about. He tried to recall the words. Was there a fag subtext? This was a well-known haunt for such activity, albeit not usually at this early hour. Apart from the title, he couldn't remember a single word. Was it a Carol King song? Someone told him she made her first demo here—in a booth. He thought of the joke that Lieber and Stoller played on the King with Jailhouse Rock—the first gay anthem.

*You're the cutest jailbird I ever did see. I'd sure be delighted with your company. Come on and do the Jailhouse Rock with me...*

He walked around the closed park looking for a way in. He found an entrance between the wire fences where a surly quintet of carney types watched him as he approached. They told him where to find Kluge and watched him go find him.

The office was the third in a row of mobile cabins which had been dropped out in the weeds in the shadow of the 'world famous' Cyclone. Marco stepped up and into the cabin which he found empty. No sooner had he scanned the desk, littered with glossy condo brochures and two battered filing cabinets against the wall, that Kluge entered behind him.

'Apologies for the venue. It's temporary. The powers have yet to decide whether the resort has enough of a future to justify building a central office.'

Kluge was short, black, bald, and of indeterminable age. Dressed in stone-washed denim, Marco wondered what his ancestors—jungle-sussed warriors of polished ebony—might have made of him. Kluge dispensed with any further preamble and spoke like a white man. 'You Kuzma's boy?'

The question was assumptive to Marco's ears, but he said 'Yeah' anyway.

'You worked the rides before?'

'Rides?'

Kluge tilted his head towards the Perspex window. Marco realised he was gesturing at the fairground attractions beyond it.

'You mean the dodgems and all that?'

29

'Yeah. What else?'

'No.'

'What about fixing shit?'

The questions were throwing him. What did this have to do with Kuzma's underworld?

'Depends on the fix. Listen… I'm sorry. Mr. Kuzma just said you might have some work for me. He didn't… you know… say what kind.'

'Well, the next season's seven months off, but there's a lot of maintenance to keep up with. Shit breaks down even when it's not being used. We keep a skeleton crew to keep everything spick and span. Y'don't stay on top of it, it can get away from ya. Course, if you're still here when the seasons starts, we can getcha on the rides.'

# 6. AVENUE X

The F Train lurched from out of Stillwell Avenue. With the taste of dusty electricity on his tongue, Marco peered through the grimy window at the gang tags and graffiti emblazoned on the desolate edifices of back yards and flat blocks… hoodlum hieroglyphics.

It was here, somewhere, that his father once spat gutter-speak and swaggered gangster to the despair of Marty and Yvonne—his grandparents—the ones who raised him. Marco was all they really had to show for their son Frankie's having lived. A teenage member of a Brooklyn street gang from back in the day—The Immortal Homicides.

All he knew of his mother was the little that Grandpa Marty managed to gasp as he lay dying in their apartment in the spring of '77. Between the rose-tinged edit at home and gang-lore on the street, it played like this: 1957—the year the Dodgers went West—was also the year Frankie fled Brooklyn for the Gulf of Mexico. His 'involvement' in a stabbing incident—a precursor to what would eventually escalate into the infamous Coney Island gang wars—was the incentive. Staying with relatives in Pensacola, Florida, Frankie got tangled up with some older broad—Cuban—whose raison d'être, apparently, was fucking boys.

Eight months seemed to be a reasonable amount of time for the heat to abate. When no sooner had young Frankie arrived back home, he was followed by a little bundle of uncalled for joy—his son—Marco Garibaldi Mascini.

It was never clear who named him but his mother got deported back to Castro-land, leaving baby Marco with the Florida in-laws who soon brought him north. But by the time baby Marco arrived in Brooklyn, daddy had already been 'iced' in a retaliation stabbing.

Grandma Yvonne would forever carry a bubble of portable distance around her, but Marty was keen—grafted his 'dad act' with nary a glitch from his dead son Frankie to his grandson, Marco. Rabbit hunting trips upstate were interspersed with tales of rabbit hunting trips of yesteryear with Frankie. Marty had fought in the war: in the 27th Marine Regiment and was a fucking great shot. Pretty soon, Marco became a fucking great shot also.

Details of the chain of events which led to daddy's murder, however, were less forthcoming. By the time he was a teenager himself, Marco had the how's and why's—but not the who's. An afternoon-long perusal through library archives of half-forgotten headlines did little to shoot the 'I's and slash the 'Ts. A page-seven column in the Eagle, dated January '57, told how sixteen-year-old Jackie Perillo of a rival gang, the Ellery Bops, was felled by a switchblade on the eve of daddy's exile to the Mexican Gulf. It's a fair bet that another Ellery Bopper faded with the vapours of urban mythology and the seldom told bon mot of how he wasted a young Frankie Mascini.

Through the carriage train window, the steeples of a church slid into view. Marco saw the steps and imagined his teenage dad dying a Cagney-esque death; "Do you know this fella?" "Yeah, he used to be a big shot."

*It was a teenage wedding and the old folks wished them well...*

Actually... they did not.

Marty and Yvonne saw Victoria Charles for the skank she was and did whatever they could to derail Marco's headlong free-fall into cunt-struck oblivion.

'Cunt-struck' was a colloquialism Marty had picked up from the British soldiers during the war. He'd never had cause to use the term since, but that summer of '76 found Marco irretrievably, unmistakeably, and hopelessly... cunt struck. Marco had rarely heard the old man cuss, especially in front of Yvonne. So, when he overheard him use the term during a terse exchange from their bedroom, Marco realised the extent of their ire.

The first time Marco laid eyes on Victoria she was turning the corner onto Knickerbocker from DeKalb—like Betsy in *Taxi Driver*—poetry in slow-motion. She wore a tight yellow dress covered in black dots. She had some kind of knot tying her auburn hair up on her head. The back of her neck invited soft kisses he was yet to give her, but somehow knew he would. She was the reason singers sang...

1976 and she was un-disco. This alone raised her way above the flares and polyester brigade that permeated the neighbourhood. But more—she knew who Jackie Wilson was. In those vapid disco-days, *she* possessed this intelligence.

The Heights played back-drop to their incendiary passions, and before July was out, Marco asked her to marry him. Why the fuck not? He knew right then and there he would never know love like this again. It was more of a decision than an undeniable truth. If you *choose* love, it ain't love. It hits you like an accident. All you can do is recover. This was the means by which Marco would come to measure the annihilation of his soul by Victoria Charles.

So, over the river they went. Got the license on Friday, booked into a Canal Street dosshouse for two nights, and sealed the deal on Monday. She moved in with him and his grandparents while they saved for a deposit for their own place. He washed dishes at a local pizzeria, and she took phone calls at her dad's junk-a-car yard... if and when she felt like it.

He had no idea his grandparents were dying and, looking back, he would always wonder if his unblessed union with

Vikki accelerated their demise. But when illness came, it came fast. When caring for them became too tiresome a chore for his new wife her true face revealed itself.

Six months after their marriage she had left him. Yvonne was dead by then and Marty was about to join her. One afternoon as the old man lay rasping and wheezing away his final hours, Marco, with some 'couldn't give a shit' nurse fussing around, saw his wife from the window, arm in arm with some old fuck. The unfairness of life going on outside as this man, Martin Mascini, a war hero, lay dying and forgotten in the next room… It was no-one's fault. No one could be blamed, but somehow a debt would have to be paid.

```
How to dispel this... rage...
```

In the schoolyard they called it getting even—a childish conceit. But in the movies, they called it revenge… vengeance. The word elevated the infantile to the biblical. But Marco knew he would kill her new fuck piece if he didn't skip town. Fast.

Marco's first lessons in death taught him two things—it was expensive… and it was boring. The sale of that two-bedroom shelf on Wilson in the face of a Bushwick Avenue Brownstone block barely took care of the funerals—and a fair to middling education at John Dewey sealed the deal. This bird had to fly.

When he handed over the keys in the summer of '77 to Mr. Square of Fuck U & Fuck U Realtors it was the end of an era. The Mascinis were the last Italians on that street. He spent his last night in the apartment in which he was raised shooting at rioters with Marty's old M1 from his bedroom window. It was the night of the big blackout, causing the neighbourhood to ignite in a frenzy of looting and hellfire. It was with some satisfaction that he remembered taking out some mook in a Grand Funk Railroad T-shirt who was stomping the roof of a Mustang across the street. That's the thing he remembered— the T-shirt—*Grand Funk Railroad*?! He deserved to die. His bullet found the guy's teeth and sent him somersaulting backwards into someone's yard. Marco was convinced he'd killed him, but on scouring the papers the following morning

as his plane took off from JFK to London, he could find no
reports of fatalities on that hellish night.

And so began the search for himself—the prize that
supposedly awaits you at the end of travelling around the
world.

He hit Europe with a vengeance.

He found London gripped by a frightening epidemic called
Punk Rock.

Prague smoked Lucky Strikes and dreamt of velvet
revolutions.

Berlin was still reeling from a shit storm of radical chic as
exemplified by hurricane Baader-Meinhof. But there was
nothing—no person, or place, or experience that exceeded his
expectations. Nothing was beyond his imagination. He realised,
of course, that he had to travel to find that out... that travel was
a false economy. Whatever he was looking for was with him all
along. That was until Paris and that call from Bangkok... with
an offer he couldn't refuse.

Thailand would define him and cast its shadow over forever.

# 7. THIS IS THIS

He was still in a state of amusement about the Coney
Island job. Ironically, he realised. Was Kuzma really
offering him work on the ding dings? Maybe he
honestly thought Marco was jerking his chain so played along
and called his bluff.

But the long of it: he still needed to find a job or go to the gun.

The short: unemployment or impending doom would not
derail tonight's plan to see the Cimino double bill at The
Forum.

He switched on the jukebox—loaded with daddy's old
records. The only kingdom he'd inherited was a vinyl citadel of
Speciality, King, Imperial, Atlantic, Chess, Vee Jay... Apart from
a box of photos, these were all that was left of his dead
teenager dad—pictures in a shoebox and a loaded music
machine.

Bobby Bland's 'Farther Up the Road' crackled and swung, and Marco wondered what Frankie was doing the last time these exact vibrations moved his soul.

*You got to reap just what you sow...*

Marco pondered endlessly on the state of music. Black music especially... Once upon a time you listened to Chuck, Little Richard, Fats... you got educated, he reasoned to himself. Now, on the odd occasions he'd turn on the TV, he'd see young black guys dressed as infants bleating over a soundtrack that sounded like a toy shop being raped by a helicopter. It was the Minstrel show in reverse. They called each other nigger and became their own slaves.

*You got to reap just what you sow...*

Back in '79, when he first got back, he was brutally aware of the cliché he became. But he was still young enough to find the prospect of self-destruction attractive. The monkey was on his back. The fucking thing had to go.

Those first months were a blizzard of cocaine and east European whores via Kuzma's Pitt Grocers. Somewhere in that blizzard he met Bonnie Rachanski who danced at the Sapphire Lounge, just up the street.

A lingering paranoia concerning his big score compelled him to stuff a few of the bills into her G-string. He followed her a few times when she left the club, watched her use them in a couple of stores... in the subway... all without incident. One night she didn't show at the club. Marco wondered if she'd been arrested, questioned...

*'Where d'ya get these fuckn' bills, sweet tits?!'*

He asked the girl on reception about her. She was cagey, pleaded the 5th. The barman was not so guarded. He knew Marco's face—God knew he was in the place often enough.

'Bonnie Rachanski,' the barman told him. 'Lives in Hicksville. No, really. Hicksville... Long Island... No, I don't know why she ain't in...'

The next day she was back. He intercepted her on the way back to the dressing room. His opener was of the direct variety. 'Wanna see a movie with me?'

She did, so they went to see *The Third Man* at the Waverly. She didn't say whether she liked the movie or not, but afterwards they danced, naked and slow in Marco's kitchen, to the Chiffons' Tonight I'm Gonna Dream. Through the window the bridge cross-faded into a tangled mess of gold lights that skipped across the river... The first time the tip of his tongue touched hers his black heart skipped too. He succumbed to the cliché... that he thought he knew her from somewhere... or had somehow always known her. The sex that night was coke-fuelled. He fucked her in the ass... at her behest. He came over her... a lot.

They awoke the following noon, huddled together under a blanket on the fire escape. It was quite the debut and barely a day went by when he hadn't thought about it since.

Things were going pretty good there for a while... a couple of months maybe. She came over nearly every afternoon and sometimes after work. They became a thing! Three weeks into it and he realised he did know her—or at least remembered where he'd seen her before. It was from an opium night in Paris. She was the Princess Leia from *Star Whores*—a porn video he'd seen at Queen Evelyn's. If he was given to embarrassment he would have been, when describing the circumstances in which he'd seen it, but she laughed big and said it meant they were *meant* to be.

One night she was supposed to come over but didn't. The next night he went over to the club. The barman had an envelope for him. The note read...

*I'm going to do us both a favour. I've had a blast. Thanks for the explosion that is you. If I'm back over this way, I'll be sure to swing by. Missing you a little, wanting you a lot. BX*

Just like that. Gone. It was the second time he'd been fucked over in this fashion. He married his first love when he was a teenager and she turned out to be the skank they all said she was. And now this. It was absurd—Bonnie Rachanski was a glorified whore; made fuck films, he knew—but that was alright. She had *something*. *They* had something. Living with the stain of murder on his soul was nothing—an icy breeze. But was he really so cunt struck that she had so distorted his reality?

Her departure would herald in Marco's long night.

From then on, he decided, time would be defined by the rhythms of his body and the alignment of the universe as it revolved around him. He decided to remove all timepieces from sight. He had no radio, and the television was only ever used when he jerked off to her fuck tapes.

Freedom was no escape. True freedom was freedom from time and for nine years he used it to bury himself in this Lower East Side tomb—a monument to himself—a 'made to measure' Treasure Island... in an ocean called Manhattan.

# 8. EXPOSURE

The Forum, like most of the area's picture houses, was on its last legs. Its foyer was littered with paint-splattered step ladders and looked like it was being dismantled. The same girl who sat behind the gloomy box office and sold him his seat also came around to serve him at the concessions stand. She barely had a chin, and her sullen service was delivered as if *he* were somehow to blame for this facial fuck-up.

Inside, many of the seats were covered in gaffer tape with DO NOT USE signs—including the entire back row which was an annoyance. But when the lights went down his surroundings ceased to exist. The next five and a half hours would transport him—first, just a few blocks away to the sweatshops and back alleys of Canal Street and then to Pittsburgh and Vietnam.

*Year of the Dragon* he'd seen when it came out last year. There was a lot of talk about how Mickey Rourke was a contender for De Niro's crown, but Marco couldn't see it. Although when they went toe to toe in *Angel Heart*, he thought, Rourke held his own. He'd first seen *The Deer Hunter* in Paris when it came out ten years ago, and by the time the lights came up, a decade had done nothing to diminish its power.

Marco remained in his seat still reverberating from its charge as the only other people in the house, a pair of couples, rose and left. It was the excruciating tension of the Russian-roulette scene that everyone remembered, but for Marco, the 'This is this!' moment cut to the core of the human condition. If De Niro was God (and up until last night's *Midnight Run* debacle, this was not such a stretch) and the hapless and doomed John Cazale was humanity, then for Marco their scene in the mountains summed up humankind's relationship with their creator...

**De Niro/God:** 'You see this? This is this! This ain't something else. This is this! From now on, you're on your own!'
**Cazale/Humanity:** You're a fuckin' bastard, you know that!

A light drizzle accompanied his walk home and seemed to put the streets around him in some misty distance. Neon-splashed asphalt spread around him. Distorted. Volatile. At night the city was prone to atmospherics that got inside you, truly revealing itself. A naked city—tantalising and seductive.

Then it hit him.

Why not tonight?

He'd been gearing up for it for years.

*Why not tonight?*

Tonight... he could die.

It's not like he hadn't considered it before, but the one thing that bugged him and stayed his hungry trigger-finger was an aftermath he could not control. He'd seen crime-scene photos of murder victims and suicides and they invariably looked stupid. Dribbling mouths hanging open—eyes staring in eternal surprise, perhaps realising in that final second that the Gods they'd followed or forsaken were not waiting for them in the next world. But stupid expressions aside, the idea of these being his final moments put purpose in his stride and seemed to galvanise his mission with every step. Could he really do this? Could he really face down eternity and fling himself into it?

Don't think it.

Don't weigh it up.

Walk in.

Grab that gun.

Check out.

The days were all the same. He would miss nothing, and nothing would miss him.

He reached his floor. Canned laughter from a television in the opposite apartment was muffled by its heavy door. Some girl lived there. He'd never spoken to her. He performed the sequence of unlocking the big Yales to his apartment and went inside. He went straight to the kitchen, left the light off, but could see the cooker clock say 3.28. He grabbed the .38 from out of the drawer and went to the bedroom. He leaned back against the wall and scanned the room for the last time as he put the barrel in his mouth.

A thin streak of light from between the blinds revealed it.

On the unmade bed, placed squarely in the centre on the throw, there was... something...

For a second, it didn't register.

Ignore it.

It didn't matter now.

But what?

How?

Its presence defied his logic. He thought for a minute of what he must have left there.

He flicked the lamp switch and saw it.

A large, padded envelope.

Confusion gave way to cold shock.

He panned the gun around the room, expecting to see someone in the shadows sparking a cigarette before announcing themselves in classic film noir fashion.

There was no-one.

Keeping the door in his peripheral vision, he approached the wardrobe—listening for movement the whole time. He slowly opened it—keeping the gun on the opening—nothing. He glanced down at where he kept the remains of his big score. In the half-darkness it looked undisturbed.

He went to the door—scanned the lounge—nothing.

He approached the kitchen, gun first—nothing.

The bathroom. The shower-stall.

Nothing.

The kitchen window—unbroken—undisturbed.

Ditto the lounge and bedroom windows.

No signs of a break in whatsoever.

Did he dream it?

No.

The package lay on the bed.

Explosive possibilities suddenly occurred. As in... a bomb?

Suicide died. The threat of an external death nixed it.

He approached gingerly—lifted one corner of the package with the barrel of the gun—turned it over. The object's innocuousness jarred violently with its ominous possibilities. An idiot notion presented itself—what does a bomb weigh?

With thumb and index, he lifted it carefully into the kitchen and placed it in the sink.

Another idiot notion—if it explodes, tuning the faucet on will save the day? Without taking his eyes off the sink, he backed away towards the front door and checked the spy hole. The fisheye lens warped the vacant hallway. The dim and naked bulb flickered as if in distress.

No one had passed him on the stairwell. He made a quick mental replay of anyone who looked like they were leaving the building as he approached it. Unless—on the rare occasion when someone commanded his attention, bums on the make, God-suckers trying to save him, or that mugger a couple of years back, on whom he pulled this very gun and ran that fucker down the street—he was blissfully off-the-air to the crowds he moved through. He barely recalled tonight's suicide stroll as he floated on the reverie of Cimino's masterpiece and the universal possibilities of 'two shots eating pussy'—let alone the few characters he may have passed on the street at this late hour.

How the fuck had they got in? And for that matter—out?!

It must be Kuzma. He'd have keys. Probably. But why sneak it in? He'd just give it to him directly or get one of his boys to drop it off. No?

He put the gun on the table. He steeled himself for sudden hell, lifted the package out of the sink, and squeezed carefully. It had one of those old fashion string fasteners holding it closed. He unwound it, peered cautiously inside, then removed the contents... one of those portable phones... the kind 'suits' yell into on Wall Street; a VHS video tape—no case— unlabelled... and another smaller envelope. The envelope contained a laminated press pass in his name for something called 'CHRISTIAN BROADCASTING NETWORK' and a type-written phone number on a blue card.

As he made coffee, he considered his mystery gifts as they lay on the kitchen table. The fucking thing was *in his apartment— in his bedroom*. The lack of break-in evidence whispered supreme professionalism. If this wasn't Kuzma, then the package's location screamed, WE CAN FUCK YOU ANYTIME!

He sipped the coffee, set it down, picked up the card, picked up the cell phone—a Panasonic—and punched in the number. Nothing happened—no tone—no answer. The green button must have appealed to some misplaced instinct because when he pressed it... Bingo! It rang.

And rang...

Misplaced instinct says red button cuts the call.

Once again, misplaced instinct was correct.

He took the tape with the espresso to the lounge and loaded it into the VCR. The image rolled and stuttered and settled into a black and white shield with the words *U.M & M TV Corp presents*. The jaunty sound of men singing indecipherable lyrics punctuated with 'Hi dee hi dee hi's...' *'Max Fleischer*

41

*presents 'Bimbo's Initiation'.* Marco sipped the coffee, sat, and watched.

A cartoon… It was old… maybe from the 30s? An indeterminable character, presumably Bimbo, happily strolls along a street not unlike the ones that constituted Marco's neighbourhood—broken lamp posts, boarded-up windows. Maybe Bimbo's a dog? Bimbo falls through a manhole, then what looks like Mickey Mouse, padlocks it shut. Bimbo slides down into a chamber where a crowd of hooded figures wait, holding planks with nails through them. They surround Bimbo and sing '*Wanna be a member?*' Bimbo says no! A reverse trap door sends him into a room above, where there is an exit. He makes for it, but it rolls up like a projector screen and he hits the wall. The hooded figures watch through a secret hatch and laugh…

He remembered seeing cartoons like this on Saturday morning Matinees at the old Paramount, but this was from another era, older. This was violent and surreal, an animated nightmare.

Bimbo is in a room which turns upside down, knives with teeth come out of the wall to attack him. Another room— spikes hover above him suspended by a burning rope. He blows out the flames, but they become flaming dancing figures. The spikes fall…

On and on the torments continue, whilst the hooded figures threateningly entreat the hero, '*Wanna be a member? Wanna be a member?*'

Bimbo is faced with four doors. The first has a skull and crossbones on it and contains a mirror. He opens the second door with '13' on it and it contains a skeleton talking on the phone. The third door with a handprint releases a boxing glove on a spring. The last door seems to be an escape but leads to a spanking machine. The beating sets Bimbo aflame so he leaps into a pool which becomes ice. Suddenly Betty Boop appears, all big fluttering eyelashes on an outsized head, and beckons him through yet another door. Bimbo tries the door but behind it is another door, then another and another… the doorway swallows him, and down another trapdoor he slides until he runs a gauntlet of axes and steel-toothed corridors. His shadow is decapitated, his heart exits his mouth and swallows it again. Another room, another hooded figure. '*Wanna be a member?*'

Again, Bimbo refuses, but the hooded figure removes its uniform and reveals itself as a rubber-limbed, self-spanking Betty Boop! *Now* Bimbo wants to be a member!

A curtain slides away, and behind it, a chorus of the hooded figures. They remove their hoods and they're *all* Betty Boop! Chorus lines of identical Bettys perform a high-kicking Busby Berkeley deal while Bimbo and the first Betty dance and spank each other...

The image warped and deteriorated into static. Marco let it roll for a while then felt around under the cushions for the remote.

Betty Boop?

The significance, if there was any, was beyond him. He was about to hit STOP when the on-screen static was replaced with a black-and-white image of what looked like a large warehouse loading area. His stomach rolled. He knew, somehow, that he was about to witness something unpleasant.

The point of view was up high, revealing nothing but a few crates in the distance by a wall. A figure in a light-coloured suit and carrying an attaché case entered, screen right. The figure seemed to be fumbling with keys and looked like he was probably approaching a vehicle—off-screen left. Another figure in a short coat and a baseball cap appeared and looked as if he were struggling to free something from his pocket as he crept up behind. The man in the suit spun around suddenly and hit his stalker across the head with the case. The stalker fell to the floor and scrambled for something which fell out of his pocket. The man raised the case again but the stalker on the floor reached his objective and pointed it at his attacker. A burst of muzzle flash and the man with the case fell on top of the man on the floor.

Marco went cold and leaned in closer to the screen.

The baseball cap fell off the stalker revealing a Mohican style haircut. The fuzzy image of a young Marco Mascini wrestled his way out from under Captain Suphatra's dead body, stagger for

43

a few feet, then vomit by the wall. Then Marco of yesteryear—
in fact, nearly nine yesteryears—approached the body,
grabbed his victim's case and ran off-screen.

And there it was… finally.

At exactly 3.55am on Wednesday 5th of October 1988,
Marco's big skeleton had shimmied out of his closet and kicked
him squarely in the pills.

# 9. WHACKING GROUND

H
e sat frozen by the grainy image of Suphatra's body
spread out on its back in that Bangkok department
store service bay. The tape continued seven minutes
after the shooting until two men in overalls appeared. One ran
off-screen as the other stood over the body. Then the picture
deteriorated painfully into white noise, fuzz, and distortion—
along with Marco's deluded fantasy of himself.

He hit STOP on the remote.

Jimmy.

It had to be Jimmy.

More coffee and a rerun. The tape had rewound. Perhaps a
second viewing would reveal… more.

He hit fast-forward, hit play and… nothing. He forwarded it on
some. Stop. Play… and still nothing. The tape was blank. Was
this some kind of flashback? He wound the tape back and forth.
Either the VCR had died, or the tape had somehow erased
itself.

He sat back and sipped the hot coffee, trying to make sense of
the last ten minutes. Did it happen?

The phone chirped loud and sent a spasm through him that
threw the drink up the wall.

He answered it.

Took a moment to figure out how.

Hit the green button.

There was static.

It sounded long-distance.

A voice. Male. Old? Said, 'One, Leroy Street. Midnight tonight. Say it.'

Marco stuttered, 'W... What?'

The voice said it again, 'One, Leroy Street. Midnight tonight. Say it!'

'One, Leroy Street. Midnight tonight?'

The caller allowed Marco two seconds to absorb this then continued, 'It's a club. Take the phone and go there. There will be an announcement. Listen to what is being said then call the number on the blue card. You are being watched. Don't fuck around. Don't fuck it up.'

'Wait! How did you get in my place?'

The line died and left Marco in the same state of permafrost he was in when he first found the package. He leapt up and went to the hallway. Again, he peered through the spyhole at the distorted vacant hallway. He checked that the Remington behind the kitchen curtain was loaded, then took it to every window and studied the gloomy streets below him. The bedroom window was level with the bridge as it ascended past his floor—a prime vantage-point for anyone wanting to case the joint. The pay phone on the corner was unoccupied. The walkway on the bridge was deserted. A few cars raced over it. Two trains clattered past each other in opposite directions beneath the road.

His heart felt like it was trying to punch its way out of his chest. He scanned the street below his window and, for the first time—illuminated by a streetlamp—he saw, painted on the broken tarmac—X-ING CHILDREN. It was faded and barely readable—a typical feature of city zoning, but it struck him as strange that it would command his attention now. In the old Howard Hawks version of Scarface, Xs appeared in every scene whenever someone got whacked.

Okay.

Rewind.

Who knew?

Two stiffs.

45

Jimmy Farragher…

… and by extension, at least two Thai police prefectures.

Sleep was not an option. He needed to scope the scene of his possible demise… now.


1 Leroy Street was no more than an iron door, studded with heavy rivets like the hull of a ship and sandwiched between a delicatessen and Grandpa's Bella Gente on the corner of Bleecker—Al Lewis' place—Grandpa Munster from the old television show. Marco had read about it in The Voice but had yet to sample an 'out of this world' Bracioline Ripiene. It mentioned that sometimes Grandpa himself would make an appearance and mix with the clientele, posing for photographs and exchanging banter. It was also the scene of a recent mob hit. Two on a motorcycle put four in a Gambino-connected man sitting in his limousine.

Bona-fide gangster shit right outside your restaurant was probably good for business—aggressive marketing, 80s style. As he approached, Marco couldn't help but riff on the idea that he was walking into a designated whacking-ground. It was five twenty-four a.m. now. Cars cruised. People would have walked through him if they could. He walked around the block. Nothing struck him as being any kind of precursor to the mayhem he envisioned taking place that night.

He ducked into the coffee shop across the street—within view of the club. He drank expressos and didn't take his eyes off that corner. The idea was to wait it out until the appointed time and perhaps intercept Jimmy, or whoever was coming, before they even got there.

Four coffees later and he saw the situation for what it was. It was going to be nineteen hours before it was midnight again.

The enterprise was goofy. Go home.

Kuzma was still the most obvious culprit. Was his mob somehow connected to Marco's shenanigans and Jimmy Farragher in Thailand? Kuzma would not be back in his shop until the next rent day. If Kuzma wasn't involved how could the subject be broached? If he *was* involved maybe he'd having reason for denying it. Marco had been exposed enough. Cards would have to be played close.

His next move was a massive, and probably futile, leap into the dark. But he would have to speak to his neighbours. Maybe they saw something—saw who delivered the package.

The whole block became a flurry of activity around six a.m. as the squares got ready for work. He entered the stairwell from the street and could hear that this morning was no exception.

It was impossible to get a fix on where the muffled sounds of television sets were coming from. All floors seemed to vibrate with the same cacophony of jingles and canned laughter.

He started on the ground and worked his way up. Most were not at home or just plain not answering. There was no answer at the doors of the hippie or 'yuppie weird-lips' but the Cyndi Lauper wannabe on his floor peered through the gap of her thrice-chained apartment door, fussing with a magenta-coloured cap which lay defeated across her head—pulled down where it failed to conceal a black-eye.

'Hi, I'm Marco. I live opposite?'

'Yeah, I know.'

He was surprised. He'd believed he'd done a fair job of achieving near invisibility concerning his neighbours. 'Has anyone called for me recently or, y'know... maybe someone hanging around?'

She scraped remnants of pink lipstick off her bottom lip with her top teeth. 'No, I don't think so. You been robbed or sumthin'?'

'No, I'm... I've received a package. Wondered if you saw who delivered it.'

'Well, they gotta get through downstairs first. Someone mustah let 'em in. I ain't seen no one.'

'Okay, thanks.'

That should have ended the conversation but the black-eye demanded enquiry. 'How d'you get the shiner?'

Her face ran blank—like it took a beat for the question to register. 'Oh... a cop hit me in Tompkins Square.'

'A cop hit you? For what?'

'In the riot.'

47

This was news. A riot virtually on his doorstep and he didn't know about it. His recluse status held fast.

'Them fuckin' cops, huh? You go easy now.'

'Thanks, I will. Thanks…'

She shut the door.

*Them fuckin' cops.*

The cupcakes upstairs were a different proposition altogether. They'd seen everybody.

'Ohmagodyesss! Two guys! Thursday! Said they were from…'

He yelled over his shoulder at his out of sight boyfriend.

'Where did those guys say they was from?'

An identical voice hollered from a distant room. 'What guys?'

'Those guys. Those… hang on.'

Cupcake's face disappeared from the gap in the door. Marco could hear indecipherable conversation. Cupcake's face, searching and earnest, reappeared.

'He can't remember *what guys*! But they were from… somewhere.'

He proceeded to run through everyone who had entered and exited the building since the weekend and even many who'd merely passed it: Cyndi Lauper's Avon rep, weird lips' 'masseuse', the mailman, various UPS delivery boys, four bums who pissed in our doorway… Cupcake's itinerary concluded with 'you been robbed or something?'

The same enquiry from two neighbours does not a conspiracy make. There was still no answer at the other four apartments. He went back to his own and thrice-bolted the thick steel door behind him.

*'You bin robbed or sumthin?'*

He broke protocol. To hell with the coffee and honeyed toast. He went to the Spanish place on Avenue A and had breakfast— Eggs Benedict and a Sapporo. His first actual breakfast since 1986. He tried to distract himself with a copy of the Village Voice. Neo-Hippy's still bleating on about Hippy shit. He glided home on a beer-buzz where exhaustion made an entrance— mental now as well as physical. Pitt Street Grocers were open, and Kuzma's kid sat behind the Perspex. Marco went in and bought rolly papers. Marco eyed the kid carefully, waiting for him to say something about the delivery. The kid gave him his Zigs Zags, his change… and nothing more.

'Do you know if Mr Kuzma or anyone dropped anything at my place last night?'

The kid's attention was back on the TV where the news was all over the forthcoming presidential election. 'Not that I know about. I know *I* didn't,' was all the kid said.

Marco told him to get Kuzma to drop in if and when he saw him next.

He went around the apartment, collected all his weapons from their various hiding places, and threw them on the bed. The Remington, the thirty-eight, the forty-four, the M9, a couple of Saturday Night-Specials and his grandad's old army M1. He didn't need to check if they were loaded but did anyway.

He put them all under the duvet except the Remington. He held it to his chest as he lay on the bed and waited for the day to die.

# 10. FAT TRAVIS

Jimmy said, 'You pick up a case containing a million dollars—you can keep it but it means a Chinaman dies. Wouldja do it?'

Marco said, 'Depends on the Chinaman.'

'Okay, how about two kid-pedalling Thai cunt fucks?'

'I do it just for the case.'

**February 1979:** Chiang Rai: Wiang Kaen district. . .

Acres of neglected paddy fields interrupted the forest's emerald imperialism. Out there in the forest Jew boys were shooting hogs. Vacationing Mossad agents, Jimmy told him. They drew the line at cows, sacred or otherwise. 2500 baht and you could take a bazooka to a beast and blow it all to hell. But today it was a hog fry—1500 baht. The Jew boy with the turned around Jets cap shouldered his weapon, braced himself and let off a blue roar at three hogs grouped around a jackfruit tree. The hollow report of the weapon folded back and forth across the field. Two beasts scattered as one took the blast. The large sinewy clump of its hindquarters spun off into the distance, hit the tree, and raised dust. The foremost half of the creature, still intact, tottered from one hoof to the other before falling snout-first in a puddle—tipping entrails over the back of its head. Its jaw worked the dirt for a moment, oblivious to death. The Jew boys laughed and slapped backs.

Marco sat on the fence popping gum and reading the Bangkok Post. '*Boogie Fever*' squawked from someone's radio. Weapons and shells lay in an orderly fashion on the grass behind him.

Jimmy had said he had an offer Marco couldn't refuse. Called him all this way from France then gave him this job: supervising the Hog Fry, loading up, maintaining the weapons and throwing whatever pickup-able remains were left to the other hogs. This had to be the warm-up before Jimmy introduced the main act.

Surely...

Jimmy was one of the first people he met in London a couple of years earlier—a scrawny little guy in tight drainpipe jeans with oily back hair smarmed back into a ducktail—banging away on some weird drum with a sextet called the Collinsmen in the backroom of some pub. They were yelling rebel songs, making rowdy and, so it seemed to Marco, overplaying the mad paddy card. Marco had a girl on his case at the time—Lisa Brown—a textbook Irish redhead, pale as an April moon and in continual pursuit of the craic... whatever that was... He'd heard somewhere that real Irish women were magical and if blowjobs were anything to go by, Miss Brown was the new Houdini. A 'nosh', she called them. 'D'ye be wantn' a nosh?'

She was part of this crowd and introduced him to it. At some point in the evening's revelry Jimmy asked Marco if he wanted to help him, and another guy called Eugene, rob a bank.

Two days later the three of them sat in a Ford Zodiac—a malformed parody of a Lincoln Continental—across the road from Lloyds Bank on a busy main street somewhere in South London. The bender they'd been on since Saturday night had continued into that Tuesday afternoon and none of them were in any condition to even remember what they for there for, let alone execute an armed raid. But what their plan lacked in criminal dexterity was more than made up for in sure-fire getting pinched inevitability: storm in, jump the counter, take all the money they could see and make a mad dash through cramped suburban roads in this god-awful piece-o-shit car. They all sat, leather jacketed, with .22s in their laps, trying to focus on the entrance doors. The next thing Marco remembered was waking up long after the place had closed. All three of them had passed out with the engine spluttering on its last drop of gas. Talk of a return attempt was vetoed by Jimmy's abrupt disappearance the following weekend.

Lisa told him she'd heard Jimmy was a loyalist snitch and that some exiled Provos were keen on sending his heart and balls home to his mother. 'Go to Thailand. You can live like a king out there,' Jimmy said to him more than once during their brief acquaintanceship. He figured if Jimmy's vitals weren't winging their way back to Derry, then Thailand was probably where he'd gone. Marco decided against passing this info on to Lisa. Within days he had quit London and was stalking his next adventure among the archaic spires of Paris. How Jimmy's phone call found him in a whorehouse De La Republic is testament to the man's resourcefulness. But find him it did.

It was at a plush apartment in the 13th arrondissement, where he pondered the pros and cons of jamming a hunk of opium up his anus. The place was a mind bender—all green paper lanterns and white Op-Art—*Clockwork Orange* meets the *King and I*. A huge television set of brown plastic sat on a marble plinth in the corner of the bedroom and played host to '*Star Whores*': two Princess Leia's going at it on the control deck of the Millennium Falcon. Even when one of the Leia's dropped her drawers and turned out to be hung like a Peruvian pit pony, Marco remained idée fixed on the other girl.

51

Never in a million years would he dream that she would one day be his girl. For a while anyway…

The apartment was Queen Evelyn's—purveyor of A-list tail to politicians, actors and pop stars. That night he'd been at Le Gibus Club watching an all-female Punk band that he'd seen previously in London. Their vocalist, a scrawny teenager of no discernible nationality, berated the meagre audience in her faux patois as Marco was handed a straight Jim and summoned to a party of crashed fabulousness. He found himself beside Evelyn, a back-combed peroxide blonde in black leather. She was forty-two—a Hell's Angel's wet dream. Up to a decade ago, Marco surmised, she was probably considered stunning. The rest of the party was all about edge—the edge of celebrity, the edge of a habit, the edge of Evelyn's orbit. They feigned obliviousness as Evelyn's fingerless leather glove groped his crotch and almost commanded that he take opium with her. Opium was a journey he'd yet to embark on and he was ready. But there was a catch.

She tongued his lobe—hot, whispered breath, 'To get the best hit, you have to put it in your ass…'

Another drink appeared before him. An act loaded with a significance he was unaware of until they rose to leave the dingy club. One of the circle—a dirty blonde with amazing teeth—pulled him to one side as the party ascended the poster-dashed stairwell to the street.

'She's been coming here since 1969. You're the only one I've ever seen her buy a drink for.'

Marco always looked at the mouth when people spoke to him, never the eyes. Without dropping a beat, she added, 'She got raped when she was sixteen.'

Marco remembered himself standing there in that apartment. When was it? A decade already? With a brown lump in one hand and wondering… wondering if opium really could be taken anally… wondering if Queen Evelyn really had been raped… wondering why the honour of a drink had been bestowed upon him and no others—at least since 1969… wondering if he somehow reminded her of her attacker… wondering if he'd been lured here… wondering if the sun would rise on his hanging upside down in her shower stall with his balls cut out...

On the TV screen the non-transsexual Princess Leia, the girl he would one day know as Bonnie Rachanski, squatted over the cosmic lady boy as he lay prostrate on the Millennium Falcon floor and returned a munificent quantity of spermatozoa to its owner's mouth.

That's when the phone rang...

# 11. THE CHROME DEVILS OF CHIANG RAI

For Marco, Southeast Asia presented a barricade between reality and... everything else. Apart from a pack on his back his only baggage was a simmering rage.

The hog fry suited the temperament of the time. He had no desire to wield one of those bazookas and send those beasts back to the soil which begat them. But these bloody scenes that took place every weekend under those gnarled trees seemed to placate a fiend in him he'd only been vaguely aware of until now.

You wanna fucking lose it? Chiang Rai province was the place. It wasn't just away from the world, and it wasn't just away from Thailand. It was away from all reasonable notions of humanity.

His arrival in Bangkok saw him do as tourists did—annoy lady boys and drink until oblivion claimed him. Fucking the whores, however, was off the menu. Apart from that marijuana model in Prague and Lisa Brown's transcendental blowjobs in London he hadn't been laid since the dying weeks of his marriage. The lustre of this routine wore off after a couple of months and already he was riddled with the same inertia he thought he'd left in Brooklyn. He took an overnight train north to see Jimmy about his offer, but the prospect of cultivating a heroin addiction seemed more appealing. He'd once promised himself (When, he couldn't recall) that if he lived to be seventy, he would become a heroin addict and murder someone who deserved it. Time, like everything else here, was mangled, wrong, warped. So, the murder-pact he'd made with himself made an early appearance.

Chiang Rai was no more than a wide, muddy half-mile strip right up in the north country, flanked on either side by stores, bars, and a couple of hotels. Undernourished horses were tethered to posts outside and if not for the gas pump outside the Rural Traders store on the east side of the street, the place could have been Tombstone circa 1880. But this was no shit-kicker's paradise in the middle of a barren wilderness. Chiang Rai was surrounded with lush green forestry which the midday sun would energise into kryptonite. And it was out there under those trees that desires were satiated, spleens vented, and darkness reigned.

When he wasn't running the hog fry, he'd while away afternoon hours getting destroyed at Connect 4 in Little Mama's Bar by a kid who called herself Amy. He never found out what her native name was. She must have been ten years of age—twelve tops, with an expressive almond-shaped face with haunted dark eyes heralding horrors behind them. She wore a necklace of tiny white flowers and would touch it before every move she made. She said her parents were dead, so she challenged tourists to the game to survive. She had a big old story to back this shtick. She claimed she was saving up so she could go in search of a Thai biker gang called the Chrome Devils of Chiang Rai. Her family were among a group of Karen tribe workers who were murdered by their employers who decided it would be cheaper to kill them all than pay them. She told him it was she who found them—thirty-one bloated, stinking bodies in a swamp near the Burmese border. She said the Chrome Devils would avenge her parents for a hundred dollars.

Jimmy came into the bar and dropped himself at their table. He watched Amy destroy Marco for a final time and packed it up. Marco handed over five Baht notes. She said, 'See you tomorrow. Kill you again.'

Jimmy watched her cross the muddy street to work more suckers in the other pile of bamboo they called a bar opposite. 'Another year and she'll be good to go.'

Marco kicked the table at him. 'Hey!'

'As far as *these arse holes* are concerned!' Jimmy thumbed at the balding fat Belgian behind him in the corner with a giggling teenager on his lap. She wore a sparkly boob tube and satin hot pants. Belgium ran fingertips up and down her calf. Jimmy held up surrender hands, 'Not me, brother. Not me.'

Thailand had transformed Jimmy from the wan shadow he struck in London to the deep-fried, tightly wrought accumulation of sinews before him—the mounds of his abdominals framed by his open waistcoat. Marco wondered how long he would have to stay here on a chicken noodle diet before his own stomach garnered such glory.

'Ye wanna make some big an' easy money, Marky boy?'

'How big and how easy?'

'Twenty Grand. Bang bang. That big 'n' easy.'

Jimmy outlined the situation of two police precincts battling over untold grievances going back years, and how the removal by a complete outsider of the two key players in this sorry psychodrama would alleviate a lot of local misery and would allow all concerned to retain face.

'It's basically the old Chinaman dies conundrum.'

'Chinaman dies conundrum…'

'You pick up a case containing a million dollars—you can keep it, but it means a Chinaman dies. Wouldja do it?'

Jimmy had run this poser by him before, but Marco had shrugged it off as the 'pass the time Christmas cracker brain teaser' it surely was. Marco would answer with 'Depends on the Chinaman' and the enquiry would end there. This time Jimmy was all gaze-holding sincerity.

'Well?'

'Twenty thousand? Not quite a million, is it?'

'It is here. Besides, we're not talking Chinamen.'

'A Chinaman is worth that much more than a Thai? I blame Bruce Lee. Them chinks were all about fireworks and laundry till he made the scene.'

Jimmy pulled in his chair and got earnest. 'The point *is,* no one's offering you a million for a Chinaman. But they *are* offering twenty-grand for a Thai.'

'Two Thais.'

'Two Thais. If the day comes when they do... then may the grace of God go widjya.'

Jimmy was momentarily distracted by the short bandy legs of a group of worn-out hookers at the bar who were bartering over the price of Preludin. He pushed the heel of his wrist into his crotch to straighten his stiffening dick and got up to leave.

'You ponder. It's a sweet deal. A piece o' piss. And don't forget, there's a hog fry in the morning: some big-deal kickboxer and some of his pals, so be nice.'

Jimmy followed the hookers outside leaving Little Mama by herself, sitting behind the bar staring out into the middle distance with that pinched and mean expression which, to Marco's eyes, adorned the faces of most women here of a certain age.

Marco pondered.

He pondered Jimmy's offer.

He pondered the consequences... of pushing a broken bottle into the face of that fat Belgium fuck who was making whistling sounds and pulling at the top of the giggling girl's boob tube to peer at her flat chest.

That night, as mosquitoes bounced off the net which covered his bed, Marco watched the slow progress of Geoff, a large lizard of yellow and black as it clung to a supporting beam in the roof of his hut. When he was first shown this place a couple of months ago, another lizard, different species, grey like a shark, about the size of a rat, clung to the cliff face of one if its Formica walls above the bunk. Its bloated, veined abdomen pumped furiously in stark contrast to its cold, beady appraisal of nothing in particular. 'Lose the beast and I'll take it,' Marco told the miniscule woman who looked after the entire row of ten huts which constituted the whole west side of the road. She left and returned with a large net and an accomplice—a tall teenage boy holding a huge hollowed-out tube of bamboo. Marco stood back, assuming they were going to somehow manoeuvre the creature into the tube with the net before it scuttled off. BAM! The boy simply hammered the thing with the end of the bamboo, sending a spray of blood and guts in a wide arc across the wall.

The stains remained. So, when this new uninvited guest made its way into his hut this morning, he let it be and gave it a name—Geoff.

Geoff's eye rolled like a security camera and Marco tried to envision himself through its cold lens. A twenty-two-year-old olive-skinned Caucasian male—234lbs, brown eyes, 'kung fu' hair—black and combed into a fringe across his forehead, laying naked across a raft-like bed in a puddle of perspiration, cast adrift in a world he had yet to find his stomach for.

He had no intention of accepting Jimmy's offer and he had no doubt that the job was real. But he knew that this, or something like it, was the real reason Jimmy invited him here. Not the hog fry.

Marco had taken scare shots at people in the park with his old rabbit gun when he was a kid—wondered about the prick he thought he killed with his grandad's M1 during those Brooklyn Riots. And then, someone getting shot was a distinct possibility had his farcical London bank job with Jimmy actually come to pass. But really? Go out with the sole purpose of killing someone?

Marco had long ago convinced himself that he was capable of murder, but that conviction was coupled with notions of the heroic... dropping three muggers who tried to take his wallet... slicing the throat of a predatory rapist in pursuit of a young mother... finding the one who killed his old man and throwing him through a skyscraper window... but for twenty grand? It would buy you a lot of swinging miles but wouldn't get you the great escape.

# 12. MARCO'S BIG SCORE

Before dawn, Marco trudged up the main street from his hut for the morning's hog fry. With a backpack full of ammo, he wore his hood up with his hands jammed deep into his sweater pockets. The sun had yet to clear those rolling hills and until it did, it was freezing. Like a microwave oven in reverse, the bitter cold bit hard into his marrow first, then worked its way outwards.

Four little hill tribe kids skipped after him as he engaged them in a call and response singsong. Marco sang, 'Start spreading the news…'

The kids copied it as best they could. 'Sta breddin da noooo.'

'I'm leaving today…'

'Ah leevee toodaeeee…'

The song made it until 'It's up to you, New York, New York,' when Marco turned right and approached the beginning of the forest. The kids stopped at this boundary and watched him disappear into the undergrowth. He giggled to himself as their voices faded into the distance.

'Eees ah too oo noo ark noo ark…'

Already he could hear gunfire up ahead, muted by the thick undergrowth. It wasn't until he made the clearing, finally, that the full boom from the weapon seemed to shock the forest to its roots. The extreme cold of minutes ago subsided fast and as he stumbled onwards, he was soon drenched in sweat. The animal's screams from out there in the clearing chilled him again. That was no hog. Whatever it was… was unfamiliar; bigger. He made the clearing and was momentarily blinded as his eyes adjusted to the morning light searing through the foliage. Another bazooka coughed and boomed and was answered again by the agonised screams of a wounded beast. Propped up against a gnarled and blood-fed jackfruit tree was a big old elephant. Three deep bloody craters in its side

smouldered with hot shattered shell pieces. He'd lost count of
the animals he'd seen die in this field, but never an elephant.
This huge, dusty, blood-streaked beast screaming in terror was
something from an acid trip gone horrifically awry. Another
blast smashed into the side of its trunk, rendering the
appendage a useless limb hanging on by a sliver of flesh. The
scream geared down to a distressed whine. Twenty feet away
was a group of four men—locals, all in dirty white vests. The
one shooting handed the gun to a taller man who went down
on one knee to reload.

  Marco removed his backpack as he ran towards them,
swinging the bag of ammo. He knocked the gun from the
kneeling man's hands which was caught on reflex by another
standing close. Reflex compelled the man to aim the unloaded
gun at Marco. He grabbed it and pushed its butt into the man's
face, breaking bone under his right eye. A flurry of fists and
kicks pummelled Marco onto the ground. He felt the gun being
wrestled from his grip but let it go to protect his head from the
melee of cheap mud splattered sneakers that were now raining
down on him. He felt his lip split, his ear tear and ring. He went
foetal and heard the elephant scream again against the thuds
of his beating...

The sky had transformed itself from the brilliant blue of the
morning to the slashed and bruised scarlet of dusk, and Marco
knew he'd been propped up against this tree all day. His hands
itched with bites of mosquitoes and his head pounded like a
galley-slave drummer in attack mode. He dragged himself to
his knees and flexed limbs. Every fibre of his being resounded
with the throbbing epilogue of sustained violence. He dragged
himself to his feet and his legs trembled with excess adrenalin.
The pitched screech of crickets introduced a piercing
headache, and Marco would quite happily have died right there
alone in that forest if he could. The shooters were gone. He
wondered how long they continued to beat him after he'd lost
consciousness. He cursed God and all his lousy creation that
they hadn't killed him. He staggered towards the rickety fence
which lined the field. Beneath the tree, a sad dark hulk

shimmered with layers of bustling ants. Flies swarmed and feasted on a mountain of gore and the warm evening breeze carried the stench of death to Marco's blood encrusted nostrils. His stomach spasmed, his lungs felt like they were snatched out of him. He fell to his knees in the dirt and cried himself beyond tears; beyond grief; beyond despair. The Chiang Rai night descended, but for Marco the dark would never again be black enough.

A puddle of cold spittle against his cheek on the pillow alerted him he was face down on his bunk. A sensation like a fiery blade pushing into the base of his spine vetoed any attempt to roll over. Devoid of even the strength to scream he lapsed back into the fitful shadows of the half consciousness he'd occupied for days.

The sound of a squawking rooster outside dragged him back again. He found himself propped up on a pile of thin pillows, dribbling onto his belly. The little travel clock on the bedside cabinet said 10:34. With difficulty he raised a bandaged hand and wiped drool from his chin. His entire body was solid and hard, like he'd been pumped up to exploding point. One wrong move and he felt his guts would be joining lizard Geoff's cousin on the wall behind him.

The air shifted and he knew there was someone in his room. The view through the less swollen of his eyes revealed Jimmy sitting astride a turned-around chair at the end of the bed, wearing an outsized pair of Foster Grants and sipping a bottle of Pepsi through a straw. Marco had the uncomfortable feeling that he'd been there a while.

'I woulda brought grapes, but I didn't think what's leftya teeth could handle it.'

Marco tongued the gummy void at the front of his mouth and found the two front ones missing. 'You should have fuckin' left me there', he lisped.

'The kids found ya. Brought ya back on a cart. Was the Connect 4 kid cleaned ya up.'

Marco considered the ridiculousness of that scenario and wondered aloud, 'How am I?'

'Broken wrist, three broken fingers, two broken ribs—one a side—and two missing teeth. Beyond that, Bruise City Arizona: Population: You.'

Jimmy had arranged for Dr Robert—that's what Jimmy called him—the main supplier of amphetamines to all the local bars, who also just happened to own a first aid kit. Jimmy had the good doctor look in on him. Amy brought soup.

What was Jimmy? Mercenary? Spy? Fixer? Some kind of modern-day Buccaneer? Certainly, an adventurer. All the pies he had his fingers in vibed underhand and, clearly it seemed, a mismanagement of his efforts accounted for his self-exile from Britain and the troubles. That mess alone suggested the outskirts of a political vibe. It occurred to Marco that this is how the world works. The West—the real world—is all cosmetics—the face. The engine room: the expenditure of real blood and guts happen here—or places just like it. The moves, the angles, the intrigues are somehow facilitated in the shadows, away from... morality, with all the hand-wringing conscience-crippling showboating that comes with it. Drugs, guns, slaves, political prisoners, the insane, looking to be sanctified... all came through places like this. All monsters, great and small, hid and ran their operations here. Jimmy's role, as far as can be ascertained, was facilitator—or as he described himself. 'I'm the can-do boy. I'm everywhere and nowhere, baby!'

Marco's increasing mobility seemed to shadow the frequency of Jimmy's visits. On this day, a Wednesday in March, Marco was hobbling around on his porch with the help of a length of bamboo and a pillow jammed into his armpit. Jimmy rode a bicycle around and around on the dusty road outside the hut whilst reassuring him that his expired visitor's visa should not be a problem, due to the certificate of exemption he'd got Dr Robert to sign.

'Go to Lao for a couple of days, get your visa re-stamped and come back.'

Marco squinted into the searing morning sun towards the town. 'You seen the kid? Amy?'

Jimmy jammed a front wheel into a deep groove in the hardened mud. 'Probably gone off to find her biker gang... hopefully. Unless she's been scooped up by 23 Precinct—'
'For what?'

Jimmy lost his balance and hopped clumsily off the bike as it clattered to the ground. He grabbed the back wheel and dragged it from the path of a rusting flatbed truck that came rumbling down the hill.

'For *what,* Jimmy?'

Jimmy left the bike on the grass verge and came across the road. 'Those lockups on the hill... The middle one's for Suphatra's little gladiator tournament next week. Very big with the Krauts.'

'Gladiator tournament?'

'Little 'uns. Kids. Strip 'em and make 'em fight. Big bonus for the winner if they throw in a rape encore—'

'Stop! Fuck!'


As soon as Marco yeah'd Jimmy's 'Chinaman dies' proposal, he figured he'd been played. But now he didn't give a fuck. Life here was cheap. Hang a number on it.

Jimmy told Marco to go to Lao... Burma... whatever... to get his visa renewed before returning. If all went accordingly, he'd best vacate Southeast Asia quick fast. The last thing he'd need was any customs or border complications.

And so... he did.

Happy people, Jimmy told him, the Laotians. Marco couldn't say he noticed as he primed himself for his leap into the abyss where, he hoped, he could tear off the monkey that climbed on his back when his wife, gramps and grandma abandoned him and just kept getting bigger and bigger.

He kicked his heels in Vientiane for a week while Jimmy set everything up. Marco's only stipulation was no knives—there was an intimacy with the blade that rang wrong. This thing would be kept at arm's length.

He installed himself at the first hotel he found. Hotel…
Whateverthefuck… and pretty much stayed there. He spent
most of his time staring at his reflection—wondering if he'd
remember himself post murder. He had his heart set on
transformation. He shaved his head—Mohican style like
Travis—like *Taxi Driver*.

One day a real rain.

# 13. I WAS A TEENAGE HITMAN

## JOURNAL: APR 19th 1979

Sak Lek district, Phichit Province.
I was a teenage hit man. Well... almost.
'Just 22 and I don't mind dyin''. Well...
almost. Smooth... real smooth.
A clear view from the rooftop of the Lucky
Beer Hotel.
The fag-end of a marathon card game.
Three players left.
The sun will not truly rise for another
twenty minutes. The air was still, so would
not be a factor.
The bolt-action was old - a Mannlicher - the
kind of rifle they use for safaris. But the
bore was corroded - a result from not being
properly cleaned after using bad ammo.
Sticky, but quick enough to get another
round off should the occasion require it: it
doesn't.
The sight's crosshairs hover around the
target's glazed face and throat. The gun
rears up, and the target slumps back in his
chair as the man opposite gathers his

winnings in his arms. No sir, this was not
your lucky day. Even before the report of
the shot has finished reverberating back and
forth across the deserted main street I'm
already halfway down the fire escape, sans
weapon. I dump the gloves in a plastic
wheelie bin and drag a bicycle from behind a
stack of soggy cardboard. The bike rattled
down the rocky pathway which cut a swathe
through two paddy fields. The first rays of
the morning sun frazzled the trees of the
distant hills. Despite the smell of damp
cardboard and stale noodles clinging to my
nostrils, the drama was Wagnerian. The
essentialness of the man I've just killed
has been claimed by the rising sun which
seems to appear just for the occasion.
Goodnight, Captain Boon-Nam Sansern.

### JOURNAL: APR 21st, 1979

Bangkok.
This job was not so smooth.
A tricky one.
Crowds.
Commotion.
A department store on Lad Prao.
Jimmy made it clear – this needs to happen
out of sight – do it in the loading bay.
Thursdays were Captain Suphatra's shakedown
day and I watch the oily piece of shit enter
from across the noisy monoxide-choked main
street. I cross and watch him ascend the
stairs of the mezzanine office which
overlooks the open-plan sales floor. I hang
back under the staggered shadows of the
stairwell figuring that he wouldn't leave by
the same way he came in. Business conducts
itself within twelve minutes. The sound of
patent Italian leather loafers, new, still

a-squeak, alerts me. Too expensive for a
cop. Too classy for a scum-bag noodle
sucker. Suphatra makes a detour and heads
for the loading bay – perfection. I clear
the stairwell and shadow my man. Suphatra
enters the emergency door and I catch it
before it closes and slide into the dim
concrete loading area behind him. Three
spots light the scene. Again, stale noodles
and damp cardboard load the nostrils: odours
that, for me, would now be forever synony-
mous with death.
'Suphatra!'
The cop turns fast, bringing an attaché case
up to his orange face. A word almost finds
its way to his tongue, but I get in close,
pull my nine and half punch/half shoot my
man – two in the chest. Suphatra drops his
case and grabs my wrist and I almost assist
him as he lowers himself crossed-legged onto
the floor. He gasps frantic words that I'd
never understand, but they are his last
whatever they are. I let him hang on to me.
I give him that much – this child destroying
piece of shit. His grip turns increasingly
feeble until the essential Suphatra relaxes
into the next world, depositing his
abandoned remains on the oil-slicked
concrete.

Marco's transition from 'aimless drifter' to hired killer had been no more profound than his quick stride from the Ladies Apparel to the Toys and Games section of the department store, where he had just left Suphatra's corpse cooling in the basement. Passing a mountain of outsized Day-Glo water pistols, he took it as some obscure, ironic message. There would be no remorse, no bad dreams… no dreams at all. He was vaguely disappointed by the absence of any feeling of elation or sense of power over having, in some small way, changed the course of human history. It was just a crazy game. He squeezed triggers—men ceased to be.

It had been just forty-eight hours since the first one: Captain Sansern in Sak lek. He'd expected some morality check but there was nothing. The overnight train he caught to this appointment with death could have been the commute of any working stiff on his way to the office.

But he knew why. It was his unique insight into the human condition. Life, death, it was all a matter of seeing things in the correct and proper way. Death is merely change. Living forever is like never becoming an adult and killing was just changing the parameters of a person's existence—a rearrangement of molecules. It's in the Bhagavad Gita: '*There's never been a time when you didn't exist and there'll never be a time when you'll cease to exist.*' Seven years it takes for every cell in your body to replace itself. Within a decade he'd be innocent.

He moved, cat-like, out into the sanctuary/chaos of a cloudy mid-morning Bangkok. The heavy glass spring-loaded door closed quickly, like it thought for you. *Are you in? Are you out? Whatever. But do it fast.* His sepia reflection of dark aviators, flak jacket and baseball cap (He realised the Travis Bickle Mohican was a stupid idea) was a single frame of a silent movie that flickered in the corner of his eye. If I was gonna get murdered, he mused, I'd want it to be by someone like me.

Was it a breeze of envy that ebbed and rose for Captain Suphatra as Marco faded into the crowds of Viphavadee-Rangsit Road?

It wasn't until he reached his hotel room when he realised: he was still holding Suphatra's attaché case.

He threw it on the bed and showered. He dressed, sat on the bed and stuffed his backpack with a couple of T-shirts and his wash bag. He flicked the pages of his passport and slipped it in the pocket of his combat pants.

Mission: Wait for Jimmy, who was due to meet him in the foyer in an hour with the other fifteen-large, then a cab to Bangkok International for the first flight out of the country. Destination? Whogivesafuck?

He thought it might be best to wait in the foyer and watch who comes and goes. God only knows what activity is now taking place as a result of recent occurrences. Here in this mouldy cockroach nest he was a sitting duck should he receive an unwanted visit. He gave the room a quick once over and considered Suphatra's suitcase for a moment as if seeing it for the first time.

If that isn't evidence...

Why did he grab it?

A nervous reflex?

He thumbed the locks and they flicked up. He opened the case and recoiled from it like it contained a cobra.

Now *that* was a nervous reflex.

Marco approached the case again—his heart storming the walls of his rib cage. The case contained money—a lot of money—shrink-wrapped blocks of hundred-dollar notes. Was this a million? Is this what a million looked like? He tipped the case up and emptied the blocks on to his bed; thirteen of them—one, half the size of the others. Thirteen...

'Thirteen...'

Loud wrapping on the door.

'Fuckfuckfuck...' He pulled the sheet over the pile and shouted, 'Yeah!'

A female voice, 'Mashini? Mr. Mashini?'

'Yeah. What?'

'Man to see you down stair. Mr. Jimmy.'

'Tell him I'm coming down.'

He listened to her shuffling away down the hall and descending the creaky stairs.

He paced and whispered frantically to himself—the mantra of a broken 45, 'What to do, what to do, what to do...'

He wiped the gun, put it in the case, took it to the window. Directly below in the yard was a row of wheelie bins. He dropped it neatly behind the middle bin. He grabbed the blocks, stuffed them in his rucksack, and pulled the T-shirts over them. He threw the pack under the bed, gripped the bed frame and took slow, deep breaths.

The foyer of the Royal Siam was crowded but Marco spotted Jimmy straight away, sitting under an umbrella-shaded table outside.

Marco sat opposite and said, 'You're early.'

'I'm sure you're in a hurry—and if you're not, you should be. I hear success stories.'

'Missions accomplished.'

This exchange was conducted without the two of them looking at each other. But then Marco felt Jimmy's eyes on him. Jimmy said, 'You don't look good.'

'No?'

'You been sick or sumthn'?'

'My back is still fucking me in no uncertain terms.'

From the moment he'd followed Suphatra into that loading bay he'd been on autopilot. The last hour or so was a total blank. Maybe he had been... sick, that is. The same thing had happen-ed up in Sek Lek and even now it required a certain effort to recall the aftermath of his murderous debut. It was like trying to access someone else's memories.

Jimmy pushed the carrier bag across the table towards Marco. Marco peered into the bag and saw two boxes of two hundred Marlboro.

'The still sealed one is cigarettes. You know what the other one is.'

'I smoke Luckies.'

'I'll drive you to the airport.'

Jimmy's white Nissan pickup truck joined the crazy race on the flyovers out of Bangkok.

A year ago, Marco had been coming the other way on this very road. He imagined that he saw himself, glaring sullenly from the back of a taxi, at the dirty high-rises that dominated the slums and shanty towns that constituted the suburbs of the city. That day was ancient history, and no misguided notions of nostalgia would suggest regret at the farewell Marco had bidden his previous incarnation by coming here.

Jimmy had made it clear that getting his money out of the country was Marco's own responsibility. Changing it up was risky, even in bite size amounts over a period of time—a potential trail should anyone be looking for one to follow.

Finally, the truck descended at the intersection and stopped hard outside the busy departure terminal of Bangkok International.

'My advice? A direct flight to anywhere where dollars don't raise eyebrows.'

'Home?'

'There's no place like it. If you get a tug, you won it in a game.'

'Of?'

'Connect 4?'

Marco got out of the truck and dragged his heavy rucksack out after him and came around to the driver's side. He dug deep into the pocket of his combats and produced a bundle of dollar notes. He counted them and handed them to Jimmy.

'That's six-shy of a hundred. Round it up and give it to that kid, will you?'

'For the Chrome Devils of Chiang Rai? Yer shittn' me!'

'Do it. Keep an eye.'

'Don't know when I'll be up country again... but you got it. Go easy, Marky boy, and good luck.'

Jimmy's truck lurched back out on to the causeway. Marco entered the noisy airport terminal and peered through the glass doors until he saw the truck engulfed by the madness of early evening traffic. As soon as Jimmy was out of sight, he exited the terminal and caught a taxi to the nearest airport motel.

The next forty-eight hours presented an even more pronounced sense of detachment than was usual for Marco. He always felt that he was somehow observing himself from a distance and wondered if there was ever a time when his body and soul were properly aligned. The night he spent at the Imperial Inn was a possibly futile, diversionary tactic should Jimmy, or anyone else for that matter, have less than honourable reasons for wanting to know where he was. It was risky spending any more time here than necessary but then, he surmised, it may be the last thing that anyone looking for him might expect.

69

At the Lat Krabang flea market near the motel, he bartered for the most unappealing used rucksack he could find. Back in his room, he transferred the thirteen sealed blocks and two cigarette boxes into it and slept in his clothes. He'd already decided that his story would be that he'd won the money in a backstreet Russian-roulette tournament, a la *The Deer Hunter*.

The sound of freedom, exemplified by the roar of jet engines, accompanied his shallow sleep.

At 9.15am at the check-in desk of TWA, he collected his boarding pass and watched his oily old rucksack disappear behind rubber flaps and onto the conveyer system.

Eighteen hours later, he ambled through customs at JFK with nothing to declare but two missing teeth, that rucksack and the words from some old WC Fields movie under his breath...

*'When I came into this town, I had nuthin' but the clothes I was wearing and a sack on my back. Now I own two hotels, three restaurants and the saloon we're standing in. And all I had was that sack on my back.'*
*'What was in the sack?'*
*'Two hundred and seventy thousand dollars!'*

# 14. WHATEVER HAPPENED TO PEGGY MAE?

## Wednesday October 5th
### 5.00pm

He awoke in a funk of amazement and confusion: amazed that he'd slept: confused by the rifle beside him— followed by the quick realisation that the events of this morning's early hours were not a dream. He went to the kitchen where he could see that it was now dark outside. He checked the clock on the stove—nearly dusk.

He rescued and resurrected a half-smoked blunt from an ashtray which allegedly belonged to Screamin' Jay Hawkins. He inhaled hard and considered his predicament.

Clearly, Jimmy was unaware of Suphatra's case at the time, but it was highly likely he would have heard about it eventually. An errant quarter-mill will always be missed by someone, somewhere. The mystery would loom large in Thai underworld folklore. But if it was Jimmy that set him up— arranged for that second hit to be immortalised on video tape—then why wait nine years to put it to work?

Jimmy had tracked him down in Paris fast enough. Why had it taken this long to track him down now? and after all this time, why bother? It's a given that by now those ill-gotten gains would be gone with the wind.

And this shit with the video tape…? Betty Boop? What the actual fuck?! Why not just knock on the door and say 'Hey fuck face, I found you! Any of that green left? Consider this a shakedown.'

There was, however, an even less appealing possibility… Perhaps Marco's name and current whereabouts had finally found their way onto the top of two Thai police precincts' 'to do' list. This had the acrid stench of vengeance—an invitation to a stroll in Punishment Park.

His tongue played with the smoke in his mouth. He realised he welcomed this crisis. This was… something. A ray of light cutting into his crypt.

The steel door, the reinforced bars at the window, guns in every room, the dagger taped to the bottom of the bathroom washbasin, the switchblade in the pillowcase… The spoils of paranoia were finally paying off.

He went to the wardrobe—to the stash—to that hole in the floor that he served. Unlocked it, took out the half-finished journal and dropped it on the kitchen table. He took the typewriter off the top of the fridge. He would finish it today— his journal—his confession; his last will and testament; his feeble shout into eternity that someone, somewhere might one day hear... and know he had been in the world.

He re-read where he started it off—his arriving at JFK; 16.30 April 23rd, 1979—a Monday, and walking the long walk through a deserted customs area with a big dirty rucksack containing $270,000.

And then the flashbacks to how he acquired it...

He never wrote a thing about how he spent it; the coke blizzard; the lost gambling weekends in Atlantic City; Rock-and-Roll memorabilia auctions; the teeth implants; meeting Bonnie; losing Bonnie... none of this struck him as being cinematic. His '79 homecoming was *Midnight Express* with a happier ending and no welcoming party. The Bonnie part was drug-loaded triple XXX filth with some kind of *Love Story* thing going on in there somewhere. With no ending—just a sudden cut to black.

But now, as he wrote about how the phone and video tape had so expertly found itself in his apartment, it occurred to him that if persons unknown wanted him dead, he would be.

He began with that...

```
If persons unknown wanted me dead, I would
be...
```

Coffee, honeyed toast and four blunts fuelled the early evening until the day began to die. Despite the logic of the situation as it presented itself, his imagination fast-forwarded to the unshakeable belief that his corpse would be lying on a slab by the time the sun returns. And should he die in a bloody shootout tonight? They'd have the ending to his movie...

He placed the updated manuscript in a mannered pile beside the typewriter where the cops would probably find it.

With death in mind, he selected fresh socks and boxers. He got dressed, put the switchblade in his top pocket and the .38 in his boot. He found and put on the fake Breitling watch he'd brought back from Thailand. He kissed his fingertips and put his hand on the jukebox. He took ten seconds to think of his murdered teenage dad then left the apartment.

It was just before ten when he got back to Leroy. He wanted to devour at least two hours of the scene leading up to whatever was going to happen to him. The club was still closed, but now the studded door had a poster scotch-taped over the spy hole.

**Game Show**
**TONITE!**
**D.J Ellie Gantz**
**Cover $8.**
**23.00**
**'Resurrection junket'**

This text was accompanied by a Grable-esque redhead showing her garter belt and holding up a big ace card. He tried the cold handle. The door was locked solid.

He crossed the road to La La Lavazza, a small coffee bar busy with chatter and cigarette fumes. A dismal attempt at a jukebox dominated the place—a flat Perspex facade depicting a Wurlitzer and, behind it, the mechanisms of a CD player. Madonna's bleating something like *'I fell in love with some dago. Girl with eyes like potatoes...'* accompanied his order for a 'blacker than night' espresso.

He found a seat by the window where he could see the club's entrance. On the table behind him someone had left a magazine—INTERVIEW. He grabbed it and flicked through. The usual gloss and nonsense—self-important nobodies that other nobodies decided were somebodies—fashion shoots of dignity-bereft fags and junkies.

It was just after eleven when an apparition of sideburns and corduroy came sauntering down the street, pulled out a bunch of keys and unlocked the big door to the club. Behind Marco, a crowd simultaneously put down their Lattes, grabbed battered flight cases and left La La Lavazza en mass. The group, ten of them, crossed and approached the key-holder who saw them and beckoned them inside. Marco's coffee had yet to arrive, but he left an Abe and hurried across the road to join them.

Music from inside the club rumbled as he walked through the long corridor into it. The walls were glass cases of antiquated eight by tens—a Mise-en-scene of bikinis and fleshy stomachs. The floor and ceiling of mirrored tiles created a vortex of eternity, completing the time-warping effect.

Marco descended stone steps and followed the music down. It was old and could have been straight from his old man's record collection. He came to a room which was less a club and more like the set of a television game show—a disastrous collision of chrome and illuminated primary-coloured panels—huge neon question marks punctuating every wall. The key holder vaulted up onto the dark stage and disappeared behind thick sequin-encrusted drapes. Stage-lights flickered on revealing an orange guitar: a big old Eddie Cochran job on a stand and plugged into a small amplifier.

The key-holder reappeared. He addressed the group who were unpacking cameras and sound equipment. He told them he was going to his office to make some calls and find out what's keeping her. It seemed they were all waiting for someone.

Marco approached a young Jap in a satin jacket, fixing a lens to a Nikon. 'What is this?'

The Jap jutted his chin towards the stage. 'One of Xtravaganza's things. She's always late.'

Extravaganza? The name rang none and Marco thought better of exposing his hand by requesting a wise up. He hung back as the crew set up. They were textbook media types—walking billboards for designer labels, destined for oblivion in some corporate wilderness. The place started to fill up with young guys and gals dressed up like they were auditioning for *American Graffiti*.

He saw her legs first: encased in seamed black stockings. The echoic tik tik tik of her impossibly high-heeled stilettos as she descended the staircase from the street were like the warning signal of a Geiger counter—radiation and science fiction special-effects imminent.

A sudden barrage of flashlights obscured her entrance—heralded by an entourage of three transvestites—each of them

74

immaculately attired in different traffic light colours—red...
yellow... green...

The photographers crowded around them as the quartet their
way across the room.

Marco craned to get a better look, but his vision rang flash-
blind. By the time normal service was resumed she had taken
the stage.

Her entourage were nowhere to be seen.

Someone turned the music off.

The key-holder suddenly appeared, stage left, and led the
applause. 'Ladies... gentlemen... the late... Erika Xtravaganza!'

Tall and pale, she seemed to drift into a dim blue light, in a
midnight-blue satin pencil dress, her hair in bangs of shellac
black. She picked up and hung that big orange Gretsch over a
slender shoulder and hit a thick wobbly pulsating chord.

For Marco, it was as if an epiphany of sound and vision had
punched him in the face. She was a dream he never knew he'd
never had. He pushed his way through the crowd for a closer
look.

'Oyez, oyez, oyez...' Her voice was throaty and deep—like
Lauren Bacall. She leaned into the microphone and
announced... 'In 1957, one of the world's most mysterious and
enduring icons left New York City and was never seen again.
The mystery, like the enigma herself, has tantalised and teased
us for over three decades and still we ask, "Whatever
happened to Peggy Deveroux?" Well... it is a mystery no more.
Peggy Deveroux... is alive and well.'

The collective gasp struck Marco as funny. Before 'who the
hell is Peggy Deveroux?' could even manifest itself in his mind,
the curtains swished open behind Xtravaganza, revealing a
collection of life-sized mannequins dressed in old style corsets,
nylons and garter belts. All five of them were topped with
identical wigs—replicas of the style Xtravaganza was
wearing—immaculate oil-black bangs.

The mannequins were surrounded by framed magazines with
fruity titles like '*Wink*', '*Cad*', '*Chicks 'n' Chuckles*', '*Sir!*' and
'*Black Nylons High Heels*'. A copy of '*Quick*' had the headline,
'*Are sex dreams normal?*' They all featured the full-figured,

raven-haired angel with eyes of hydrogen blue. The magazines named her as Peggy Deveroux, or Peggie, as some of them spelled it: the spitting image of the woman who now stood before him on this stage. He recognised Deveroux from a couple of framed photos in his hallway. Now he had a name to go with the face.

With the magazines was a collection of glossy blow-ups featuring Peggy with other girls in campy bondage situations. The hairstyles and make-up dated the pictures—probably the 40s or 50s, but the costumes looked somehow recent—modern. Xtravaganza's uncanny resemblance to the girl on the covers made him wonder if a lifetime of marijuana intake had given him brain damage. She spoke as Marco stood mesmerised by her sloe eyes... her mouth—sapphires and rubies set in ivory.

She indicated with a manicured hand the tableau behind her. 'Here we present part of a recently discovered collection of personal items some friends had put into storage shortly after she disappeared. They were thought to have been lost forever but the complete collection will form the centrepiece of our next event. Ladies... gentlemen... and...' she smiled mischievously, '... miscellaneous... I announce... *Resurrection!* A celebration of a pioneer of sex and fetish culture—a legendary pin-up whose work appeared in private stashes across America in the nineteen fifties and set the stage for the sexual revolution. *Resurrection* will present to the world—for the first time in over thirty years—a personal appearance from the Queen of the Pin-ups, the Dark Angel... Peggy Mae Deveroux!'

A tsunami of questions hit the stage. Xtravaganza, bemused by the commotion, seemed to enjoy the building hysteria: like she got off on the crowd's kinetic charge.

The Jap photographer raised a hand. 'When and where's this thing gonna be?'

Xtravaganza strummed the guitar once more and waggled the tremolo arm. The chord shimmered. She grinned. '*When*? This very weekend. *Where*? South of the border.'

This raised the odd guffaw. Confused murmuring among the group ensued. A thin-faced woman, power-dressed in grey, bleated, 'How south?'

Xtravaganza leaned in close to the microphone and said, after a drama-loaded pause, in an exaggerated Latino accent... 'Meh-he-coh.'

With a sweeping arm she led the room's focus to the screen behind her. 'At midnight on this screen, a phone number will appear for 30 seconds. The first twenty callers will get a reserved seat on the plane that will be taking off from a New York airport this Friday morning! To ensure maximum secrecy, the exact destination will not be announced until we are in the air.' She stepped back, away from the microphone. She yelled, her voice thinned by the distance, 'Buena suerte, ladies, gentlemen and... miscellaneous!'

Loud music twanged out of the loudspeakers—a trashy Rockabilly song that sounded like it was recorded in a kettle. The place suddenly leapt into action as if King Kong had thrown a Buick down the stairs. The journos moved back. The floor was suddenly invaded by an invading army straight out of *The Wanderers*. Circle skirts rose, revealing pale bum cheeks and stocking tops. Stiletto heels stepped and kicked. The place was a bop and strolling mass of velvet, chiffon and sharkskin.

Someone cut the stage lights. Xtravaganza unplugged the guitar and exited, stage right. The dancers ignored her exit, but all journo eyes were on her as she disappeared behind the curtains.

Marco craned his neck to see she where she went. As soon as she was out of sight, he began to question his sanity. The display remained on stage, and he shared the general astonishment at Xtravaganza's creepy resemblance to the long lost Deveroux woman.

It was twenty to midnight. Marco hit the bar. Foreign bottled beers. He pointed at the one with the most appealing label, leaned against the bar to watch the bopping crowd, and knocked it back. Beer, fear, orders from persons unknown, to do an unknown thing, to make midnight phone calls...

```
Today.
Was a day.
To remember...
```

On the other side of the dancefloor, beneath strobing lights, he saw the Jap put his camera in a backpack and pull out a cell phone—not dissimilar to the Panasonic he'd been given. He realised he—they—had the advantage. As soon as that number came up, he and the Jap would be on their phones. Marco pulled it out of his pocket and re-familiarised himself with it. Punch the number. Hit green.

The countdown to midnight began. Journos around the club's dancefloor were checking their watches, testing their pens, scratching biro on notepads.

The clock struck twelve.

Big red characters hit the screen at the back of the stage...

212-763-0042

Marco memorised the digits—the N.Y. area code; Buddy's birthday; the year Kennedy got shot; two zeros and the age Elvis was when he bought the farm—and ran up the stairs and outside—hindered by the rush of journos who all scrambled up to street level with him and ran for the nearest phone booths. He punched the number and connected. A girl asked for his name, the name of the publication he represented, and his phone number. He gave his name and tentatively offered, 'Christian Broadcasting Network? I don't know the number of my phone. It's new. It's one a them cell things. Can I call you back?'

There was an agonising beat and half before said 'Yes, if you can call us back within the hour.'

He half spluttered that he would and said, 'don't forget me!'

He found a drop-down with the number he'd been given and called it. It rang... and rang. He cut the call and tried again. This time someone answered. The man on the other end said yeah. This was not the same guy who called him last night. He sounded out of breath, but he got right to it. 'Talk to me.'

'This thing. It's in Mexico.'

'Mexico, where?'

'That's the thing, they're not giving that out until we're in the air.'

'Until we're in the air...'

'It's all top secret. They're giving twenty seats on a plane, for members of the press, to some undisclosed location in Mexico. I got a place, but I don't have a passport.'

Silence.

'Hello?'

The voice said, 'relax, I'm still here.'

Marco waited and then remembered. 'What's this number?'

'Huh?'

'This number - they want it - the people who are organising this thing. They need to call me back. They're gonna need the number of this phone.'

Reluctantly, the voice told him. 'You gonna remember that?'

Marco made a quick translation into celebrity birthdays and dates of famous disasters.

'Yeah, I got it. I'll call ya back!'

The man said 'Hey!' But Marco cut him off, punched the Peggy Deveroux hotline and connected.

'Hi, It's Marco Mascini from the Christian Broadcasting Network...'

The same girl said yeah, and Marco gave her the cell number. She said, 'We will call you with full details. Make sure you stay close to your phone.'

Marco confirmed that he would and called the mystery man right back. 'It's done. They're gonna reserve me a place. But I can't go to no Mexico without a passport. Fix it and I'll go.' Marco waited. The line cut. 'Hello? Hello!'

He punched the number again. It rang... and rang. He cut the call and tried again. Nothing. No answer.

Heading east, his thoughts raced ahead and were already home to his hallway, where a collection of framed photos hung. A shot of King Elvis with his arm round the stripper Tempest Storm, flanked by two black and white eight by tens of the woman he now had a name for—Peggy Deveroux. If that *was* her real name.

She disappeared in '57—the year of his birth. Why were people looking for her now? If there were no repercussions, no other occurrences connected to this, could he go his entire life without knowing? and live beneath the blade of his secret held by persons unknown? What could he expect when he got home? A unit of Thai cops waiting to pounce out of his fridge? Did he now have to live with the threat of one day being invaded? He saw visions of himself defending his castle against a marauding army of east-Asian mafia.

The last twenty-four hours had changed everything. Someone somewhere knew who he was, what he had done; that he existed. The possibility that this would be the end of the matter was unacceptable. He would try the number again. Failing that, he would track down Erika Xtravaganza. Clearly, she's the connection. Whatever happened to Peggy Deveroux had put the hooks in him. But whatever was about to happen to Marco Mascini had got him all tore up.

The cat had it easy. Curiosity killed it outright.

# 15. LONG DISTANCE INFORMATION

Leonard Borg cut the call on the cell phone and checked through the gap in the door from the shower room. Carlo Madden was strapped naked to the bed in the half-light of a darkened bedroom. Borg had left the axe against the wall where Madden could see it: to consider its possibilities. And in doing so, Borg knew, the desired order of things would come to pass.

Madden blurted it out... 'She escaped three years ago. Back in '85!'

And there it was.

80

Borg dialled Minister John Stevens' number. 'I have it on very good authority that Deveroux escaped from Patton three years ago. Also, your man in N.Y has just called claiming that she's in Mexico. I detect amateur hour.'

'Of course. He's a nobody.'

'Nobodies are a fallacy. They come from somewhere.'

'From an old patsy directive. Off the books. A scrap from yesteryear. Completely disposable.'

'So… Mexico. Your man's keen but needs a passport. Friday.'

'Where in Mexico?'

'To be revealed. Says he won't know until he's in the air. Some top-secret location bullshit. But we can use him, to at least show us where. Can you arrange it—the passport?'

'Do you trust him?'

'Do I trust him? He's *your* nobody, remember? Give him hot creds. If he tries to get cute, we'll know where he is. According to—'

Out in the bedroom, Madden started crying. Borg covered the mouthpiece and shouted through the door. 'Shut! Up!'

Madden did his best to stifle his terror and wind it down to a faraway whimper.

'According to my sources…', Borg continued, casting a languid eye over Madden's trembling form, '… the bird has flown— three years back, adding credence to the freak's claim that she knows Deveroux personally and that she's making some kind of a comeback.'

'And you believe this? On what basis?'

It was no small effort to suppress his impatience, but Borg managed it through gritted teeth.

'Given the proximity of the bughouse she escaped from to the border, it rings right. Tijuana or surrounding areas are a fair bet. An escapee wouldn't dare pull this shit on this side of the line.'

The hesitation on the other end of the phone was one of those moments that felt like eons. Finally, Stevens ended it. 'Where's Mascini flying from?'

'Mascini? That the kid's name? JFK, he said.'

'Okay, Leonard. Consider it done.'

81

Borg cut in. 'A hot passport, remember! As soon as his plane takes off, there will be a flight plan. Get it and get it to me. Wherever your idiot lands, I want to be there.'

Borg cut the call before he heard the Minister's agreement.

Borg went outside for some fresh air. It was too warm to be fresh. He sat on the low wall outside the decrepit motel and gazed over midnight traffic at the distant mountains. The border was just a hundred and twenty-five miles away. The idea that she might be in such close proximity put fire in his guts.

Rookie cop fire.

Korean War hero fire.

Hollywood fixer fire.

He imagined he could smell her: her whore pheromones drifting across the hard line that said, '*You are Mexico, and I am America*.' He could taste her on a wild and wayward wind that swept him up and dumped his bloody screaming mess... right back in the middle of 8th Avenue.

Right back to 1957...

Leonard Joseph Borg's daddy, Charles, was a Mormon Fed, a St. Paul SAC, 'Special Agent in Charge', in the days of Dillinger. Leonard was two when daddy and his six wives and their eleven children moved to Utah from Minnesota in 1930. His mother, Dolores, was the first wife, and Borg, the second child.

A fervent and meticulous adherent to the Latter-Day Saints and its codes of chastity, dress and public comportment, young Borg graduated, inevitably, from Brigham Young. Aged twenty, he entered the Police Academy in Ogden, expecting to join the Bureau before he was twenty-five.

He got posted to San Diego and distinguished himself on a regular basis to the point where the higher-ups were muttering FBI noises. The only thing between young Borg and the corridors of power was the sticky topic of his father's polygamy. The Bureau favoured the Mormonite doctrine—but only up to a point.

At the grand old age of fifty-three, daddy fucked up and brought down all the acid rain that comes with getting his ten-year-old niece to jerk him off. The transcripts made for savoury reading, *'...do it till the milk comes... that's it... that's it... so sweet...'*

No-one knew who fingered him: a colleague within the department or an enemy without. But it didn't matter. Whoever it was fucked two Borgs for the price of one.

Daddy's dark shadow cast long and wide and the FBI noises around young Borg became an abrupt silence.

He knew he had plateaued.

If he was lucky.

As it turned out... he wasn't.

Effectively a shamed samurai by association, young Borg found himself edged out to the side-lines until it was clear that the name Borg was about as desirable as a negro in a Vegas steam room. Which is almost exactly how an SAC in San Diego put it to him, '... Leo, the name Borg is about as desirable as a nigger in a Vegas steam room...'

*'Polar Bears be my saviour now...'*

With vague hopes of getting himself killed, Borg joined the army and they put him in the 31st Infantry Regiment which, in 1950, meant Korea.

Kim Il-sung had swung his considerable Commie dick over the 38th Parallel, so all bets were off.

The Polar Bears were a tenderizer unit for air sweeps—which meant maximum and unchecked carnage. Borg killed his first men in Iwon. Long-distance stuff. Swept the hills with his M3 and, minutes later, stepped over the smoking results. If wholesale slaughter conflicted with his LDS codes, he couldn't say he'd noticed.

The Bears met with little resistance and dealt death like poker hands. The term 'overkill' was made for the B26s that would swoop over afterwards and effectively kill the already dead. Their campaign was shaping up to be no more than a bloody hike. But by the time they'd got to the Yalu River the whole deal went meat-machine.

Manchurian hoards descended from out of the sub-freezing fog and decimated Borg's entire unit. Both his guns jammed. He jabbed and sliced blind with his bayonet, shredding every one of those chink fucks that got within arm's length. Later, when Borg cast his mind back to this massacre, as he sometimes did, he figured he'd sent at least fifteen of those godless savages to their great reward. Sometimes he'd fret that in his passion he'd taken out some of his own men.

His unit's commander was killed, along with the hapless fuck they'd sent to replace him. Borg had taken shrapnel which left him with his jaw near hanging off. A miracle had him stagger for six hours across the nightmare terrain and straight into an X Corp stronghold where they were dug in tight and holding ground. Their medic had morphine, but the intense cold rendered it useless. Borg plunged his face in the snow and let it do its work, which is how they found him the next morning when they scooped him up and made a suicide run for the Marine lines at Hagaru-ri.

Officially, this was the end of Borg's active service in Korea. While convalescing in the military hospital in Daejeon he re-located some of his missionary zeal. His Latter-Day Saints codes, he thought, would find purchase in the bombed-out ghettos of Taejon. He, and a handful of like-minded grunts, converted South Koreans and American servicemen alike to the ways of the LDS. They even got a temple built—a flimsy construction of corrugated iron and bamboo at the end of an alleyway behind Yongsan Station—a rag tag congregation looking for salvation in a place where gods came to die.

While Borg's missionaries were converting all-comers to the ways of Brother Brigham, twenty-one American servicemen had converted in ways unimaginable to any right-minded American, and gone Red. The war was coming to a close in '53, but no-one could talk of anything but 'The Twenty-One'—twenty-one defectors who shat in Uncle Sam's face and went commie chink.

When Borg heard a rumour that one of them had shacked up with a local girl nearby, he took it upon himself to find him. Strangely, the papers reported that Sergeant Rufus Douglas had died in hospital of a rheumatic heart disorder with complications. The only complication that Borg could recall was the young Sergeant's girl arriving at their apartment to find Borg's hands around her beloved's throat. He killed her too. But this could never be enough. He sat the Sergeant's body on the nearest chair. He dragged the dead girl up onto the table, ripped her dress aside and fucked her so the traitor could watch from wherever the deserving dead peer into the world of the living.

The papers didn't even mention her, let alone how she had been violated. This, Borg now realised, is how the world worked and was a precursor of things to come.

In the aftermath of what would be remembered, ironically Borg thought, as the forgotten war, they had him driving for Operation Glory, transporting dead PVAs up to the border and swapping them for dead Americans.

In '55, another three defectors realised the turncoat game was for the birds and defected back. Incredibly, Uncle Sam accepted their appeal.

A clear-cut case of keeping your enemies closer.

Surely.

If those three thought their Stateside return would be anything but closely monitored, then they were even more stupid than their treacherous conduct suggested. Hoover had every man jack of them shadowed... and Borg was one of the shadows.

There had been no fallout from the Sergeant Rufus murder, but the fact they took Borg off Operation Glory and put him on defector detection duty suggested an inkling had reached the right people, and that they liked the way Borg's flag flew.

They sent him home where he spent eight months in Washington staking out one of those scumbags. Once confirmed that his quarry had nothing to offer in the way of compromising intelligence, and nothing that might threaten American sensibilities, Borg was invited to work as a private investigator for a Republican-connected defence attorney he met during his service.

85

His feet barely touched the ground in Utah, where he left his Purple Heart and Bronze Star with his mother and bounced into California.

They worked out of a two-room office in Glendale: exclusively high-profile scandal-avoidance stuff: the removal business, be it evidence, money trails or embryos. Eighteen months in and Borg got a call from Howard Hughes' head-hunters. It seemed Leonard J. Borg's reputation preceded and exceeded him.

It was common knowledge, at least to those with even a vague proximity to the power people, that Hughes 'the man' was barely a breathing rumour: a Codeine-obliterated Nosferatu with a hard-on for clean living who slept in his own shit. Hughes 'the brand', however, was still a force to be reckoned with and there were those who were fixed on using that force like a biblical storm.

It soon became clear to Borg that Hughes' control over his regime was marginal and was actually controlled by a small but powerful group of (largely Mormon) corporation executives; some of whom were 'juiced in' at Hughes Tool; others with empires of similar political clout. They referred to themselves as the 'Kingmakers'.

The Kingmakers ran a stable of political 'stars' who they were grooming for powerful government positions. Hughes still had his old fuck-pads all over town, but he'd long since tired of bringing in would-be starlets from around the country with a view to *maybe* auditioning, but *definitely* fucking them... before sending them on their way. Uncle Howard may have been bored, but the system stood and many within his organisation continued to exploit the facility as a matter of course. Wire taps and clandestine movie footage would always reap dividends when it came to controlling errant influencers.

Clearly, Deveroux had been summoned to that December '57 soiree, but probably high-tailed it before the evening went Hollyweird. Unfortunately, she may now be in possession of an anecdote that could not, and will not, ever be told. At just twenty-nine, John Stevenoski was a new kid on the brink of political stardom and had to be protected like an endangered species. So, it was just another day in the secret history of

America that saw Diane Stevenoski hanging from a piano wire in the presidential suite of the Roosevelt Hotel... and just another day of housekeeping for Leonard Borg.

And then there was that chase across 8th Avenue... and that truck... and the end of everything...

# 16. THE SECOND DEATH OF LEONARD BORG

The darkness he was propelled into was punctuated by three distinct explosions.

The first was a universe of screams.

Endless screams.

... Bellevue.

It was only when the screaming stopped that Borg realised that the screams were his own. Then shouting, not his own, panicky—urgent. Falling head-first as lights... a ceiling of hooded strip-lights rolled downwards. Medics raced him through a dim corridor. A rubber gloved palm across his brow held him. He forced his head to one side and caught a reflection in a dark window. Something had emerged from his abdomen. His gloves were wet.

Fade to black...

The second was an explosion of... calm.

A cathode screen fixed in the air before him... alone with the screen... floating in space together on a bed of endless darkness.

Was this death?

Was this hell?

There was movement on the screen. Occurrences. Tales woven. But they were... complicated. Too alien to assimilate.

The sound comforted.

The sound was low.

The twittering voices of cartoons—endless cartoons. Advertisements for automobiles… cigarettes… candy… but a voice… a twittering voice—reoccurring. 'Boop boop e doop!' They questioned him. The questions seemed to drift in cartoon form, visible from the television. He outlined his account. That he intercepted her on 46th St. outside her apartment and put her in the dumpster that he remembered was doing its rounds outside that night. His phony account that rendered Deveroux birdfeed on some New Jersey landfill appeased his interrogators. They made conciliatory noises and told him they would come back to see him soon.

Fade to black…

The third explosion was a flurry of visitors moving at unimaginable speeds. He understood he was static—bedridden. But why was everything so fast? Medics who assessed him, the nurses who tended his ablutions day after day, seemed at first to be in a frantic hurry, but then they would enter and leave the room faster and faster until they were nothing more than sudden drafts. The world escaped his grasp and sped off without him.

Fade to black…

The garden was beautiful… drenched in the sun's love. Bloody Dahlias splashed immaculate jade lawns. The doddering gait of shuffling old men, shared like an open secret by everyone in it.

Sports-shirts hid pacemakers.

Bermuda shorts hid colostomy bags and diapers.

A girl in a hard-blue uniform steered a drooling fat man by the elbow up to the house where Borg was watching, as always, from an upstairs window. He could see her mouth moving.

What was that?

She was… *speaking to the man*.

Words…

Borg moved his mouth. He could speak too. He said 'Mother'. A concept occurred, like a cold raindrop on the forehead. He'd been sitting at this window all day. Then he realised he'd always sat at this window. He couldn't remember a time when he hadn't sat here. He'd been here forever.

He was the man…

… who sat at the window.

Again, he found the word on his tongue. 'Mother.'

Another cold raindrop.

Then another.

He was filling up.

God was pouring him back into himself.


'How do you feel, Leonard?'

Borg considered Dr Haas's off-the-peg concern but couldn't conjure up an off-the-peg response. It would be easy to answer honestly, but Borg's instincts—what there were of them—told him to remain hidden.

Haas, bifocaled and earnest, perused the reports spread across the desk in front of him. 'Physically, I mean.'

He spoke as if addressing the reports directly rather than Borg himself. Maybe that was hardly surprising. Until his resurrection six weeks ago, bi-weekly ward visits and reports had been Haas' only mode of contact with him. Borg felt competition with his file and dossier self. Borg on paper was malleable, but Borg in the resurrected flesh? He still had an eternity to transverse for that rendezvous. He needed to straighten his story with himself first before opening up to this figure of starch and whiskers before him.

Framed and archaic deeds—accolades on parchment hung on walls around Hass' office—to Haas directly or to The Strong Memorial Hospital in general, certificates of privilege, of righteous upbringing, of progeny with great teeth and patted shoulders of assured futures.

Borg grunted harshly and croaked, 'I don't feel… like I can walk.'

'You'll walk, Leonard. Do you remember anything? About the accident?'

89

The chaos and horror of that Bellevue corridor—the bones of his pelvis splintered and thrust through his guts. He looked past Haas' wispy head towards the large open window at azure skies. It was the sky of another world. The scents of the flowers outside were alien to him—they weren't the same—skies and aromas of the future. He understood that this was not 1957.

He could feel the time—the vast dark ocean he'd floated across—back to the shore of himself. On that shore there were sparks of turbulence—at once repelling and beckoning—and now, finally, he landed.

Borg gripped feebly at the arms of his wheelchair, sucked future air through gritted teeth. 'What day is this?'

Hass told him. 'Monday... June 3rd... 1963.'

When Hass presented him with the concept of his having spent six years in a coma in this Rochester facility, it was news but no surprise. Soon, Borg received visitors... men with gifts of history and tomorrows lost. They questioned him... wanted to know what he knew... what he *remembered*. Curiously, they didn't question him again about the Pin-up. To all appearances they bought his story. Mission accomplished.

They reciprocated. They filled him in on the life and times of Leonard Borg to which he had been absent. Kid Kennedy had reaped the kingdom. They'd sent a man to space.

They told him his mother visited him every week, Thursdays, until she died last year. Some form of Septicaemia, they told him. Something wrong with her blood.

The men with gifts brought effects... items his mother might have taken away in bag had he waved the big adios on that New York street... a ring of keys to doors he was yet to remember: his wristwatch... stilled now, the times it told consigned to vapour: a heavy gold signet ring heralded by a red stone with an insignia that meant nothing: his wallet... leather and stained with dry blood. Someone had tried to clean it, but nothing doing. It contained bills, crisp with antiquity; his Hughes Tool ID card and another one with a name he couldn't recall.

Regimes of physiotherapy brought his body back to him. Eighteen months had passed since his resurrection, and now he was on weights—real ones. Two men, 'APTA therapists' Hass called them, came on alternative days to work manicured thumbs into the recesses of his pudgy legs. Endless sessions of traction, massage and shock treatment filled his days. They taped wires to him, sometimes stuck him with needles and turned on the juice. A mild execution—strapped to a gurney with a hunk of rubber in his mouth. He'd convulse, pass out and recover in time to feel himself being lifted from a puddle of hot piss and drool.

These last few months saw the transformation of the two useless sandbags beneath him become actual limbs again. He'd lumber in the corridor from wall to wall, up from his window-less room to Hass' office and back, palms smacking against glossy green painted brick walls. Now his confident stride had won him an accompanied tour around the grounds outside. The first thing he did when he took his place among the nappy-fillers out in the garden was look up at the window where he'd spent his lost years. He saw a hulking shadow in blue striped pyjamas leaning against the window frame. Big ruddy baby cheeks threatened to render the sweaty face itself an irrelevance. The thin streak of black hair gave his head the appearance of a deformed piggy bank. Borg squinted and wiped the sweat from his eyes, and the figure was gone. The man at the window didn't sit there no more. *He* didn't sit there no more.

They sent a nurse, three days a week—a girl, really—dressed in the uniform of the hospital. She talked about TV shows she liked, jerked him off and gave him suck jobs, often while relating what singers had been on Sullivan that week... a courtesy he suspected was not on Strong Memorial's standard roster of treatments, even here in the future. Sometimes she would bring in a bottle of Old Forester, which she would pour into plastic beakers. Her visits suggested a powerful force of a machine still in place. He believed it was only a matter of time before he would know his part in it.

Just in time for Christmas 1966, they discharged him.

91

# 17. SHOWTIME

They'd given him a riverside bungalow in Bridesburg, Philadelphia, an air-conditioned limbo somewhere between New York and Washington. The location suggested accessibility—that he was still in the gang. He married the nurse, Margaret Rose Randell. Ran it by the powers first. The fact they did not baulk should have clarified his situation. Her people were from Chester, just on the other side of the Schuylkill, so she was happy. It was fair to assume she held some sway over where they would be located. The notion that she was somehow assigned to him did not exceed his scope. He didn't love her exactly, as far as he understood the concept, but figured he would eventually, if at all possible. Their sex was good. She liked it as far as he could tell. Coltish and enthusiastic, and she didn't say anything about his inability to ejaculate. She had the hips, the lean thighs—was built for motherhood. But Borg thought maybe it was something about the way she was made *down there* that couldn't give his glans the necessary purchase. Then one night his war years drifted across the desolation of his mind—about how 'America the beautiful' was so unfairly insulted by the Twenty-One... Sergeant Rufus and his whore... Another one of those raindrops hit his forehead.

From then on, their lovemaking was conducted in total silence, with no more of that dirty talk—and with Margaret keeping still. Very... very still...

He figured she understood men like himself—men that had seen combat—understood that they were devastated in wildly differing ways. He figured that's why she said nothing about his being able to ejaculate from that time on.

The fact that her happiness was of no small importance to him was reason enough to embrace the straight life. And more, he believed that she loved him. His only concern was how his work would sit with domesticity.

He needn't have worried.

In the first few of his wilderness years, he would receive regular visits for information about this or that incident. They always came in twos. Sometimes one of them would be female. The world was changing. They came at night when Margaret was at work. She understood the nature of these conferences and would make herself scarce on the rare occasions she was home. He wondered if she was more wised-up than he was—that she was more 'in the gang' than he was. These meetings would be conducted in his office. The questions were often candid—obscenely so—*what became of that corpse? What became of the hands and teeth?* Sometimes the questions would just be plain loco and nuts. '*When Monroe was living at Doheny Drive, where did she buy her maxi-pads?*' '*Can we verify the brand?*' Borg learned to assess the level of paranoia assigned to a case by the sheer randomness of the questions. The devil was in the detail and the more obscure the enquiry, the more pressing the situation.

The decade was punctuated by assassinations, and the conferences that exponentially followed them. He'd missed the first half of the sixties, but '68 was busy. Dr King and Bobby K—loose ends kept to a minimum. Slick. Bobby's clock was cleaned in L.A., so conferences concerning the Ambassador Hotel and who might have been in place rang relevant. Other visits followed the Martin Luther King hit and again enquiries zeroed in on the L.A. area. King was shot in Memphis. But it was clear from the line of enquiry that the MLK endgame began in the City of Angels.

No one mentioned the Pin-up—the Deveroux woman—his nemesis. Clearly, they had believed him when he told them she was dead. Maybe she was. Whatever happened to her stayed under the radar. Case closed.

Somewhere along the grapevine he heard that Senator Cornelius Stevenoski's son, John Stevenoski, had body-swerved the whole politics game, changed his surname to Stevens and became a television evangelist with his own station.

Within a couple of years, the visits stopped and were replaced with phone calls. By the middle of the 70s, the phone stopped ringing. He knew, now, that the generous allowance he

93

continued to receive, and the rent-free bungalow, was the big fuck-off.

He was out.

He got involved with the local community. His Mormonism belonged to another life, but Margaret buzzed Protestant in this one, so he helped organise fetes and fund-raising efforts for her church on Kirkbride Avenue. He had to do *something*, right?

The straight life bemused and horrified him, and in the midst of this bemusement and horror (and with Margaret's being very... very still) the straight life blessed them with two daughters. The older one, Georgina, was an undeniable beauty in the conventional sense of the term. His army and Hollywood years had exposed him to true ugliness, so he recognised beauty when he saw it. 'Gee Gee' was certainly that.

The younger one, Geraldine, would struggle as a female. The puppy-fat of her teenage years, along with a surly temperament, would remain a fixture and warp her ascent into adulthood.

The notion of his being a showbiz Golem never left him. This was the definitive Leonard Borg—his signature role. He was consumed by the notion that his daughters could never know the man he really was, only the no-mark he pretended to be. For Leonard Borg, fatherhood was an acting gig.

Gee Gee was thirteen when she got in with a bunch of coloureds that he knew were giving her drugs. She came home one evening with eyes like saucers and talking gibberish—an even more demented version of the hipster-speak he used to hear from the mouths of beatniks back in the day. He grabbed his old automatic and silencer. He went over there—in the early hours of the morning—to the dilapidated house they all hung out in. He parked the car and walked the remaining two blocks. The neighbourhood was going to hell, and the house was either a symptom or the cause. He kicked the door in, forced the small crowd that sat around in a mutual stupor down into the basement, and peppered them all with mute bullets. Splintering wood, exploding plaster, and muffled screams filled the night air as he made his way back to the car.

The story made the papers—three dead—four wounded: one seriously. He half-expected to get a call from the powers about this lapse of protocol. In fact, he kind of hoped he would. But the powers never rang that phone again.

By 1980 he was alone. Margie had died in '78. She was twelve years younger than he was, but she checked out first. Liver cancer. Where's the justice? Took her four months from when they told her she had it to when they buried her. Georgy and Gee Gee stuck around long enough to accompany the casket to the cemetery.

Georgy married some highfalutin hedge-fund manager prick and moved to Hawaii, of all places. The last he heard; Gee Gee was beach-bumming it in Florida some place. The once in a half-decade postcard he received from her would precede a letter about needing money.

He worked the garden until it was as immaculate as the one at the Strong Memorial Hospital. He'd take a rest from mowing the lawn, break open a beer with increasingly unsteady hands and gaze at the darkened windows at the back of his house. These moments reminded him of those lost years propped against the hospital window, drooling. The panorama of dark glass was an aquarium of ghosts, and in its reflection, he was one of them. He rarely thought about his army-years. Korea was a half-forgotten dream and figured his '57 accident had pretty much erased much of it from his mind. Hollywood, however, was seared into the forefront of his consciousness like a cattle-brand. Watching old movies would send him back to dark hotel corridors, back-lot dressing rooms, underground car parks—where the real moves took place—where a currency of guns, narcotics and human beings were traded freely against a backdrop of glamour; all for the acquisition of control, for power. On arriving at the end of '54, he found Los Angeles a skewed and nightmarish place. In Hollywood, he'd seen men and women demean themselves to a degree beyond anything he'd seen on the killing fields of Chosin—a weighing station of painted flesh—sold for a moment in the sun. Show business was not about entertainment. Show business was where you bought people. It went without saying that he was far from enamoured with Tinseltown, but he could pinpoint the exact moment when his general disdain putrefied into gut-wrenching disgust. One-night backstage at Pantages, he saw the spots on Peggy King's back as she was about to sing at some awards ceremony and in that moment his hatred for humanity went ironclad. For Borg, all of human ugliness would be forever encapsulated in those pancake-smothered shoulders.

But now, life had become one endless day, with intervals of light and dark. He'd never been much of a drinker but these days his intake was in the upward direction. Beer created a fuzzy dimension which kept the world around him at arm's length—as if near reclusiveness hadn't achieved this already.

In the autumn of '87 he was amused by the news that Stevenoski—now calling himself Minister John Stevens, was seeking the Republican nomination for the presidency, the actual *President of the United States of America*, presidency. Borg recalled the announcement last year of Stevens' seeking the nomination. It was funny then, because he also remembered Stevens' prediction all over the news, years earlier, that the world was going to end in 1982. It seems the man's addled state was not exclusive to that one murderous night at the Roosevelt.

It was the summer of the following year when, slumped in his armchair watching the game, Borg was on his fourth Colt 45 as The Dodgers fucked the Cincinnati Reds to the tune of 13-5. The painful twinge he always got down his left side, when stressed, began to loom—the momentary loss of depth of field—where everything in front of him flattened into one dimension—the prelude to those migraines. He drained the tin, crushed it, and threw it at the trash can in the kitchen.

He aims…

She shoots…

He sco…

His arm jerked out unexpectedly, the tin hit the wall. The limb shook uncontrollably, and it took the other hand to hold it under control. No sooner had the event occurred, it stopped just as suddenly. He got up to retrieve the tin from the floor and walked into the wall. He spun around and hit the floor— his right arm involuntarily spasming again like an electrocuted snake. The mild shakes he had since... he didn't know when... maybe after Margie died? had become more pronounced in the last couple of months.

He put it down to getting on.

The body got away from old people, right?

Ignore it and it'll go away, right?

Driving back from the mall the next day, it happened again, only this time it was preceded by a wave of euphoria. He snapped out of it and found his entire body spasming violently like some out-of-control clockwork robot. The car careered across the lanes of the busy 95 as he fought with his possessed musculature to regain control... of himself and the car. The spasms settled into mild tremors. Mild enough to wrestle the car home and on to the driveway. Exhausted, he leaned against the door and fell out onto the ground.

And that's all she wrote...

'The scans show nothing, but you're responding favourably, Leonard. This suggests our diagnosis is correct.'

'Will it kill me?'

Doctor Sams sighed. 'It can, but we're a long way from that possibility.'

Borg was almost disappointed. A conclusion to the Leonard Borg story was way overdue. In so many ways, he'd been dead for decades.

'Surgery then?'

Sams sat casually on the corner of his desk—a disturbing posture for a man of his advanced years. 'Surgery won't cut it—pardon the pun. Well... *perhaps*. Like I say, we have a long way to go before we hit that pitch. Of course, somewhere down the road it could be a possibility: DBS—'

'DBS?'

'Deep brain surgery. It involves the placing of a neuro-stimulator. But that would be the last chance saloon.'

*'Parkinson's...'*

'We're going to begin a course of L-Dopa, then we'll review our situation in a month.'

*'Our'*, thought Borg. *Prick.*

And so, the sentence had been passed. Borg's long and slow execution had truly begun.

# 18. THE COMEBACK

They got him home with a bag of drugs and a Warren Commission-sized tome of directions—all of which helpfully pointed out they were pills and needed to be swallowed at specific intervals. Most of the directions were 'get out of jail free' declarations—of how the manufacturers were not libel for unforeseen side-effects or, and here's the kicker, *improper* use. He knew the pharmaceutical industry worked just like all the other corporations and assumed he was one of a million lab rats on whom all this shit could be tested for free. Instinct told him to can the lot and let nature take its course. But morbid curiosity about his own demise stayed his increasingly shaky hand. So, he followed the directions—did what the pamphlets told him—how many and when. The shakes abated, so faith was not so much restored as given birth. His diet had to change. Despite the catastrophic damage his guts had sustained in his '57 accident, he'd pretty much eaten what he wanted—classic American fare—cheeseburgers, steaks and pork chops. There were periods where he couldn't shit right, but those episodes were few and far between. But now he had to avoid the iron, the meat, the cheese... apparently the Levodopa doesn't take kindly to it.

Third side-effect: this shit sent his libido through the roof! He was jacking off like a teenager. At this rate he would jerk himself into another dimension.

A month of this and he got to wondering who, exactly, was he trying to make better? His actual self or the no-mark Jerk-off he'd been all these years whilst upholding this straight-life schtick?

This reminded him...

The medics that scraped him up told him he was found on the driveway by the two broads that lived next door. Dykes, Borg surmised, found him sprawled on the concrete, with his head under the car. He didn't remember the drive home, but he must have had some presence of mind to have stuck the parking brake on before rolling out and under it.

He took over a box of Krispy Kreme's. The women were fat, so he figured they'd appreciate the gesture—a *thank you,* for turning him over, stopping him from swallowing his tongue and calling the ambulance. He kind of wished they hadn't, but... they had, so... the shtick continued. It's what neighbours did, right?

They wanted to know everything. Questioned him earnestly at the door. Their two chubby faces furrowed with concern, both clutching silk night robes around themselves. He obliged and gave them an abridged version that featured a fictional heat-stroke and no mention of the true diagnosis. As he related the tale, he stumbled over it for a second when he saw a kid, who lived up the street, appear for a split-second behind them at their kitchen doorway, bare-ass naked with a boner that would have done Johnny Stompanato proud. The two women betrayed no sign of the interruption, but Borg wrapped up the story fast and left them to it.

Later, as he brushed his teeth, he glanced out of the bathroom window that overlooked his neighbour's kitchen and saw the kid, couldn't be any more than sixteen, laying on the table while the two now naked women, sans night-gowns, and in fancy lingerie, ate the donuts off his prick. So much for being dykes. He watched in a fever; then brushed and flossed thoroughly. His way-off-the-mark assessment of his neighbour's orientation reminded him just how far off-course he'd gone. His ability to read people and situations was now rusty at best. The scene took him back to his Hollywood years—some of the shenanigans he'd witnessed—been a party to. He'd been living in a cloud for decades. If he didn't know better, he'd swear his entire life before 1957 was a hallucination. He swallowed the pills he was supposed to and

watched as the two women finished the kid off. Then the three
of them went back to sitting round the table, smoking, and
playing cards as if nothing had happened.

Borg went to bed and put the television on. He liked to fall
asleep to it and was about to do just that when he saw *her* face.

He thought he was dreaming—as he sometimes did about the
Pin-up. But no. There she was, exactly as she looked back in
'57, giving an interview on some talk show.

The drugs were fucking with him.

Surely.

Then shit went Chinatown.

The woman was *not* the Pin-up, but an exact double; Erika
Xtravaganza; claiming to know the real Peggy Deveroux.

*'... yes, she's alive and well and very much looking forward to
meeting all the new fans she has from around the world. She
really had no idea that she was so well remembered, and that
people were still interested in her....'*

He found the remote and hit the volume. The interviewer
asked what Deveroux had been doing all this time. Xtravaganza
smiled that smile. Deveroux's smile. A perfect storm of teeth,
lips, tongue...

Three decades died.

The double continued... 'She has dedicated herself to God and
has worked tirelessly for the church. In fact, she has a very
important message for the world...'

The interviewer cut in. 'Which is?'

Xtravaganza laughed, 'Well... we'll just have to wait and see,
won't we? She will be making her first public appearance very
soon...' She winked at the camera. 'So, stay tuned!'

Cross-fades of Deveroux's old photographs danced around the
screen to Guy Lombardo's Tennessee Waltz. A voice-over
explained how Deveroux had retired from modelling in 1957—
the very year of his own near-fatal encounter with her—how
she had studied to be a missionary and worked for evangelist-
superstar, Billy Graham. The photos were all beach-shots and
cheesecake. None of the *'by special order only'* bondage stuff

he'd found scattered around the murder scene at the Roosevelt made the cut. Thirty-one years evaporated, and he was right back in that Presidential Suite... Right back in her 46th Street apartment in Manhattan... Right back in that Grand Central concourse, waiting with his flick-knife and then chasing her across 8th Avenue into the oblivion he'd been in ever since.

The segment wound up with the interviewer thanking Xtravaganza. The camera zoomed out, revealing an entourage of Deveroux look-a-likes standing behind her—all sporting those glossy black bangs. The interviewer said 'For all those fans who have been asking whatever happened to Peggy Deveroux? Well... It looks like the mystery is about to be uncovered.'

Xtravaganza popped her head back in to view. 'Remember, watch this space—don't touch that dial!', signing off with a coquettish giggle.

Tomorrow's weather forecast followed. But Borg sat upright in his bed, staring snow-blinded into the distant past.

Had Stevenoski seen this? And Deveroux was working for Billy Graham? He thought of his own long-abandoned codes of the Latter-Day Saints and his paedophile father. He never forgot, but his recently adopted mantra sang again, *Religion: The Devil's masterpiece.*

It took a while but eventually he faded into a listless sleep as yesterday's winds swirled around him—churning hurricanes and tornados in the now.


He took it upon himself...

... to transverse a thirty-one-year-old circuit and intercept himself somewhere along its endless loop.

The women spurred him to it. Their leaving him. The empty house now presented Borg with possibilities denied him for years. A four-bedroom, two-in-the-roof, Bridesburg bungalow was too small to contain his burgeoning consciousness, and too big to be a coffin. Peggy Mae Deveroux gave flight to those possibilities and returned them to him.

Now, he would return to her.

The paper boy woke him when his stack of papers hit the lawn at 06:16. Borg worked out in his garage, chest, back and abs— 500 reps. No legs. That hip still protested. He showered and squeezed fresh orange juice and thought of Minister John Stevens. His Senator dad, Cornelius, was surely dead by now, so he wondered if the 'Kingmakers' were still in currency and how 'juiced in'—if at all—Stevenoski/Stevens might be.

He wandered into the office, sat at his desk, and looked at the phone. The one that had not rung since... '78? The one, when something had escaped him during one of their in-person visits, he would call and wise them up retrospectively. Would anyone still be manning it now? He knew the line was still connected, because he'd pick it up from time to time to check— an endless tone to his flatlined career. He knocked back the orange juice, grabbed the phone and dialled. Someone answered it quickly and cheerfully.

'CNP office...'

The acronym was a new one on Borg. He hesitated and tried to remember how he opened these calls. Your name. Always state your name. Upfront.

'Good morning. My name is Leonard Borg, and I would, if at all possible, like to speak to Minister John Stevens' office, please.'

The voice—young, male—repeated Borg's name back to him and said, 'Just a minute, sir.'

Borg stared at the framed pictures of his dead wife and absent daughters and somehow felt more distant from them at this moment than he ever did. He had slipped, momentarily, back to his pre-showtime self.

In exactly forty-four seconds, the phone came alive with the declaration that he was about to be transferred. Another older male voice spoke. 'Mr. Borg. I'm Phillip Conway, advisor to the Council for National Policy. How are you today?'

'Good, sir. Thank you.'

'And what can I do for you, Mr. Borg?'

'Apologies, Mr. Conway, but can I assume you know who I am? Beyond my name, of course?'

'I…' Conway employed the corporate 'we'. '… Indeed, we do, Mr. Borg. We understand you did sterling work for us. How can we help you now?'

Us? Borg had to wonder what 'Us' consisted of these days.

'I would like, if at all possible, to speak to someone from Minister Stevens' office.'

'Minister *John* Stevens?'

'Yes, sir.'

Borg detected a clicking sound. It was a given that the call was being recorded but then realised the sound was Conway's nails tapping a desk as he contemplated the request. Borg interrupted the moment. 'With the Minister directly. If at all possible.'

Finally, Conway responded. Mr. Borg, can we suggest having someone visit you? A member of the Minister's staff?'

'I'm pretty sure, given the nature of my…' Borg felt suddenly exhausted, '…need to speak to him. He would probably prefer we did this one-on-one.' Borg let the statement hang in the air. 'Sir.'

'Understood. I… will approach the relevant parties and we will come back to you as soon as possible. Thank you for your call, Mr. Borg. We will speak again soon.'

The phone flatlined again.

Why did he call? Was he going to confess? That he fucked up? That he never offed the Pin-up and never put her in that dumpster? That she's alive and well and about to give interviews because he failed to clean her clock when he was supposed to? And just what was her *message for the world*? Could it possibly be an exposé? About the Roosevelt? Maybe she was dying and wanted to take Stevens down with her. Whatever the case, back in the day, Borg's call would have been turned around within the hour.

But this day faded on its silence.

And the next.

And the next.

# 19. THE LONG GAME

H e lay contorted on the settee, picking at the dead skin on his feet, waiting for the coffee to kick in. He took it to the window and slugged it back with the morning's medication. The boulevard outside was a vista of twenty-four carat suburbia. A girl twirling a baton on the lawn opposite. Kids in the road, stick-balling to kingdom come. One of the 'probably not a dyke' women next door, pruning the Rhododendrons that separated her slice of the American dream from his. And this, he thought, is the prize at the end of all those wars. They were kept at a distance now: wars. They were showrooms—for selling hardware. The Pacific theatre of WW2 sold nuclear superiority and the loooooong shadow of threat. Korea sold the first jets. Vietnam... *well*... Napalm was an own goal. What was on offer with this Nicaragua fiasco was yet to be seen.

He still hadn't bought that sink plug for the kitchen and was considering the wisdom of attempting a drive to the mall again. Then the phone rang; not the one in his office, but the one in the hall. It could still be from Conway. Or who knows? Even Stevens himself, figuring they would have both his numbers. The meds hadn't kicked in yet, but his hand was uncharacteristically steady as it hesitated before grabbing the receiver. Borg listened. If someone called *him*, he never spoke first.

'Mr. Borg?' It was Doctor Sams.

'Yes.'

'I'd like to make an appointment for you up here at Strong Memorial this week. Would that be convenient?'

Borg told him it would and agreed to be at the clinic at 10am that Thursday. It was only when he put the phone down that he realised he hadn't even asked why Sams wanted to see him.

Was there some fresh development in his diagnosis?

*'According to my findings, Mister Borg, you've been dead since 1957...*

No such luck.

Thursday morning, Borg took the hour flight and got to the hospital thirty minutes early. The receptionist told him to go straight through. Sams got him to take off his shirt. Padded his chest and back with the cold stethoscope, got him to move around some and asked him the same questions, word for word, as his last visit three weeks ago. Borg got the feeling the doctor was stalling for some reason and realised it could only be one of two things.

Either the old doctor was descending into the first throes of dementia and forgot that he'd gone through this rigmarole already or... and the certainty began to grip him... he was about to reveal the timescale of Borg's endgame.

The doctor continued to fuss. A scoreboard flickered in Borg's mind's eye. What would he do with six months?

A week?

Days?

He thought of his daughters and the difficulty of trying to reach Gee Gee.

Sams stopped fucking around, shot his cuff and checked the watch on the inside of his wrist. 'Can you give me a moment?'

Sams left the room, and the door closed behind him. No question: the old doctor was acting funny. Borg considered slapping it out of him when he got back. The door opened behind him and a man in rolled up shirtsleeves came into the room and took Sams' place on the corner of the desk—adopting the exact same disturbing posture. The man hooked his jacket over his shoulder like a post-show crooner. He was around his seventieth summer, but his dyed auburn hair pleaded younger. Borg's elephant memory was intact—the man's aroma was familiar, but for a second, he could not be placed.

Then the dime descended...

John Stevenoski's old face smiled, revealing teenage teeth. 'How are you, Leonard?'

'Mr. Stevenoski?'

'*Please*. Stevens. Minister Stevens. The eastern Europeanism proved to be somewhat cumbersome.'

They had never met face to face—Borg's enduring image of the man was the crack of his ass as a whore's face bled down it in the presidential suite of the Roosevelt Hotel three decades back. The lines flanking his mouth reminded Borg of shark's gills.

'I have heard great things about you Leonard—*great* things...'

The old Minister appraised the old killer and, with a sweeping gesture, directed his attention to the half-open window where a warm morning seemed to freeze outside.

'You know Strong was home to the Manhattan Project, Leonard? That building across the way there? The Annex, the Atomic Energy Commission, had an office there. The experiments... they pumped patients with Plutonium and tracked them forever after. Even beyond the grave. What do you think of that, Leonard?'

This assumed familiarity irked Borg, but he maintained the general good humour.

'They didn't know—the patients?'

'Of course not! But the tenacity of it. The long game. Always thinking of the long game...'

The strangled spectre of Diane Stevenoski swung between them. Borg felt the overwhelming desire to exorcize it.

'You've dropped out of the race.'

The Minister's face hardened and softened within a beat. 'Have you any idea of the scrutiny they subject you to? The sheer pathological dismemberment that comes with being within even a sniff of the big chair. These people literally analyse your trash, and I'm not being metaphorical. I mean, they literally empty the trash cans in your yard and take it away for... God only knows what.'

This meticulousness struck Borg as prudent, given the stakes, but Stevens' whining made him realise that *he* had to be the man in this fucking thing. What *did* Stevens remember about *that night*?

'Can I assume you know why I tried to contact you, Minister Stevens?' Borg surrender-smiled. 'This ambush suggests you do.'

Stevens sagged—defeated. Borg had no idea how long a moment could be, but Stevens had surely exhausted its limits when he finally said, 'Leonard... Diane was... troubled. I believe that what happened to her that night, she bought on herself. She ran with a... an exotic bunch, whose tastes were intriguing, especially to the adventurous young man I was in those days. It's ironic that the very thing that attracted me to her in the first place would be the very thing that would kill her. A cliché, I know, but even then, I knew that the intensity of our... relationship... was due to the fact that we were on borrowed time. Diane was someone you just knew was never going to see old age: that her enthusiasms would get the better of her.'

Borg cut to it. 'Do you remember the brunette?'

'I... she was someone Diane was interested in. Some kind of bondage expert, I understand. Diane invited her to the party. I have a vague recollection of our being introduced, but beyond that—'

'And the redhead?'

'A friend of Diane's. She was a regular attendee to our soirees. Her name escapes me...'

Borg was not given to pangs of sadness, but he might have felt one right then for the forgotten redhead who had dissolved along with her name into the vapours of time.

'Did it ever occur to you,' Borg suggested, 'that your wife was murdered? By the brunette?'

Borg knew he'd offered a 'get out of jail free' card and waited for Minister John to play it. Stevens' response was either genuine or worthy of an Oscar. He looked shaken, as if an ironclad belief had been suddenly demolished. 'Murdered...'

'She high-tailed it and has never been heard of since. You gotta wonder why.'

'But I thought—'

'No. She skipped. I went after her and I fucked it up. Got mangled in hot pursuit. Intended on making it right as soon as all the king's horses and all the king's men did their thing but, it was not to be. I had to assume it had been taken care of. But now, after all these years, she's out there somewhere and about to talk.' This brought Borg to his next point. 'Erika Xtravaganza—is the name familiar to you?'

'It is not.'

'To put you in the picture, she's some creepy impersonator—'

'Impersonator?'

'Of her!' Borg lowered his voice. 'The brunette… of Deveroux. Xtravaganza claims Deveroux is alive and well and about to make some big comeback appearance. Seems they're both cult figures to the weird queer brigade. Says Deveroux has some big announcement… some news for the world. What do you think that might be, Minister? I mean, what's so important that after thirty years *now* she comes out of the woodwork? Right on the back of your… current situation. Co-incidence? I think not.'

The force of the confession Borg had been wanting to make for three decades came like an avalanche. 'I fucked it up! I want to make it right.'

Stevens leaned in by way of appeasement. 'Leonard… I… *we*… commend you for your zeal.' He smiled teenage teeth again. 'Leave it with us. We will look into it. If this Deveroux woman is really still alive, we will find her soon enough and, if necessary, discuss appropriate action.'

Stevens slid off the table and slam-dunked a firm hand on Borg's shoulder as he made his way past him and out of the room. A musky cologne insulted Borg's nostrils.

Before Borg could process the encounter, Dr Sams reappeared and went behind his desk. He scribbled on a notepad, tore off the page, and handed it to Borg. 'Take this to the reception window and they'll give you what you need.'

Sams said nothing about Stevens' appearance and seemed so oblivious as to what had just occurred that Borg had to wonder if it even happened.

Now Borg's antenna was up—the Minister seemed to be everywhere.

On the six O'clock news, a harassed Steven's, in stark contrast to the relaxed and amiable figure he cut at Strong's, ran the gauntlet through a crowd of reporters outside the House of Reps.

*'Stevens is now the subject of an ongoing FBI investigation into sexual impropriety allegations…'*

Borg hit the news channels—scoured the papers. Within days, he had the lowdown on the life and tawdry times of Minister John Stevens. It seemed he had rose phoenix-like from the debauched chaos of his first wife's death, turned his back on the political life he was reared for, found God, become an insanely popular Televangelist, married again (poor bitch) and, bolstered by four million God bothering campaign volunteers, tried to fly his ticket all the way to Capitol Hill after all; declaring that it was time for a 'Spirit filled presidency!'

But now he was in trouble.

Initially, it was just an investigation by the Internal Revenue Service into whether $10 million of tax-exempt funds had been used to propel Minister John's candidacy. That can of worms revealed his financial dealings with a number of African despots—some of whom were known to control a stable of high-end sex slaves who were sent all over the globe to service our elite degenerates. Now that 'HMS Sexual Insinuation' had been launched, it inevitably ran into a tsunami of escalating historical sex allegations. By now, it was clear that no tomb would go un-raided. So, if there were any loose ends concerning the Roosevelt (And Borg could think of a few— such as what happened to the confiscated film and Chauffeur Lee, for instance?) it would be the old bastard's endgame. The curtain was closing on the Reagan show and with only a month away from the election, all the rats were jostling for position. Stevens was a big rat. An old rat. And when they get old, they get mean. They have a God-given right to the power and privilege to which they have become accustomed, and woe betide any elements that think they can wrong that righteousness. Stevens had abandoned his presidential campaign early in an attempt to evade the media hounds, but now they smelled blood, they would not stop until they bit meat. Deveroux, emerging now with what she *may or may not know*, was impermissible. If she thought thirty-one years was long enough for bygones to be bygones, then she was one stupid broad.

De beaux rêves, mon amour.

# 20. BERDO

Borg's hijacked appointment was last Thursday morning. This Monday morning, he got a call, on the office phone, from Minister John himself. Stevens cut to it. 'We found her. She's in a mental hospital in California.'

'Mental hospital...' Borg weighed it. 'So, this big comeback is a put on?'

'Well... perhaps.'

'Seriously? You think they'll let her broadcast an interview from an asylum?'

'Why not? Charles Manson just did Geraldo.'

'Maybe...' Borg considered aloud '... whoever this Extravaganza freak is talking about... isn't actually *the* Peggy Deveroux. Maybe she's being metaphorical or something. I mean, she's her exact double. Maybe she's talking about herself. But we know where *our* Peggy is now so, what do you want to do about it?'

'Do?'

'For a start, is she a dribbling sack of piss, or is she... you know... coherent? Establishing her competency might be prudent. I'll go. To see her. See what the state of play is.'

'I...' Stevens stammered, '... don't see the point. It's fair to say she's out of the frame.'

Borg brought it home. 'Tell me, how long has she been in for?'

He could hear the rustling of paper as Stevens shuffled through whatever he had in front of him.

'Are you ready, Leonard? Six years. *This* time.'

'This time.'

Borg could hear the shuffling again, and then Stevens came back on the line. 'She has quite the curriculum vitae. To cut a long and eventful story short, she is a violent schizophrenic.'

For Borg, this was enough. 'Deveroux may see… or may have *already seen*… the coverage of your… situation. And one way or another, this Erika Xtravaganza bullshit, whether she's involved or not, might rouse her from her dormant state. We need to make a positive ID… establish, either way, whether she's a concern or not, and then act accordingly. Consider this… worst-case scenario… *The* Peggy Deveroux has been granted permission to do a live broadcast, and she spills about thirty-year-old events at the Roosevelt. As unlikely as that narrative is, we want to avoid that possibility, no?'

'But she's mad. Who'd believe her, anyway?'

'Not the point. It's something the press will use, regardless.'

The line hummed as Stevens considered this, then said, 'You might be better off talking to the Xtravaganza freak, directly.'

'Fine. Where is she?'

'We don't know yet. Obviously, Erika Extravaganza is a showbiz name, hence the delay. Sit tight, Leonard. We'll get back to you.'

'Can you fax me a copy of Deveroux's rap sheet? Oh, and the hospital? What hospital is she in?'

Stevens gave it up. 'Patton State. It's in San Bernardino.'


While he waited for Stevens to get back to him, he tried a few of his own sources. Within the hour, he had the name and direct line of Patton State Hospital's director, Carlo Madden. He dug out one of his old phony press-passes, gave it the once over, got into character and called the number.

'Good morning, Mr. Madden? This is Bob Mayhew from the Los Angeles Daily News. We're working on an investigative piece and there are a few patients at Patton we would very much like to talk to. It's a long shot, I'm sure, but how might we go about arranging some interviews?'

'I'm sorry. Who did you say you were again?'

'Bob Mayhew. Los Angeles Daily News.'

111

'Well, good morning to you, Bob. May I ask how you got my direct line?'

'Oh, we're pretty good at what we do, Mr. Madden but, to be absolutely up front with you, we're working closely with the LAPD and… well, let's just say they've been liberal with the lowdown.'

Borg felt the words being absorbed—long distance.

'Well… that's very fortunate for you, Mr. —'

'Mayhew. Bob.'

'Mr. Mayhew… as I'm sure you can appreciate, interviews, or any other type of disruption to our patients' treatment, would only be considered in very extreme cases. And to be honest with you, would require both legal and medical authorisation.'

'Understood, Mr. Madden, but we have it on good authority that at least one of your patients is about to speak to the press—'

'About what?'

'Nothing to do with the hospital or any of your staff—as far as we know.'

'For your trouble, Mr.—'

'Mayhew.'

'Mayhew, yes—I can categorically state that none of our patients are currently scheduled for any such event. As I say, a thing like that would only be granted in very rare cases and even then, with the most stringent of protocols first being met.'

'Again. Understood. We're just trying to establish that what our sources are telling us is accurate.'

Madden cut in fast. 'Can I ask which patients you were interested in?'

'No, Mr. Madden, you cannot. Disclosure of any aspect of our case *would only be granted in very rare cases and even then, with the most stringent of protocols first being met.*'

Borg put the phone down.

*Prick.*


Borg's plane landed at Norton Airforce Base at 22:08. He bought a cell phone at the airport for $849.98 + tax, picked up the Hertz Chrysler he had booked in advance, and escaped the bedlam of the airport's access roads and service ramps.

Twenty-two minutes later, he booked in at the Days Inn on East Highland—just another ten minutes' drive from the asylum. He wore his old olive drab M-1965 Field Jacket, dark grey khakis, and steel toe-capped work boots, which, to his mind, struck just the right note of ambiguity. He could be anyone. He could be anything. And thus, he could be nothing at all.

The sullen jerk-off on reception treated him as such, checked him in, and gave him his key with minimal acknowledgement. The hotel—low-rise roadside—was nothing also. It had a no-frills restaurant with a dirty outdoor pool. The carpets had seen decades of wear and the lamps were hanging from wires. All along the corridors, television sets behind closed doors were turned up and served as a sonic backdrop to the icy, near silence of Borg's room. Fusty odours tempered with notes of semen and rubber told him whores worked here with impunity.

Stevens would not be happy. Taking things upon yourself seldom sat well with others. But fuck him. He threw his duffle bag on the bed, unwrapped, and charged the cell phone. Then, after an hour, called him.

'I'm in San Berdo. I'm going to see her and get this thing cleared up, once and for all.'

Borg could almost feel the Minister's 'thousand miles away' composure as it moulded itself frantically in his politician mind.

'Jumping the gun somewhat, aren't we, Leonard? Perhaps your reputation for measured endeavour is something of a myth.'

Borg didn't much care for defending his reputation. 'This is a question of thoroughness, Minister. But I will confess; I need to know what happened to her. I can't sleep on this no more. Don't you? Want to know?'

'Leonard...' Stevens sighed big, '... I barely knew she existed until you dragged her faded visage in front of me.'

'Well, she's well and truly in front of you now. I need creds, so I can make a positive ID. I need to get into that hospital. I want medical papers. Whatever it takes…'

'These things take time to arrange…'

'We both know that "immediately if not before" is the order of our day. Or have things really changed that much? One way or another, I'm going into that hospital and the best way is with as little fuss as possible. Neither of us want me getting caught climbing the wall now, do we?'

Stevens knew he was up against it. 'Forget the fake doctor nonsense. Your best chance is to go as a police officer…' Stevens re-calibrated, 'Better still; go *with* a police officer. *You're re-opening a very old case*, etcetera. I'll send someone over in the morning. They will brief you.'

'In the morning?'

'In the morning, yes.'

Borg didn't ask what time. It would be early, and he would be up early.

'Minister Stevens, how are we doing with that rap sheet?'

Stevens signed off, telling him he'd have the police officer bring it in the morning.

# 21. RAP TRAP

**Tuesday October 4th**
07:07

H e slept in his clothes but was awake when the desk clerk called at seven of seven. 'There is a Detective Koenig here to see you, Mr. Borg.'

Borg told him to send him up and watched the man through the blinds as he ascended the stairs and came along the balcony looking for his room. Stocky, bow-legged, grey buzz-cut, matching grey suit. The bull-dog type. The kind they unleash on a suspect when due process fails. Borg let him knock. The man introduced himself almost jovially. Close to retirement, Borg thought. Happy about it. Koenig handed Borg

114

a heavy folder and told him he'd wait for him in the burger place next door. Borg closed the door and went back to the blinds to watch the detective make his way across the parking lot.

Borg removed the documents, freshly faxed, from the folder and placed them in a row on the bed. Four groups of A4 held together with a paper clip. He started with the basics and was surprised to see that she was older than he thought.

**Peggy Mae Deveroux**: D.O.B 4/22/1923.
Nashville, Tennessee
Identification Information:
Sex: Female
Race: Caucasian
Hair: black
Eyes: blue
Height: 5.5ins
Weight: 181 pounds

The rest was an even bigger eye opener. Note attached from...

Jackson Memorial Hospital, Florida:
**Attention**: Diagnosed schizophrenic –
paranoid type chronic

He skimmed the full discography and tried to focus on the greatest hits...

**1972**
**January 17**th – Threatening behaviour. Runs amok with a gun at Bibletown, Boca Raton Community Church, Florida. Deveroux is arrested and collected by her third, and recently divorced, husband, Larry Frear who takes her back to their home in Hialeah.

**April 13**th – arrested at home after threatening Frear and her ex-adopted family with a kitchen knife. Forced family to stare

115

at a picture of the Virgin Mary for four hours. Frear claims she told them that "If you take your eyes off this picture, I'll cut your f****** guts out!"
"Arresting Officer J. Oakes reports that she was charged with breach of the peace and confined in Jackson Memorial, a state hospital, for four months."

**August 15th** – discharged into Mr. Frear's care

**October 28th** - Hialeah policeman, James Fitzgerald, was called to the Frear household, where Deveroux was tearing the place up. He managed to get her in the patrol car while he took a statement from Frear. Returning to the car, Fitzgerald "saw Deveroux in the back seat, with her dress pulled up, panties around her knees, masturbating, screaming in tongues and broke her hand punching the roof of the car." His report: "defendant psycho."

Assault and battery and disorderly conduct charges were dropped after she voluntarily recommitted herself to Jackson Memorial, where she spent six months, part of it under suicide watch.

The accompanying mugshot clipped to the sheet was undeniably Deveroux, taken from her October '72 arrest. But the haggard and defeated forty-nine-year-old woman that stared vacantly out of the photo was light years from the 'piece of ass' he'd seen for just a second across 8th avenue three decades ago. You had to wonder what another sixteen years had done to her.

He flipped back and forth. Had he missed a section? If the file is complete, it seems things go quiet until she shows up again in 1979 having moved across country to California...

**1979**
**April 19**th – Deveroux living in a trailer at 14723 1/2 South Firmona Avenue – attacks elderly landlords Ellen and Humphrey Toussaint with a kitchen knife. Taken to Lennox Station in Lawndale – "Suspect mentally unstable."

**May 11**th – preliminary hearing

**May 25**th – arraignment - bail set at $1000, but judge XXXX (name omitted) finds her mentally incompetent and orders her involuntarily committed to Patton State Hospital.

**1980**
**May 1**st - Motion for bail granted

**May 22**nd – judge finds defendant **not guilty** by reason of insanity

**July 24**th sentenced to five years incarceration and treatment.

She puts in 20 months, and then they let her out, February 81...

**1982**
**February 3**rd - Outpatient status renewed

**June 12**th – Linda Lane, Sunset Park, Santa Monica, Cal: Deveroux attacks housemate Leanne Szabó with a knife and arrested that morning. Deveroux sent back to Patton for observation and to determine her competency to stand trial.

117

**1983**
**September 26**th – stands trial for attempted
murder. Ruled insane. Guilty by reason of
insanity – second Cali incarceration - sent
back to Patton, indefinitely.

PROSECUTORS NOTE: "Defendant carried kicking
and screaming from the court room."

The last sheet were her priors to 1972...

**1946: March 25th:** Living at 1129 South Van
Ness Street, San Francisco. Trial for
misdemeanour assault and battery with her
sister Grace of their landlord.
Both women handed 30 day suspended
sentences.

**1951: July 10**th**:** South Salem Dairy,
Westchester County – Camera club arrest –
indecent exposure and disturbing the peace.
$5 fine.

**1955: May 28th:** Subpoenaed in the Kefauver
trials due to a seventeen-year-old boy
('Eagle Scout' Benjamin Grimes from Coral
Gables, Florida) who choked himself, trussed
up, (found by his father) surrounded by
bondage photos featuring Deveroux and
others. Subpoenaed with Igor Krane and his
sister Patty who specialised in such
material. (Film Fan Fotos - 212 East 14th
Street "Damsel-in-distress" photos of
actresses being bound and gagged, spanked
and flogged)
Deveroux waited sixteen hours but ultimately
never called to testify.

**1957: September 30th** Questioned and
cautioned by federal agents about obscene

photos of her that are circulating in and
around Times Square and extended Tri-state
area.

**October 5th:** Deveroux reports receiving
death threats to police (sexual sadistic in
nature) Federal agents believe they're from
a wanted serial killer. Deveroux agrees to
be used in a sting to draw out the perp.
Turns out to be a teenage boy who is
questioned and cautioned. Deveroux refutes
the Feds assessment and claims to be still
receiving threats.

And this is only what they knew about; what they had on
official record. Deveroux was a disaster in waiting. Her history
of violence led credence to the notion that maybe, just maybe,
she *did* have something to do with Diane Stevenoski's death.
Okay, the M.O contradicted: knives and a single firearms
incident contrasted somewhat from Diane Stevenoski's
strangulation. But, if this were a 'good old days' frame up,
Deveroux's conduct would have delivered her on a plate.

Big gap, Borg thought, between the '57 Roosevelt Hotel
incident and the next time she shows up on police files in 1972.
She stayed under the radar because no-one was looking for
her. Until now, nothing had contradicted Borg's claim that she
was dead.

He made coffee in the room, washed down his medication, got
dressed, and left to meet Detective Koenig at *Tom's Famous
Original Super Burger*.

He stepped out into a morning that others might describe as
balmy. Borg, used to the more reasonable climes of Philadelphia, might describe it as oppressive.

He found Koenig at a table overlooking the hotel parking-lot,
nursing a coffee. Borg ordered another to go on top of the one
he'd just had.

'So, Detective Koenig, where are we?'

Koenig explained he had already called the hospital and told
them who they wanted to see. This was annoying. 'Why did

you do that? I wanted to catch them unawares. In case they were thinking of giving us the run-around.'

The outburst caught Koenig by surprise. 'And why would they give us the run-around?'

'I called them the other day about an interview Deveroux's supposed to be giving. They completely denied it. I think they may be earning from it and don't want it exposed.'

'If that's the case, they could use that as an excuse *not* to play ball: that their *not knowing* who we want to see means they had no time to check her availability and so on…'

'Check her availability? She's locked up. What's she got, a heavy schedule?'

Koenig ignored the sarcasm. 'We're seeing the hospital director, Carlo Madden, at 10am.'

'Madden himself, huh? Hellova name for the boss of a nuthouse… Madden!'

Koenig yukked twice unconvincingly, as if he agreed that it *was* funny, but clearly, he didn't really think so. Borg suspected the irony had escaped the detective, and was, perhaps, irked that his powers of detection had been found wanting.

'How long have you been with the force?'

'I put in twenty-seven years. I'm retired now, but they keep me around for this kind of stuff.'

Borg gave him a moment to see if he would expand on what 'this kind of stuff' might be. Koenig sipped his coffee as Borg's arrived. Professionalism stood firm. Both men studied the other—a silent reckoning. Koenig broke it. 'So, this is *the* Peggy Deveroux we're going to see?'

'You've heard of her?'

'Sure. There was a time when you couldn't pass a newsstand without seeing her on some cover. Couldn't get away from her. Not that you'd want to. I mean, seriously, have you ever seen a finer piece of ass?'

Showtime: Borg needed to get in character, get to know his co-star and join Boy's Town. 'I was more for the Ann Sheridan type.'

'Cute but sassy, huh?' Koenig sipped again. 'I have to say, I got mixed feelings about this. As you can imagine, I've come face-to-face with all kinds over the years—from gutter-junkies, out-and-out crazies, all the way up to whacked-out movie stars but never got the willies over any of 'em. But this... a bona fide 10-96. The prospect of seeing her in the flesh ...'

'Yeah, well, don't forget, she's sixty-six now. Her ballroom days are over. You saw the mugshot, right?'

'That's what's givin' me the willies. Time is a fucker, ain't it?'

'It's a fucker,' Borg agreed.

# .22 THE RUNAROUND

They went in Koenig's Ford Fairmont and headed east on Highland Avenue. The distant mountains were a snow-capped wall, as if all of San Bernardino itself was incarcerated. Koenig outlined how they were going to play it. He would perform the preliminaries, and Borg would introduce his specifics as and when.

The highway was an identikit parade of real estate offices, fast-food joints, and gas station forecourts. All standard issue So Cal, until they emerged from under the flyover where one building leapt out and disrupted the monotony. On the left, as they sped by, Borg saw a circular red brick construction—a small citadel. 'What is that?'

Koenig didn't need to look to know what Borg was talking about.

'It's all that's left of the original hospital. The rest got taken out by an earthquake. In the 20s, I think...'

At the next left, they saw the grey brick edifice that said...

PATTON STATE HOSPITAL
**3102 E Highland Ave**
**Patton, CA 92369**

... and weaved their way through a neighbourhood of bungalows until they came to a twelve-foot-high fence topped with barbed wire—not the monolithic stone walls that Borg had envisioned. They followed its perimeter around to the

121

entrance. Koenig wound down, announced who they were into the intercom, and the gate rolled aside.

They pulled into the visitor's bay. Borg got out of the car and stretched. He half-expected some shift in the air, some Chernobyl-like disturbance caused by the proximity of all this consolidated insanity. But the relentless heat remained untroubled.

They made their way across a vast and busy carpark to what Koenig already seemed to know was the main entrance. The complex was a vast collection of buildings—none of which were any higher than a couple of floors. The palm trees tastefully interspersed around it reminded Borg of the old naval base at Pearl Harbour before they shipped him to Korea.

The cold conditioned air was a welcome shock. The receptionist told them to take a seat, and that the Hospital Director would be with them shortly. Banal framed watercolours decorated the white walls. Borg eyed them suspiciously and wondered what mind triggers they were supposed to pull.

Carlo Madden appeared suddenly and introduced himself. Crisp white shirt, blue checked tie, grey slacks, medium height, thin greying hair, wire-framed glasses. If the word 'average' could scream, it would scream *Carlo Madden*. Koenig introduced himself, flashed his badge, and introduced Borg as Detective Leonard. Madden led them down a series of hallways until they reached a make-shift office. He apologised as he ushered them in, explaining that his own office was being redecorated. Madden bid the two men sit in a couple of office chairs as he continued to stand—which said to Borg that this is a man anxious to keep this short. He eyed the two phones on the desk and knew that one of them will ring within ten minutes, requiring the Director's urgent attention. He anticipated a performance. The dance began...

'How can I help you, gentlemen?'

Koenig took the floor. 'We're re-opening an old case that we believe Miss Deveroux may be able to help us with.'

'Miss Deveroux?'

'I'm sorry, were you not notified?'

'My secretary left me a message saying that the police wanted to speak with me today about one of our patients but didn't specify who.'

Koenig's peripheral vision seared with Borg's angry glare. 'We need to speak to Peggy Mae Deveroux…' Koenig removed a piece of paper from his inside pocket and read. '… admitted on the 26th of September 1982. Date of birth…'

Madden cut in. 'Deveroux? Let me find out who's treating her, and I will see what I can do. As I'm sure you can appreciate, she may be in no fit state to *be* interviewed. So, I need to establish where she is with her treatment as well as what ward she's on.'

Now it was Borg's turn to cut in. 'But we can see her today, right? If, y'know, she's able?'

'Uh… unlikely,' Madden spluttered. 'I only wish we'd had more notice so that we could have prepped the situation before you came all the way out here.'

Borg knew he already had. Koenig tried to save the day. 'Which is why we *did* specify who we wanted to see when I called your office this morning. As I'm sure *you* can appreciate, time is of the essence.'

'Just how old is this case, detective?'

'Too old and well overdue. Would it be possible to at least make a positive ID? No questions. Just to see her. It may well be that she is not who we need to speak to after all.'

Madden's face scrunched with helplessness. The phone rang. Here it is, thought Borg, textbook run-around,

'Excuse me.' Madden picked up. He hummed and hawed in response to whatever he was being told and said he'd be over as soon as he can. He put the phone down. 'Gentlemen. I have—'

Borg interjected, 'A pressing matter to attend to?'

'Indeed, detective. Specifically, the Joint Commission, conducting one of their unannounced visits. I need to show them around and convince them to keep our funding fluid and unmolested. I am *so* sorry about this mess up. I guarantee I will chase this today,'

Borg scribbled his cell phone number on a notepad.

123

Madden tore it off, pocketed it, and offered his hand. 'I will call you by this evening at the latest. If the patient can be made available, you will know by this evening when you'll be able to see her.'

Koenig shook the director's hand reluctantly. Borg even more so. He could barely suppress his rage. Koenig read it and took pains to dispel. 'How many patients do you have here, Mr. Madden?'

'Nearly two thousand.'

'Two thousand, huh?'

'So, as I'm sure you can appreciate, finding her will take time, but the task will not be as daunting as it sounds. We have fifteen full-time psychologists. I just need to go through their rosters and see which one of them is treating her.'

'What about her medical records?' Borg said. 'Can we see them?'

Madden did that splutter again. 'All confidentiality protocols would veto that, I'm afraid. That would have to be signed off by numerous bodies, her psychiatrist and whoever is representing her legally, if she even has anyone.'

Madden opened the door and motioned for them to step outside. Borg pulled a Columbo. 'Has anyone else been asking about doing interviews with Miss Deveroux?'

Madden's eyes narrowed and knew in that moment that they had spoken to each other on the phone two days ago. 'Funnily enough, a journalist from one of the L.A. papers called recently. Can I assume their enquiry is related to yours?'

'I wouldn't know. Was it Deveroux they wanted to talk to?'

'They didn't say.'

Madden walked them back out to reception. 'Again, I am so sorry I can't be of immediate help, detectives.'

Koenig fired one final volley. 'I hear Patton has a high incidence of escapees, Mr. Madden.'

The statement caught Madden off-guard. Borg glommed it. Madden collected himself. 'What facility of this size doesn't have that problem, detective?'

Borg said, 'Let's hope our person of interest isn't one of them.'

124

'Ha! What are the chances, Detective... Cohen? Is it?'

'Leonard.'

'Apologies; Detective Leonard.'

'But not impossible?'

Madden ignored this. 'I will locate the patient for you and let you know what the situation is. Today.'

Borg headed for the entrance as Koenig thanked Madden for his time. Those banal watercolours pulled mind-triggers now... and saw Director General Carlo Madden full of holes.

Sure enough, when Madden called him just before nine that evening, it was a no no. Madden told him Deveroux was currently unfit to receive visitors, or any other kind of disruption, due to some ongoing complications with her treatment. Madden adopted a tone not present when they'd spoken to him that morning. Cockier. Borg asked him if he'd been approached by Erika Xtravaganza and told him about the TV spot—that this woman claimed to know Deveroux and was about to do an interview with her. Madden pleaded ignorance of any such person, but re-iterated that the story cannot be true. Borg put it to him that this could be cleared up if he could just see Deveroux and make a positive ID. 'No interviews. Promise.'

'Detective... I'm sorry. I just *can't* help you.'

'Director, you realise that we can raise our game here. This is a police case and that we will get access eventually...'

'Then, I suggest you do that very thing, *Detective Leonard.* I have done a bit of investigating myself and discovered Detective Koenig no longer even works for San Berdo PD. And I have a question for you: are you familiar with a Bob Mayhew? Works for the Los Angeles Daily News...'

Borg killed the call.

*Absolutely... a prick.*

Almost immediately, Koenig called. Said he checked with the Joint Commission, who Madden had claimed to have had an appointment with yesterday. Turns out they did their accreditation check two months ago. If Madden was lying about that, he was lying about other things.

125

'If you can give me anything else. Anything I can run by my guys still on the force, we can try another angle,' Koenig offered.

Borg nixed it. Told him they had been compromised. Thanked him and cut the call. It didn't matter now whether Madden was lying or not. Borg had already decided what would happen next.

# 23. INTENSIVE CARE

## Wednesday October 5th
### 07:59

Borg got up and emptied his duffle bag out on the bed. Underwear. Socks. His meds. A spare pair of Foster Grant's. A clean shirt, passport, driver's license, credit cards, the phony Los Angeles Daily News press-pass in the name of Robert Donald Mayhew, a thermos, two identical orange shaving bags. One for his creds and meds. The other, for the licenced Ruger P-85 automatic, pimped to take the silencer.

He made a mental itinerary of the rest of the items laid out before him, took fresh socks, briefs, and his meds, got dressed, then put everything back and pushed the bag under the bed. He washed the meds down with cold coffee and got with it.

He drove out and scoped shit-hole motels near the airport. The Astro had three derelict cars on its cracked lot and, at first glance, looked like it was closed down. The door to one of the upstairs rooms was hanging off. Some of the windows were boarded up. He found the reception window and booked two nights. He insisted on a downstairs 'away from the main road' room which the old crone behind the counter issued without static. Borg took the keys and found it, in a far corner flanked by a low wall. It stunk and made his room at the Days Inn look fit for Liz Taylor. There was a large single bed with a jailhouse mattress, an armchair, haemorrhaging its stuffing, a small table

126

and an overlarge television set bolted to the wall. Somehow, he knew this room had seen death.

He drove to a nearby hardware store. He bought gaffer tape, nylon rope, and a medium-sized axe with cash. He wasn't hungry, but it was midday now, time to take his meds. He wanted something to wash them down with. He walked a couple of blocks towards what he instinctively felt was the main drag. As he passed a bookstore he thought his meds, or lack thereof, were fucking with him again.

*'There was a time when you couldn't pass a newsstand without seeing her on some cover.'*

There she was, plastered all over the left-side of a window display. Comic books, posters, garter belts and brassieres strewn all over it like the fag-end of some stripper's routine. He went in and found an entire corner dedicated to her. Flanked by a couple of life-size cardboard cut-outs, the racks carried Rocket-Man Magazine, Peggie Deveroux: Private Peeks, The Peggy Pages...

He thumbed through them, grabbed three of the extortionately priced vintage items, and took them to the counter. A point-of-sale rack sported a fanzine—UNTER-ZONE—which had her on the cover, laughing in front of the World Trade Centre, with the headline 'The Resurrection of an icon'. But this was not Deveroux. This was that creepy clone he'd seen on television—Erika Xtravaganza. He took the magazine to the window, where his feeble eyes could better sweep the article within. It was mainly an interview where she expounded on her idée fixe, and of how she had become close friends with the apparently reticent star—pretty much the same spiel she gave on her TV spot. The upshot seemed to be that Deveroux was virtually forgotten until recently and had now become something of an underground cult figure, due to the efforts of a handful of fans who had become missionaries for her faded star. But the article wound up with an announcement—that Deveroux had agreed to appear at some big comeback gig—the whereabouts were to be finally announced tomorrow… in New York!

Borg went outside and tried to call Stevens on the cell. No answer. He went back into the store and bought the fanzine along with *Peggy in Bondage*, *Eyeful* and *Male Life* at forty dollars a pop. He considered grilling the prissy fruit who served him for what he might know, if anything, about Peggy Deveroux, Erika Xtravaganza, and the cult that they seemed to be a part of. But the haughty service Borg received voted against it. If he got any more static, Borg knew he would get annoyed and end up doing something noisy to the uppity little fuck.

He drove back to the Days Inn and cursed the hard reality of not being able to be in two places at once. A solid lead was about to be announced in the east, and here he was in the west. He flipped through the Unter-Zone fanzine. Perhaps there was something vital he had missed. Apparently, Erika Extravaganza ran a bunch of fag bars and clubs in an around the Tri-state area and was something of a face on that scene. It outlined the clubs she ran. Currently there were two, one in the Village and another one, inevitably Borg thought, in Queens.

He was about to try Stevens again when the portable chirped. The Minister was returning his missed call. Borg waded straight in. 'Tonight, they're making a big announcement about the Deveroux comeback, at a club in New York. I want someone to go and get the deets.'

'I take it your hospital visit bore no fruit.'

'About that—the guy running the place is giving us the run-around. I don't know why. But he's sure acting funny. Absolutely would not let us see her, even to make a positive ID.'

'Perhaps Xtravaganza has insisted on an exclusive,' Stevens offered, 'so they're shutting out all other enquiries.'

'It's a fair bet that this announcement in New York will confirm either way, whether this thing is going to be at Patton or not, and if it is, I'm exactly where I should be. Minister, get a man over to that club tonight and get them to call me as soon as they know for sure.'

'Relax, Leonard. Where exactly is this thing?'

Borg read him the name and address from the fanzine—some club in Greenwich Village.

Stevens told him he'd see it done and hung up.

Borg removed one of the vintage mags—Wink—from its resealable bag, sat back on the bed, and jerked off. He saw himself between the orbs of her creamy, dreamy derriere—felt his fingers dig into her fleshy hips. Holding her still. Oh, so still...

Around seven that evening, Borg drove around the perimeter of the hospital again, until he came to the entrance where he and Koenig were so unceremoniously ejected yesterday. Borg had made a mental note of the vehicle in the director's parking space—a brown 1987 Lincoln Town Car. Now, Borg got out of his rented Chrysler and went to the fence where he could just about see the Lincoln. Madden was here.

He drove back along the perimeter and parked on some scrub under a tree on the corner of Miller Lane... and waited. As the sun sunk into the horizon, the lights around the hospital flickered on until the whole area glowed within an anodyne ochre glow. He could only guess at the fevered cerebral riots that were contained within.

Three cars had exited the hospital's gates and passed him. At 20:05, Borg saw the light shift and shadows move in his wing mirror a fourth time. Madden's Lincoln cruised past and took a left towards Highland. Borg turned the key and started after him. He maintained a respectable distance from Madden's car as they cruised through the light evening traffic. The drive took them south, past the airport, and south again. Within twenty minutes, they were in a residential street near West Colony Park. Madden took a sudden turn onto the driveway of a large, high-end, two-story house. Borg drove on a piece, pulled over and watched in the rear-view as Madden entered the house. Borg got out and stood at the foot of the driveway. There were no other cars. A couple of kid's bikes littered the otherwise well-tended lawn. This wasn't a visit to some squeeze. Madden lived here. Knowing this would make forthcoming events a lot easier. All the windows were dimly lit. No activity could be seen from the street. Borg walked right up and rang the bell. Silence reigned, but he could sense movement on the other side of the door. He was about to ring again when it opened slightly, and Madden peered out. Borg didn't give him a chance to go into his act or even to signal recognition.

Borg's gun was in his face. 'Let's go for a ride, fucko.'

They took Madden's car. Borg made him drive, giving directions as they went. Madden's countenance exuded rabbit-in-the-headlights shock. Borg couldn't read him. These situations normally produce a deluge of 'What is this? I don't know anything!' 'Whatever they're paying you, I'll double it!' type bullshit. Carlo Madden exhibited all the emotion of a waxwork.

It was nearly nine when they got to the Astro Motel. The evening heat ratcheted the death smell in the darkened room up another couple of notches. Madden looked around, confused, then gasped when Borg switched on the light. The director recognised a crime scene-in-waiting when he saw one and backed up against the nearest wall. Finally, his situation caught up with him. 'Please! What is this?! What do you want?!'

Borg made himself comfortable in the armchair and placed the pistol on the table. 'Now? I want to you to get undressed.' All colour vacated Madden's face. Borg told him, calmly, that he wouldn't tell him again. The portable phone rang. Madden started at the sound of it. Borg ignored it and stared with calm but significant intent into Madden's fearful eyes as they frantically searched the room for an escape, a reprieve, another gun... that both men knew the director would never have the gumption to use.

The ringing stopped, and so did Madden's search. He unbuttoned his shirt, slowly. 'Quicker than that!' Borg barked. Madden stepped it up some.

Finally, Madden was strapped naked to the bed, and for the first time, noticed the axe leaning against the wall.

130

The phone rang again. This time Borg answered it. It was Stevens' man in New York. Borg took the phone into the shower room. Cockroaches ran for cover across the tiled floor. 'Talk to me.'

The idiot on the other end proceeded to give him a ton of horse shit about *top secret locations'* and that *it's happening in Mexico*, and *not having a passport*... Borg's heart sank. If this is the current calibre of Stevens' men, the old Minister's stock must have fallen irrevocably. Borg had had enough and cut the call. From the bedroom, Borg heard Madden cry out. 'She escaped three years ago. Back in '85!'

And there it was. All hail the gentle art of force.

Borg called Stevens, quick fast. 'I have it on very good authority that Deveroux escaped from Patton three years ago. Also, your man in N.Y. has just called claiming that she's in Mexico. I detect amateur hour.'

'Of course. He's a nobody.'

'Nobodies are a fallacy. They come from somewhere...'

'From an old patsy directive—off the books. A scrap from yesteryear. Completely disposable.'

'So, Mexico. He's keen but needs a passport. Friday morning.'

'Where in Mexico?'

'To be revealed. Says he won't know until he's in the air. Some top-secret location bullshit. But we can use him to show us where. Can you arrange it—the passport?'

'Do you trust him?'

'Do *I* trust him! He's *your* nobody, remember? Give him hot creds. If he tries to get cute, we'll know where he is. According to—' Out in the bedroom, Madden started crying. Borg covered the mouthpiece and shouted through the door. 'Shut! Up!'

Madden did his best to stifle his terror and wind it down to a faraway whimper.

'According to my sources...' Borg continued, casting a languid eye through the gap in the door over Madden's trembling form, '... the bird has flown—three years ago. Adding credence to the freak's claim that she knows Deveroux and that she's making some kind of comeback.'

131

'And you believe this? On what basis?'

It was no small effort to suppress his impatience, but Borg managed it through gritted teeth.

'Given the proximity of the bughouse she escaped from, to the border, it rings right. Tijuana's a fair bet. An escapee wouldn't dare pull this shit on this side of the border.'

The hesitation on the other end of the line was one of those moments that felt like eons. Finally, it ended. 'Where's Mascini flying from?'

'Mascini? That the kid's name? JFK, he said.'

'Okay, I'll get it done.'

Borg cut in. 'A hot passport, remember! As soon as his plane takes off, they'll log a flight plan. Get it to me. Wherever this Mascini idiot lands, I want to be there.'

Borg went outside for some fresh air, then filled it with Marlborough smoke. He sat on the low wall outside the motel and gazed over the midnight traffic at the black and distant mountains.

*Over the border* rang right.

Tijuana?

Tijuana was just two hours away. If you're going to escape a U.S jail or, in this case, a mental hospital, where else would you be able to stay under the radar for years? He'd never been. But Tijuana sounded like the kind of place where insanity might just blend in, and just the kind of place where freaks like Erika Xtravaganza, and by extension, Peggy Deveroux, were likely to find it.

Borg went back in, untied Madden's restraints, and told him, 'Get dressed!'

# 24. BACK TO THE HEAD SHRINKERS

It was ten thirty-one when the Lincoln approached the hospital entrance. A shaken Carlo Madden pulled up beside the intercom. Borg reminded him that he was now on the shit-list of those who knew where he lived. He said it. 'Remember; you're on the shit-list of those who know where you live.'

Madden made a convincing job of affecting a neutral tone when he announced himself into the intercom. They buzzed him in and said, 'Good evening, Director.'

He led Borg across the darkened reception area but took a different route to the one that led to the makeshift office he had taken him and Koenig to yesterday. They came to a door with Madden's name and position emblazoned in gold and maroon on a metal plate. Madden fumbled with keys and unlocked it—aware of Borg's scrutiny. Even now, Borg half-expected him to pull some more diversionary horse shit. Was the office full of shrinks, waiting to declare him insane and consign him to the soft room forever? A gang of agreeable psychopaths, perhaps, recruited in advance to dismember him and dump his body parts into some basement incinerator?

Madden moved quickly over to his desk and turned on a lamp which threw oblique shadows around the room. As expected, there was no evidence of renovation, but Borg said nothing. They were way past petty deceptions now.

Using the same bunch of keys, Madden unlocked the filing cabinets and quickly located a large file, quick enough to suggest to Borg that Madden had visited it recently. If Borg were a gambling man, he'd put an even hundred on straight after Koenig's call yesterday morning. Madden dropped the file on the desk, followed by a large envelope that clattered plastic.

Borg peered inside. 'What's this?'

133

'The tapes she was arrested with. Said it was some kind of prophesy. They provided the starting point of her treatment. She was working on some kind of book. I believe she was trying to get it published.'

Borg pulled out a cassette and studied it. *Chapter 3* was written in biro on the label.

'Prophesies...'

'The police thought we should have them,' Madden elaborated. 'She tried to murder her roommate and when the cops came to arrest her, they had to be wrestled from her grip. They thought they'd help with her treatment.'

'Did it?'

'I believe it helped, yes. She only really opened up when talking about them.'

Borg replaced the tape, pushed the envelope aside, and reached for the psychiatric reports.

'Is this everything?'

'It's the overall history. The specifics are with her doctors...'

The documents within were unkempt and barely contained, but, for the most part, looked like they were in chronological date order. Borg flipped to the back. The last entry was Friday, May 31st, 1985. Borg went to the cabinet and checked the files before and after. Nothing more on the torrid and tempestuous times of the Queen of the Pin-ups appeared to be in evidence. Borg threw Madden a warning glance.

'That's all.' Madden offered. 'As you can see, the last session she had was more than three years ago. She escaped the day after.'

A note was clipped to the final entry saying the patient had absconded, and the case was in the hands of the San Bernardino P.D. 'It was reported to the police...' Madden offered helpfully, 'but it never made the papers.'

Borg wondered why Koenig had not been privy to this. Maybe his 'in' was shallow.

'How did she escape?'

'During a recreational day out, with eight others.'

'And they all got away?'

'Three. They rounded the others up that same day.'

'So, three still at large…'

'In this instance. As your… *colleague* so accurately pointed out, we had something of a problem in that regard.'

'And you don't now?'

'We've stepped up security. There's the odd lapse. Nothing on the scale we used to.'

'What about visitors?'

'She's had none. She's got a brother in Lawndale, and she writes to a sister in Missouri, but no one ever came.'

'Popular girl.'

'She made it clear she would not accept visitors. But until now, no one had ever requested one. So, even if she were still here, it would be difficult… for you to talk to her, I mean.' Madden seemed to re-locate his inner director. 'Mr.… Detective Leonard…? What is this about?'

Borg realised that all this effort, the chase, the abduction, declared importance. Like *governmental cover-up* importance. If it weren't for the plain fact that making Madden disappear would only make more noise, Borg would have no qualms about ending him. But fear tended to be a reliable device. Madden was full of it and would only spill about tonight's events if he absolutely had to.

Borg closed the file and put it with the tapes in his knapsack.

'You can't take that?!', Madden bleated, despite himself.

'What?'

Madden answered the question with silence, then countered with another. 'Why are you looking for her?'

'I just want her autograph.'

The Lincoln glided out onto Highland Avenue. Borg told Madden to head home. They got out and Borg watched him go inside. Once satisfied that the director was safely ensconced in his house, Borg made his way quickly up the street to his hired car and took off.

He went back to the Days Inn and started packing his stuff. He could do nothing but cool his heels now. Stevens' New York idiot wouldn't be leaving JFK until the morning. He pondered the value of making a visit to Deveroux's brother in Lawndale.

Could she be there? No, he was convinced of it; Erika Xtravaganza's *extravaganza* was going to be in or around Tijuana, certainly over the border. In a more reasonable, less car-lousy universe, it would be a two-hour drive. But in the here and now, he'd be lucky to get there in four—even at this time of night. In the interests of making good time, he considered leaving now. But he was right near the airport. If he was wrong about Tijuana, he might need wings.

He took the phone and the envelope of Deveroux's cassettes out to the car. The stereo came on. Talk radio and Country stations bombarded him with everything he didn't want to hear. He took out Deveroux's cassette tapes. There were seven of them—all numbered. He found number one and loaded it. As expected, it was the ramblings of the chronically unhinged. He struggled with her thick, lazy drawl against the low rumble of Highland Avenue's midnight traffic. The hollow acoustics suggested she had made the recording in the bathroom. The years she spent in New York, and subsequent decades, had done nothing to cool her Dixie-fried twang. The word 'prophecy' dominated the sermon, occasionally rising to a rant. Apparently, there were seven of them—prophesies—the 'Coming of the Seven Apostles': one prophecy per cassette.

That brief appraisal of her medical records back at Patton mentioned something about her having once been a schoolteacher. He pictured her testifying the gibberish he was now hearing in a road-side church—a spirit-fevered Laura Ingalls. The gist of the first tape was that the second coming would appear in the year 2167 to thwart humankind's invasion of Heaven and an assassination attempt on God.

*'Humankind would rise up against their father, but the Second Son will be waiting for them... He would be born into a wanting world and was lost in the Blacklands, but the whore would find him... would find him and bring him home...'*
After ninety minutes, the tape flipped and started to repeat itself. He loaded the next tape despite the danger of the unhinged prophetess pontificating him into the grace and favour of the Sandman. Tape two spent an inordinate amount

of time riffing on the subject of an epidemic of genital deformations, and how this would almost bring about the end of humankind and how, in order to survive, we would create a breed of androids capable of recalibrating their reproductive organs to engage with any deformity they may encounter— thus saving the human race. But then, according to Deveroux, it pans out that this breed is the work of the Devil, (surprise surprise) harnessing the power of the human soul to gain entry into Heaven where they intend to assassinate God. The second coming—or Second Son, as she sometimes referred to him would recruit a human army, who would commit a mass suicide to get to the next world the honest way and wage a universal war on the rolling prairies of Heaven...

*'He would lead us. Hear himself in the scream of debauchery and make us hear him and rise up... and lead us...'*

The green dash-lights illuminated the thick veins on the back of his hands and wondered if they were destined to touch her. No matter how much he tried, he could not reconcile this voice with the visage of the woman that had haunted him all these years. The sound of it was not something he had considered. His heart stopped momentarily when the possibility of Stevens' intel being flawed—that this was not the real Peggy Deveroux. But no, he could *feel* her. She was within reach. She was still with him in this world, and he would meet her one final time.

04:10: The portable chirped and Borg realised he'd descended into a deep sleep and had now awoken to a dark morning. It was someone from Stevens' office. The hot creds they'd given to the idiot in New York had raised an alert. He had just taken off from JFK—New York time 07:10, in a privately hired 727 and was en route to Cabo San Lucas—with a refuel in Austin.
  Cabo San Lucas?!

Borg scoured his maps and found it at the foot of the Baja peninsula—a thousand fucking miles away! Right neighbourhood—wrong address. Or more accurately, right country—wrong end!

It would be a simple matter to call Stevens and requisition a military plane. But it was now time to go off-piste. It was time to let go. Shake off officialdom.

Borg grabbed all his stuff from the room, checked out, and headed straight for the airport. He ditched the car in the multi-story and bought his own ticket from Norton Airforce base to Aeropuerto Internacional de Los Cabos... one way.

# 25. FAG AIR

### Friday October 7th

The 727 sucked its wheels up into its guts and left JFK's runway at 7.10am, precisely. The plane banked starboard as Marco peered glumly at the majestic curve of a grey Hudson River, obscured by Universal Horror movie mist. The last time he saw the city from this elevated advantage was when he flew in from Bangkok nine years ago. From up here nothing had changed. It could have been the same day.

The intercom bing-bonged. The captain announced that they would be cruising at *whateverthefuck feet* at *whateverhtefuck altitude* and that they would be making a brief landing in Austin. It had occurred that the Mexican location was a red herring—but Texas was certainly in the right direction.

After last night's confusing events in the village, he had gone back to his apartment and was vaguely disappointed that the night hadn't descended into the bloodbath he'd half-hoped for. But he understood, implicitly, given the ease with which 'persons unknown' had entered and planted the package in his apartment, *that if they wanted him dead, he would be*. However, the effort with which they were expending on the search for the Deveroux woman suggested that her re-emergence was proving troublesome for said 'persons'. It was a fair bet that her permanent disappearance was the endgame in mind. Could

138

he save her? Could he be a Travis to her Iris? He always imagined himself to be some untested savour. Was he about to be tested now?

Despite his *If they wanted him dead, he would be* summation, he had checked all his weapons again, still half expecting an attack from a crack-squad of Thai assassins. He removed the two framed Peggy Deveroux black-and-whites from the hallway wall and placed them on the kitchen table; made coffee; drank and stared at them...

One had her out in a jungle somewhere in a Flintstones outfit with a baby tiger. The other, standing in a living room next to an ancient television set, wearing a short black negligee, black stockings and garter belt, encasing perfect legs, stood apart imposingly on patent leather stilettos. In the tiger shot, her full mouth smiled coyly. But the eyes, almost certainly California blue, betrayed the kind of mischief you'd chance a jail term for. The negligee shot could almost be another character entirely, occupying the same body. An arched eyebrow and the heavily lip-stick'd mouth sneered cruelty beyond depravity.

Who? Was She?

They called him again—on the cell phone, at 2am. A man—not the one he'd spoken to from outside the club, said... 'You're on. Be at JFK at six, sharp. Someone will be there to give you your passport. You're a freelancer for the Christian Broadcasting Network. You're on the payroll. Bring the phone, bring the press-pass.'

The whole deal vibed big budget. Marco had to ask. 'Is there any money in this thing?'

'Money?'

'Y'know. My fee?'

After ten seconds of long-distance static, the voice said, 'Sure. Ten grand.' Then added tersely, 'Call us as soon as the destination is known. Do *not* fuck around.'

He packed the portable phone, the CBN press-pass, two extra T-shirts, five pairs of boxer shorts, five pairs of socks. Hand luggage only. A large black leather satchel. When he travelled, he travelled light. He pondered essentials and remembered the fake Breitling watch he'd bought in Chiang Mai. He fished it out of the bedside cabinet, wound it up and put it on. He wanted to take the .38 but, being unlicensed, knew he'd never get it on the plane. Ditto the switchblade and its ankle scabbard. The only thing between him and his immediate destiny was that fast-tracked passport. But if all this apparent professionalism was anything to go by, it was being made right now.

He hit the typewriter and spent the next couple of hours updating his journal—his confession—his last will and testament.

At 4.50am he left for Delancey St. subway for his JFK-bound trains. He left the journal propped up on the table.


A woman had approached him almost as soon as he entered the departures lounge. She was pushing a buggy with a kid in it. She challenged him with his own name. 'Marco Mascini?' The kid's presence took him by surprise. It looked up at him with big baby browns. Marco was about to shake its tiny hand. The woman challenged him again. 'Marco Mascini?'

'Yes.'

Pushing forty. Dirty blonde hair. Chopped short, with a faded galaxy of freckles across her nose, he figured she was the kid's grandmother. She wore an outsized blue anorak with yellow slacks. She studied him right back, making, Marco would guess, a positive ID. Without another word, she handed him a folder and pushed the buggy towards the exits. He watched her go and realised she was as juiced-in as he was. As in *not juiced in at all*. The realisation that there was an entire echelon of society peripherally connected to powers they couldn't even imagine, because of some past transgression, came to him in that moment. She was with him in the cracks. Between what needs to happen and the forces that make them happen.

He opened the folder and there it was—his fast-tracked passport. They'd used the same photo from his last one—pushed the contrast, which put bags under his eyes. Gave him that last nine years. He felt naked. Secrets were a myth.

Being back in an airport, preparing to fly, eradicated the last nine years. It was like his travelling days had never ended. Finding check-in was a pain. The information boards offered no clues. After walking the entire length of the lounge five times, he spotted a girl in a silver dress holding a sign that said 'RESURRECTION?' She was talking to a group of guys with camera cases. He recognised the Jap who he'd spoken to briefly at the club last night. She pointed them off towards the far end of the concourse and made diversionary shapes. It was only when Marco got closer that he realised the girl was a boy.

'Hi, I'm Marco Mascini? From the Christian Broadcasting Network?'

He/she fluttered false eyelashes, checked names on the back of her sign, and pointed in the direction she sent the others. 'Over there, God boy.'

He followed the others and found the check-in desk at the end of myriad tunnels which, Marco felt, seemed to be away from the general public. Celebrity routes, he guessed. He joined a short queue. It reminded him of an excursion to Israel during his world travels. In the interests of some security bullshit, they had their desk situated underground, away from the others, and grilled him about his motives for wanting to go there. This morning there was no such interrogation and within the hour, he was on board, in his seat, and in the air.

The earphones were uncomfortable and made his ears sweat. The music was that disco shit he thought was buried safely in the 70s. The plane emerged up from out of the clouds and was, according to the intercom announcement, now cruising at twenty-five thousand feet. 'Cruising' being the operative word if the high incidence of queers among the passengers was anything to go by. They seemed to cover the entire spectrum of fag-dom as far as Marco's marginal experience of that scene went—tight-jeaned, capped T-shirts—like an identikit parade of that guy with the huge cock on the back of Lou Reed's Transformer album. Positively Christopher Street... At the other end of the spectrum were the pretend girls—the glamour overloads that would put those lady boys in Thailand to shame. Everything about them was immaculate. His heart

141

sank slightly when he noticed the sensational blonde on the other side of the aisle rummaging through the overhead… with her overlarge hands. He lowered his gaze, discretely. Nothing about the plump curve of her pubic region suggested it was anything other than what it promised. The Monroe locks cascaded over one shoulder. Marco had to admit, she was a knockout… for a man.

Within the hour, lunch was served. He ate astronaut food and fell asleep. It would be another three hours before touchdown in Austin.

After that… things got weird.

## 12.55pm

He had no more sleep in him when they hit the runway at Robert Mueller Municipal Airport. The plane taxied to the terminal gate. No one got off, but a trio of bikers—sans hogs, naturally—emerged from the boarding tunnel and did a 45% degree turn straight into the plane's VIP area. He was in Dixie now. Home of Rock-and-Roll. He had the vague feeling that his body and soul had aligned for the first time.

Twenty-eight minutes later, the plane sucked its wheels again and the big bird was airborne. The intercom bing-bonged, and the captain announced this would be a three hours and fifty-minute flight. It bing-bonged again. The husky contralto of Erika Xtravaganza's voice introduced itself and spilled with the big reveal: to *where*, exactly.

*'We would like to announce, girls and boys, that the final destination will be Cabo San Lucas, where a shuttle will be waiting to take us to the Resurrection. We will be announcing the exact pickup point shortly before landing. Be sure to listen out for it.'*

Cabo San Lucas? He caught the attention of the Monroe knockout. 'Hey hon, Cabo San Lucas—that's Mexico, right?'

She shrugged and said, 'Search me, daddy.' She turned to ask the girl-man next to her who answered, 'It's in the Baja. Right at the bottom. About as far south as you can go.' The Monroe knockout turned to Marco. 'There you have it, daddy; as far south as you can go... without getting wet.'

The pair of them found this funny and raised a loaded giggle. Marco left them to it and pulled out the phone. He punched the number, but the thing was dead. No tone. Nothing. The little green light showed power, but no signal. Then it occurred to him... Fuck them. He had everything he needed—a slab of bills in his pocket and this fast-tracked passport. That old travel bug re-infected him. With money and a passport, the world is yours.

So...

Mission.

Find Deveroux and warn her that people with dubious intent were looking for her. The obvious place to start was with Erika Xtravaganza. Now that he knew she was on the plane, he would wise her up first chance he got. If whoever was behind this thing caught up with him, he could legitimately cite the fact that he could not get a signal from up here to call it in. Maybe he could when they land, but yeah, fuck them. He would not be making that call.

From his seat, Marco could now see Xtravaganza and her twenty-plus entourage holding court at the front of the plane— a thick red cord denoting the division between very important people and... people. The VIP area was crowded. As far as Marco was concerned, the cheap seats were the place to be. There were only around twenty other passengers scattered around the main body of the cabin. He peered through the gap in the window and could see water. The Gulf of California? He closed his eyes and tried to shut out the building chaos. Forty minutes into this second leg of the flight, the VIP area got rowdy. Some of the entourage spilled out into the rest of the cabin. More of that fucking Disco music issued forth from the tinny intercom. Marco sensed movement and opened his eyes.

'Wakey wakey. You look like you could use this.'

He looked up to see the silhouette of someone leaning over the seat in front. Marco sat up. His eyes adjusted to the light. The level of androgyny this girl possessed meant she was

143

undoubtedly another 'he'. Shame. He/she looked like Jean Seberg in *A Bout De Souffle*.

Elfin features?

Check.

Joan of Arc hair?

Check.

He peered into the cup he/she was offering him. It looked like a G&T. 'No thanks.'

'Go ahead. It'll change your life.'

'It's been changed enough already for one day.'

Erika and a couple of the Austin bikers emerged from the VIP area. They sat and chatted to a couple of guys on the other side of the plane—a journo and his photographer. The Queen and her court had decided to go among the peasants.

Marco still could not get his head around Xtravaganza's likeness to Deveroux. It was beyond eerie... like she'd leaped right out of those old magazines he'd seen at the club... like the photos on his wall. All eyes were on her, and Marco realised the only possibility of gaining her attention might—just might—be with feigned nonchalance. Absentmindedly, he took the beaker from 'Seberg''s slender hand and sipped. It was only *then* that he realised how dehydrated he was. He necked the rest of the cold drink. It brought him a new level of consciousness.

'Hey!' His/her protest killed Marco's trance. 'Seberg' said, 'You wanna meet her?'

*Does the Pope shit in the woods?* Marco thought. Then he said it. 'Does the Pope shit in the woods?'

'Seberg' grabbed his hand and led him across the plane between the empty seats. He slumped into the chair opposite the aisle from her with what he imagined might be the right degree of cool. She wore a black silk shirt and a black and white stripped pencil skirt. He could almost see his warped reflection in the shellac-vinyl gloss of her hair. Photographers snapped away. Marco wondered if he should avoid their hungry eye. The Jap journo he'd seen at the club asked Xtravaganza how she came to know Peggy Deveroux.

'She knew about me and got in touch. The next time I was down south…' This got laughs. '… I met up with her. In Mexicali where I was… having some work done. It seemed we were attending the same clinic, so we met up and… well, what can I say? It was like coming face to face with your maker. A fascinating woman, so full of stories… just the sound of that voice… but she was reluctant, y'know, to appear. But she had no idea that people still loved her.'

The Jap asked, 'Why did she retire?'

She waved a glossy red nail at a hostess, pointed at her empty beaker, and mouthed '*please?*'.

'Why does any model retire? Violated by gravity and brutalised by the clock.'

This too, got laughs. The hostess filled her cup.

'What is she doing now?'

'Well, she's quite religious, does a lot of work for a commune…' She paused. That Alaska melting smile again. 'Let's leave a few questions for her, shall we?'

*Quite religious.* Was there a connection between that and his phony employment by the Christian Broadcasting Network? For this journo ruse to fly, it had to be a real thing, right?

*The Christian Broadcasting Network…*

Marco gazed forlornly as Extravaganza sat surrounded by her entourage, trying to figure out how he might gain a private audience. Her freakish visage alerted him to the idea that he could be dreaming. He looked back over at his seat and half-expected to see himself still sitting there, asleep. The seat was empty. The plane hit turbulence and shuddered briefly. He thought he was going to throw up. He made it to the restroom without incident. The bile burnt his throat. As he urinated, he felt a surge of energy wiggle its way down his back. He checked his reflection. His eyes were enormous black saucers which stared back manically at him. His vision flickered.

The drink…

… that 'Seberg' gave him…

He staggered out of the restroom, holding himself against the moulded walls of the cabin. 'Seberg', along with others in the group, danced up and down the aisles. Someone had hooked

145

that shitty music up to bigger speakers and was now pounding. He felt great—invincible! He grabbed 'Seberg' out of the conga line he/she began to lead.

'What did you give me?'

She laughed big and declared, 'The future, baby!'

A neat flip of her arm liberated him/her from his grip. She jumped on the seats and climbed to the other side to re-join the crazy line. A wave of total pleasure washed over him. He collapsed into the nearest seat. His mind was turning in on itself—an entire body orgasm. Souped-up horny thoughts hit him from all sides. If this is dying, he thought, he should have done it years ago. His vision flickered uncontrollably and rendered everything an old movie—jammed frames—slipping spools, then a jump-cut, much like that beating he took all those years ago in Thailand. By the time the stuttering visuals eased off some, he realised he was back in the toilet cubicle. 'Seberg' was giving him a blow job that bordered on the quasi-religious… his first for half a decade. He looked down to watch his prick disappear into 'Seberg''s mouth; it was Bonnie's face he saw…

Bonnie Rachanski.

She pulled on his balls, looked up at him and winked big. His entire body from the chest down disintegrated like splintered glass…

# 26. BAJA BROUHAHA

## 6.02pm

The scene around the Aeropuerto Internacional de Los Cabos was fast becoming a polite riot. No heads had been busted… yet. But the margin of orderly conduct was narrowing fast. Journos and cameramen milled around the pickup area, with no picking up in evidence. Beyond the perimeter fence, a solitary phone booth had a line halfway down the street. Somewhere out in the world, editorial offices received frantic calls. Unprepared for this influx of the world's media, the local car-hire places were maxed-out and were either closed or were in the process of being so. Hertz had a sign behind the glass saying CERRADO.

The next one had the same sign.

VOLVER POR LA MANANA was scrawled on a billboard and propped up against a third one.

The few available cab drivers were recruiting on an ad hoc basis.

*'Hey, Hector! Call your useless fuckin' brother, mang! Earn a few pesos for the first time in his life!'*

Travel-ragged anchor men and their producers stood bewildered among flight cases on the drop-off apron as their cameramen had gone in search of alternative transport. It was only twenty miles into town, but without wheels, it might as well have been twenty thousand.

Erika Xtravaganza's efforts at exclusivity had backfired. The return of Peggy Deveroux was not to be the controlled explosion she had planned for. The pin was out.

Emerging from the chaos of the arrival suite, Marco staggered into the confusion outside. The early evening heat sucked the breath out of him. The air was thick and seemed as reluctant as the bustling crowd to move aside as he forced his way to a wall where he threw up. A sheet of frozen sweat burned into him. The sun was going down. He went dizzy and went down with it. A kaleidoscope of horny images still swirled around his blown mind. Bonnie Rachanski was the star of this psychedelic brain-show. He'd thought he'd done a sterling job of banishing her from his internal legend.

Clearly not.

The surrounding cacophony of crowds squabbling over taxis and aircraft engines firing up began to create a demented soundscape of horror-movie sound effects. Nausea came to town on a rubber horse. He threw up again and faded to black.

Maybe it was a moment later. Maybe it was a million years; but he seemed to be receiving a signal from a distant galaxy; that

147

he was propped up against a wall and that a plastic container
was being held to his lips.

'Here.'

The cold water hit his throat and coated his insides. His body
jolted, and he sensed light at the end of a vortex of noise and
writhing flesh. Eyes tightly shut—he could *see* the sound of a
plane taking off like a silver bridge soaring up and out into said
galaxy. He tried to focus on a miniscule blur of clarity and saw
the silhouette of a big man squatting in front of him, blocking
the sun.

He had no recollection of landing on the runway or leaving the
airport; any more than he could remember how he now came
to be propped up on a stool in this noisy bar.

'Drink the orange juice.'

The voice jolted him again, out of his trance. The relatively
familiar scene of a dark cocktail lounge ignited a semblance of
order. Journos and their crews sat around tables, glumly
outlining their meagre options. Was he back in New York?

His surroundings began to morph into something
comprehensible. A woman behind the bar was looking at him
with casual concern. 'Él está bien?'

Marco turned to see the man sitting one stool away from him,
who said again, 'Drink the orange juice.'

He saw the glass. Large. More purple than orange under the
ultra-violet lights. He gulped it back and felt that jolt again.

Back to life.

Back to the world.

He felt the scrutiny and finally took stock of his… saviour?

The left side of the man's jaw had seen devastating violence;
scared and off-centre. Heavily built, he reminded Marco of…
someone that he couldn't place. His severely short black hair
looked like it had been styled with a piping bag—two stark
segments bitterly resenting each other's presence. Leaning
against the chair at the man's feet was a large duffle bag, not
unlike the kit-bag Marco had used to smuggle his big score
from Bangkok all those years ago. He met the steely dots of this
stranger's myopic regard. Marco put the man's age at around

forty. Although glazed with perspiration, the man's face suggested a calm serenity while his hands betrayed the shakes. An unfamiliar brand of junkie.

Then it hit him.

With the almost non-existent jaw and cubist's wet-dream hair, Marco suddenly placed who this guy looked like.

Himmler.

Himmler with, it had to be said, a phenomenal set of forearms. Captivated within a tight grey T-shirt, he looked like he was made of steel. The man held out a now firm and steady hand. Reflex demanded he shake it. He was immediately sorry. It was cold, wet, and clammy.

The man asked the barmaid for a glass of milk and said to Marco, 'What's your name, son?'

Marco focused and refocussed again. He needed to know that what *seemed* to be happening was *actually* happening, that he wasn't about to engage in small talk with a hallucination. The guy looked fucking weird. No question. But in the interests of trying to make it back to this planet, he would have to chance it.

'Mascini. Marco...' He regretted this revelation the second it left his mouth. Should he have given a phony name? Fuck it. Too late.

The man inspected the lanyard hanging from Marco's jacket and eyed him slyly. 'Christian Broadcasting Network, huh?'

Everything was confusing to Marco in this moment, so he let go of whatever that look was supposed to mean. He realised suddenly, and with much relief, that his satchel still hung across his shoulder. He patted his jacket and could feel the wad of twenties still in his inside top pocket.

The man reciprocated. 'I'm Bob. Mayhew. Los Angeles Daily News. What happened to you? You look like you've survived a car crash.'

The barmaid brought the man's milk. Without taking his eyes off Marco, he pulled a small phial from a pocket, tapped out a capsule, and slugged it back.

Marco refocused again and scanned the room, half-hoping to see 'Seberg'. He'd like to know what the fuck she/he'd given

149

him and see if she still looked like Bonnie Rachanski now that the effects of the drug had eased off some.

'Someone slipped me a mickey on the plane… which… seriously disagreed with me.' A mild rush of pleasure wiggled its way down his back again. 'Although, I have to say, it didn't at first.'

'Bob' took a closer look into Marco's eyes. *Again, with the scrutiny.* This guy was waaaaaaaay too familiar. He saw Marco's big black saucers and laughed a lipless laugh. 'You are *flying*, my friend.'

The place was getting busier as the stranded came in, searching for some temporary salvation, bringing the building hysteria from outside with them. Marco's mission began to reform in his addled mind. On the plane, they told them there would be some kind of shuttle taking them to the event. He needed to lose this freak, whose shakes had now abated, and try to remember where they said the pickup point was going to be. He slid unconvincingly off the stool.

'Listen Bob… Bobby? Thanks for the juice. I've got a bus to catch.'

'A bus?'

'They've got a shuttle laid on. I gotta go find it before it leaves without me.'

The man grabbed Marco's arm to steady him, but also, Marco sensed, to stop him from getting away. The man's countenance darkened. Marco tried to pull away, but no cigar. The grip was vice-like.

'Turn me loose, you fuck!' People turned around.

The man sat him back down. 'Who do you think I am, you fucking idiot?'

Marco played it defiant but knew he would not be able to shake that grip. 'I don't know and I don't give a fuck!'

The man laid it down. 'You are Marco Mascini. Born November 1st, 1957, Pensacola, Florida, parents deceased, raised by grandparents in New York…'

The dime descended.

The man on the phone.

'*You* left that shit in my apartment.'

'... Flunked school—John Dewey High—in '77, Got married to a...'

Marco muttered, 'Fuck you.'

The man lowered his voice. '... April 1979, you murdered two police captains. One in Sak Lek and one in Bangkok...'

That skeleton again. The one that shimmied out of his distant past and kicked him squarely in the pills.

'... You've been living at your current Pitt Street address since '81...'

'Okay, enough!'

The man stopped and let Marco absorb it.

'So, how d'you find me?'

'Seriously?'

'Fuck it. So, what is this?

'*You* will fill me in on absolutely everything you know about Deveroux... Xtravaganza... this event. Be liberal with the lowdown. If I get the feeling you're holding out on me, I will throw you over this bar. First question: Do you know where the Deveroux woman is?'

'No.'

'Xtravaganza?'

'She was on the plane, but now she's probably on the bus I'm about to miss.'

Marco spilled the same meagre info that he'd already given him given over the phone from N.Y.—that's all he had. 'Bob' seemed to buy it. Another dime descended...

'If you knew where this thing was taking place, why did you need me?' Bob said nothing. Another dime... 'You *didn't*. You just needed to follow the passport.'

The man eyed Marco's empty glass. 'You want another drink? Down here you should stay hydrated.'

'Tea for two? I think not. So, Bob Mayhew. That's your real name?'

The time for subterfuge was over. The interloper gave it up. 'Leonard Borg.'

'Borg?'

'You want me to spell it?'

'I know already. P.R.I.C.K.'

151

Marco tried to read him, but the man's guileless face had little to go on. 'As far as I know,' Marco said, 'Xtravaganza is the only one who knows where Deveroux is. So… shall we?'

# 27. ENQUIRING MINDS

Chaos also reigned around the bus-less terminal. Marco asked around, flashing his Christian Broadcasting Network lanyard like a priest might wield his cross. Someone bit.

'The Resurrection bus? You missed it. Left about twenty minutes ago.'

'Left for where?'

'Cabos, I guess.'

'Anyone know if Erika Xtravaganza was on it?'

No-one bit.

'Fucking fuck fuck fuck! This is your fault!'

Borg ignored him and said he would go see what the car hire situation was. Marco steadied himself against a bus shelter and tried to formulate a plan to escape the clutches of his dubious benefactor. No plan presented itself. And within minutes, Borg was back.

'Not happening.'

'What?'

'They're out of cars.'

'Out of cars?'

'They're bringing some more down from La Paz… in the morning. Seems like this thing caught 'em on the hop.'

'Well, how far away *is* Cabos?'

''Bout twenty miles, but it's not *in* Cabos, my sky-high amigo. The general consensus says this thing is in Todos Santos, about an hour in the opposite direction. North, to be precise. And if we're going to get there, we are going to have to get creative about it.'

'Yeah? Who says it's in Toady whateverthefuck?'

'Todos Santos,' Borg reiterated. 'It's an open secret. The car hire place said they've been taking production crews up and down there all week.'

The heat wouldn't quit. With the sun's sinking, a menacing, fiery glow began to rise behind the distant hills. Marco stuffed his jacket in his bag and scanned the desert terrain. The wires of old-style telegraph poles seemed to skip into oblivion. He couldn't remember the last time he wasn't hemmed in by walls... buildings... His heart fluttered and he felt faint with whatever the opposite of claustrophobia was. Cars, trucks, and Winnebago's passed. Marco stuck out a thumb. No takers. He had no intention of hanging with Borg any longer than he had to but couldn't see how he was could give him the slip. Leonard Borg's appearance had confirmed Marco's belief that Deveroux was on some shit-list. He had to lose him and get to her first. But for now...

'So, what have you got in mind, Lenny?'

Borg put on a pair of Soul Brother shades, smiled that lipless smile again and said, 'Let's lose this madding crowd.'

They walked along the highway until, twenty minutes later, they came to a gas station. Through the service window, they could see one guy behind the counter. The forecourt was busy with broadcast trucks, but with only one guy pumping gas. Borg told Marco to go in and hold the counter guy's attention. 'There's gotta be something round the back.'

'Hold his attention? How?'

'I don't know; riff.' Borg eyed Marco's unruly mop of hair. 'Ask if they got lacquer or something.'

'Oh, so you're cute now?'

'Do it!'

'Y'gonna boost a car? With all these people out front?'

Borg had already made a tangent and disappeared around the corner of the place.

Marco took the entrance. The AC froze the sweat on him. He returned a desultory nod to a hollow-cheeked cholo in overalls, slouched at the counter. A genuine thirst had Marco take a beer of unfamiliar marque from the over-crammed fridge. By the time he got to the counter, the cholo was gone. Someone from the back room shouted, 'Hey!' Marco leant over the counter and saw an open door, stage-left, and the cholo running through it and out back. Marco pocketed the beer and raced back outside onto the forecourt. He turned the corner and almost bounced off someone using the pay phone. A woman all in khaki. Dark as a native but her *'Hey, take it easy!'* was generic stateside.

Marco made it around to the back of the building in time to see Borg throwing the cholo and another guy, wearing identical overalls, around like rag dolls. Marco hung back, popped the beer, and watched the show. Borg left his two would-be assailants lying on the ground when he got into a nearby Dodge Ram van and started the engine. Borg finally noticed Marco standing at the corner chugging the beer and shouted to him, 'Let's go!'

As addled as his mind was, Marco had no intention of jumping in a stolen vehicle with this whack job. But even before he could respond with any kind of protest, both cholos leapt to their feet, pulling identical pistols from their identical overalls. Borg's surrender-hands shot up and he slid back out of the van.

Nice.

And.

Slow.

One of the cholos swiped the butt of his gun across Borg's head, knocking his glasses off. He rolled with the blow and staggered slightly. 'Okay fellas, big mistake.' He attempted a disarming smile. 'You wanna sell this thing?' Hire it out?

Their response included the word 'Puta'. Borg swiped his glasses from the ground and took another kick in the back as he walked away—both guns aimed directly at his head.

Marco feigned nonchalance as the guns were now aimed at him as Borg passed. Marco gulped beer—Alla salute. They put their guns away, one spat, and they both went back to whatever they were doing before—property rightly defended.

The woman in khaki at the payphone slammed the receiver down and muttered, 'God... dammit!'

Marco eyed her as he followed Borg back to the forecourt. She was about to dial again when she said, 'You guys going to Todos Santos?'

It was only when she muttered '*asshole*' for ignoring her that Marco realised she was addressing him. Her thick black hair was tied up with a red bandana. Her nose was thin and equine. He put her in her late thirties. A few years older than him, at least. Borg had wandered out on to the highway, duffle bag at his feet, hands on his hips, pondering their next move.

Marco seized his chance. He led the woman by her arm and steered her quickly away to the far side of a news truck. 'Listen, I need to lose that fucking idiot. He just tried to steal a truck and got royally fucked. And, if I'm not careful, I'm gonna get arrested with him, or shot by the natives. What do you need?' Satisfied that he'd established an outlaw vibe, he pulled a twenty out of his inside pocket. 'I got funds, see?'

Her scowl was replaced by a sly smirk revealing a missing premolar. 'I'm going through there, but I'm out of gas. My office was supposed to wire some cash, but for reasons beyond all comprehension, it hasn't happened. Is there any way you can lend me, say... forty bucks? My office'll vouch for me. I'm with the Enquirer—'

Marco put up halt hands. 'Wait up, Little White Dove—you got wheels? Well, let's go!'

He gave her the forty. Her car was an orange Opel, at least a decade old and in the opening rounds of a losing battle with rust. They got in and drove to the Pemex on the other side of the highway. Marco scanned the road. Borg was nowhere to be seen. She pumped thirty in, took the car to the road, and waited for a break in the busy traffic. The car lurched forward, but the passenger door was wrenched open suddenly and Borg was in Marco's lap. 'Scoot over, Sky-high!'

Before Marco could yell any kind of a fuck off, Borg had forced him into the back seat—face-first. Little White Dove said, 'This your grand theft auto buddy?'

With a struggle, Marco turned himself the right way around. 'Yeah, this is him. What the actual *fucking fuck*!'

155

Borg lowered his shades and fixed him with his 'two bullet-holes in the wall' stare. Marco stared back. A loaded standoff. The girl read it. 'Okay guys, take it easy.'

Marco addressed the big man. 'Problem?'

'I nearly took bullets, and you were gonna slope off?'

'What are we, a fucking item?! Thanks for the orange juice. Sayonara. What else?'

Borg turned back around, grunted, and squinted through the dirty windshield. 'Sneaky little fuck.'

She pulled out onto the highway, gunned it, and joined the exodus north. She said her name was Echo Hernandez, reiterated her Enquirer association to Borg and drove crouched forward, peering through the dust encrusted windshield with her breasts pressing against the wheel.

Borg gave her a sideways glance. 'The Enquirer still owned by the mob, sweetheart?'

In the aftermath of his failed car boost, Marco figured this was Leonard Borg's way of asserting himself... as the guy with the 'inside dope' on whom nothing was lost.

Hernandez didn't bat an eyelid. 'Yeah, I heard that story. Maybe. I dunno...'

They hit the 19 and curved right and north. On the left, the Pacific Ocean scored its blue line between heaven and earth.

Agoraphobia.

That was it.

Too much space.

The opposite of claustrophobia.

Marco felt less agoraphobic remembering this. His mind went Sinatra—like it was making a comeback. Whatever that shit 'Seberg' had given him on the plane was finally abating. He needed to focus but the very strong possibility that he had been blown by a male took center-stage in his addled memory.

Fuck it.

Put it down to experience.

Brando and Dean were half fags, right? Hell, maybe even De Niro.

The Opel found itself between two ABC news trucks. Hernandez was about to overtake but thought better of it when they passed a crashed car on a plinth of oil drums—a warning rendered futile by a pantheon of bloody wrecks not a mile further on. Along with the crashed car display, the road was also littered with crushed armadillos. Out in the distant desert halos of vultures circled the unseen dead.

'It doesn't matter what you're driving, your car is only as good as the piece of shit you're stuck behind,' shouted Marco.

The car had the windows down and the radio on.

A Spanish talk show...

No music.

Hernandez shouted back, 'I was here a month ago! These roads were completely deserted! Now it's a fucking L.A. Freeway! You're covering the Peggy Deveroux event, right?!'

Marco glanced at Borg who seemed to be falling asleep. 'Yeah, what else?!'

'Not me! This Deveroux thing is a fucking nuisance—of all the lousy timing! I'm following up a story about an *actual* resurrection... Check it out... should be a copy somewhere in the back!'

The back of the car was littered with clothes, empty food containers and cassette cases. Marco found a recent copy of the National Enquirer behind his head rest. Among the 'DID WHITNEY GIVE CYBIL AIDS?' and 'GERALDO CYBORG RUMOUR' type headlines, was... MEXICAN RESSURECTION.

He thumbed the pages and found a center-page spread featuring some tanned and naked messiah-type standing in a graveyard—his meat-rack tastefully blacked out—a crowd gathered at the gates. One photo showed him collapsed at a graveside, with what looked like an old-style Mexican soldier being pulled from the ground by a couple of girls in white smocks. Hernandez yelled over her shoulder at Marco, 'Staged—*obviously*! I'm going back to find out how they did it! I'm guessing he had oxygen down there or something. But that ground looked pretty un-tampered with!'

Another picture had the resurrector and the ressurectee embracing, laughing... 'Who's the miracle man?!'

'Mr. Kite—the Prophet Mr. Kite! He was some kinda half-assed country singer, but he's a prophet now. Founded the

157

House of the Son of Man! Runs a commune out in the desert!
Their whole thing is based on the unhinged ramblings of
Charles Manson! Kite gives all his favorites Beatle names—'
　'John, Paul and Ringo?'
　'From the songs—hence, Mr. Kite!'
Marco's painful recovery in Chiang Rai sprang to mind—when
he got his teeth kicked out.
　'I knew a Dr Robert, once!'
　'Yeah, they got one a them too!'
　'They fucking ruined Rock-and-Roll, the Beatles.'

# 28. TODOS SANTOS

18:08

T he sun was drowning in its own flames when they
approached the town. The endless sky was slashed and
bruised like the aftermath of a gang-fight between
hoodlum angels.

　Borg woke up and said, 'It's gonna rain.'

　Hernandez dropped them off near the crowded town square.
Unable to continue onwards, they watched her turn the car
around; presumably to pick up the junction they'd passed five
minutes ago, catch a clear road around the town and on to her
big resurrection reveal.

　There was a church to the south of the square, a theatre to the
west and grilled-windowed buildings of ambiguous purpose to
the north and east. On the corner, the smell of fried chicken
from the taco stand set their guts-a-growl—albeit for opposite
reasons. Electric light seemed scarce and burning torches had
been ignited on most corners. Above them, sneakers and torn
prophylactics-a-plenty hung, bobbed and weaved. Those
telegraph wires that skipped into oblivion from the airport
seemed to have collided here and exploded into a web that
captured the town.

　Some kind of carnival had begun to fragment. The two
elephants that led it were tethered to a post outside a bar

158

where a mob of drunken newsmen sang a Springsteen song. Again, ghosts of Chiang Rai slithered past Marco like cold snakes.

On the bandstand at the north of the square was a crowd of Peggy Deveroux look-a-likes, a few deluded distortions, and the rest, Hollywood knockouts. But none quite achieving the heights of Erika Xtravaganza's uncanny clone. Some of the girls posed nervously with some raw looking bikers as photographers devoured the scene in explosions of epileptic flash. The rest of the parade carried on out of the square.

The smoke from the taco stand wouldn't quit. Borg bought one and chewed into the greasy meal. Marco didn't trust his churning guts and gave it a miss. They made their way across the square to the theatre where, it seemed, Deveroux was to make her big comeback.

The press accreditation tent was behind the theatre. The chatter from the throngs of media personnel inside bordered on the hysterical. Marco got in line. Borg told him he would wait for him out front. Marco had every reason to believe just that. Whatever further use Borg had in mind for him remained a concern.

Everyone had a theory as to Deveroux's current whereabouts. It was rumoured that Xtravaganza's HQ was one of a legion of luxury Winnebagos, south of the town. Marco remembered passing the trailer-park city, which stretched all the way out to the ocean when Hernandez drove them into town. Someone said they thought Deveroux was, or will be, there before making her grand entrance tomorrow evening. A woman wearing an Azteca 7 News badge declared she knew *for a fact* that Deveroux was staying back in Cabos and would be helicoptered in at the appointed time which, thought Marco, would be a drag considering the effort it took to get up here.

Twenty-eight minutes later, Marco reached the desk, finally. He showed them his CBN lanyard and the press pack they gave him at JFK. The girl ticked him off some list, then wised him up to here and now. The rooms they had booked for the Game Show winners had been invaded. She looked out at the rising mayhem.

159

'Those bikers are supposed to be the security, but all they've done is fuck around and chase the girls around the square. If we can get them to do their fucking job, we might get the rooms freed up. In the meantime, we've got a camp set up out on the beach. Look out for the big Game Show flags.'

Marco was irked to find Borg waiting for him as promised but the symbiosis began to appreciate. Borg had the inside dope—and probably the whole story. Marco wanted it. As for himself? Well, he was a bona fide Game Show winner. He might have access somewhere along the line that Borg didn't. Perhaps therein lay his value. He'd seize his chance when it presented itself. He'd play along... for now.

'Have you booked up? Cos they've fucked up on the accommodation. They got a bunch of tents set up in case they can't get these biker dudes to clear out the invaders.'

'Tents?! I told you, there's gonna be a storm. We don't wanna be out in it when it hits.'

Marco scanned the near cloudless evening sky. 'A storm? Really? I don't see it.'

'All the same, it's coming.'

'So, are you booked up or what?'

'No. But if we find Deveroux quick enough, we won't need to stick around any longer than we have to.'

'We? What do you need me for?'

'I'll let you know.'

Marco flashed his lanyard at the theatre door. Leonard had a press pass and did the same. *Teatro – Cine* was painted in a flowery design above the entrance. The stockade-like doors were flanked by huge posters depicting the delectable Miss Deveroux in glossy knee-high lace-up boots, brandishing a bullwhip—across it, in garish B-Movie typeface...

RESURRECTION
THE RETURN OF PEGGY DEVEROUX!

The old theatre had been transformed into a pantheon of archaic eroticism—part shrine, part 1920s cathouse. Jumpy old movies projected back and forth across the expanse of the main hall. A triptych of screens had Peggy shimmying around a lounge with a creepy stuffed clown... Peggy feigning cartoon shock, whilst being spanked by another woman similarly attired in garter belt and stilettos... Peggy suspended off the ground by a complicated series of pulleys and weights, a gimp-ball stuffed into her mouth... eyes wide with cartoon terror.

Deathly pale mannequins, draped in lingerie and 'Peggy' wigs, were arranged on the main stage under blue lights—a tableau of frozen compliance. Among them, formations of Peggy look-a-likes rehearsed their clumpy routines to some sleazy reverb-laden guitar instrumental.

Marco watched as Borg stood before a series of huge Peggy blow-ups; seemingly absorbing some supernatural charge.

Compliant Peggy...

Haughty Peggy...

Laughing Peggy...

Zany Peggy...

Cruel Peggy...

'What's with you?'

The question partially dragged Borg from his trance. He adjusted his vision of Marco as if seeing him for the first time and fixed him with that two-nail stare.

'I've just had an epiphany.'

'You need a Kleenex?'

Borg snorted. 'I bet you're quite the smash, back in your natural habitat.'

'I get along.'

Inevitably, Deveroux was nowhere to be seen, nor was Xtravaganza. They asked around. A couple of security bikers... the guy directing the dancer's routine... some of the other photographers...

Nobody knew shit.

'Where is this hotel you're supposed to be staying at?'

Marco opened the folder. 'Hotel California. But the girl said it had been invaded. There's a map...'

Borg gave the map the once over and ran the idea of storming the room, evicting whatever inebriated camera or newsmen they might come across, beating the shit out of them, and

161

taking it. But the climate of rowdiness that met them an hour ago was escalating into a riot. From outside the theatre, they watched as the handful of bikers who had been hassling the Peggy wannabees on the bandstand had now grown to a small squadron. Leathers hung on rows of bikes—green and red insignia—Vagos MC. Loud, proud declarations of outlaw endeavour. Marco thought of Amy—the Connect 4 kid in Thailand—and wondered if she ever found the Chrome Devils of Chiang Rai and bloody justice.

The girls on the bandstand were gone—replaced by boozed-up reporters. At least two fights were in full swing—the Springsteen-singers across the road had swelled—they chanted Born in the USA like a rebel song. Some fool staggered into a bike and knocked it over. The cops were conspicuous by their absence. Things were about to go nuclear.

Borg said, 'We better hang back. It's only a matter of time before the militia arrive. We don't want to be in this when they start rounding everybody up.'

They made it to the church on the south side of the square. The contrast between the candle-lit calm inside and the heat on the street outside was of Oz/Kansas proportions. A young priest nodded a terse acknowledgment as they walked in and told them he was locking up soon.

Apart from an old woman sweeping up, the place was deserted. Borg strode down the aisle and read out the sign above a small statue at the altar. 'Nuestra Señora del Pilar. Apt.'

Marco took a pew. 'Apt? Apt how?'

'Our Lady—the Virgin herself... she could appear in multiple places at once. Just like Xtravaganza's Peggy Deveroux freak show outside.'

Marco eyed the statue. Our Lady gazed at the marbled floor in motherly admiration, hands held out, accepting anything you might want to subject her to. Borg sat on the other side of the aisle, dumping his duffle beside him.

Marco eyed it and said, 'So, what is this? Spooksville?'

Borg scanned the ceiling. 'It's a church.'

'Don't be a fucking idiot.'

'*You're* the one talking like a fifties Beatnik. *Spooksville*! Learn to tell the fucking time.'

'So, you *are* a Spook.'

'I'm a reporter. Deveroux has a brother in California who wants us to find her.'

'Us? Define *Us*?'

'I told you. *Me*, Los Angeles Daily News. *You*, Christian News Network. There's a story in this, no?'

'Horse shit. I'm no journo and neither are you.'

Borg smirked. 'No?'

'Breaking and entering apartments, delivering cell phones and phony journo creds, issuing marked passports... following my ass all the way down here... it's got government-level skulduggery written all over it.'

Borg scoffed. ''Wasn't me—breaking into your apartment. Anyway, you think an old stripper is worthy of that kind of attention?'

'No-one is beneath those fucks.'

'And you know this, how?'

'My little Thai adventure. You know all about it, right? Not exactly common knowledge, and that shit didn't happen in a void. It was plain as day that *moves* take place down there. Political moves. Moves that are basically dry runs for shit that goes down in the real world. The place was crawling with officialdom. If *I* can get involved in something that's gonna bite me on the ass after all this time, then anyone can. No-one's under the radar, right?' I got no illusions about that.'

'No, just *delusions*. You were scouted, plain and simple. A casual recruitment sweep, probably.'

'Probably? You don't know?'

'Don't know. Don't care.'

'*Los Angeles Daily News*', Marco spat. 'Prick. And what about my money? When do I get that?'

'What money?'

'The ten grand. They told me I was getting ten grand.'

'That what they told you?' Borg's oily smirk meant that was never going to happen. The two men locked eyes. This standoff would yield no fruit. Marco knew he was being fucked with and

163

looked at the statue again. The held-out hands no longer offered acquiescence. Now they suggested, *'What the fuck do you want from me?'*

The priest appeared and ushered them out with an open hand and a smile.

They took the road they came in on—back out of town. Marco still couldn't see it, but Borg insisted it was going to storm that night, so finding cover in trailer city was the best deal on offer. Marco stopped and gazed back down at the road to town. A hellish glow illuminated the sky over the tiled roofs.

'Careful Mascini,' said Borg. 'You'll turn into a pillar of salt.'

# 29. CHIEFTAN

The first camps were set up about half a mile from the south-west side of town. The outskirts of this makeshift metropolis comprised tents which intensified to mobile homes and Winnebago's to the centre. Fox News, ABC, NBC... media tribes from across the nation sported their colours and logos as loud and as proud as those marauding bikers in town. Satellite dishes on top of remote broadcast trucks panned blindly to the heavens in preparation of live feeds to and from distant civilisations.

The smell of myriad barbecues assailed Marco's nostrils. His appetite cried vengeance. He was now ready to give an Andy to anyone that would sell him a hot dog. They walked over uneven brush land, through narrow alleys between the caravans of the vast camp, until they came to the beach. The ocean flashed fitfully under a distant storm that Borg was sure was coming inland. It raged silently on the horizon—crackled and fizzed. Marco could only guess at how far out it was— anywhere between a mile and a thousand. They had hardly seen anyone in the portable shanty town—perhaps a few conscientious runners and interns—making busy and showing willing. But now as they approached the beach, campfires punctuated the Land's End, around which sat groups of people staring into the flames.

Someone somewhere strummed a guitar.

Waves crashed against the unspoilt beach. Marco sparked a Lucky and marvelled at the storm which, he now realised, had indeed wandered closer.

Borg dropped his bag on the sand and weighed up the possibilities. 'When that storm hits, the bars are gonna max out, and everyone else will head back here. I say we hot-wire one of those trucks while we still can, take it up to the hills until it passes.'

The Game Show flag spasmed in the near still air. 'The camp's right there. There's probably tent with my name on it somewhere.'

'No. Let's go get one of those trucks.'

Marco sucked the last of his cigarette but arrested himself before flicking the butt into the waves. This place will be ruined one day. He would play no part in its demise. He stubbed it on the sole of his boot and pocketed it. Borg headed into the vast camp.

Marco watched him for a moment, then followed.

They peeked through the windows of some of the more impressive vehicles.

'Would be a blast, wouldn't it, if we found Deveroux in one of these things?'

Borg ignored him and kept going. Marco kept his eye on Borg's duffle bag, slung over his powerful shoulders, as they sauntered onward. Having seen the speed and force of the man when he took on those cholos back in Cabos, Marco knew that Leonard Borg was nothing more or less than a self-contained lethal weapon. Any physical exchange with this monster was not an option.

*Los Angeles Daily News,* my Guido ass.

It was a newish black and cream Chieftain Winnebago. Or maybe maroon and cream. In the failing light, with only a few camp lights hanging on tents nearby, Marco couldn't be sure. Borg found an open side-door, did a quick recon of the interior, found no-one, and proceeded to the cabin. The reflection of the dark glass of the driver's window obliterated Borg as he sat behind the wheel and fooled with the wiring underneath the dash. Marco stood back, partly to keep watch, partly to distance himself from the situation should the owners return, and it all go to shit... again.

Then Marco saw it—Borg's bag just inside the Chieftain's entrance...

Borg manoeuvred the vehicle out of the camp, hit the road and headed another half-mile south, before taking a hard left across rocky terrain uphill and over the other side. By the time he stopped at what he thought was a satisfactory vantage point, the underneath of the vehicle was ripped out with the exhaust hanging off. Night had well and truly fallen. The sun was gone and took the heat with it. The cold started to bite.

Borg rummaged through the cupboards, looking for milk, found some, sniffed it and put it back. Outside, Marco stood at the peak of the hill and watched the distant town smoulder in the darkness. Where were the people who lived here? Had they abandoned their homes? Or were they holed up inside their stucco-clad bungalows, cowering from the invasion?

Marco yelled to Borg, who he didn't realise was now standing right behind him. 'I'm guessing building a campfire is off the menu!'

Borg yelled in his ear. 'Correct!'

The shock jerked him forward. He lost his balance trying to correct himself and partially slid down the hill on his ass. He scrambled quickly to his feet. 'Yeah... cute.'

He stormed past a smirking Borg and climbed aboard the stricken Chieftain. The fridge contained cheese and ham. Plastic tubs contained things not readily identifiable. From outside, Borg shouted, 'Leave the milk alone!'

Apart from the beer he'd stolen from the gas station in Cabos, nothing had passed his lips since the astronaut food on the plane. He rolled the ham and stuffed it in his mouth. Borg climbed inside and dropped himself in the seat opposite the open door. The vehicle rocked.

Marco said, 'You know this thing is useless now. I doubt we'd make it back to the road.'

Borg put his feet on the seat opposite. 'It'll serve its purpose.'

Marco decided to bring it all home. 'So, how's Jimmy?'

'Jimmy?'

'Jimmy Farragher.'

Borg fiddled with the overhead lights. 'The name is unknown to me.'

'He was the guy in Thailand who arranged those hits. He still around?'

'I have absolutely no idea. He was probably a handler of some kind. A recruiter… Unless they're very good, their shelf life tends to be fleeting.'

'So, what has this got to do with my Thailand adventure? Obviously, you know most of it's gone… the money. If the sucker punch is a shakedown, you left it too late. So just cut to the fucking chase.'

Borg said, 'I already said, I don't know who Jimmy is, nor do I know what money you're talking about. But I offer this…'

Marco waited. 'What?'

'You bought in.'

'Bought in?'

'If I'm talking to you now…' Borg pinched his own wrist, his bicep, his nipple, '… and I believe I am, it's *your* actions that put you here. There are sleepers… aaaand there are sleepers.' Borg held his big hands open in a welcoming gesture. 'So, wakey wakey!'

'C'mon man. What do you want her for, anyway?'

'Tut tut.'

'Tut tut… what?'

'Not professional. Ours is not to reason why.'

'Yours maybe. I told you, I'm not a professional. I'm not even a fucking amateur, okay? And no, I don't *wanna be a member.*'

'What is that? *Don't wanna be a member*?'

'The incentive tape they sent. The old Betty Boop cartoon on it…'

Borg was suddenly far away. Marco saw it. The statement was significant.

'Do I hear ringing bells? What's *that* about? Betty Boop…'

Borg's two-nail stare fixed him. 'Your guess is as good as mine. Your involvement in this thing is as much a mystery to me as it

167

seems to be to you.'

'What do you mean, *seems*?'

'I can see no reason whatsoever why a complete no-mark, such as yourself, should be involved in this in the first place. You just said it yourself, you're not even an amateur.'

Marco opened the flap in the top of a window and sparked up. 'After all this time, what do they want her for?'

'Search me. Her re-emergence is probably awkward.'

'Awkward?'

'Awkward.'

Borg's almost featureless face seemed to achieve an even greater height of banality. Marco had seen expressions of this level of vacancy before.

'You want to kill her.'

'I don't want to kill her.'

'Someone does. Why?'

'I'm sure no one *wants* to kill her...' He did that c'est la vie shrug that French people do with their shoulders, and the down-turned mouth, '... but life is full of what we don't want to do.'

'What did she even do?'

'Enough, I guess.'

Marco realised this guy wouldn't spill if he were tortured. It was time to surmise. 'Okay. This storm passes. Then what?'

Borg suddenly froze, staring into nothing. His hands began to quake.

'Borg?'

Borg snapped out of it and got up. He took milk out of fridge and went back to his bag.

Here it is, Marco thought ...

Borg rummaged around for a moment and seemed to freeze again. Those eyes, like pin pricks into the void, fixed themselves on Marco like bolts holding him in place. Borg's right hand jerked around violently. 'Where are they?!'

Marco leapt to his feet and dodged Borg's clumsy lunge at him. 'Where's what?!'

Borg stumbled and hit his head against the cupboard. Plastic plates slid out and clattered around them. A lamp cracked off the wall.

'Don't fuck with me!' Borg fell to his knees and seemed to hyperventilate. His huge hands shot out and grabbed Marco's throat whose vision went to purple and red as if his brain had been squeezed into his eyes. The explosions of colour began to blacken. And then ease off. The darkness went back to purple and red, and then back to the beige ceiling of the Chieftain. Borg's grip weakened. He was passing out. He grabbed at the hem of Marco's jeans. Marco stamped to remove Borg's clamp-like grip.

No avail.

Borg seemed to convulse with a series of violent stop-motion-like movements. Was he dying? What the fuck was wrong with him? Borg seemed trapped in a kneeling position; the left leg of Marco's trousers still clamped in his huge hand. Marco kicked and scraped at Borg's fingers and knuckles but could not remove that grip. Would he have to remove his trousers before Borg regained consciousness? *If* he regained consciousness.

Should he kill him while he had the chance?

With what?

Maybe he was dead already.

He heaved Borg onto his side. His small eyes were half shut. A string of drool hung from his mouth and seemed to connect him to the floor. Marco put his hand to Borg's chest. He could detect no under-the skin-activity.

His pulse...

Marco checked the wrist of the hand that still held his trouser leg in its vice-like grip.

Yes. A rapid series of palpitations.

Marco stumbled and stepped over him and stretched for the cutlery drawer. The knives were of the picnic variety. He hacked away at the garment but was unable to even penetrate the denim. He had better luck with a fork. Ten minutes later he'd made enough mess with the tiny, pronged instrument to tear away his leg.

Borg lay in a foetal position at his feet, still clutching the tiny

169

piece of fabric. Marco upended Borg's bag: cell phone, shorts, socks, T-shirts, and an orange shaving bag, identical to one he'd randomly grabbed when Borg was hot-wiring the Winnebago down at the camp. He opened the shaving bag; blister packs of pills, a couple of syringes and the mother lode—a Ruger automatic and a silencer. Whatever Borg was looking for was in the other bag—the one he hid behind a nearby boulder. He put the gun in his pocket and went outside to find the other shaving bag. He found it, tipped it out on to the ground, keeping one eye on the open door of the Winnebago where he could see Borg's frozen visage.

Six vials in the name of L J Borg.

A passport elaborated: Leonard Joseph Borg – DOB 8.10.1928. Minnesota.

1928!

The guy's sixty tomorrow?! Marco had put him at forty. Tops.

Probably a phony name, probably a phony DOB. But then, it would have to be believable so, the DOB nixed the theory.

L-Dopa: that's what it said on the vials. Borg had popped one with his milk at the airport bar.

Marco remembered the shakes.

Marco remembered said shakes abating.

L-Dopa. Bells remained un-rang as far as this particular pharmaceutical was concerned. But a lack of whatever it was rendered the Samson on the floor of the stolen Chieftain… bald.

Okay…

Plan…

One: get this thing back to the road where it will be found. Leave Borg in it *with* his drugs. Hopefully, whoever finds him will know what to do, or get him to someone who does. He didn't really want to see the guy dead. Nor did he want to see him again anytime soon.

Two: Find Erika Xtravaganza. Get her to spill Deveroux's whereabouts. If she proves difficult? Wave the gun around. Get your hard-sell on. Tell Deveroux all. Warn her off of this big comeback tomorrow. Tell her she's on radars unknown; that she's within shadows of nefarious origin; that she's lining herself up for the big knock off.

170

If the little he knew of Deveroux's long chase told him anything, it was this: Nowhere to run to, baby. Nowhere to hide...

Music must be faced.

Instruments must be mastered.

Fate now demanded a performance.

# 30. ECHO

8:20pm

Getting the outsize vehicle back up the hill was the *real* fucker. Marco stomped the acceleration and the gears screamed accordingly. Something beneath the chassis cracked loud. Big birds fluttered and took off in a shrill night-borne display. He thought the whole thing was going to see-saw at the peak, but he hit a boulder port side and put it into a downhill skid.

Over rough ground and rocks, the Chieftain rolled. Marco struggled with the wheel, desperately trying to prevent a roll-over. Borg was unsecured in the back and probably bounced off every surface available. The terrain levelled out. The Chieftain rolled on some, then came to a creaking halt. Marco checked on Borg who was now jammed under the fold-out table. He was pretty beaten up, but his position was otherwise unchanged. Dragging him to the roadside was do-able, but fuck that...

Marco stuck the drug pouch under one of Borg's arms—sans a couple of vials. He might encounter Borg later and some ill-formed notion suggested he hold on to something this animal might need. The contents of the bag were scattered all over the inside of the vehicle—including a Wal-Mart carrier bag. Inside was a bunch of old collector item magazines—*Peggy in Bondage*, Eyeful, *Male Life...* all with Deveroux on the covers. Marco appraised the centre spread of one of the magazines. Deveroux was bound and gagged. Two girls led her to the open trunk of a waiting car.

There was a bunch of cassettes with a heavy portfolio of thick mottled brown card. Keeping Borg in his peripheral vision, Marco flipped it open—official papers—medical records? Deveroux's name leapt out.

He hauled Borg up to a sitting position and turned all the lights on.

Borg moved!

With that creepy stop-motion movement, Borg turned his face towards Marco. Those steely dots nailing him again. Marco's heart accelerated. Even in this stricken state Borg's ire was a frightening prospect.

Marco stood at the side of the road. The big, wrecked Chieftain lay forlorn, like some sunken vessel on a bed of black rocks. In his satchel he put the Wal-Mart bag with the magazines, cassettes, and portfolio. He would give them a proper look once there was enough distance between him and Borg. He glanced back at the vehicle—satisfied that it was easily visible from the road. The cabin glowed dimly in the desert dark. To Marco's mind, it was a clear SOS scenario to any passers-by. It couldn't be long before it was spotted, possibly by the poor sap they'd stolen it from, who by now must surely be looking for it. They'd find Borg and get him... somewhere.

Erika Xtravaganza must have a direct line to Peggy Deveroux. The Teatro-Cine was the centre around which this circus revolved. He would go back and start there.

*'You'll turn into a pillar of salt...'*

A towering fire had been started in the square—around which whoopin' and-a-hollerin' bikers drank and sang. On the steps leading up to the bandstand sat a few inebriated palefaces— newsmen trying to get their Hemingway on. The 'Return of Peggy Deveroux' had become a free-for-all. Someone some-where set off firecrackers. Or gunfire. Not a cop in sight.

The Teatro-Cine was locked up now. The two heavy wooden doors on either side of the front entrance afforded no view inside. Peering through the tiny windows, Marco could see that everyone was gone. Likewise, the accreditation tent at the back

172

of the building—dismantled or stolen—and with it, the crowd of frenzied journos.

Marco tested the strength of a drainpipe and climbed up to the roof. Now the sky was void black. Todos Santos was a war zone.

On a flat area above the entrance, before the tiled roof, he found a small window which overlooked the main theatre inside. The three projectors, positioned on the balconies around the hall, had now been turned off. The chairs had been removed—standing room only. The mannequins on the stage were the hall's only occupants. Dramatically lit exhibits of ancient lingerie radiated with an otherworldly luminance—the gel-lit tomb of a 20th century Cleopatra. He thought of his own apartment—laden with artefacts of similar vintage. If things go to shit here, and should he never make it home, he felt some misplaced satisfaction that his final domicile would evoke him entirely. His stuff was his story.

He scanned the roof to check he was still alone. He found a corner that offered some protection from the elements and buttoned his jacket. He sat and pulled Borg's Wal-Mart bag out of his satchel. The cassettes were labelled with biro—part 1 to part 7. The rap sheet, along with the psychiatric reports, were all headed with Patton State Hospital, San Bernardino. He flicked through them at random. They were basic progress outlines.

Dates… times…

So *that* was it?

She was an escapee?

They just wanted to take her back?

At the back of the portfolio were her arrest sheets. Paper clips and loose documents tumbled out. Marco snatched them back from the churning winds. His eyes narrowed with intensifying interest. The words 'violent schizophrenic' leapt out. He read on. She was arrested on more than one occasion… several, in fact, for attempted murder. Was Borg looking for revenge? For himself or on someone else's behalf?

He read random passages. It would take a day to read the whole thing in detail, but it was clear that she was crazy. Was he now trying to save a killer? As he stuffed everything back into his satchel, he flicked through one of the vintage mags. *Peggy in Bondage*. Gagged and bound to a chair. Her eyes pleaded convincingly. The truth of Deveroux's violent past served only to amplify his desire to save her. From the world and herself.

If nothing else, the last forty-eight hours had forced him to be more sociable. No mean feat after a near decade of inertia. As uncomfortable as he was with the prospect, Marco realised, once again, that he would have to interact with other people.

He packed all the stuff into his satchel, patted the reassuring bump of Borg's gun in his pocket, and climbed back down onto the street. He crossed the road and sat among the journos on the steps at the north of the square. The guy next to him was nursing a bloodied face. He recognised no one from the airport that he could even begin to strike up a conversation with. He thought, at first, one of the Japs behind him was the photographer he'd briefly spoken to at Xtravaganza's club. It wasn't but Marco asked him anyway, 'Were you at Xtravaganza's club on Leroy?'

The Jap seemed fixed on the antics of a couple of the bikers who were pulling wheelies across the square. After what seemed like a delayed action he turned to Marco and simply said no.

Marco stood and shouted a general address. 'Where's Xtravaganza? Anyone know?'

A girl on the bandstand shouted back. 'She's at the big house.' The girl was one of the less convincing Peggy wannabes. But...

Oil-black bangs? Check.

Stacked accordingly? Check.

Thick foundation barely concealed pock-marked cheeks, but striped pedal-pushers captivated legs till doomsday. She sat with another look-a-like—a remaining duo unperturbed by the attentions of the inebriated pack of bikers around them.

'Big house? Big house where?'

She deftly side-stepped a chunky denim-clad Latino who was about to tongue her ear.

'Which way did you come?'

174

Marco thumbed south. 'That-a-way?'

'Right, about five miles before you hit town, there's a turnoff—'

Someone shouted, 'Bullshit!'

One of the palefaces sitting on the steps stood and came over.

'It's bullshit. Xtravaganza's people are feeding this line to everyone to put 'em off the scent. Truth of the matter is, even *they* don't know.'

The girl with the doomsday legs smiled coyly and went back to her Vagos M.C tongue-squiring.

'So, this thing's pretty tight...' Marco said to the paleface, 'the whole secret location shtick...'

'Planned months ago and holding fast.' The man wore a short-sleeved checked shirt, and like most guys of around forty, wore it loose. 'This place might as well be another planet. No one knows anything. Talk about dicks swinging in the wind...'

The guys he was with got up. One of them announced they were going to get a drink.

Newsroom renegades prowled. Presenters, cut loose from their idiot boards, engaged in new idiocies. Jeering drinkers sat on the roofs—spectators at a circus of chaos. Everyone seemed to have abandoned their assignments and were now on the hunt for something... *anything* more tangible. It was as if a mad panic had descended upon a doomed population—Pompeii's morning-before-the-day-after or New Year's Eve in Hiroshima, 1944. A sexual hysteria gripped the town like the Chancellery basement at the fall of Berlin...

Marco glanced at a couple fucking on a barrel outside a vandalised grocery store. For a moment it required no small effort to make sense of the scene. Beyond the blowjob 'Seberg' gave him on the plane, he hadn't been laid since 1981.

The streets leading off from the square were little more than alleyways. The bar which Marco now approached was on the corner of one of them. It said 'El...' something or other above the entrance. Marco followed his adopted gang as they fought their way to the bar. The two bartenders, an old guy and a woman about half his age, were under siege. Marco grabbed a half-finished bottle of wine from a table and took it outside. He

175

checked the contents for butts, sniffed and swigged. The drink hit his stomach and made him want beer. The siege at the bar continued to rage, Alamo-style. He took another swig and scanned the street for a clue as to what to do next. The wine suddenly engaged with his system like someone turning on a light. He now recalled an orange Opel Ascona on the forecourt of a motel that he passed a block back. He finished the bottle, tossed it, and followed his tracks back along the uneven sidewalk.

Sure enough, there it was. Echo Hernandez's car on the overcrowded forecourt of L'America Motel; rust lining the door sills and wheel arches. He peered into its dark windows and could just make out the magazines and food wrappers on the floor. He crouched and touched the exhaust. It was hot.

Hernandez, though, was nowhere to be seen. All the rooms on the ground and on the balconies overlooking the forecourt looked occupied—all lights were on. Some betrayed movement within as shadows rolled back and forth across closed blinds. The coloured lights and bunting that hung across the forecourt were in stark contrast to the mess of wires which crowded the skies of the rest of the town.

The receptionist may or may not be helpful, guest-information-wise. He shouldered his way through heavy glass doors and there she was—Hernandez behind the desk on the phone.

On sight of him she jumped back and hit the wall behind her. 'Fuck! Oh, it's you...'

She started hitting the buttons of the till.

'Are you robbing the joint?'

'No, but I need to make phone calls and... well, there's no-one around to ask.'

She picked up the phone again and told him to wait. She dialled again. Whatever connection she was waiting for wasn't connecting. Marco, joking, said, 'You got that forty?'

'I won't stiff you,' she assured him. 'I promise.'

'Ixnay, I don't care. Where's the receptionist? Has everyone taken a powder?'

Her expression declared she was unfamiliar with the term 'Powder'.

'Gone. Like, absconded. Like, quit this crazy scene...'

She came around the counter and peered out into the forecourt and saw marauders with suspect intent.

Marco said, 'Don't worry, your car's still there.'

She said, 'Where's your friend? You got any more money?'

'I gave him the slip. Money? Some...'

She turned to face him. Not too close but enough to suggest... possibilities. Beads of sweat on her long nose—the spoils of exertion... suggested others. 'I might have news for you that you will appreciate.'

He intercepted—prematurely. 'You know where Xtravaganza is?!'

'What?'

'Erika Xtravaganza—the architect of this madness?'

Hernandez grinned; enough to reveal that missing tooth. 'I know where *Peggy Deveroux* is.'

# 31. RANCHERO PINEDA

11:10pm

They sped north on the 19 and away from the rape of Todos Santos. The impenetrable blackness around them gave Marco the feeling they were flying through deep space. He side-longed her as she leant forward into the wheel as if trying to urge car faster. She chattered incessantly. He suspected she was wired on something of the upward variety. In quick-fire delivery she described her visit to Mr. Kite's House of the Son of Man at the Ranchero Pineda, twenty minutes ahead of them—the destination to which they were now headed. She had arranged another interview with this outlaw-priest via one of her old high-school buddies who was

177

also giving her the inside dope on the cult's goings on. But tonight, this buddy, Tabetha, now known as Polythene Pam, had met her at the compound gates and told her that the interview with the prophet wasn't going to happen. Kite disappeared weeks ago.

'… now, apparently, the cops are involved. His family, the Haines clan—Carter Haines is Kite's real name—suspect foul play. But get this; with his disappearance, there's been a change of leadership.'

She glanced at Marco, expecting him to pick up the slack.

He had nothing.

She picked it up for him. 'Their new High-Priestess is none other than the Queen of the Pin-ups, herself.'

'Deveroux is running a church?!'

'She's founding a religion.'

Marco pondered the implications. Maybe this was the point. Running and hiding wasn't working for her. Maybe raising her profile was an alternative measure to protect herself. Maybe the hope was that the more visible she was, the trickier it would be for her pursuers to put her out of the frame. That might explain why someone on the run would expose themselves this way.

Hernandez continued, 'She's using this big comeback to promote their church, only *now* they've jettisoned the whole Manson/Beatles thing. Now, they've got a whole new tenet. Get this: The Sisters of the Seven Prophesies.'

Marco glanced at his satchel between his feet and remembered the cassettes. 'Does the tape player work?'

'Usually.'

He loaded a random tape. It was wound half-way through. He hit play. The thick, trance-like drawl seemed to suck the life out of the warm air.

*'The genitals were deformed… deformed… relations were near on impossible… God saw the wickedness. He saw his own wickedness. But more… he knew his creation saw his wickedness and knew the children would come to find him. He had to stop the children…'*

Marco and Hernandez exchanged *what the actual fuck* glances. Marco asked, 'Recognise it? Is this her? Is this Deveroux?'
 Hernandez said, 'I think it is.'

 *'... from finding him, from killing their father. He deformed the genitals... to stop them from their parricide. They were full of wickedness, but he would stop them from committing this one crime. The second son was lost in the Blacklands, but the whore would find him...'*

 Hernandez said, 'Turn this shit off! It's giving me the all-overs.' She swerved hard to avoid the squashed carcass of something dead. 'Where did you get it from?'
 'I got a bunch. They were with her rap sheets.' She side-longed him. He caught it. 'Don't ask.'
 'Yeah, Polythene Pam—Tabetha—said something about Deveroux being in a mental hospital.'
 'People *are* looking for her. Do you think she's an escapee?'
 'It would explain what she's doing down here.'
 'Doesn't explain why she would get involved in a big event like this, though... y'know... if she's on the run. All this attention...'
 'I don't think it was meant to *be* a big event,' Hernandez considered aloud. 'The whole thing's got a little out of hand, don't you think? I don't know the ins and outs of it, but she's threatening not to appear unless Lucy Hartman... you know Lucy Hartman? From Showtime Tonight?'
 'Never heard of her. Never heard of it.'
 'The TV show—she's one of the hosts. Well, according to Pam, Hartman is somehow integral to the completion of the prophesies, and a no-show from Hartman equals a no-show from Deveroux. She's driving the organisers nuts with this shit.'
 'So, what's your interest in this thing now?' Marco asked. 'They still raising the dead up there?'
 'Kite's one and only miracle has, as you say, taken a powder too.'
 'The dead soldier?'

179

'The dead solder... I want a proper gander at that grave site, but anyone seen near it is given short shrift. Pam says the only chance would be to come at night. I'm hoping your audience with Deveroux might offer a distraction.'

'How do you see her?' Marco asked. 'Can you just walk in?'

'I don't know. When Kite was running the place, it was an open house. But now... all the men are gone.'

'All the men?'

'Pretty much. It's a matriarchal regime now. She might see you, she might not.'

Eighteen minutes later, they saw a sign for El Cardonosa, but she pulled a hard right off the highway on to a dirt track and into a darker oblivion than the one they were already in.

'Are you sure this car can handle this terrain?'

She peered into the void beyond the windshield. 'It did earlier.'

A sudden roar came out of nowhere.

Had the universe collapsed?

Hard rain smashed down onto the vehicle like biblical vengeance. Hernandez said Jesus! Marco said Fuck!

She hit the wipers. Visibility was still zero. The thunderstorm threatened their progress. The dirt track became instant mud. An irrigation ditch beside them overflowed. The car waded on...

'Shall I stop? Wait for this thing to pass?'

The windshield was a wide-screen cascade of visual gobbledygook.

'Yeah, stop. Can't see anything...'

The car lurched to a halt.

They sat and waited. Borg was right. About the storm. Marco wondered if anyone had found him yet. He checked his watch—11.30pm 'I guess what happens next depends on the state of this road when the rain stops.'

She stared blankly at the windshield. 'Yeah... *when*.'

Marco side-longed her again... her bare arms, where her ear met the curve of her jaw. Her skin was caramel perfection. A sleeveless t-shirt hung on a torso, lithe and braless. Painted black nails drummed on the wheel. He was about to ask her where she was from, but as soon as he drew the breath to say it, it felt ridiculous in his mouth. He pulled down the sun visor and checked his reflection. He could only see his eyes. They were as sullen as any man whose life had been turned upside down, drugged, blown by a person of ambiguous gender, nearly strangled, caught in a near riot, all in pursuit of an old damsel who has caused her fair share of distress. All this struck him as heroic. He realised Hernandez was watching him, watching himself.

She said, 'This place is beautiful, believe it or not. When it's not being invaded.'

He'd only seen it as the sun was going down. Apart from the airport and the town, the Baja had been a litany of dark distant mountains and inhospitable terrain. She added 'Do you surf?'

An image of himself in Speedos, let alone riding a board, was Camus-Grade absurd. The boardwalk at Coney Island was as close as he got to the sea these days. But he played with it.

'Do I look like a surfer?'

She eyed him up and down. His olive skin, Kung-Fu-black hair and wiry frame were the antithesis of the beach boy.

'Guess not. But if you're looking for a new kick, you're in the right place. The beaches here are the best.'

He met her gaze, wondering if this could, or should, be interpreted as anything other than the micro-talk it surely was. A frantic fuck in a car, in a desert, in a storm, was beyond cinematic.

Then the rain stopped.

The moment's potential stopped with it.

Hernandez turned the key.


The ridge overlooked a recessed plain—a vast crater containing the compound and the surrounding ranch. The temple was a flood-lit yellow twinkle and could just about be seen from their vantage point a mile away. She had stopped the car, too close to the edge for Marco's liking.

'I'd move back if I were you. After that downpour, we could end up avalanching the rest of the way.'

181

She reversed a few feet. 'The cemetery is on the far side of the ridge. I'm thinking, drop you a little way from the entrance, and while you make your introductions, I'll go check out this grave. Wait for me afterwards and I'll come get you.'

He considered the proposal with pursed lips. 'No. You kinda know these people. *You* can make the introductions… I mean, you seen her, right? You've met her.

'Seen her, yeah. I didn't meet her. She was Kite's number one lady a couple of months ago, but I gather she was… eh…'

'She was what?'

'Usurped.'

'Usurped?'

'Usurped. Side-lined. But now he's disappeared, and she's running things.'

'Kite's number one lady—'

He glanced into the back seat where copies of Hernandez's Enquirer's lay.

'He was into older broads? Is she still a looker or—?'

'Not really. She's about sixty. Looks it.'

'Older. Her rap sheet says she was born in twenty-three.'

Hernandez continued '… fat. It's kind of sad. She still wears her hair the same—the wide fringe, the bangs—dyes it black. She's a disaster to be fair. You've got her rap sheet?'

Marco looked across the vast crater in the direction of the temple—its meagre light reflecting off a fleet of vehicles parked beyond its walls.

'Yeah. She tried to kill some people…' He was thinking aloud. 'Do you think she offed Kite? To seize the kingdom?'

Hernandez weighed this up. 'Plausible… I don't know.'

It hadn't occurred to Marco until now that Deveroux might be anything other than receptive of him and his warning. But the woman *was* an escaped whack-job. The stone-cold panic he felt years ago in Paris, at Queen Evelyn's apartment, and his imaginary slaughter at the alleged rape victim's hands, made an unwelcome return to the pit of his stomach.

They got out of the car. Hernandez grabbed a red Puffa-jacket from the trunk and Marco stuffed his satchel under his seat and outlined his plan. 'We'll do this. We'll go to the grave

182

together. Check it out. See what we will see. Then we'll go to the temple and see if we can get an audience with this pornographic pope-ess.'

That thundercloud had moved further inland and revealed a wan and lonely moon. The old graveyard was in the centre of an unremarkable acre of scrubland with a low chain fence around it. There couldn't have been more than fifty plots, all in poor condition. The inscriptions were eroded with age and caked in moss. They'd driven to a six-foot wire fence on the other side of the ridge. They left the car there and climbed the fence and walked about a quarter of a mile to the cemetery.

The illuminated bell tower of the temple was just visible as the ground ascended. They couldn't be seen from the compound, but it also meant that if anyone came, they would not see *them* until it was too late. But then what could they do, anyway? It wasn't like they were robbing this grave. It had already been robbed.

Hernandez had a flashlight and quickly located the site of Mr. Kite's big miracle. Marco joined her at the graveside. It had been left largely unfilled. Pieces of splintered wood lay scattered at the bottom. Only the year on the headstone was legible—1848.

'Impressive. When *Jesus* pulled this stunt, Lazarus was only a couple of days dead. But *this* guy had been dead for a hundred and forty years.'

Hernandez said, 'Yeah maybe. Here. Grab my hand.'

'You're going in?'

She grabbed his arm above the wrist. 'What else?'

He braced himself for her weight, dug his heels into the wet earth, and lowered her down.

'Careful!'

She stood for a moment in this bed of death. It was deep, by only about four feet. She crouched down and started picking at the fragments of wood. It was a mud bath. The red jacket she'd put on was caked. Marco scanned the area. Apart from the beacon of light from the distant temple tower, the place was desolation personified. Marco watched her poking around. 'If they had oxygen or something down there, don't you think they would have removed it by now?'

She stood up and peered over the edge in the direction of the temple, frustrated in the certainty that the answer lay somewhere within its hallowed walls. Suddenly, she slipped. Lost her footing. At first, he thought she'd fallen to her knees, and then saw she had sunk to her waist. Calmly, she said fuck. Then the mud beneath her made an obscene slurping sound. And she was gone.

His first thought... hope... was that whatever drug he'd taken on the plane was still fucking with him. Her flashlight sat on the edge of the grave, barely bathing the scene. He refocused on the mess of mud and splinters below him. He shouted, but not too loud, 'Hernandez!' Nothing. 'Echo!' Nothing.

She was absolutely and irrevocably gone.

He ripped at the mossy reeds that strangled the nearest tombstones. They came away too easy to support human weight. He threw them aside and stumbled to the edge of the cemetery. The fence was a series of flagstones about six feet apart and joined by spiked chains. He kicked at the link connecting a chain to the stone. His feet slid off and around it.

He grabbed a small boulder—might have been a small headstone—and cracked it down on the link.

Nothing.

Again.

Again.

Again.

'Fuck!'

The beacon of light over the hill may not be one of hope, but it was the only other option. As he ran down the rocky, puddle-splattered pathway that led out of the cemetery, his mind went into overdrive. Could there be a long enough rope or wire or something in the car? Even if there was, he remembered she locked the car. She'd have the keys.

No.

Go to the temple—admit they were snooping—fuck whatever indignation they might greet him with. His warning for Deveroux will be his get out of jail free card. He looked above, thinking of Todos Santos' ceiling-like web of telegraph wires. He tripped, pratfell, and skidded on his chest down the incline towards the compound walls. He almost laughed. To have witnessed this would have been hilarious. He sat up and tried to wipe the mud from his arms and face. All he was doing was smearing it from one part of himself to another. He stayed put and resumed his appraisal of the sky. Above him, those telegraph wires skipping on poles from a corner roof of the temple to a big house up on a hill. Real Munsters style. Could he shimmy up the pole and get those wires down without blowing himself to fuckery? His only hope was that Hernandez had fallen into some kind of vault. Otherwise, she might have even drowned.

The temple was the only game in town.

# 32. SISTERS OF THE SON

The walls around the temple were ten-foot-high orange stucco, or looked that way, illuminated by the small spotlights planted in the ground around it. Marco walked through the open entrance where it felt like gates should be. It was like entering a derelict theme park or some crazy, animated landscape. The building was a bunch of extensions on what was probably an old farmhouse. The whole thing had been painted cartoon yellow. The stained-glass windows were adorned with grotesque, hellish figures, given a Disney make-over, being vanquished by a long-haired blonde superhero in Evel Knievel Stars and Stripes. The face in all of them had been spray-canned out. The twin doors were riveted steel, like the side of a battleship. Marco peered through the red tinted potholes. At the end of a long aisle, he could see Erika Xtravaganza, who seemed to be in a heated exchange with a group of women. Only these were not her usual trans/fruit/fag entourage. Naked children played and ran around the vestibule, oblivious to the adult's aggression.

There was no obvious means of alert around the doors, so he banged with cold, wet hands. All the women turned to face the door. Somehow, he knew he'd interrupted something underhand. He could just about hear Xtravaganza shouting at the women, '... tell her from me, if she doesn't show tomorrow, I'll kill her!'

He watched as two of the women approached the door. They were wearing identical red robes and were holding shotguns.

Marco backed away from the door as they unlocked it and instinctively offered surrender hands. The door opened, and both guns were in his face. One of them screeched, 'Get in here!'

Marco stepped inside 'I need help! A woman has fallen in a hole out there!' He thought better of mentioning the real location... yet. 'I need something... a rope. Have you got some rope? Anything like that?!'

He thought the statement would remove the quartet of barrels from his face. It did not. The younger woman on the right barked, 'What woman?! What hole?!'

He reiterated this time with feeling. 'There's been an accident. Someone... a woman's in trouble out there. We need to get to her real fast.'

The barker's eyes narrowed. She nodded in the direction of the altar. 'Join us.'

Marco felt the barrels in his shoulder blades as they marched him to the altar. Some of the kids followed the procession, intrigued by the presence of this newcomer. As he got closer, he could see Erika Xtravaganza was ashen faced and harassed. A far cry from the assured Uber-model she exuded on the plane. He thought of Deveroux's bondage shots—the fear in her eyes inciting rescue in the hearts of Lancelots everywhere. Feebly he said to her, 'You remember me?'

The younger of his escorts barked again to Xtravaganza. 'You know this fella?'

She seemed unsure of how to react and nodded affirmation, as if it were a lie. She mumbled, 'He's a reporter.'

Another bark, 'From Showtime Tonight?!'

Marco had to play his ace. 'Is Peggy Deveroux here? I need to see her—URGENTLY! She's in danger. This is NOT a joke. I'll tell you all about it… everything, but there's a girl out there that needs our help, NOW!'

The two girls just kind of stared at him as if he were speaking Klingon. Marco looked at the other girls. Seven of them circled around, his look of astonishment failing to get the desired response. In fact, *any* response. They stood mute, waiting for the shotgun sisters to speak.

The older one was honey-blonde with high cheekbones—about forty. Could have been a '70s Playmate. She said, 'Let's go.'

They poked and pushed Marco up the few steps to the pulpit—Un Objet d'art—a highly polished construction of wood and chrome. A row of those old 50s microphones—like Elvis had—were fitted across the top. The entire hall looked like it was carved from a single mountain of dark wood with chrome fittings, like the hull of an old ship adorned with motorcycle parts.

Behind the pulpit, there was a stairway leading down. He looked back and saw Xtravaganza watching; her face frustrated with anger. He thought of all those movies where they grab the barrel of the gun, wrestle it away and turn the tables. But there were two on him. He tried to remember how they handled *that* in the movies. Nothing presented itself.

In the distance he could hear Xtravaganza shouting again, 'If she doesn't appear to tomorrow, I'm going to fucking kill her! You hear me!?'

The trio descended into a long hallway. The door they came to was a like bank vault. Playmate kept her gun on him while Barker braced hers under her armpit and spun the big lock, like a giant roulette wheel.

He tried to sound casual—merely inconvenienced when he said, 'Look, what *is* this? Do you know Echo? Echo Hernandez? She did that story on you guys… girls… whatever. She's the one that needs your help. She's right outside. She's the one in trouble. Whatever this is, let's go to her first, and then we can do... No? You don't know her?

*Then he remembered...*

'Pam! Pam—she's a friend of Hernandez.'

They kept on walking, but Barker said to Playmate, 'Pam? You hear that? He's a friend of Polythene Pam.'

Her tone told him he'd declared the wrong association.

They stepped into a shorter corridor—red lights—like 'emergency time' in a submarine. After the Fort Knox-like barriers they'd just passed through, the next door was the kind you'd find in a dorm: Formica—standard doorbell.

Barker rang it. The lock clicked, and she shouldered it open.

The women urged him into a circular room of mirrors. The explosion of repeated images made him lose all perspective. His eyes fought to adjust to the kaleidoscopic barrage. Two racks of steel shelves were packed to the ceiling with weapons—assault rifles, boxes of ammo, grenades and fuck knows what else—instruments of death he could only guess at. Four concrete arches supported the room. Tethered to one of them was a naked Latino male, maybe twenty years old, whining incoherently.

Thunk!

A dart hit the Latino in the chest, where it joined another four. It hung for a second, then fell out. Beyond a stack of television sets was a huge circular bed. The TVs were placed haphazardly like electric bricks of a wall and faced the thrower. Barker and Playmate nudged Marco around the front. Propped up on massive Turkish cushions was a podgy faced woman whose large veiny breasts flopped tragically over the edge of the quilt. Her immaculate raven-black Peggy-Do looked like it had been kicked onto her head from a distance. Across the bed lay two more young naked Latinos. At first, Marco thought they were dead. But he could see the bloody tracks on their arms and realised the lot of them were zonked to horse town.

The scene stunk of sex and blood. Clearly, this was the fag end of a gargantuan druggy fuck-fest.

Barker barked, 'Tell her what you told us!'

Before he spoke, he side-longed her, to make sure she was speaking, or barking, at him. He was about to speak when the dime descended.

The woman in bed.

*Peggy Deveroux.*

Through little mean eyes, she glared. Not *at* him—*into* him. 'Who th'hell are you?'

Finally, he'd come face to face with the whole reason his world had been turned upside down. She *was* flabby. Not in good shape. Just like Hernandez said. The fact she'd had work done was more than evident by the waxy tightness around her eyes and at the apex of her mouth.

She out-barked Barker. 'Well?!'

Where did he even start? For once, letting his mouth do the talking, then his brain following suit, seemed to be the best course of action.

'There are people looking for you.' If a statement like *that* doesn't get a reaction, what does? 'I've come to warn you—'

'You've c'hum tuh *warn* me?!'

That heavy Tennessee-twang sounded guttural, raw, like someone shouting across a swamp. 'Ah'm the one doin' the warnin'! I *know* them laws bin watchin' us from up a there'n them mountains, fer a month!'

She swung her legs to the edge of the bed, pulled on a quilted night coat and kicked into leather slippers. She came up close and examined him as if by smell more than sight. 'You a cop?'

'No, ma'am.' *Did he actually say, 'no ma'am'?* The hillbilliness of the situation was getting the better of him. 'I'm not a cop. But people... someone is here to... probably take you back.'

She backed away towards the bed, not taking her eyes off him for a second. Three decades of running scared, and God knows how many years in the screamer's lounge, had turned them from California blue to deep dark watery pools. She scrambled around on the bed and found a huge half-smoked joint. She sparked it and waited for its effects to galvanise her to a decision. Marco filled the musky void. 'I don't know nothing about cops in the hills or whatever, but I'd seriously think about getting out of here if I were you.'

Her waxy face contorted as best it could. 'Let 'em come! We ain't goin' no place! This ain't no *end* o' th'line. This is the beginin'! We're gonna petition the lord with our prayer. Our *mass* prayer! And we're gonna take as many a them sumsobitches with us. *He* abandoned us, but we'll find him and bring him back. He cast hiself out with his own vanity, but we gonna bring *him* back!'

She refocused her address at the shotgun sisters. 'God's been a beatin' hiself up over his vanity, An' we'll tell 'im—s'alright to be beautiful! Right, ladies?!'

The shotgun sister's response was immediate and in unison. 'S'right, Sister Peggy!'

'S'right.' She gave Marco the up and down. 'I reckon we should take us a little trip to Golgotha.'

She blew on the tip of the joint. The shadows it threw on her altered face distorted it some more. She sucked on the wet butt, flicked it in Marco's face, and told him, 'Git yer fuckin' duds off.'

The ten minutes it took for them to march Marco naked across rocky land behind the temple felt like an eternity and a half. It was only now that he remembered Borg's gun in his jacket, left on the floor of Peggy Deveroux's bedroom of mirrors, guns, and zonked out Latino boys. They'd bound his arms so tight behind him they felt like one big throbbing limb. The image of an angel with its wings torn out danced across his mind's eye. Was this it? Were they going to kill him? He had fantasied about his death all his life. But shot-gunned by a mob of religious nut jobs in the Mexican desert was not on his list of probabilities. He thought of his journal, propped up on his kitchen table with this fucked up ending missing. He expected, now that he faced it, that his lifelong belief that death was merely a painful transformation might desert him. But it held strong. All he felt was a profound sadness that no-one will ever know what had happened to him. Who was going to miss him? An irrational hope that must infect those about to die was the only thing that stopped him from breaking down and begging for his life. If he cried, it would be for the child he once was, fated to be murdered absurdly, and not for whoever he was now.

They descended into what looked like another crater. The freezing cold started to bite. Barker and Playmate led the way, through a rocky pass and descending again into what looked like a natural arena. Walls of black rock loomed up high around them.

Up on a small steep hill was what looked like a row of four scarecrows, silhouetted by the low moon behind them. They were doing a lousy job. Big ravenous birds circled and swooped and tore away chunks. The cold wind changed and gave him a gut-churning nose full.

These were not scarecrows.

This crucified quartet had been stripped naked. One of them was either black or had been beaten so badly he'd changed race. Another was a young woman, around twenty, with her chest ripped out. Another male had a gaping black hole where his groin should have been. Sister Peggy followed his eye line. 'You heard the sayin', "hung by the balls"? We tried it...' She shrugged dejectedly and smirked. '... didn't work out.'

She shooed the birds—threw rocks. There was panicky fluttered ascent. He could hear them directly overhead but only caught their fraught silhouettes as they passed the moon. Playmate put her gun down. Marco could hear her dragging something heavy behind him. He was looking at his bloodied feet on the rocky ground. He had lived his life like he was watching himself from another galaxy, and the stark reality of this death—sick and unspectacular—didn't fail him now. It was like he'd abandoned himself and left his carcass to it. All senses went into overdrive. The screeching birds were deafening, the silver moon seemed to burn. The cold chewed the marrow out of him. The inner sensation of hurtling into a void at unimaginable speed made him vomit. Someone shoved him hard in the chest and he fell flat on his back, onto a post of slimy wood. His numb arms took the brunt. He felt no pain, but his throat groaned regardless. Where was that storm now? To wash these women away like sins.

A flash obliterated his meagre view of the moon and stars above.

But it was not a flash of light.

It came from somewhere inside of him.

It was only when Playmate hammered the nail further into his right foot again that he understood what had happened. His scream sent those birds fluttering into space. Sisters Peggy and Barker watched blankly. For them, crucifixion was a familiar procedure. Barker told Playmate to cut his arms free. 'I'll hold 'em!' Be ready with that hammer, now...'

The pain stabbed up through his entire system. Adrenalin and shock arrived cavalry-like. The pain became a throbbing alert.

His body vibrated.

Small wet rocks around him began to flip and dance.

A roaring sound came not from his stomach, but from somewhere out in the desert.

A bad exhaust coughed, and the roar got louder.

A vehicle!

A truck was approaching—approaching fast.

It sounded like an avalanche—like this enclosed arena of rocks was about to collapse.

Marco could get no sense of its direction—still completely immersed in a vortex of excruciating pain and confusion. He tried to twist himself off the post, but the nail holding his foot held fast. Cold, sharp sheets of agony sliced up and down his nervous system. It was more than his shattered psyche could process. What sounded like a truck skidded down into the arena, sending sprays of dirt and debris in a wild arc. Marco twisted around to see Deveroux's pudgy form rendered an X-Ray in the truck's blinding headlights. She seemed to be trying to wave the vehicle to a halt. It sped up and splattered her into oblivion.

Marco twisted again and tried to make sense of the head-lit scene.

Hernandez?

It must be.

192

He tried to shout, but nothing came. He had to re-learn quickly.

All he could see were the red taillights of what was probably a heavy pickup truck.

He yelled… something. Probably, 'Hey!'

His throat was working, and it was making some kind of noise. That's all that mattered. The engine rumbled salvation bass. His next shout was drowned out by the growling gears and roaring exhaust as the truck raced up the pass and out of sight.

Once again, Marco found himself in total darkness until his retinas re-negotiated with whatever the moon offered. The rumble of the departing truck diminished, replaced by distant screams and whimpering.

His entire leg throbbed up into his waist like it was pumping lava into him.

Deveroux was dead. Surely.

That truck hit her head on.

Then there was nothing but complete silence and burning cold. Even the birds had disappeared. Around him were only shadows—thrown across the enclosed landscape by the ghostly moon. He was sure he was alone now. The women must have gotten Deveroux out of here. Back to the temple. Perhaps hoping to save her.

If it was Hernandez driving that truck, did she see him?

But why did she run down Deveroux? Did she see what was happening? If the driver was trying to save him, why have they left him here?

Something squawked.

The birds were back.

They tore at the crucified dead as they hung over the scene—ruined and eyeless.

# 33. KANGAROO

## Saturday October 8th

4.24am… It wasn't broken, his watch. So that must be the time. That's all they left him wearing. He hobbled, pitifully, by the side of the road.

The 19.

South.

Back to Todos Santos.

If a car came, should he wave it down? He made one of those pacts with himself—a vague one—to hit the weeds; what there was of them; see if it looked friendly, then leap to his feet and hope they'd be prepared for a naked hitchhiker covered in vomit, mud and blood.

Leap to his feet?

The nail had missed bone, but he was beyond pain now. Adrenaline had hosed down his smouldering nerve endings. He thought of the beating he took from those elephant-slaughtering kickboxers in Thailand all those years ago. Thinking of this put some purpose in his stride. It knocked some of the pity out of his hobble.

It was pointless trying to make his way back to Hernandez's car. She had the keys. Plus, the longer he spent on the Ranch, the more likely it would be that those women would find him. Maybe it was Xtravaganza who ran Deveroux down. When he saw her at the temple, she was angry. Maybe she had cause. Something had gone awry between her and the Pin-up.

*'If she doesn't appear tomorrow, I'm going to fucking kill her!'*

Hernandez had mentioned that Xtravaganza had been unable to get some celebrity—Heart? Heartman—to come to this thing.

Hernandez…

Curiosity.

Cat.

So, now he knew what happened to Peggy Deveroux. It was ugly and staggering but now he was consumed with a new kick. Whatever happened to Echo Hernandez?

He couldn't wait to tell Borg—about Deveroux. And it was only for that reason he hoped he was still alive. But he had to get help for Hernandez first. It took over an hour to get off the ranch and find his way back to the highway, stopping only to clean his crippled foot in a ditch.

5:55am

The journey had taken no more than twenty minutes in Hernandez's car last night. He'd been stumbling along this highway for nearly three hours now. More panic—albeit a ripple—was this even the right road? Perhaps his estimation of how fast he walked was fucking with him.

Two-lane blacktop stretched into nowhere. The glistening ocean to his right reassured him. This was the road. The edges of the mountains started to sizzle and dissolve. The night had minutes to live.

There.

In the distance.

Red lights.

The taillights of a car abandoned by the highway.

It hadn't passed him. He hadn't seen a single vehicle the whole time. Had it come from the town and was now turning around?

It took him a while to make some distance, but it hadn't moved at all. Then it hit him. Is that the pickup?

The one that hit Deveroux?

This stopped Marco in his tracks.

It was.

It was getting lighter now. Long shadows crawled to the beach. He scanned the endless horizon. There was no sign of life. Not human anyway. Birds still circled over the unseen dead out in the desert—some roadkill—and this, a dusty red Ford pickup flatbed. He snuck up and could see the driver's side door hanging open. If anyone was inside, they were hiding, unconscious or dead. He crept along the side of the truck. He scanned the area one more time before peering around the door into the cabin.

195

The keys were still in the ignition. The back of the truck was empty except for a few loose vegetables and fruit. He wiped the dirt from a few tomatoes, got in the truck and munched. The tangy fruit lit up his system like a Times Square billboard. His stomach protested, but he wolfed the rest down, anyway. He searched the glove compartment. Receipts, paper... He found an oil-soaked cloth and was going to make some attempt to wipe himself down. But no.

He felt savage.

He should look the part.

He took a breath and turned the ignition.

The Ford lurched and rolled.

Shock spasmed up his right-side into his neck when his foot touched the accelerator, then went numb. The truck trundled along unconvincingly. The motor protested and whined when he tried to take it over twenty. But he would hit town soon and the vehicle would serve another purpose—it would save him from wandering into town bare-ass naked—savage as he felt. He'd head for the Chieftain where he'd left Borg. If it, and Borg, was still there, there may be some clothes too. Failing that? He'd burn that bridge when he came to it. Ha ha...

Within minutes, Todos Santos loomed into view.

The engine was shot. The noise was circus clown time.

Steam billowed out all over the hood.

The impact, when it hit Deveroux, must have fucked the radiator and belt.

Ahead, there was a roadblock just before the edge of town. Dark blue uniforms on a highway are as welcome as Don King at a KKK Fun Day. Two patrol cars formed a barrier. Rifle-toting Federales stood by.

It was too late to turn off and go cross-country. As he slowed down, he could see one of the cops start the ignition in his prowler—a precaution should Marco try to make a break for it. Fuck it—he'd tell them the full story—how he came to be naked, how he came by the car, and most importantly, get help for Hernandez.

The truck came to a grinding halt. Something under the hood finally snapped and screeched. To Marco's ears the engine had spluttered its last. Three cops approached with their guns on him. One came around the side and calmly said, 'Poner sus manos en la cabeza. Lento...'

This couldn't have meant anything else, so Marco put his hands on his head.

The others gathered around the front, assessing the damage. One pushed his hat back on his head. The other took his off and made the cross. The one with the gun on Marco kept it that way but opened the door and said 'Fuera.'

Marco stepped out. The cop up-and-downed him. He thought they might find his naked state funny. They didn't. He looked to the other officers, but they were engrossed with the damage at the front of the truck.

The cop with the gun on him bade him forward. The other cops didn't bat an eyelid.

Marco stood beside them and saw what they saw.

The woman's bloody carcass was jammed face-first into the grill. Her black hair was matted and stuck to her freckled shoulders. The right arm from the elbow and the entire right leg were missing—torn out by the force of the impact. A leather slipper hung from the remaining foot.

They put a plastic sheet around him and took him back to town. The backstreets and alleyways were littered with debris. They sped past at least three overturned cars. They kangarooed over hard, uneven roads until they pulled up behind a one-story building with a bunch of archways that led into a small courtyard. They hauled him out of the car and shoved him across the yard and inside. They took him around a busy reception desk and through the main office, hectic with behind-the-scenes cop shit—straight out of Hill Street Blues. Arresters and arrestees yelling, typing, signing—due process in full effect. They came to a door, pushed him inside. Blinding light lasered into the room through closed blinds. The room was another, albeit deserted, office. The two Federales dumped him in a chair by the wall, then sat opposite and watched him from across the room.

His entire leg was numb now. The pain had emigrated to his hip and throbbed accordingly. He examined the wound. The nail had gone straight through the flesh between his big toe and second. Marco said Si to the two Federales and gestured to the pitcher of water on the table nearby. Their languid appraisal remained languid. Marco poured the water directly into his mouth. His entire system went Elvis concert and screamed. He finished the jug but saved a little and poured it on his foot. He scratched away at the congealed blood, mud and desert dust, revealing a puncture surprisingly small. A commotion from somewhere outside suddenly got louder.

Shouts.

Protests.

He tried to dismiss the unavoidable fact that he was seriously cut adrift from all and any rational notions of law and order. Not a word had been exchanged on their journey, but now seemed like the time. 'English?' He called across the room. They had PJF on their badges.

Police 'something' Force?

'Speak English?'

Two men entered—another cop and a medic. The cop spoke to the other cops—a gruff and unintelligible exchange. The medic attended his foot. Freakishly hairy forearms were betrayed by warm slender hands. He worked fast. Poured some shit on it that hurt and wrapped him up tight. The foot throbbed anew. Clean and reassured. So enthralled in the medic's industry was Marco that he hadn't noticed that someone had dumped some clothes on the table beside him— tan slacks, a T-shirt that said, 'Channel 5' and a forlorn pair of sneakers. The slacks were looser than he would have preferred but being dressed again felt like he'd emerged from an era of savagery.

7:58am

The noise outside was getting louder. The noise of a mob invading the building. The medic left without a word. All three cops turned and looked at him. One fumbled for keys and the others flanked him and led him back out of the room. They led him to a heavy wooden door. The commotion came from beyond it. Marco envisioned a public hanging.

*His.*

How would it compare to Borg's onslaught in the Chieftain? His throat throbbed with the memory.

The door swung open, and Marco was blinded by an explosion of flash guns. His pupils went to pins, and the room was in uproar. Sound deafened him; vision was slowly restored. The cops positioned him in front of a division of microphones. A baying mob of photographers and journos were crammed into the room. As his eyes met the temper of the light, he scanned the over-lit room, hoping to see Hernandez among the sweaty mob. Video cameras on tripods had been set up at the back of the room. He recognised that Jap directly in front of him, from the club; the arrivals lounge of the airport... Marco's 'What *is* this?' was drowned out by the noise.

Someone screamed 'Don't talk to him!'

Another five cops entered through the door behind him and began to quieten the noise. A tall, balding Latino with a handlebar moustache and wearing a brown suit appeared. He introduced himself as Captain Gael Mendez of the Policia Municipal. He stood beside Marco and attempted to calm the crowd with a waving gesture. It was working until someone shouted,

'Did you kill Peggy Deveroux?'

It took a beat for the realisation to sink in. It was Lee Harvey Oswald time. He glanced around furtively. Who would be his Jack Ruby? What was he going to say? I'm just a patsy? What did they know? What did they *think* they knew?

He tried to speak. 'Wh...' His throat misfired. A combination of sucking desert air for the last twenty-four hours and the diminishing returns of Borg's attack. He swallowed and tried again. 'I didn't kill her. Why do you think I did?'

A hoarse answer called from the back of the room. 'You dragged the evidence into town, numb nuts!'

Marco's retort was rendered a mumble. 'Not my truck. I found it that way.'

A shout. 'What?! Speak up!'

Marco shouted back. 'It wasn't my truck! I found it like that!'
The Jap said, 'Can you say your name, please?'
Marco's hesitation declared guilt. 'I'm a freelance writer...'
Camera-flash obscured the owner of a shrill voice to his left
yelling, 'Who for?!'
'For a Christian TV show.'
The big window to his right exploded. Hot bullets peppered
the wall to his left.
Everyone hit the ground.
Everyone screamed.
Many hands grabbed him and hurtled him towards the door.

'I'm Federal Agent Ian Strauss, this here's Agent Bill Portland.'
They wore cheap grey suits and sported buzz-cuts. What was
left of Strauss' hair almost matched his suit. Portland's was
sandy-red and Brylcreemed to fuckery. Globs of oily sweat
bordered his hairline. Their shared preciseness of movement
suggested military training. The bigger of the two men,
Portland, leant beside the locked stationery door with his thick
arms crossed and his eyes on Marco, who sat wedged between
two metal shelves on reams of paper. Strauss' pale blue eyes
scrutinized Marco's face for giveaway ticks; microscopic
flickers of subterfuge. Marco knew this and let him search.

*Fuck you and good luck, fuck head.*

Strauss crouched before him and looked up into his face.
'What are you doing down here, son?'
Marco would run with the official narrative. 'I'm a free-lance
writer. I'm covering this Peggy Deveroux event.'
'Who hired you?'
'Christian Broadcasting Network. I got creds, but all my stuff
is up at that ranch.'
'You see who killed the woman?'
'Deveroux? No. I see her get hit, but not the driver.'
'Why were you there, at the ranch?'

200

'I went up there with Echo Hernandez... another writer. She's doing a piece for the Enquirer. I think she's still up there. We gotta go back... she might be dead...'

'Woah. We will. Okay? But you need to tell us what we're dealing with. The quicker you fill us in, the quicker we can get up there. Continue.'

'I went up there to warn her...'

'Hernandez?'

'No. Deveroux. To tell her someone was gonna kill her... I went up there to tell her, and she tried to kill *me*!'

'Slow down. What makes you think someone wanted to kill her?'

'What does that matter *now*? It came to pass, right?!'

Strauss brought it back. 'How did she—Deveroux—try to kill you?'

'They tried to fucking *crucify* me, and I'm not being metaphorical. Okay? They literally tried to nail me to a fucking cross with the rest. They got their own little Golgotha up there. The woman was fucking insane. They've got a whole commune of shotgun nuns up there...'

Last night's horrors were starting to catch up. Strauss held up a halt-hand. 'Okay, kid, relax. Who are the rest? The crucified...'

'I don't know. One was a girl. I think it was one of their own who was rattin' 'em out about the place to Hernandez... if she *is* the one, they called her Polythene Pam. Which is why she was heading up there...'

'Hernandez?'

'Yes. She thought this Pam chick had a lead on some story she was writing about.'

The agents exchanged glances. Exotic minutiae were threating to engulf their line of enquiry. A straightener would be required.

'What about the others?'

The silhouettes of those ragged, nailed-up, crow-mutilated corpses, with the moon coming up behind them, gripped Marco's fevered mind. He saw himself among them this morning. Face and guts torn out, flies feasting on the gore...

'Mascini! The others?!'

Marco snapped back, 'Three guys. One might have been black. I dunno, it was dark. Maybe he'd been there longer than the others… you know…' Strauss looked at Portland. Portland looked to the slit of light coming through the window.

'… and then that truck came out of nowhere…'

'You see who was driving?'

'Fuck no. I was on the ground half nailed to a post staring at the Milky Way… My money's on Xtravaganza. She was at the temple—they got a temple up there—she looked mad as hell. They'd been arguing about something. Something was definitely up. She actually said she was gonna kill her.'

'Xtravaganza said this?'

'Yeah. She said I'm gonna fucking kill her if she doesn't show.'

'And she said this to Deveroux?'

'No. Not to her. She wasn't there, then. This was to her girls—about her. Extravaganza stormed out of the place… and the shotgun sisters… the girls—they had shotguns—took me to see Deveroux. I tried to explain to her that her life was in danger. She didn't go for any of it. Then they led me out for the big nail up.'

'And what was she—Deveroux—doing when they were nailing you up?'

'Fucking supervising. I guess while she was distracted with me—nailing my ass to the wood—the driver made his move. Or her move—if it *was* the Xtravaganza broad. That truck came out of nowhere.'

Strauss sat back. This info seemed to satisfy him somehow.

'What makes you think someone was after Deveroux?'

Marco weighed it. 'There's this guy—Leonard Borg. Said he was from the Los Angeles Daily News, but he had all her stuff, rap sheets, psychiatric reports and a gun.'

'You think he was here to kill Deveroux, too? But you said your money was on Xtravaganza.'

Marco pondered. 'Maybe Borg put her up to it. Forced her… I dunno.'

'And this Borg,' Strauss said. 'You know where he is now?'

# 34. AGENTS AND ACQUIESCENCE

09:22

Strauss and Portland made calls on the phone and on the radio. They put out an APB for Xtravaganza and got the Policia de Los Cabos to check the airport. They backed up their Chevrolet to a service entrance in the courtyard of the Delegación Municipal. They bundled Marco into the trunk and maneuvered the car through the agitated crowd of media crews outside. On the outskirts of town, they got him out, put him in the back seat, and followed his directions to where he said he left Leonard Borg.

This was Marco's first view of the Baja in daytime. Agoraphobia came to play again, and Marco longed for the polka dot walls of his cluttered apartment.

The vast encampment to the right seemed to have grown even bigger. He guessed that many of the new arrivals were yet to learn of Deveroux's death. Within minutes, they all saw the wrecked Chieftain on the side of the road. Three men stood around it, searching the area, assessing the damage. They all turned as the Chevrolet appeared in a cloud of desert dust. The agents left Marco in the car and introduced themselves to the unhappy trio—a sound and cameraman in their fifties and their teenage runner. One of the older guys took the lead and told the agents that they found a couple of guys dragging an unconscious man out of the Chieftain and took him away.

'Who took him, and where?'

'We dunno. Hospital, I guess. Couple of backpackers were giving him the once over when we got here. Got kinda testy. We thought it was them that stole it at first. Was looking to give 'em a beatin.' They rolled him into their station wagon and took him away.'

'Yeah? How long ago?

203

''Bout an hour.'

'Long shot: you get the registration? A partial, maybe?'

'Nope. But it was beige and white, the car. A Ford I think.'

Portland peered into the dark cabin of the stricken Chieftain. 'You mind if we have a look?'

'Go ahead.'

Portland stepped inside and assessed the wrecked interior. Strauss stayed outside with the owner. 'Anything missing?'

'Not that we can tell. Wasn't much to steal anyhow. We had our cameras and sound stuff with us. Just a bunch of clothes, and they're still all under the bunk.'

'Anything in there that shouldn't be?'

'You mean drugs? Don't touch 'em—don't take 'em.'

'I mean, anything that's not *yours*.'

'Nope. There was a bag. Like a duffle bag? But I handed that over to the guys that took him away.'

'You look in it?'

'No.'

Strauss fixed him.

'I said no.'

The agents got back in the car and Portland drove. He got on the horn and requested the local hospital number; got them to leave a message with the admissions desk at the Centro de Salud for any patients that matched Leonard Borg's description. Strauss stared out at the sea in sullen reflection. Portland 'over the shoulder' questioned Marco some more.

'This fight you two had. What time was it?'

'I dunno. Eight?'

'What was it over?'

'He was cramping my style. I wanted rid. He didn't go for that, so we got into it. But then he had some kind of seizure, maybe an epi.'

'Saved by the bell, huh?'

'Saved by something.'

'You say this Borg fella was out to kill Deveroux? Any chance that he could have got up to the ranch, run her down, dumped the truck and got back to where they found him this morning?'

'I doubt it. Maybe. Anything's possible...'

Borg's stop-motion, pin-eyed face made an unwelcome return to Marco's mind. He re-calibrated. 'He looked pretty fucked up when I left him. Thought he might be dead.'

'And you left him.'

'He tried to fucking kill me. Check this!' Marco pulled down the collar of his borrowed T-shirt, exposing black bruises all around his collar bones. 'At the time, I didn't *give* a fuck. I just wanted to get out of there.'

Strauss told Portland to stop the car at the edge of town. Marco protested. 'Fuck that hiding in the trunk shit! I'll duck down.'

Once inside the station, they handed him over to the fat cop on desk duty, who took him somewhere in the back.

They got a call from the Policia de Los Cabos. Xtravaganza's hired 727 was still in the hangar and not scheduled to leave until tomorrow morning. There were no domestic flights booked in the name of Erika Xtravaganza, but then, they were yet to receive word on her real name. They ran AKAs by their Central Office who, again, told them they would get back.

They got another call from the hospital.

They've got Borg.


The Centro de Salud had been unable to handle the night's siege. Extra medics, requested from La Paz and Cabos, and unfamiliar with the facility, had served only to amplify the climate of hysteria and confusion. As the corridors became blocked with admissions, the clinic's directors made a snap decision to send most of the help back, and to take as many of the injured as they could with them. Most of the intake had suffered alcohol-related injuries, via fights, accidents, or brutal assaults—including four rapes—two of them male.

There was no room for the big man that they brought in this morning, so they put him in the canteen. A cursory once-over told the beleaguered morning shift staff that he was dead. A nurse searched the bag he came in with and realised he was still very much alive. L-Dopa was exotic. Frantic calls to Cabos put them through to their Parkinson's unit, who furnished them with administration and dosage advice.

## 10:47

Leonard Borg had seen his fair share of flickering strip lights.
The mental white noise that served as his only sensory input
for the last... (Who knows how long?) ...finally morphed into
the over-lit ceiling that constituted his field of vision.
Movement flickered fast around him. But now it was slowing
down and making sense. His mind was synchronizing with the
tempo that the rest of the world beat its drum to. The spasm
that suddenly arched his back and slammed him back down on
the bed was not his nervous system expelling some random
energy, but blind panic seizing his entire being. The last time
he was in a similar predicament was back in '63, when he
awoke to find he had lost half a decade and, subsequently, his
raison d'être.

He looked around and saw closed canteen shutters and a
snack dispenser. Notice boards were in Spanish. A second
spasm was headed off at the pass. It took a second to figure out
that the room was an emergency measure. Yesterday's
invasion of Todos Santos would have made for a hectic
evening—to say the least. They'd abandoned him on a gurney
in a room that had been cleared of chairs to make way for an
unprecedented influx.

He was sure of it now.

Mascini was Stevens' man.

The one who would execute the big knock off once Deveroux's
clock had been cleaned.

No open cases.

The brown blur in front of him became a face—a woman's
face. Her furrowed brow bridged her weary but thorough
appraisal. 'Can you tell me your name?' The husky Latino
accent helped him re-calibrate himself—where he was and
why.

'Yeah, Lex Barker.'

'Don't be an asshole. Do you know who you are?'

The passport in his top pocket would already have told them
who he was pretending to be—if anyone had even bothered to

206

check. He decided to fuck with her anyway. His ID, real or otherwise, remained on a need-to-know basis.

'Tyrone Power.'

She took her dry palm from his forehead, pulled the stethoscope plugs from her ears, and left him alone in the room.

The last thing he could remember is clutching the hem of Mascini's jeans in that stolen Chieftain, while the idiot rained kicks down on him and then… hospital strip-lights and 'Nurse Wetback' breathing in his face.

But he was alive.

Did Mascini pussy-out when it came to administer the big so long? Did he fuck it up? Thought he was already dead and got it oh so fucking wrong?

But if Mascini wasn't supposed to kill him, what was Stevens' point in getting the kid in on this shebang? Borg refused to believe Marco Mascini was a random addition—a bona fide wild card—and anywhere near as stupid as he made out. As sure as chance is the enemy of art, amateurs are the enemy of government-sanctioned death. A wave of clarity awoke him to the very real possibility that he had been played. His was to clean up his long overdue mess and then he himself would be cleaned. Such was the way of their world. It was clear now; Mascini was the sucker punch at the end of a rigged game.

He tested his limbs. His feet scrunched. His hands became fists. He was not hooked up to anything, nor was he strapped down. He could leave. Who was going to stop him? He began to ponder his next move when the door swung open, and two men entered. They came around the canteen tables and stood on either side of Borg's gurney. They wore cheap grey suits, buzz cuts and reeked of Fed. The one on his right flashed his badge. 'Leonard Borg?'

So, they already had his name. Borg's expression tuned in to Non-Committal FM.

'I'm Federal Agent Ian Strauss. This is Agent Bill Portland. 'Where were you around midnight?'

Borg did what he usually did when confronted with potential human threat: make a quick assessment of their physical prowess. Strauss was around 5.9 tall—slight build. Portland—6.3—powerfully built and would be his first target if necessary. Tentatively, Borg pulled himself up, swung his legs and let his feet find the floor. 'Bit out of your backyard, ain'tcha, boys?'

Strauss reiterated. 'Midnight. Where were you?'

'Here. Probably. I've only just come around.'

Again, Portland took the door. Partly to guard it, but mainly to let his elder do his thing.

'You were admitted two hours ago. Where were you before that?'

'Two hours?' Borg shrugged. 'Until just now, I've been out of it since last night.'

'So, whatcha doin' down here, Leonard? In Mexico? You're a little out of your backyard yourself?'

Borg thought better of running the Los Angeles Daily News routine. They wouldn't buy it. Not now. But thought he'd fuck with 'em, anyway.

'Research. Thinking of writing a book.'

'A book?'

'Yeah. You know, a travel book. Top Ten Baja Beaches; sumthin' like that.'

Strauss wouldn't entertain it. Too much time had been lost already. 'Okay, fuckeroo. Main event: Peggy Deveroux: Describe your involvement.'

'There is none. I just happened to be travelling through and came across this hoedown. I'd never heard of Peggy Deveroux until...' he thumbed in the direction of where he guessed the town was, '... all this.'

'Marco Mascini: Describe your involvement.'

Borg hid his surprise expertly and had to wonder what the idiot had done to put himself on the Fed's radar. Had he gone ahead, done the deed, and managed to get himself caught?

'I don't... know no... Marco Mascini.'

'Well, he's a suspect in a murder enquiry and he's blaming you.'

'Well, fancy that. Who'd he kill?'

The agents exchanged glances. Borg read it. 'Hold on now... *Deveroux*?! She's *dead*?'

Portland called across the room, 'If that hunk a blood 'n' guts that was found hangin' offa that Ford flatbed this mornin' is her—then I guess yeah.' He delivered all this in a West Texas monotone—as grey as the suit that hung on him.

Strauss laid it down. 'God's honest truth? The two of you reek of wrongdoing, but we don't give a flying fuck who you are or what you're about. We got two missing men—probably dead— who we think are up at that ranch. Mascini was up there last night, and what he's saying gives us reason to believe that is the case. We're going up there and we don't want to go half-cocked. So, if you got *anything* you can give us to help us along, then we'll be eternally grateful. Failing that, we'll stick you in the cooler together and you two can fuck each other to kingdom come, or whatever it is you Yankee fags do in your spare time.'

Tempers were frayed. Borg ignored the slight. 'Where is the body now?'

Portland said, 'Fuck it. Let's lose this prick.' Strauss nixed it.

They let Borg get his duffle bag. They took him, and it, to a vacant office, searched it in front of him, found the blister packs of aspirin, hypodermics, and vials of L-Dopa. Borg made a quiet assessment of the contents. Marco had left all but two of his vials of medication, (what a fucking saint!) but had taken Deveroux's rap sheet, psych reports, tapes... and his pistol. The silencer was missing, also. The kid was gun-wise.

Borg asked for milk and got it. He washed back one of his pills. He also asked to make a call. 'There's a pay phone in the foyer; you got any change?'

Strauss protested. 'No! No phone calls. Absolutely not... not until you spill, shitbird.'

'I'm gonna level with you. People of significance...' Borg let that hang in the air a beat. *People of significance* '...are looking for Deveroux. I can square this whole thing right now. And maybe help you with your missing men. Just one phone call. You got nothing to lose.'

'No calls. Fuck your rights,' Portland exclaimed. 'This ain't Kansas, Toto.'

'Not for *me*: for *you*. I got a number. Call your Special Agent in Charge and give it to him and get him to call it.'

Strauss said, 'Our SAC is a *she*.'

Borg snorted and said, 'Of course *he* is...'

They went out to the hallway. Borg picked up the receiver and offered it to the agents. They backed off like it was a poisoned chalice.

Portland said, 'I fuckin' *knew* it. This has got black ops written all over it.'

Borg sized the agents up. 'You military men?'

Their lips were tight. Borg said it again.

Portland piped up. 'Afghanistan, school of '81'

Strauss spat and mumbled something that could only have been 'Nam.'

'Then you're all wised up, right? Ours is not to reason why.'

'I didn't go for that cloak and dagger shit then,' Strauss drawled, 'and I don't much care for it now.'

'Nevertheless, darkness reigns.' Borg put the phone in Strauss' hand. 'Make the call.'

Strauss wasn't going to take the chance of being bluffed or smote down in some remote Yankee-fag beef. He had to know for sure. He dialed.

'Jeanne? This is Agent Strauss. Hold on.' He beckoned Borg to him. 'Borg... the number...'

Borg reeled it off from memory. Strauss repeated it into the phone. 'Can you have Special Agent Brenda Reynder call it and then call me back, please? Thank you, ma'am.'

He hung up and went down the hall to the big window and stared out onto a derelict side-road. A group of bare-chested marauders marched past—press-hounds fruitlessly trying to pick up the bloody scent of a dying scoop.

Borg asked Portland, 'You've ran the prints... from the truck?'

'We have.' Portland looked to his despondent colleague, bathed in morning light. 'And naturally, we wait.'

'Where's the body?'

'Let's wait for—'

'We don't have to wait,' Borg interrupted.

The phone rang loud. Portland grabbed the receiver. Strauss
came over and grabbed it from him. 'Agent Strauss ... yes.'
He listened.
His brow darkened.
Fears were confirmed. 'Yes ma'am, *Leonard Borg.*' He listened
some more. 'Yes ma'am. We have a possible suspect and few
leads and expect to have an update before the day's out. We
ran some prints by the APD office an hour ago. *Any* help in
moving that along, ma'am will be greatly appreciated ... Thank
you ... thank you, ma'am.'
Strauss hung up, looked at Portland, and shook his head. '*Taco
circuit.*'
Portland spat on the polished floor and rubbed it in with the
toe of his slip-ons.
Borg said, 'Taco Circuit?'
Portland flicked the hanky from his trouser pocket and wiped
grit from a corner of his eye.
'It *means* this is a bullshit case.'
Borg reiterated. 'We don't need to wait for print results. I can
make a positive ID right now. Take me to the body.'
The agents didn't even bother to display their disgust. The
taco-circuit demanded indolence.

The men stood around the corpse, shrouded with a blue sheet,
as Doctor Ramon Espinoza read out the injuries like they were
today's specials. 'Gross trauma to throat and jaw... multiple
fractures of the pelvis and both upper femurs. Right hand
missing at the lower elbow...'
Borg interjected. 'Right hand missing?'
Espinoza looked up and over bifocals at the interjector. 'Yes,
*missing*. At the elbow...' He waited a beat. His re-iteration
raised no further questions. The doctor continued. 'Right leg,
from above the knee missing. Multiple lacerations on the entire
front of the body...'
Borg interjected again. 'Right leg? Where is it?!'
Again, the doctor squinted at the uninvited trio. 'Which part of
*missing* are you having difficulty with, amigo?'

Only her black hair and remaining dirty foot were visible at either ends of the sheet. The toenails were long and unkempt. Someone had taken the trouble to comb her recently dyed hair, which hung over the edge of the metal table like a freeze-frame waterfall of oil. Borg wanted to see her face. But not with these interlopers. Borg glared at the doctor, who continued... 'All injuries indicative of a large vehicle impact...'

Borg bade the agents out into the hallway.

Strauss hissed, 'She got tats on that missing leg or sumthin'?'

'How long these prints gonna take?'

Strauss looked at Portland, who said 'I'll call 'em again. I dunno. We already asked 'em to fast-track it.'

'So, no timescale whatsoever?' Borg scoffed. 'No guarantee that it would be quicker to just go find those missing parts. Have you *any* idea where they are?'

'According to our suspect she got run down at that ranch we wanna take a gander at. By the time they found her, the truck was just on the outskirts of town. The body was stuck in the grille, with the arm and leg already gone. They could be at the place of impact or they coulda fallen off anywhere along the road.'

'Has anyone even looked?'

'We're taking the suspect back up to that ranch to where the hit and run happened. They could be still there. But wherever they were, the wildlife probably had at 'em by now.'

Borg said, 'Let's go get your suspect.'

# 35. A SECOND STORM

12:00

They quick-marched Borg towards the north end of the square. They passed the damaged bandstand and up the steps into a building that said Delegación Municipal above the entrance.

Portland brought him up to speed. A naked Caucasian male, black hair, brown eyes, average build, thirty years old, was apprehended by the local Policía Judicial Federal, but still not formally charged. He was found driving south towards Todos Santos at around 6am this morning in an unregistered Ford flatbed truck. Tangled in the front grille of the truck was the body of an as yet to be formally identified woman of around fifty or sixty, who the suspect claims is Peggy Deveroux. Apparently, she's some old bondage queen who was to appear at this here event in Todos Santos. When news of her death got around, Captain Gael Mendez succumbed to the demands of the invading media and granted an impromptu press conference in the back office of the Comisaria. Before any meaningful questioning could begin, someone blew the windows in with a shotgun.

'Those idiot reporters have done gone vigilante and are fixin' on turning your boy into a piñata.'

Borg had to ask. 'Why was he naked?'

Portland smirked. 'You tell me, sweetheart?'

The square was all but deserted. A burned-out, overturned car on the steps served both as effigy and tribute to a fading fit of mass psychosis.

Portland continued. 'Meanwhile, he keeps bleatin' on about some girl who needs his help. Hernandez? Up at that ranch, where Deveroux got splattered.'

Borg knew he meant 'Miss Enquirer' but kept schtum.

'They've taken your boy to a basement cell for his own protection.'

'How is he *my* boy?!'

'Ah, will you quit it with this shit!' Strauss exploded. 'The two of you have wrongdoing written all over you, so let's stop jerking each other around, okay?! You are CIA or some other government spook! We don't give a fuck. We just want our guys!'

With that slight build, Borg thought, the man should avoid hostility. Clearly his law-enforcement attributes lay elsewhere. Borg said to him, 'You a good shot or something?'

'What's that, a cryptic question?'

213

'Not really.' Borg thought it prudent to change the subject and sustain the line of ignorance. 'So, what are they so het up about—this vigilante press corps—about the woman?'

Portland said, 'She's the whole point of this circus. They came all the way down here to see a resurrection and got robbed. So, now they want to see an execution.'

Marco had been staring at the glossy grey ceiling for some kind of forever. The realisation crawled upon him that this was not the dullest dream in Narco-ville. He was awake.

To the left, a tiny window, about six feet from the floor, was that wall's only distinguishing feature. To the right, a thin line up, across, and down again suggested the strong probability of a door. The bulb in the middle of the ceiling had its own cage.

When they first brought him in this morning, they put him in a stationery cupboard. But now this was a proper cell. He figured he was really under arrest now, but no-one had told him anything. Or if they did, it escaped him beneath the cover of Español.

The cold frame against his knuckles summoned him to proper consciousness. He swung his legs off the bunk. His bare feet hit cold tiles. He would swear his lungs were scratching his spine. The frightening power of Borg's assault made those elephant-killing kickboxers in Chiang Rai look like a slap-fest with Erika Xtravaganza's entourage. His throat throbbed with a slow, lumbering rhythm. For the happy few who ever survived a lynching, this was the price.

He had pondered his situation for no more than a couple of minutes when he heard keys rattle outside. The thin line that suggested a door became one. Agent Portland beckoned him out. 'Come on, fucko. We're gonna get your gal.'

They stopped the car north of the town. They got Marco out of the trunk and put him in the back seat next to Strauss. Marco's heart missed myriad beats when he saw Borg in the front passenger seat. Borg barely glanced back. Everyone felt the heat in the car go up a notch. Strauss laid down the ground rules. 'This is what we're gonna do. We're going up to this place. We're gonna find our guys. We're gonna find those missing body parts and then, *maybe*, depending on how that pans out, we'll go look for this Hernandez broad. As I'm sure you both know; there's a lot of moral latitude down in these parts. So, consider the possibilities. I do not care what bad blood has gone down between you two but know this: if at any time you two start up, I will shoot you both. *Governmental black ops* bullshit or not. Don't care. I will *kill* you. We square? Fabulous. Let's go.'

Portland stabbed it and steered.

Borg said, 'Can you remember where you found the truck?'

They had hardly covered a hundred yards when Marco announced. 'Here!'

Borg and Portland got out and inspected the area. Pools of congealed black blood marked the spot. Portland kicked stones aside. Borg looked up the 19. No body parts could be seen. The hard ground beside the road wasn't footprint friendly. Strauss looked out towards the sea and saw a small group of beach houses. He got on the horn and requested any spare officers to check out those beach houses. 'Whoever was driving that truck might have hunkered down there.'

They continued their journey. 'So, you believe me?' Marco enquired. 'That I found the truck as it was?'

Everyone ignored him. Borg told everyone to keep their eyes on the road for anything that might be those missing limbs.

Captain Gael Mendez of the Policia Municipal Todos Santos watched with some satisfaction as a heavily armed task force, twenty-strong, sent down from Tijuana at his request, arrived at Pineda Ranch.

He got out of the car and waved the first of their assault vehicles through the ranch gates. It barely slowed down, ignoring him as he stood by waving like a fool.

He told them he would be there waiting for them and assumed they'd report to him for instructions and invaluable information about the surrounding terrain. By the time the cloud of dust had drifted over him, the truck was already halfway down the hill heading towards the temple. This snub

215

served only to remind him of his place in the grand scheme of la ley Mexicana y el orden.

Justice here in the Californian peninsula was controlled by unsanctioned hired guns. In this case, the Baja Security Force. A gang of glorified drug dealers, with local biker gangs as their muscle and Mexico City councillors as their brains.

His Policia Municipal was a mere facade, used to present a veneer of officialdom to anyone from the international community that might be looking to make moves down here. Inevitably, the BSF assumed responsibility to oversee the festival in Todos Santos with inevitable results. The event had gone from debacle to warzone within hours of the first news crews' arrival. The Deveroux woman's subsequent murder pitched it blitzkrieg. Admittedly, the scale of the event had caught them all by surprise. Even the BSF. Mendez's dream of helping promote Todos Santos as a desirable tourist destination was as dead as the woman all this had been for.

Two months ago, when his department had received the applications for camping facilities, power hook-ups etc. he could see that it was a potential money spinner, and because of that, knew that whatever his microscopic department may demand for the safekeeping the town and its inhabitants, would be overruled.

Chaos was a given.

Of course, he was aware of the activities up at the ranch— some of them at least. As to be expected, the people kept themselves to themselves, so there was no cause not to leave them that way. Only once had his department been required to call at the temple, a couple of years ago, to caution someone about a traffic violation.

This morning when their suspect, Mascini, revealed the dead woman was from the commune, Mendez hit the files for whatever they had on the place. Ranchero Pineda... There was nothing but basic sale information—a derelict sugar mill and colonial mission house, surrounded by a couple of thousand square acres of arable land. The lease was bought from the Baja Trust in 1982 via a realtor in Clovis, New Mexico. The traffic violation pertained to a Pedro Terán and a Mustang

216

stolen in La Paz. He'd been arrested but released without charge within the hour. The BSF at play again, thought Mendez.

He'd already sent the dead woman's prints, and those lifted from the truck that killed her, to Cabos, but it'd be weeks, if ever, that he'd receive a response. And now, out of the blue, two Texan FBI agents appear, wanting to search the ranch for two of their missing men. As was usual with American investigations, he and his department were consigned to the need-to-know shit-can.

It was inconceivable that the BSF didn't have some involvement with the people at the ranch, if only to make their presence felt. But when Agents Strauss and Portland requested back-up, Mendez knew the job would require complete outsiders. His call for help would, he hoped, insulate his department from the controlling criminal element and, who knows? win a few brownie points for the Policia Federal Todos Santos.

He had made the call yesterday, and now they were here. A twenty-strong task force was beyond overkill, he felt, but, as always, his was not to reason why. The first of the assault vehicles were out of sight now. Mendez signalled to the patrol car on the other side of the dirt track containing the best of his department, Valverde, Marquis and Sandor to follow him. Pasquala they left behind. *Someone* trustworthy had to answer the phones. He got in his own car and drove. He always drove alone. With a department as small as his, it was important to dispel any notion of a close-knit family or, Mary forbid, a gang. *The margin* must be maintained at all times.

Mendez had never been to the ranch before. Tucked away as it was, east off the highway and at the end of little more than a stony irrigation ditch, it was a place you would only go if you had business there. Last year he understood there had been some people from the American press in town asking about the place. He'd given it no more thought until he saw the story in the Enquirer about an alleged resurrection. The story was typically sensational and obviously some kind of put on, but it brought an ominous wind that he knew would leave the town with some dubious repute.

The driveway became a steep hill down and curved to the left, revealing a lush valley, an abrupt contrast to the surrounding desert terrain. Their descent elevated the distant Sierra de la Laguna mountains further up into the gods. From half a mile away, the noon sun hit the roof of the temple. It was only as Mendez got closer that he realised what an outlandish structure the building was. All evidence that the place had ever been a sugar mill was obscured by the huge yellow and black panelling, punctuated by stained glass portholes. To Mendez's mind, it was more like a theme-park attraction than a place of worship. In addition to the temple and colonial mission house were three new large two-story buildings to the rear of the temple. Of his being unaware of something like this on his patch provoked new pangs of inadequacy. Maybe he *really was* the hic-spic that out-of-towners took him for.

# 36. TANGENT

'I'd play it cool,' Marco announced apprehensively. 'The woman slept in an armoury. Thing is, as war ready as they are, I think they're planning on making a mass exodus into the next world. I mean, that's what these cults are all about, right? End of days? Shit could go Jim Jones.'

Portland drove fast, Strauss chain-smoked and narrow-eyed the glistening Pacific. Borg sat in silence. As they approached El Cardonosa, they all saw the big six-wheeler hurtling towards them before it threw a curve to the east, off the 19 and trundled cross country. Portland muttered, 'What the fuck is this now...'

Borg knew an assault vehicle when he saw one. 'That, Agent Portland, is a Panhard personnel carrier. Someone's either expecting trouble or bringing their own.'

Marco was unsure whether he'd remember where the turnoff was in the hot light of day, but now he didn't have to. 'This is it!'

The Chevrolet turned sharply and followed the Panhard. The car straddled the narrow irrigation ditch beside the sorry excuse of a road with Portland struggling with the wheel. Rocks popped and exploded beneath their tires.

They lost sight of the Panhard until they took the bend that revealed a secret Garden of Eden. Lush, well-kept fields humped over the land like a deep green sea.

They pulled up beside a row of four Panhards and found Captain Mendez and three of his men in a heated exchange with a couple of members of the task force. Portland got out of the car and sauntered over there. It seemed he possessed at least a workable grasp of Spanish. Federales... the FBI... solders... The only thing missing is the Boy Scouts, thought Marco.

The exchange between all the men seemed to escalate. Strauss got out to join them and shouted back to Borg and Marco, 'Stay there!'

Borg got out and grunted painfully as he stretched. This guttural noise stopped the quarrelling officials for an instant, who all looked round, then picked up from where they left off.

One of the men flung his arms up. Stumbled backwards and fell to the ground.

Then they heard it.

Shots fired.

From the direction of the temple.

Borg hit the dirt and yelled, 'Mascini! Get out and get down!'

Marco slid into the footwell of the car, kicked open the door and slid out feet first. He saw boulders twenty feet away. He made a mad dash and dived over them. Before he could even register the next second, Borg hurled himself over and head-butted him. A rain of bullets from the temple churned up the dirt around them and drowned out their screams. Both men got to their knees, still clutching their heads, still screaming in mutual agony. Now was not the time for blame games. Borg yelled. 'Mascini, where did this hit and run happen?!'

Still nursing his throbbing forehead, Marco tried to get his bearings from the limited view from behind the rock. 'I don't know. Maybe on the other side of that temple!'

'Well, fucking think!'

A bullet whizzed past Marco's ear, hit a rock, and ricocheted into the sky. He made another mad dash up the hill and out of the firing line. This time he turned, ready to kick Borg's face should he hurl himself into him again. From the new vantage point, he got a better view of the area. The cops and soldiers were dug in behind the four Panhards, which were lined up in what looked like a parking area about fifty yards outside the temple walls. Within the walls were a few more vehicles, and some statues vandalised with florescent spray paint. Now in daylight from up on this hill he could see that the temple had been turned it into some kind of giant cartoon submarine, complete with periscope and portholes, but was now near derelict. The ground rose up from the temple gates to a wide plateau with no obstruction of the distant mountains. Remembering the direction from which he found the temple last night, he was certain that the cemetery was up on that plateau somewhere. Shots whistled wild over his head. Suddenly, there was movement to his right. Borg had made it and was scrambling towards him. 'You nearly fucking brained me; prick!'

Marco was trying to search the results of the shootout with his ears alone. 'Seriously?! You want to do this now?! Anyway, it was your fucking fault!!'

Bullets rang. Borg's priorities returned. 'Okay, let's get away from this.'

Marco led Borg further up the hill, then across open ground just beyond the perimeter. The contrast between the lush greenery of the ranch and the desolate terrain that surrounded it was enough to induce a cerebral whiplash. The movie— Silent Running—entered Marco's mind. Bruce Dern curates a jungle in a dome out in space. It was as if Bruce's paradise had landed right here in the desert.

'I might get my bearings better if I can find that cemetery. Anyway, fuck them Feds. I want to find Hernandez first.'

He remembered the walk from the cemetery to the temple was no more than ten minutes. The ground became a sudden steep incline, and they found themselves at the edge of a fragile ridge.

'So, Deveroux,' Borg asked, 'did you kill her?'

Marco kissed his teeth and muttered, 'Fucking idiot.'

'Relax. I'm not mad.' Borg shrugged big shoulders. 'If you did, mission accomplished.'

Marco pressed it. 'The truck was like that when I found it.'

'And you missed the little detail of a corpse draped all over the front?'

'Yes, *Leonard*, I did. I just wanted to get the fuck out of there and back to town. Performing a road-side service wasn't exactly top of my to-do list.'

No sooner had Marco said this when Borg's scrutiny shifted gears and he seemed in a faraway place. He snapped back and said, 'So what's the story? Be liberal with the low-down; starting with our little dance in the Chieftain.'

Marco sighed big. 'Yeah, about that…'

'Spare me the guilty plea. I want to wrap this up, immediately if not before. Where are my pills?'

Marco had to think for a second. 'In my bag…' He scanned a distant ridge where they left the car last night. '… in Hernandez's car.

'And the gun?'

'Probably still in my jacket on Deveroux's bedroom floor.'

Neither of them said anything more until they came to the obelisks and tombs of the old cemetery. They stepped over the low-chained perimeter. Marco looked across to the gated entrance he and Hernandez had walked through last night. He took this as his reference and figured the grave she'd fallen into was near the centre. Borg followed Marco's progress around the long-neglected plots. A few of the moss-covered headstones were legible.

Borg called to Marco, 'This is a soldier's cemetery.'

'Yeah, how do you know?'

'They all died on one of two days. March 29th and 30th 1848. This ain't the first time this place has hosted heavy artillery,'

'That's… *supremely* interesting.'

'You really are a prize prick, Mascini.'

'I like to think so…' Marco remembered Hernandez's Enquirer story. 'The guy they resurrected was an old-style soldier. I

221

guess you got to give it to 'em for their attention to detail.' He stopped suddenly. 'This is it!'

Borg looked into the sorry void at their feet. Rotten broken planks were embedded in the mud about four feet down.

Marco shouted the woman's' name into the grave.

'There's more to this hole than meets the eye. That storm hit last night, right?'

'You *were* right about that. So what?'

'Look around, puddles everywhere. But not in this hole. That rain went somewhere.'

Something in the distance exploded. Stones vibrated at their feet. They saw black smoke spiralling up into the blue. Marco blurted, 'The temple!'

Borg looked in the direction of the shootout, which was somewhere over the ridge.

'Welcome to the showroom.'

'What the hell does that mean?'

'It means... everyone's getting the trouble they're looking for. Those soldiers weren't National Guard, they were paramilitaries. It's amateur night. Which means people are gonna to die.'

'There's kids in there...'

'Then I guess kids are gonna die.'

Borg kicked over a headstone and hurled it into the grave. The headstone crashed straight through the bottom, leaving a gaping hole.

'What the fuck are you doing?! If she's down there, that'd kill her!'

'Shut up! I'm trying to hear.'

'Hear what?'

Borg kicked at another headstone until it came loose. 'Help me get this fucking thing out!'

Marco squatted and got his fingers underneath the slimy rock. 'What are we doing?'

'This, Mascini, is a vault or a tunnel. If you can shut the fuck up, we'll know how deep it is.'

222

The girl's either dead from the fall or, if it is a tunnel, she's got out wherever it goes. I'm guessing it leads right into that compound. Now shut up.'

Marco envisioned Hernandez captured and nailed up with the others. He hoped Deveroux's being out of the equation had chilled those mad bitches out. But the shots he could hear now from over the hill suggested otherwise.

'Wait. If this takes us into the temple, I might be able to figure out the way to where Deveroux got run down.'

Borg got the stone in his arms and dropped it in. Marco heard a sloppy thud. 'So?'

'Twenty-foot drop.'

Close by, a few plots were surrounded by thick chains, linked to flagstones at each corner. Borg grabbed a chain and pulled.

Nothing doing.

'Borg, that was the first thing I tried last night. There's no way.'

Borg wrapped some chain slack around his lower arm and pulled again. He froze for a second. Tension sent a bolt flying out of the flagstone like a bullet. A second bolt whizzed past Marco's head. 'Fuck you, Borg!'

Borg used the chain to pull another flag stone straight out of the ground. Marco couldn't believe this guy was sixty years old. Borg swung the chain, smashing the flagstone on a tomb wall. The flagstone crumbled, leaving a chunk of rock on the end of it.

'Okay, grab the other end.'

'What are you gonna do—*lower me in*? Fuck you!'

Borg swung the chain around. 'You're going in. With or without the chain.'

Marco licked his lips and peered into the hole. Another physical exchange with this animal was not an option. 'Did you say twenty feet?'

'Give or take. Grab it.'

Marco picked up the end of the chain, still attached to the smashed piece of flagstone. The option of throwing it into Borg's face suggested itself, then scurried back to the idiot part of his brain from whence it came. 'So, what are you gonna be doing while I'm making like Indiana Jones?'

'I'm coming with. But *you* first. Wait... we need a light. Fuck!'

Marco spotted Hernandez's flashlight still sitting on the grass. He grabbed it, switched it off/on. 'Dead.'

Marco emptied the batteries, rolled them around in his hand, replaced them, hit the switch. Nothing. 'Forget it.'

Borg snatched the torch out of Marco's hand and tossed it. 'No. We're doing this. Let's go.'

'Without a light?'

'If there's a wall down there, we'll follow it. If not—if it's just a vault—we'll go back to the temple, see what the state of play is.'

'It could be full of water. Have you thought of that? I could fucking drown.'

'*Not* if you keep a hold of this.' Borg offered Marco the end of the chain. 'Now come on!'

Marco's borrowed sneakers sunk into the sides of the grave as Borg lowered him in. Marco yelled, 'Okay, easy. Not so fucking fast!'

He dangled one leg into the abyss, expecting... water?

Solid ground?

The flames of Hell?

Borg stood above him. The chain wrapped tight around his forearm. 'Can you feel anything?'

Marco prodded the darkness with his soggy foot. 'No.'

Borg let some more chain slip through his fingers. Marco white-knuckled and closed his eyes. *'I don't wanna do this, Borg!'*

'You're fine. You're nearly there... swing your legs around. See if there's anything to get a hold of.'

Marco could feel the floor of the grave touch his shoulders. He looked up, realising this might be the last time he ever sees the sky. Borg's bulky silhouette blocked whatever life affirming azure magic he was hoping for. Then suddenly he smelled it.

Putrid.

Sickly.

'I think she's dead, Borg. That smell...'

'Pipe down! Could be anything, probably rats... Get ready, I'm gonna give you another couple of feet.'

Another jolt. The sides hit his shoulders, and Marco was in total darkness, hanging in a cold abyss. He could hear Borg's muffled shouts. Panic began to rise in him. He was losing his grip. Figuratively. Actually. He thrust his hips around, trying to get a swing going. With toes pointed, he kicked into sheer nothingness. For all he knew, this hole could be a million miles down and million miles wide. Panic escalated to fear.

He swung harder.

Something...

His toe hit something.

He swung again and hooked his foot underneath... a rung?

The rubber of the sneaker slipped out. He swung hard again and again. His foot hooked under a slippery piece of wood. With one secured leg, he pulled himself towards it. He got his other foot underneath the rung. His grip gave out and slid down the chain. His feet held fast, and his stomach seemed to drop out of him. His back hit a wall and knocked the air clean out of him. He yelped. The void extinguished the noise. His hands found whatever was behind him. He was upside down and tangled in a mess of slippery wood. Then... he lost contact with everything. Before he knew he was falling, he hit the ground, shoulder-blade first.

He was cold. His eyelids flickered. He knew they were open wide, but he stared into an abject nothing. The earth was sloppy. He was embedded in it. He pushed against it. It sucked on his escape. His legs trembled. He held his arms out, scrambling for the sanctuary of solidity.

Fingertips brushed surface.

Fingertips revealed a wall. A stone wall.

He turned and threw himself against it. He moved his face toward where he thought 'up' was. 'Borg!'

Borg barked something back. That meagre bar of light disappeared, obliterated by Borg as he climbed down into the hole.

'Grab my legs! Lower me down!'

'Borg, I can't even fucking see you!' There's some kind of ladder in front of you. Grab it!'

Marco could hear Borg scrambling for the slippery wood. Then a couple of grunts, then a dull thud. 'You down?'

Silence.

'Borg!'

Loooong groan.

'Yeah… I'm down. Where are you? Reach out…'

Marco flapped his hands around idiotically in front of him. Sharp, sudden contact. Borg's clammy hand slapped him on the back of his hand, hitting a nerve point.

'Ow!'

Marco felt big hands gripping his wrists. 'Okay, up against the wall. Find the wall…'

'Ooh baby… no dinner first?'

'As far as comedians go, Mascini, you've got to be *the* most mirth-slaughtering fuckeroo that *ever* sullied God's green creation.'

'Hey! I've got a fucking hole in my foot, and I damn near broke my back. I think it's important to maintain the… y'know… general good… whatever, don't you?'

'C'mere!'

Marco felt Borg's hand on his back and grab the neck of his T-shirt. 'Stay close, follow me, keep your hands on the wall.'

Wooden struts flanked the walls. A ceiling of railroad sleepers kept the world above them. The tunnel curved slightly, and they could see shelves of machine parts and tools.

'This is part of that sugar mill…' Borg punched the ceiling. '… where old General Pineda probably stashed his kill cache.'

'Lazarus' lair… Maybe Hernandez—' Borg threw up his halt-hand and interrupted Marco's '—got out okay.'

'There's light! See it?'

They stopped and let their retinas adjust. 'Okay, this is it,' Borg stage whispered. 'Watch yourself and keep your mouth shut.'

The light was blinding as they neared its source. It glared from behind a wall of glass. Marco recognised the room beyond it. 'This is Deveroux's bedroom! The hall of mirrors.

'Mirrors?'

'Two-way mirrors. Like that Bruce Lee movie. S'one dragon I wouldn't want to enter now.'

Borg peered through the tinted glass into the room. A large, round, unmade bed, the gun racks and Marco's muddy clothes in a pile on the stone floor. The wall of television sets were still fizzing with white noise and static. Borg pushed at the glass. Nothing doing. He got his thick fingers in a gap and pried. The panel opened silently inwards.

They stepped into the room. The naked Latino was still tied to the post; darts hanging from his punctured chest. Marco peered up into his face. A long string of bloody drool hung from his top lip. This boy was dead.

Marco remembered the other guy with the smack-tracks in his arms on the bed. He scanned the room. Maybe he'd crawled off somewhere, but he was nowhere to be seen. Marco retrieved his clothes from the floor where they were left last night after being stripped off him. He removed the policia-issued slacks and sneakers but kept the Channel 5 T-shirt. The logo appealed to him. He put his own clothes, muddy as they were, back on. Borg inspected the shelves of weapons that lined the walls. 'I guess this is what the task force are down here for.'

Borg stood and assessed the circular mirrored room, disoriented by the thousands of images of himself and Marco that surrounded them. 'Grab that bag on the bed. We might need it.'

Among Deveroux's big Turkish cushions, Marco could see a large Cheyenne style hold-all. Marco tipped out the contents. A book, *The Stanislavski Method by Sonia Moore.* A small sheet of dotted cardboard was being used as a bookmark. The tiny Vishnu images could only mean one thing. LSD. He folded it and put it in his pocket. There was also a driving licence. He gave it the once over and handed it to Borg.

LICENCIA DE AUTOMOVILISTA – PEGGY MAE DEVEROUX

'We still need that leg?'

227

Borg gave the licence a once over and handed it back. 'Phony as the day is long. Yeah, we still need that leg.'

# 37. UN GOLGOTHA MESSICANO

Borg grabbed a torch from the shelf out in the tunnel. It worked. 'Mascini, you remember the way from here?'

Marco put the phony licence back in Deveroux's holdall. He saw the door the shotgun sisters had led him in and out by. 'Yeah. I think so.'

Borg followed as Marco led him through a series of long, narrow corridors. Finally, they came to the emergency exit through which the shotgun sisters hustled him through last night. They stood for a moment in the blinding sunlight. The low rumble of the distant shootout seemed to abate. A portentous silence reigned. There was only one way forward, a narrow pass between high walls of rock. The pass weaved haphazardly. Marco felt a pang of joy that he was alive to take this route again—a revisit to his own Via Dolorosa. This day should not have found him.

The narrow pass opened into the natural arena that Marco had only seen last night as an encephalograph of jagged shadows. Up the incline, to the far end of the arena, they saw them, the four crucified dead.

Borg looked around. 'Where did that truck hit?'

Marco approached the dead quartet as if trying to recognise himself among them.

'Mascini?!'

Marco was lost to the horror of the apparitions before him. Borg grabbed his collar and turned him around. 'Get with it, shit-bird!'

Marco re-occupied himself and looked around. The long slope to the right of the arena helped him get his bearings. He followed the tire tracks and orientated himself to where they tried to nail him to that post. He saw the discarded pieces of wood. Borg followed Marco's eyeline and went over to where his wary gaze fell. Borg followed the tire marks up the opposite incline. Marco stared back at the crucified. The fiery sun behind them rendering them wizened silhouettes.

'Son?'

Marco, startled, jumped back. Strauss held out an open hand. 'Easy, son. It's me.'

Marco's vision adjusted to the man before him. Portland climbed the hill for a closer look at the nailed-up corpses. Strauss followed his colleague to the foot of the hill. Portland looked down at him and nodded affirmation. They both knew their search was over. No one noticed Borg join them. The four men stared ruefully at the naked and the dead. Borg said, 'Who are the others?'

'According to your boy here,' answered Strauss, 'she calls herself Pam... something...'

'Polythene.' Said Marco.

'Pam Polythene,' Strauss spat. 'Freaks.'

Even in its mortified state, the corpse of the blonde male seemed to command centre-stage; the groin and stomach a ripped-out gaping hole. Strauss made the introduction. 'I think this is Haines.'

'Haines being...?' Borg enquired.

'Carter Haines. He owns the place... Owned. Comes from old money. Old *Texas* money. His family own the fertiliser plants. They had a falling out. Kid went his own way. They hadn't heard from him for a couple of years and filed a missing person's case. Looks like our guys found him.'

'Looks like they all found each other.' Borg interrupted the reverie and said to Marco, 'Here. Put this in that bag.'

Borg was holding Deveroux's shattered leg. 'Fuck! No!' Borg snatched the holdall from around Marco's neck and put it in himself. 'It's a leg. A dead one at that. Her kicking days are done.'

Strauss said, 'You find the hand?'

Borg surveyed the terrain one more time. 'Can't see it. Don't need it. Let's go.'

229

Strauss grabbed the hold-all, took out the leg and held it by the foot, stump down, and inspected it. It was waxy white, splattered in mud and blood. 'Coulda done with a shave...' He saw the scar down along the left side of the calf. 'This whatcha lookin' for?'

Borg fixed him with an affirmative two-nail stare. 'Check out some of those blow-ups at the theatre. Beach shots. It's her.'

Borg's standing trance-like before those huge photos at the Teatro returned to Marco's mind. Borg dumped the leg back in the holdall and punched it into Marco's chest.

'It don't fit!' Marco protested. 'The stump's sticking out, man!'

'Well, turn it the fuck around, then!'


Marco led everyone back the way he and Borg had entered the kill site, through the narrow pass towards the back of the temple. Dirty toes protruding from the corner of Deveroux's own holdall.

Borg said, 'What is going on up there? They done, yet?'

'We thought you could tell us.' Strauss listened. The shooting had stopped. 'They were negotiating on the phone with someone inside the temple when we broke away. So... you two are pleading no involvement in this siege?'

'I've got nothing to do with anything!' Marco shouted back.

Strauss continued. 'Mendez called the militia for help with the riots in town. They weren't innerested 'till he mentioned the little detail that ol' Marco gave him; 'bout the rockets and guns. So, they came down alright, but diverted their attention here. Neither of you two would know anything about that either, I suppose?'

Marco confirmed it. 'I told him—Mendez—that Deveroux's bedroom was an armoury. S'all I said.'

Borg threw him a glance that projected surprise more than anger and followed it with, 'If I had to guess, I'd say it was an old-fashioned show and tell. But you Feds know all about that doncha? Exaggerate the threat to justify the means.'

'Zat a fact?' answered Strauss dryly.

They entered the narrow corridors of the temple. When they reached Deveroux's 'hall of mirrors' bedroom, the sheer lunacy of the place astounded the agents, as it had Marco and Borg. Marco, experiencing it again through their eyes, supported Borg's unhinged 'in the know' claims about the world at large and Peggy Deveroux's place in it. It also supported what he'd read of her psychiatric reports. The woman was Looney Tunes, personified.

The agents stood aghast at the wall of military-grade weapons against the endless backdrop, which seemed to create a vortex of reflections into eternity. Strauss said, 'I guess this is what they're after. How the hell did you guys get in here?'

Marco nodded at the panel among the mirrors and put on his best anchor-man voice. 'Follow me, won't you?'

Portland examined the dead Latino still tied to the post. 'He's dead.' Marco offered helpfully.

Portland said, 'You'll make detective yet. You know who he is?'

'No. Deveroux was using him as a dartboard. There was another guy here, on the bed. I thought he was dead too, but he's gone, so… who knows…'

Borg went over to the two-way mirrored panel. 'We can get out this way. Mascini, you still got that flashlight?'

'Yeah, it's here in the bag… WITH A FUCKING LEG!'

Again, Marco led. The Feds behind him. Borg hung back, lost in some internal vault of his own. Already Marco had transported himself forward, to New York, to his apartment, to his air-conditioned limbo. The last two days had served only to amplify his desire for exile, for his return to meaninglessness; back to a time before he carried bags with severed legs.

Now that they could see, the walk through the tunnel back to the grave took no more than a few minutes. As they approached the resurrection site, light dappled in from above. The stench got thick and inescapable. A quartet of guts spasmed in unison.

Portland said, 'You see any bodies down here?'

'No.' Marco answered.

'Well… there is.'

Beneath the gravesite, the narrow tunnel opened up into a large, vault-like tomb supported by ornate concrete arches.

The flashlight was feeble, but it was enough.

Marco saw her first.

He saw her red jacket.

She lay face down in the dirt, her legs akimbo and her arm twisted beneath her at a demented angle. He crouched beside the body, ran the back of his hand against her cold cheek. He looked around the tomb and saw the other bodies. About ten of them scattered around the edges of the room. As far as they could see, they were all men in advanced stages of decomposition.

'She said all the men were gone.' Marco declared absently. He looked at Hernandez's poor, beautiful, dead face. Their non-consummated moment in the car in the storm came to him. Nights with Bonnie on the hood of his car completed the reverie. 'I guess shit went *Onibaba*.'

'*Shit went Onibaba*.' Borg repeated, flatly. 'What does that mean?'

'It's an old Japanese movie, where these two chicks dump a bunch of dead Samurai in a hole.'

'Does anything come out of that hole of yours that ain't out of some movie? Borg began to climb out of the vault. 'You sound like you're trying to escape yourself.' The agents followed Borg up out into the world.

'Hey!' Marco protested. 'We can't just leave her here.'

They all ignored him and left him alone with the dead. Marco placed his hand on the girl's head, prayed a prayer of nothing then searched the inside pocket of her jacket. He found the car keys he was looking for, then followed the others up into the world.

# .38 UNHOLY REUNION

15:45

Figuring Borg and Mascini had exhausted their use, the agents left them to it and edged around the ongoing siege. Members of the task force were still dug in behind the Panhards. Brief exchanges of gunfire popped and clattered. Desert dust and gun smoke drifted across the plain.

Strauss crawled up the hill to watch the action. Portland got in the car and radioed the Comisaria Todos Santos. 'We got a Priority 5—running hot...' It took a moment before he could generate whatever it would take to form the next words. He knew Hubbard's wife. She was in his Science and Geometry class at Stephen F. High. He wondered who they would send to knock on her door. Into the handset he managed a 'matter of fact' tone. 'We've found Agents Hubbard and D'Oyley... They're both dead. We'll need a recovery team to come down here, but we have a siege at the murder site, between an unidentified paramilitary force and the people that live at the ranch. Repeat: we have a Priority 5. I think we have the CIA, or some other governmental entity down here fucking around, so the lines of command are unclear. Tell HQ I'll call 'em direct with more when we back to town. In the meantime, can you find someone to clarify our jurisdiction?'

In the eight seconds it took for someone to answer him, he thought of the bodies in the vault. There was too much going down already to throw that into the mix. Its implications suggested epic proportions. He would report this later. Whoever was on the other end of the line said, 'si. Yes, sir. Relaying now.'

Strauss got in the car. Portland turned the ignition.

Whoever killed Peggy Deveroux was still at large, and Erika Extravaganza was still a suspect. But they had found their missing men and, probably, their killer. So, if they were to be tasked with finding Deveroux's killer, so be it. But right now, they didn't care if it got handed it over. Put some other saps on the taco circuit.

They hit the highway. The Delegación Municipal called back; told them they had just received word that Extravaganza is at the Teatro-Cine Theatre. 'Do you want to us to pick her up?'

'No. Just get someone over there and make sure she doesn't leave. We're on our way.'

Plumes of black smoke continued to billow up into the endless sky as Marco and Borg trudged back across the graveyard to Hernandez's car. An explosion threw rubble into the air. Even here, half a mile away, fragments rained down. Clearly, negotiations were not going well. Marco said, 'There are kids in there!'

'Yeah. You said that before.'

They got to the ridge. The car sat like a pet waiting for an owner that would never come. They got in. Marco took the driver's seat and twisted the ignition. He half expected the engine to splutter and die, but it choked into life. He drove the car around the inside perimeter of the ranch, found the unguarded entrance that he and Hernandez had come in by last night, and followed the half-filled irrigation ditch back to the 19.

He paused at the edge of the highway. 'We're done, right? You wanted to find her and make her dead. Someone saved you the trouble. Congratulations.'

Borg stared ahead. Marco wondered if he was about to have another one of his seizures.

'Borg?'

Borg snapped out of it. 'Take me back to town.'

Beyond his demand to return, Borg said nothing during the ride. The crashed vehicles on their oil cans whizzed by like a pantheon of autogeddon. News trucks raced past them in the opposite direction—headed to the burgeoning carnage taking place at the ranch. The town loomed into view. Borg unscrewed a thermos and washed down one of his pills. Marco hit the brakes and skidded to a halt. 'Those beach houses...'

Borg looked around. 'This where they picked you up last night?'

'Around here somewhere. It's a fair bet that whoever killed Deveroux went there. I wanna see—'

'No. Afterwards.'

'After what?'

'Drop me off in town. You wanna go there afterwards, s'up to you.'

Marco drove on. Borg navigated.

'Take a right on Obregon, then second left.'

Marco struggled to see the signs. The road was barely a road in some places—pocked-marked with craters and unfinished sidewalks.

'Right, here!' Borg yelled.

'Where are we even going?'

They took a few turns deeper into the town until Borg said, 'Stop!'

The building looked like a casino, painted orange with stripey white pillars flanking the big glass doors. Borg got out of the car, grabbed the hold-all with its torn-off leg from out of the trunk, and headed for the entrance of Saint Judes Medical Center.

Marco wound down the window and shouted after him, 'We done?!'

Borg ignored him and disappeared inside. Concealing the holdall with his thick forearm, Borg flashed Portland's badge to the solitary girl in the sky-blue uniform at the desk. Told her he was here to see Espinoza in Pathology. She pointed the way, without static. He found his way down grimy corridors, the air warm with the smell of Clorox and sugary deserts. Staff and patients alike ignored him. They had ailments to cure and recover from. A series of swing doors led him to fifteen steps down... to the morgue. He peered inside. Espinoza was gone, and there was no one else. He took the severed leg out of the holdall and put it on the side. He jammed a chair against the door and slid open the big stainless-steel files built into the wall—two rows of four—flanked by two larger ones on either side.

Most were empty.

Three were old men.

The fourth was no more than a ribcage, a pelvis and both femurs.

The fifth was the one.

She slid out of her vault like a prize in a game show. After three decades, Leonard Borg was alone with his quarry. He pulled off the sheet and gazed at the smashed corpse that had once been the Queen of the Pin-ups. He placed the severed leg, with its scared calf, beneath the stump where it should have been. It flopped on its side; the foot pointing inward, stupidly. He gazed at her collapsed breasts; her bruised black stomach, greying mons and wondered at the ballpark tonnage of doomed spermatozoa this woman had inspired during her lifetime. He wondered if this would count against her in the next life or make her a new god.

Her jaw had been completely impacted into the back of her throat, but from her top teeth upwards, she was unscathed.

She'd had work.

It was good.

Expensive.

Recent.

If he were given to pathos, he might feel it now for the old woman who had gone to the knife in a desperate attempt to recover her power; to please cameras she hoped would be kind.

And now, once again, his entire being was loaded with her as it was thirty-one years ago. The lazy right eye. The high forehead, disguised by those bangs. The little things evoked her; crossed the decades and beckoned him to the shore of himself—as it once did, back to his comatose body in 1963.

Then he drifted further, back to 1957, back to her New York apartment.

Cold dusty rooms...

The demented chessboard floor...

Absorbing her...

Becoming her...

... finding her rhythms.

236

He stripped off, leaving his clothes in a heap on the floor, and climbed onto her. His perspiring chest and hips welcomed her clammy skin. Her rough pubic hair bristled against his raging prick... He laid his cheek against her cold, collapsed chest, and waited for her essentialness to come to him... De beaux rêves, mon amour...

# 39. HALLS OF HUBRIS

16:34

The town square was desolate and abandoned. Over shattered tarmac, Portland pulled up outside the Teatro-Cine, in front of a dusty white 1984 Cadillac Eldorado, with cow horns on the hood.

They went inside and there she was: cool as a popsicle. So much for skipping town. Erika Extravaganza stood at the stage's apron with a small male entourage; a gay parade of slim-fit suits, cut to beg attention to the svelte man-boys within. Extravaganza wore a red silk shirt, open wide at the neck with a black pencil-skirt and kitten heels. The seams of her stockings rendered her legs sections of a model kit— Identikit components of a wet dream. She supervised the re-location of the on-stage mannequins of her idée fixe and science fiction twin. It appeared the show must go on. The fingertips of one slender hand to her pale chest, the other waved and flipped like a conjurer sprinkling mild miracles. The agents glommed it. This was not a woman with murders to run from.

A Federale from the Comisiria hung around the entrance and made a hash of trying to act casual while he kept an eye on her. The agents were mesmerised by Extravaganza's Peggy Deveroux facsimile. Looking at her was to be confronted with a living ghost *and* suffering hallucinations both at once. Being in the woman's orbit was a distortion of time... space... physics... They gazed up at the huge blow-ups that were hung around the hall. They saw the beach shot Borg had told them about.

Deveroux in a cream bikini, with black frills. Bare footed on white sand. Hands on hips. Pouting over a shoulder. That ass— probably considered big nowadays. Legs—probably considered short nowadays—were perfectly proportioned. Both men felt the torment of some primal need. Both felt some unspecified loss of themselves; even in the presence of a mere 15 x 13-foot dry-mounted photo. And there, as clear as the Miami summer day Deveroux once cavorted in, they saw it. A raised track of white tan-proof skin.

Right leg.

Right calf.

A couple of blow-ups along, another beach shot—hugging a palm tree, same scar. Absurd and obscene was the existential abyss between these images of carefree fantasy and the now smashed flesh and bone that lay in a file just a few blocks away.

It seemed they had made their positive ID.

Portland checked with the Federale in Spanish, 'Has anyone checked out those beach houses I asked about?' The Federale radioed it in, waited a beat and said, 'No' in English. Portland expected nothing less. Law and, especially Order, meant for shit down here.

They went over to interrupt Extravaganza's meeting. One of the man-boys, in a purple tonic suit, cha-cha heels and heavy make-up, saw them approach and smiled by way of a friendly interception. 'Hi.'

Strauss up-and-downed him. 'You ever been to Austin, son?'

'Noooooo,' the man-boy purred. 'Is that an invitation?'

Strauss had to smile. 'It's not, I'm afraid, sweet pea. I can give you some advice, though. Don't ever come to Austin in that getup.'

Man-boy fluttered lashes. 'Why not? Your daddy can't get enough of it.'

Strauss sneered by way of a limp response and turned to Extravaganza. He brandished his badge and asked if there was some place they could talk. She left her entourage with some final directions and led the agents to a backstage office.

Desk.

Shelves.

Neat.

Orderly.

Many shades of grey.

The agents blended right on in.

They took their positions.

Portland flanked the door.

Strauss asked her to sit down.

She remained standing. 'Do you mind if I smoke?'

'Not at all. Please...' Strauss flipped out his Zippo. Extravaganza tapped out a Capri, accepted Strauss' light and drew big and slow.

Strauss led. 'How long had you known Deveroux?'

She let the nicotine hit her system as she pondered. 'Couple of years? But until about a month ago, our involvement was strictly long distance.

'How did it come about? This involvement?'

She hesitated and seemed to find the ceiling of interest. Strauss was quick to interrupt the appraisal. 'Miss Extravaganza?'

'I got a call from her out of the blue in New York. She didn't say who she was at the time, but she asked me when I would be back in Mexicali. Somehow, she knew I had been there.'

'Any idea how she would know this?'

'At the time, no. Later, of course, I realised that she was visiting the same clinic, and this, apparently, is where she first saw me. So much for patient confidentially... She told me she would very much like to meet me and that *I* would very much like to meet *her*. I asked her to elaborate, but she kind of changed the subject and then asked me a lot of questions about Peggy Deveroux. I realised the implication... that this woman was claiming to be her... so, as you can imagine, I was intrigued. Anyhoo, long story short—and a lot of phone calls later, we finally arranged to meet.'

'Which was when?'

'August? Mmmmm, might have been... September.'

'Okay...'

'I met her at a Mexicali diner. She was already there, alone, waiting when I arrived. She seemed excited. Not so much with meeting me, but with what she wanted to tell me—which was who she was. It was kind of sad. She wore a sweat suit and sneakers. She wasn't in great shape. I'd say she'd had it rough. She had something of the jailbird manner about her. Of course, now I know that was pretty much the case. Obviously, I was suspicious as to her identity. That it may have been some kind of a stunt. I played along and asked her if she would be interested in appearing in public again, and she was all for it. I figured that even if she was just some joker pulling a scam, then a highly publicized event would smoke out the real Peggy Deveroux, if she was still around. But as I got to know her, it became clear she was the real deal. I have come to know many of her old associates in New York and too much tallied to be a put on.'

'These appointments at the clinic... Can I ask what they were for?'

'Whose? Mine or hers?'

'Both.'

'No, you cannot. Hers, I wouldn't know.'

'You realise we can easily find out?'

'Then knock yourself silly, Agent Strauss.'

'So, this first meeting. What else did you talk about?'

'Well, at first, she repeated pretty much the same questions she asked me over the phone, and then asked me about my obsession with Peggy Deveroux. I explained that it wasn't really an obsession, as such. I had just capitalised on my likeness and became a big fan in the process. And who wouldn't be intrigued? By the mystery of it? Of her disappearance? Most people who disappear leave a big dark hole. Deveroux left a beckoning light.'

'It's more than a *likeness,* Miss Extravaganza. Don't you give yourself the creeps just looking at yourself?'

'You're quite the flatterer.' She looked over at Portland guarding the door, who appeared to be transfixed. She was used to transfixion, so it didn't faze her.

'Don't mind him,' Portland offered. 'I won him in a game.'

'The booby prize, I take it.'

Strauss brought it back. 'I understand you were having some kind of disagreement with Deveroux. What was it about?'

'We'd been having a dispute about someone she wanted to attend the event, the host of some TV show. Lucy Hartman. Showtime Tonight. Heard of it?'

Both agents shrugged negatives. Extravaganza dragged on her smoke and blew slow.

'For some reason, the delectable Miss Deveroux felt that Hartman's presence at the show was essential. By now, we'd invested a lot of blood, sweat and tears in this thing, so we looked into it… couldn't get past her agent. Deveroux was having none of it. She was adamant that she would not appear without Hartman.'

'And you have no idea what her involvement with this Lucy Hartman was?'

'To be honest with you, I don't think she was involved with her at all. I don't believe she had ever met her. I don't think she had even spoken to her on the phone. When we spoke to the agent…'

'Hartman's agent?'

'Yes. The name Peggy Deveroux certainly didn't seem to elicit any interest or recognition.'

Extravaganza dragged again and stubbed out the cigarette in the ashtray.

'Personally, for reasons I am not privy to, I think she baulked at appearing at the eleventh hour and the whole Lucy Hartman angle was an excuse to not appear.'

'What would make her… *baulk*, as you put it?'

'I have no idea. Maybe the size of the event spooked her. This was only meant to be a low-key event, a glorified photo shoot. I think we were all stunned by the media reaction to it. Ill-prepared to say the least. And then, with Deveroux's insistence of hiring a local biker gang for security… well…' Extravaganza shrugged, helplessly. '… untold carnage was a given.'

Realising she was assessing the situation aloud, she changed direction. 'Can I assume you know she did jail time, right?'

'Yeah, you said. Last night, up at the ranch. Did you see what happened to Mascini?'

'Who's Mascini?'

'Part of your group that flew in from N.Y.?'

'One of the reporters? Longish black hair. Thirtyish. Italian looking?'

'Well, Italian looking, for sure.'

'He did turn up at the ranch last night. At the temple, saying that some girl needed help.'

'What time was this?'

'Around… midnight?'

'Then what?''

'I guess… they went to help the girl. I left.'

'A girl needed help, and that didn't get your interest?'

'Detective…' Extravaganza sighed. 'Up at that ranch, it was a cavalcade of chaos. Most of them were on drugs, I think.'

'So, you left and did what?'

'I came back here.'

'To the theatre?'

'No. I have an artist friend I'm staying with, in El Pescadero.'

'He bring you back?'

'*She*. No, I drove myself.'

'No-one with you?'

'No.'

'Where's your car?'

'Out front.'

'The Eldorado with the tinted windows and cow horns on the hood?'

'It's hired, but yes, that's the one. Agent…?'

'Strauss.'

'Agent Strauss, are we done? I have a show that must go on.'

# 40. NO OPEN CASES

5:59pm

J unk washed up against the shore—totems of a mass psychotic breakdown. It took him back. To Coney Island.

One Sunday afternoon, a couple of years ago, when the beach was awash with medical supplies.

The beach houses were derelict, one-floor bungalows. Seven of them. Identical. Two bedrooms, a bathroom, and a lounge area. Fifty years ago, this was probably some kind of resort. The invading media had trashed them and added another fifty years of dereliction in half a weekend. Whoever killed Deveroux last night may well have headed here after dumping the truck.

But then what? Could they still be here?

He searched the huts and found only booze bottles, food wrappers, car batteries, soiled underwear… In one, he found a deflated blow-up doll in a Peggy wig. In another, someone had taken a shit in the middle of the floor.

Fucking animals.

Out on the beach, near one of many still-smouldering bonfires, half stuck in the sand, he found a half-empty litre bottle of Jack Daniels. He inspected it. Opened and sniffed. Beautiful and kosher. The drink lined his innards.

Again. Elvis concert.

That inner scream…

The archways leading into the resort area presented the nearby highway in episodes, balmy and idyllic, an oasis away from the post-riot desolation of Todos Santos.

He slugged the Jack again and saw Echo Hernandez dancing across the sand. What she said…. He tried to envision himself on a surfboard. The absurdity held fast. The impossible fantasy of her, dead as she was; of her long, tanned legs wrapped around him as they fucked in the dunes was still a more likely scenario than Marco Mascini making like Dennis Wilson.

He watched a couple cavorting in the sea. A middle-aged man with a girl too young for him. The girl's heavy hips and short solid legs seemed to contradict her small breasts. The last time he'd seen a woman in a bikini was when he and Bonnie went swimming at the West Side YMCA.

Bonnie… She had come to him in the moment of certain death.

*She had come to me in the moment of certain death.*

From the direction of the town, Marco saw a big man walking towards him. The looping gait—limp not withstanding—suggested joviality. It was Borg, barefoot, with his duffle bag over his shoulder and holding his boots. Borg stood beside him and watched the couple, who splashed and laughed.

Marco broke the silence. 'Happy birthday, by the way.'

'What?'

'According to your driver's licence. Or is that phony too?'

'Ha. Oh yeah…'

'Where did you go?'

'Oh… a little party.'

Clearly the celebrations were over. 'What the fuck is happening up there, Borg? At the ranch?'

Borg put his bag down and put his boots on top. 'Just a good old-fashioned show-and-tell. It's like I told them Feds— *'exaggerate the threat to justify the means'* routine. That's how they launch any new directive. It's how they launched the FBI back in the thirties. Strauss and Portland could tell you all about that. Fuckin' hillbillies. The war on crime… Hoover picked a buncha two-bit crooks at random, got the papers to front-page their efforts, gave 'em crazy names, 'Pretty Boy Floyd, Machine Gun Kelly or whatever; let 'em run wild for few months, then it's cleanup time. Boom! The Federal Bureau of Investigation are go! Korean war? Same thing. All Commie considerations aside, if that conflict was about anything, it was about selling a shit load of F-94s… M20s. The Massacre of Pineda Ranch, Mr. Mascini, is about to enter the pantheon of folk-law, but at heart, it's a marketing campaign. In the end, everything is. There are cults, communes and Cartel factions like this all over the place and they've got 'fair game' written all over 'em. The important thing *is*, is that they're nobodies. No-marks. You use 'em for target practise; show whoever you're trying to impress what you got, and in comes the backing. This world spins on the weapons industry. Beyond a few squeaks of protest in the press, everyone will have forgotten about the Pineda Ranch Massacre within a month. 'S'pecially down here.'

For Marco, all this rang right. Borg's concise secret history of America evoked Chiang Mai and the engine room, where the controls behind the alleged 'free west' were operated in the shadows of the third world. It was clear to him now; Jimmy Farragher was some kind of spook handler, for some agency or organisation that the world at large will probably never hear of.

'The CIA… FBI probably…' Borg continued, '… are about to take the presidency and they're gearing up for some major moves down here. They need some on-site muscle they can control so they're bankrolling some heavy artillery. They'll sell it as a 'war on drugs' enterprise or whatever, but first they need some working demos; show and tell. And, if the truth be told, this is one of many dress rehearsals.'

Marco was still wondering what M94s and M20s were, but figured they were some kind of military hardware. 'So how come you're so clued up?'

'My daddy was one of the first Feds and I was in Korea. Seen it all for myself. Aggressive marketing. That's all it ever is.'

'What do you mean, the *FBI are about to take the presidency*? The election ain't' till next month. No one knows what's gonna happen.'

'Get real. Dukakis? Get the fuck… Ronnie's cleared the floor for ol' Georgie boy. Bush is an old ex-Fed. The perfect facilitator for what's about to go down here. And when I say here, I mean *here*. Mexico, and shit holes just like it.' Borg let Marco suck it up. 'You got my pills?'

Marco fished them out of his satchel and handed over the L-Dopa. Borg didn't ask for the gun, which was still in his jacket—or for Deveroux's stuff, the rap sheets and cassettes—which were still in the car.

Borg put the vial in his bag. 'What happened to your wife, Mascini?'

Marco's immediate and angry surprise quickly melted into acquiescence. 'You *even* know about *her*?'

'Only that you were married for about eight seconds.'

245

Marco slugged. Swallowed. 'She was a phony.'

'She was a phony when you *married* her? Or she *became* one?'

Marco swigged the bottle again. Acquiescence... anger...

'Fugazi through and through. From womb to tomb.'

Marco slugged a third time and offered the bottle to Borg. 'If you're so juiced in, you could probably find out about my mom.'

Borg, ignoring the bottle, said, 'What happened to her?'

'That's it, I don't know. She was Cuban, living in Florida, illegally. Had me and got sent back. Trail goes cold. If you can find Peggy Deveroux after thirty years, you could find her.'

'Why would I do that?'

'To show me how *worldly fuckin' wise* you are. You got the 'in' on everything. Riddle me that one, prick.'

Borg zoned out and stared into nothing. Marco shot him a look of disgust that died in its own moment. Finally, Borg came back. 'They're going ahead with it, you know. The show tonight.'

'What? How? Without Deveroux?'

'Operation save ass. The show must *always* go on.'

'I want to see it,' Marco declared. 'Remember her as she was; not that maniac that tried to kill me last night.'

'Rehabilitate her.' Borg muttered vacantly. 'Re-energize and rehabilitate *your* Peggy Deveroux.'

Marco looked up into Borg's freakishly smooth face, waiting for the punchline, or the point. Borg seemed to have forgotten that he had even spoken, so Marco headed for the huts. It was shelter, and the floor would do just fine. He had already decided which one he was going to use; the one furthest away from the one someone shat in. He could see Borg out there, gazing at the ocean. He stuck his jacket deep under the bed and used his satchel as a pillow. Darkness began to creep up around him. He let it come and take him wherever it would. The show was at 9pm tonight and the plane home was tomorrow at noon. He would head back to Cabos straight after the show and sleep in the airport car park if need be. If he gave a fuck, he would wonder what Borg was going to do now. But he didn't, so... he didn't.

When he awoke, it was night-time. Or at least it was dark. It took a moment to make sense of the big form sitting with his back to him. That shot-up elephant in Chiang Mai, its huge sad vermin-infested outline against the setting sun, drifted across the desolation of his half sleep.

'Borg?' Marco sat up and shook some of the funk out of himself. 'What the fuck are you doing?'

Borg didn't look around but handed something back in his ham-like fist.

'Take it. I'm ready.'

Cautiously, Marco held out his hand and Borg dropped the Ruger into it.

The gun was cold and heavy in his hand, like it understood the gravity of itself.

Borg said it again. 'I'm ready. Let's go.'

'Ready for what?'

Borg spat the words over the hill of his shoulder. 'Don't fuck with me, Mascini. Time to close the account.'

Marco could sense the beginning of an episode. He saw the tiny, half-lidded eyes and the same vacancy he'd seen when the man had nearly strangled him in the Chieftain. Maybe a change of tack would divert this coming storm. Marco put the gun on the floor and got up.

'Let's go find a bar.'

Borg arose like a one-man storm. 'I said don't fuck with me!' His arm shot out like a jackhammer, grabbed the chest of Marco's t-shirt, swung him around and threw him through the wall.

Unconsciousness was a walk down memory lane in an old, familiar neighbourhood. He pondered the likelihood of permanent damage. What actually happens to the body when all senses are forcibly shut down? Marco likened the process to that of leaping from a car before it crashes. The essentialness saves itself and leaves the vehicle to crash and burn. The damage he'd sustained was yet to be known. A recollection of plasterboard giving way at the impact of the side of his face brought with it a sharp jolt, a hot wire from somewhere behind his ear all the way down his right side to behind his knee, and onward to his pulsating punctured foot. The smell of damp concrete helped beckon him to sentience.

There was a hissing sound.

Escaping gas?

Something brushed his face.

Something scuttled across his forehead. A violent reflex action shook his head.

Something scuttled down his neck. Under his shirt...

His hands were a-buzz with movement.

His entire body shivered with violations unknown.

His eyes flashed on and open and struggled with the dim light.

He was in the bath.

The black water shimmered and enveloped him in a way that defied his understanding. Logic, horror and all five senses collided in a crescendo of shock.

Then he understood.

His scream went to splutter. The bugs were in his mouth. His terror propelled him out of the tub and through the hole in the wall that Borg had smashed him through. He spat and spat. Chunks of writhing bugs stuck in his teeth. He ripped off his t-shirt and whacked it against the wall; against his leg; his back. He ripped his pants down and stamped at the legs until they were off him. He slapped them out of his hair. He stepped back through the hole in the wall and tried the sink taps. They coughed dust. He ran out of the hut and threw himself into the sea. The cold water jerked him back into himself. Panic abated and reason returned. He crawled back to the sand.

He stood at the hut door, livid, freezing wet, and peered inside. The tiled floor was littered with broken, wriggling bug pieces. The tub still writhed, a glossy surface of black. The realisation that he'd been submerged in it made him heave. His guts were near empty. He retched bile over the unholy scuttling mess. He became aware that Borg was still sitting there, on the floor in the corner, still lost in whatever reverie that consumed him. He didn't look up when he said 'Relax. You must've disturbed a cockroach nest when you went through that wall.'

248

Naked, but for his sneakers, Marco flew across the room, grabbed the gun off the bunk and put it against Borg's forehead. 'I oughta whack your fucking mind right outta your fucking head!'

Borg got up and faced him, pressed the middle of his eyebrows against the barrel.

'*Now* you're talking, tough guy! C'mon! What are you waiting for? No open cases, right?!'

*Crime-scene litany: Borg lay spread-eagled before him—churned brain and skull pieces pebble-dashed the walls and floor—bug pieces everywhere, crawling aimlessly...*

*An alternative timeline...*

The overloaded switchboard of Marco's brain geared down. He closed the portal. He lowered the gun.

'No open cases? Am I *supposed* to kill you? What is this? You gone samurai? Is this how it works? Black ops, or whatever the fuck this is? Shutting you down is the big closer?'

Borg looked at him. 'There are sleepers and there are sleepers...'

Marco aimed the gun at the nightmare in the tub—visible through the hole in the wall. 'Sleepers? I must be so asleep I'm in a coma.' He fired six shots. Bam! Bam! Bam! Bam! Bam! Bam!

Borg stood up, steadied himself against the bathroom doorjamb, and looked at the tub of unaffected bugs. 'You're about fifty thousand bullets short.'

Marco sat down and took a big swig from the whiskey. He sat and nursed it and let the drink settle inner riots. He offered Borg the bottle. 'Do yourself a favour. Please.'

Borg eyed Marco with diminishing, watery eyes and slugged one. Then another. Fuck the meds. Borg took the bottle to the door, slugged again, looked out to sea and said, 'There is no way on God's green earth that you are the random element you're trying to make out. No. Fucking. Way.' Borg handed back the bottle. Marco said, 'Keep it. I'm going to see the show.' Marco, now dressed, grabbed his satchel, and stomped off towards the town, muttering under his breath, 'Enjoy the trip, fucko.'

The bodies from the ranch started arriving now. From the steps of the Delegación Municipal, Strauss and Portland watched the motorcade roll into town. The body bags had been unceremoniously thrown onto a cortege of flatbed trucks, which made their way to Saint Judes Medical Center's morgue. Both wondered which of them contained the bullet riddled Captain Gael Mendez.

A provisional calm had returned to the town. The biker gangs were gone. Most of the marauding news crews had found some compensatory pay off with the Pineda Ranch Massacre. On entering the reception Strauss was met by Mendez's man on desk duty, Sergeant Pasquala. Strauss told him he was sorry about his captain. Pasquala nodded a vague acceptance of Strauss' commiserations and told him, 'The prints have arrived.'

Pasquala handed the fax to Portland, who placed them on the desk without interest. They had seen the blow-ups. The scar on the calf. There was no need to over-egg the souffle.

The squad room vibed aftermath. The personnel oozed exhaustion. Activity in the office continued to buzz. If anything, it had increased exponentially to the new equilibrium outside. Portland made coffee. Strauss sat at the desk they had commandeered as their centre of operations. Strauss pencilled bullet points for his over-the-phone report of what they had on the murders of Agents David James Hubbard and Antoine Marcus D'Oyley. Unhinged psychopathy had reigned up at the Pineda Ranch, so the full report would be a doozy. Portland put their black coffees on the desk and produced a bottle of Wild Turkey. 'Let's load these fuckin' things.' They didn't say it, but they sipped the scolding drink and toasted their fallen men. Strauss picked up the faxed paper with Deveroux's prints. One half of his mind seemed to stop for a split second, creating a stuttered echo in his mind's eye. His cognition synchronized... and he saw it.

The prints from the body in the morgue were absolutely and categorically... *not* from Peggy Mae Deveroux.

## PART 2

# 41. ZOMBIE BOULEVARD

### 1985
### Saturday May 18th

The burial ground stretched off until it became the foothills of San Bernardino, which dissolved up into the heavens. Once upon a storybook this would have been Eden.

Peggy Mae Deveroux worked the orange grove north to the asylum which neighboured the graveyard—the final resting place of the unclaimed patients. She toiled out there for as long as they would let her, churning the earth and pruning the trees until the cows came home. Or in this case, orderly Alice 'The bull-dyke', bleating threats and waving everyone back inside at the day's end. You couldn't see her cattle-rod and hypodermic, but Peggy knew Alice had them secreted somewhere on her person.

Alice put Peggy in charge of the group—six human wrecks with at least some semblance of bodily control—utilising her natural enthusiasm for the dirt—an enthusiasm which she imparted with conscientious determination to the sextet in her charge. Some of her happiest memories were working her garden into the early hours, back in Florida, when Larry gave her a room at the back of the house long after their marriage crashed and burned.

She took a rare break and leaned on the spade. Her bad shoulder and hip protested these endeavours, but they were just parts of her body, and her body was not important. Everything but her failing physicality spoke to her now, and the majesty of the distant mountains were no exception. It had taken twenty years to admit the unthinkable. But the one

252

upside of insanity was that nothing was unthinkable. So, she could damn well go ahead and think it.

*God was insane.*

The prophesies declared it. And as soon as the notion came down from the mountains, into her brain and found itself on her tongue, she could *say* it.

'God was insane.'

And because she could say it... she knew it was true.

The television room was usually busy by eight o'clock on Saturday nights, but this evening was a rare exception to Patton State Hospital's many rules. She had the room to herself, so she placed herself front-row and centre. The weekend edition of Showtime *Tonight* had been her weekly ritual for the eighteen months she'd been sent back here.

The television set was bolted high in the centre of the wall. Lucy Hartman co-hosted the show and exuded just the right balance of piety and glamour, as clearly announced by a wardrobe of pastels and lipsticks that rarely erred beyond *'don't kiss me. Don't ever fucking kiss me!'* shades of magenta and cream.

But the words Peggy waited for and would memorise until she could get back to her dormitory were not from Lucy's carefully maintained mouth, but from off-screen, from her vagina, from where the Seven Apostles issued forth their prophesies. For reasons it was not Peggy's to question, the talk show host's reproductive organs were a receiving device connected to the Aural Corridor: a dimension in which all the sound that has ever been made on Earth was trapped. The Aural Corridor was the barrier between this world and the next. Somehow, unbeknown to Lucy Hartman, her uterus was tuned into these prophesies and was the vessel through which they were delivered into Peggy's fevered mind. It was Peggy's fate to be charged with the mission of recording the prophesies, which she would one day deliver to a wanting world.

The TV star discharged her messages, which spilled in liquid neon from the bottom of the warping screen and spread across the floor like a flood. Peggy removed her moccasins and let the sound fizz between her toes. Her feet sucked the words like sponge and her brain swelled with knowing. Time died in those moments, and she was soon giddy with beatific scripture. After forty-five minutes, the show ended, and on quaking legs she got up fast and headed for her dormitory. Thankfully, the hallways were quiet tonight. Clearly, something was happening elsewhere on the ward. Only Maud Pafko, twittering inanely into a corner, and some of the girls from the opposite dorm, shuffled aimlessly across Zombie Boulevard, the patient's name for the main concourse, which connected the four dorms and the nurse's station.

With urgent steps, Peggy made it to her bunk without interception. Any interruption or delay could result in forgetting precious fragments of the prophesies before they could be put to paper.

Of the twenty-two beds in her dorm, only five of them were occupied—three asleep and two reading. She was fortunate that her bed was on the far right-hand corner. Her endeavours were easier to conceal from intrusive eyes. She got under the covers, facing the wall. She glanced over her shoulder. Manny Leigh was lost in one of her well-thumbed romantic novels. Sarah Crank, her large, slightly bent-to-one-side nose, buried in a magazine. One of the sleeping three snored like a broken engine. Peggy reached down into the gap between her bunk and the wall. She flipped up the tile and retrieved the notepad and pencil. She got under the sheets and glanced at the room again. Confidant she was being properly ignored, she scribbled in code as fast as she could. Her mind overflowed, and her hand struggled with the information as it gushed down the subways of her flabby arm. In minutes, the entire right side of her body ached. But her body could go to hell because her spirit's place in God's glory was already signed, sealed, and delivered.

She cursed the fact that her tapes, of the original prophesies, were lost. The ones she had recorded before they put her away again. Would the cops still have them, or were they here in this hospital somewhere? She would open every session with her shrink, Dr Niedermeier, with an enquiry as to their whereabouts. But Niedermeier would plead ignorant, and they would endlessly explore their content; of her claims that she was being tormented by androids from the future. These androids, E Queens, as Peggy related it, had sex organs that could adapt and pro-generate with humans whose own genitalia would one day mutate into multitudes of new genders. Since the 1950s, way back before she got into all this trouble, E Queens had been sending her violently obscene letters written in a language she didn't know but somehow understood; with instructions on what they would do to her when they caught her. Things with gynaecological tools; tools designed to rip her apart and re-make her so that they could use her as a machine to produce more androids... more E Queens.

But here, in the hospital, she was safe. Her other selves, an army of faceless Peggys, stood guard every night outside her window. Only once did she look at them. She stood on the head of her bunk, while the rest of the dormitory slept, and peered through the meshed window at the fields outside. Legions of herself stood in silence, all facing her window, waiting. They wore their hair like she used to, years ago, in solid black bangs, but their faces were featureless, opaque and white. She knew that one day she would know what it was that they wanted from her. After that one night when she saw them, she never looked at them again. She knew they were always there and took comfort that the E Queens could never exact their horrific desires upon her.

## Sunday May 19th

She didn't know if it was the same for all the other wards throughout the complex, but on Unit 35, the patients had to be up and out of bed for nine a.m. Unless they were ill, very few exceeded this limit. But Peggy was one of the few. If not for the prophesies, she would sleep to the end of her life, until the Lord, insane as he was, called her. Only the rustle of hard starched uniforms, the squeak of sneaker on polished chequered tiles, and the pills that rattled in their paper cups disturbed the order of the ward. The few dashes of colour, the blue of the four big rugs and the green of the curtains whispered in pastels. Even the total imperialism of white throughout the building never gleamed; it suggested in opaque degrees, much like its anesthetised residents. Ghosts who could barely haunt themselves. By the prescribed hour, Zombie Boulevard was a hustling, bustling concourse of activity. The nurses and orderlies went among the population, directing them to the lines for their medications, appointments, and the group therapies that they were to attend. It would take a lot of noise and a kick to the bed frame to turf out the slugabeds. And this morning, for Peggy, it was one of the new trainee nurses on bed-kicking duty.

She headed straight for breakfast, found a vacant table, and wolfed down the fried eggs and yogurt. She had the last of the week's three therapy sessions at eleven and, as always, would not do it, or anything else for that matter, on an empty stomach.

'Whut's the deal with them oranges?'

'Oranges?'

'We got a whole grove out there and they only find their way onto our plates once a week.'

Dr Phillip Niedermeier glanced reflexively at the window. Peggy usually opened these sessions asking about the tapes the police had confiscated from her when she was last arrested; to which Niedermeier always pleaded with all honesty to be oblivious. Today she had finally moved on… to oranges. Was this progress?

'I really have no idea.' Niedermeier added notes to his pad. 'I shall certainly make enquires for you.'

'Any news about my cassette tapes?'

Ah, there it was. 'Still nothing on that front, Peggy, I'm afraid.'

Niedermeier was tall—gangly—you could say. Peggy joked to herself that he wasn't balding, just so tall he was growing through his hair. He wore suits in varying shades of grey; perhaps eager to avoid leading these sessions by wearing anything that might be considered mentally incendiary. He blended in. His was to be an extension of his patient's egos and a mere soundboard for their untethered minds. He was not a fly on the wall. He *was* the wall. And the walls were all ears.

After eighteen months of asking, Peggy's tape enquiry was rhetorical now, and she had given up on an answer. No. The question was a verbal tick. It had replaced, H*ello. How are you this morning?*

'Only once a week I get 'em. I love oranges! Whut's with that?'

Niedermeier let the question die on the ventilated air and then began.

'On Friday, we ended the session when we spoke about a curse that had been put on you in Haiti. Shall we begin with that?'

Peggy scrunched her face in confusion. 'We talked about *that*?'

'You don't remember? You had witnessed a voodoo ceremony and thought you had been cursed because of it. I'd like to continue with that.'

Peggy rolled the words around in her head, searching for the file that contained *Haiti* and *last Friday*. 'Oh yeah. We did. Talk about it...' She let the recollections fully arrive. 'You'll haveta forgive me, Phil. Whatever they make me take of a mornin' slows everthin' down a little.'

Niedermeier waited, doubtful of the claimed amnesiac effects of the chlorpromazine she was prescribed. The more coherent patients often revealed to conceal. Deveroux was certainly in that category.

'Haiti... It was just after I left mah furst husban, 1947. I got a job down there and pretty soon I was lovin' it up with a guy.' She chuckled and winked mischievously, 'Whut y'might call a *torrid affair*...'

'What would *you* call it?'

Peggy smiled with the recollection. 'I'd call it just that; a Torrid affair.' Then she sighed and shrugged. 'Another louse. Married.'

'So how did witnessing a voodoo ceremony come about?'

Peggy composed herself with a theatrical huff, but Niedermeier suspected she was also composing what she was about to tell him. He crossed his long legs.

'We'd gone exploring,' Peggy said. 'Went up the mountains, walking for hours. Mighta bin days. I cain't recall. But it was nighttime. And it was hot. We hid out in the jungle and watched the goin' ons in a clearing through the trees. It was just like one a them 'ol Paul Robeson movies, or King Kong or sumthin'. They had these big drums beatin'. I mean it whuz *real* loud! Y'know what I mean? And everone was hollerin' around, dancin' it up around a buncha fires. In the middle they had a circle of platforms, made outta bamboo an' whatnot, and they brought these girls out, black as ants and bare ass naked and got 'em to lie back on these platforms. Then this big guy, don't know if he was the chief or sumtnin', but he had this big mask on with plumes of feathers going everwhere. He was naked too, 'cept for this big mask. And he started… you know… puttin' it to these girls. Went from one to the other, stuck it in, humped her for a little bit, 'an moved on to next one. In the meantime, the louse, Mr. Torrid A-fair, was gettin' all hot watchin' this and got on me. I'd be lyin' if I said I minded, 'cos I sure did nhut…. out there in the jungle an all. But when he… you know… finished up… I felt something else inside me.'

Niedermeier ignored the expectation to noticeably respond to this revelation and continued to make notes. 'Beyond ejaculation?'

'Nah, I mean… yeah… that happened, but it was with sumthin' else. An it's bin with me ever since.'

'Can you describe *what* has been with you?'

'A darkness? Like a shadow across my soul. Sumthin' like that…' Peggy stared for a moment into the distant past. 'It wasn't the Devil exactly. I guess it's whatever the black folks have for a devil.'

258

'You don't believe we have the same devil; black and white people?'

'There's only one Devil...' She stared again. 'So... a demon, then. Maybe one o' his demons.'

Peggy slumped back in her chair as if newly exorcized.

Niedermeier scribbled and assessed the worn-out, overweight sixty-two-year-old woman before him. It was quite the performance. But it was the *usual* performance.

*Reveal to conceal.*

In their sessions, she always spoke freely. It never took much to get her to open up, to get her talking. But all her revelations wound up in a cul-de-sac of some extreme sex scenario. Peggy would divert his most innocuous lines of enquiry into some borderline pornographic fantasy. Maybe they happened. Maybe they didn't. Most likely a bit of one, bolstered by a bit of the other.

He'd covered her known history when she was admitted here for the first time in 1979. He understood that she had been some kind of model in her day. He began to explore the possibility that, with whatever beauty she had once possessed being irretrievably lost, she was now trying to compensate with these overt exploits. Was Deveroux attempting to extend her sexual prowess with these accounts? Was this some deluded attempt to seduce him? A final gasp of her waning powers?

*I can attract men!*

In one of their early sessions, she had talked about having been a member of various religious organisations and had offered herself up as a means by which she could seduce men into receiving Jesus as their personal saviour. She had claimed that she had saved hundreds via this method. She also claimed to have worked for Billy Graham. Niedermeier had to wonder what the evangelical superstar would have made of Miss Deveroux's endeavours.

'So, after the voodoo ceremony, when did you realise you were cursed?'

'Straight away. The guy I was working for tried to rape me. So, I left Haiti and went to New York, then a buncha guys tried to

259

rape me there too. From that day on everthin' I put my hand to turned to went to pot.'

'You were no more than... thirteen? When your father first molested you?'

Thrown by this sudden tangent, Peggy re-calibrated. 'Twelve. And he made me molest *him*.'

'But this was a long time before the curse. And your marriage—which had failed *before* your Haitian adventure.' Niedermeier let this sink in.

'*That* failure whuz a damn success in mah book!'

Niedermeier looked into Peggy's open face, framed by greying hair tied back into a neat bun. Her pale blue eyes, like a vibrant suburb of her high forehead, declared naïve innocence. He imagined that she had acquired some acting skill somewhere along her dubious journey. Or perhaps, like many patients in Niedermeier's experience, she was a natural actress.

'We're playing games again, aren't we, Peggy?'

Peggy sat up and met his earnest regard. 'Well... if we are, I guess we're both losin'.'

# 42. GODS AND HUSBANDS

The session finished. Peggy thanked Niedermeier for the flowers that his wife always sent her and went out onto Zombie Boulevard.

'Kike Claptrap...' is what Willy used to say. One of the few things her first husband said that made any sense, was that psychiatry was one big fat racket. '... a billion-dollar concern! Too many ah them perverts' livelihoods depend on it.'

She had to agree. All they did was turn everything upside down. If you hate something, it's because you really crave it. If you love something, or someone, deep down you really hate them.

Claptrap.

And kids wanting to have sex with their moms and dads? Sick. Sick. Sick. That might have been how it was in the Greek days, but no. Not now. And bringing up that stuff with her Pa? *He* was the one that wanted it, and *she* was the one that needed money for the movies. If she needed better proof that the Devil walked among us, she'd tell you to look no further than these dirty disciples of Freud. Yeah, she read up on all that. Back in her New York years, with the kind that hung around Igor's studio, the Beatniks on Bleeker; they all went for that sick stuff and tried to make her go for it too. Yeah, she knew what these doctors wanted. So, when feeling inspired enough, she'd give it to them, and a whole lot more. Just keep feeding them the dirty stories they wanted to hear, and they'd be happy. Her suicide attempts were none of their damn business. The creep landlords that lured her into their homes with promises of friendship and care, only to try and cut her up for the E Queens, were none of their damn business...

But she was slipping. Those oily louses had a way of getting under her skin. A way of making her say things. Things that are none of their damn business. And the drugs... You couldn't fight them drugs.


Monday. The morning stint: The psychiatrist's office was decorated in a trio of cool blues—before the 'H-Bomb white-out' of the annex and main wards of Unit 35—like an instalment of degrees between the generally crazy and the stone-solid freakin' bat-shit crazy.

Peggy typed with trained hands, reams of crazy-related administration. 10am to 12pm and 3pm to 5pm every weekday for her therapist Niedermeier and the little fat Dr Ben Simon. She could almost forget she was incarcerated. They had given her her old secretary's job back. Her desk was organised to a fault. The in/out trays were perfectly aligned with the edges of the desk. The typewriter was dead centre. The edges of the square vase were exactly the same distance from the corner edges of the desk's corner, creating a four-inch perimeter around the vase's base. Mrs Niedermeier's spectacular flowers transported Peggy like an old Hollywood movie. Peggy first

261

met Mrs Niedermeier in this office during a rare visit to her husband the first time they put her in here. For reasons that would remain forever mysterious, the doctor's wife was quite taken with Peggy, and from that day forth, sent them every week. Gazing at Mrs Niedermeier's Rhododendrons took Peggy outside of time...

Space...

Here....

... back to a time before all these doctors hung a big sign on her that said, *schizophrenia, paranoid type chronic*. But the ones who hung that sign had never known the glory of *Him*. *When God prepares us to meet him, he at first makes us mad.* She heard that somewhere. Or something like it... And knowing this made sense of why *He* had put her here. *He* was lost to madness, and in order to bring her closer to him had made her mad also.

*He* had been whispering to her for a long time. As far back as she would care to remember. But the first true epiphany was when she was making a movie back in the fifties, a wrestling short for the Krane's. She was struggling around on a tiled floor with another one of their top girls, Jane Prince, in their New York studio. The fight was energetic and spiteful, but being the professionals that they were, maintained big smiles.

They pulled hair.

Big smiles.

They spanked.

Big smiles.

They twisted... they strangled... they slapped... they... cracked!

Loud!

Jane fell hard on Peggy's knee and a wild high-heeled stiletto jagged deep into the back of her calf. The pain seemed to scream in like an explosion through the window. Patty, Jane and the cameramen fluttered around her in a blind panic. The doctor came and set up a hospital appointment for Monday. In the meantime, they got her home and put her to bed. But once she was alone, the scream became a soft voice, and it sang. It sang a song of revelation and it revealed that she would be

alright. It told her you don't need these doctors. You don't need
no hospital. And it was right. The pain was cast out and her
knee was cured, right there and then. She didn't go to no
hospital. You don't need doctors when you have *Him*. For the
raw scar she was left with, she was grateful. In time, you had to
really look to see it. But it was the proof that the accident
happened, and it was the mark of *Him*. It would be a long time
before she heard that voice again, and although many
calamities would befall her, she believed that it would never
leave her. She had questions… so many questions… but *He*
would stand mute in the corners of her consciousness. This
enraged her. But what could she do? Later, when she got
caught up in the Krane's obscenity trail, *He* watched her
agonise for sleepless months as she found herself embroiled in
their legal troubles. The Kefauver trials went on and on. Some
kid, an Eagle Scout, had strangled himself, having been
inspired by some of the bondage pictures he'd seen of her.
Finally, she was subpoenaed, hauled down to the courthouse to
testify, waited all day and all night and they never even gave
her a coffee. Then, after all that, told her they didn't want her
to testify after all.

  Then the first letter came. *He* stood in the corner as she read.
It contained diagrams of female reproductive organs, drafted
with an expert hand, with instructions of how her parts were
to be re-arranged using the same tools for mending machines.
She reported it to the cops, but they didn't do anything. She
received one letter every week for four weeks, then thankfully,
they stopped. But then there was a man who stood every night
under the streetlamp, staring up at her window. But then, like
the letters, he went away. She wanted the voice to sing to her
again. She'd finger the scar on her leg. It was still there, so she
knew she hadn't imagined that voice. But in moments of doubt,
she would taunt it to intervene. What would it take to make
*Him* speak to her again? Once she had to throw herself out of
her window for *Him* to finally respond. *He* had Mervin, one of
her many suitors, suddenly appear and catch her before she
cleared the sill, dragging her back into the apartment, kicking
and screaming. Months later Mervin killed his brother in a car

crash and his parents blamed her. She started to suspect that this presence that never left her was not *Him*, but the Devil.

Then the letters started up again. This time, the cops listened. She told them about the man who used to stand outside her window. They said it was a serial killer who they'd been after for years. A new letter told her to meet its writer and bring her bondage pictures for him. The cops told her to play bait. She agreed, and they intercepted some kid, a teenager. Questioned him and let him go. They closed the case, but the letters kept coming.

Weeks later, the same Federal agents grilled her about photos that were doing the rounds in the dirty bookstores around Times Square, the ones she did for the rich guys, the *between the legs* ones. Shush! She had relied on these louses' reputations and thought they would never bleat about them, but somehow some had got out. She knew the Feds had their own hard-on for her and were leaning on her for sex favours to make this new devilry go away. When she got that December '57 audition for RKO in L.A., she jumped at it. Anything to get out of town. The audition turned out to be another waste of time, a couple of Krane's 'special customers'—bona fide strangos. But when she got back, she saw someone waiting in her apartment. Was it a Fed? An E Queen? The Devil? Was he the same man who waited outside her window months earlier?

Even the next day, having spent the night in some doss house, and after arranging to stay with Beattie in Miami, a man was waiting for her at the station. She ran and had been running ever since. Hiding behind gods and husbands, to no avail. They always caught up with her. But here in the hospital, she was safe. Her silent army stood on guard outside. *He* had gone insane and abandoned not only her, but all of humanity. The Prophesies of the Seven Apostles would show us how to find *Him*: free him from the chains of madness and bring him back to the fold.

# 43. DARK WHITE

## Saturday May 25th

The television room, Saturday night. The spirit was with her, and it was time for the next instalment of the prophesies. Unlike last week, she now had company. Two wheelchairs—each containing a long-vacated carcass—had been left either side of the door to fart and drool. They were chronics and unlikely to disturb her. Showtime Tonight's Co-Host, Paul Robb, wound up his on-the-scene coverage of San Bernardino's first female Mayor. Then it was back to the studio and Lucy…

Peggy took a deep breath and prepared herself for verse 12…

But the revelation she was about to receive snatched that breath right back out of her.

*'And next: A mystery which has endured for over a quarter of a century…'*

A full colour close-up of Peggy's face filled the screen. A crop of one of her old Beattie Yale shots.

*'In 1957, 'Queen of The Pin-ups' Peggy Deveroux, disappeared from the face of the earth. She featured on the cover of a thousand magazines and then suddenly… she was gone. We talk to some of the people who knew and worked with her and ask… whatever happened… to Peggy Deveroux?'*

At first, she assumed a neural hiccup in her meds had occurred when she heard Lucy saying her name. Then it was like an electro-jolt to the cerebral cortex when she saw her own shocking blue eyes fill the screen—or at least eyes from nearly thirty years ago.

The image drew back, revealing a Santa hat and a bauble-decked Christmas tree. Surely, they wouldn't reveal the entire picture, not here, not on Lucy's show. She recognised the image

265

from her Playboy centre-spread—Christmas edition 1955. She had only seen it once since it was published when, in an increasingly brief period of marital bliss, she'd dragged her second husband into a second-hand bookstore to see it. Mercifully, the image on screen faded before revealing her breasts but was replaced by a series of bikini beach shots. The images seemed to sear her retinas from across the decades. The entire wall hammered her vision until she realised that she was rocking to and fro—a dance of dementia. She smacked her palms down hard on the metal frame of the chair. The pain offered a bolt of clarity and control. Somehow, in the cacophony of Lucy's shame-born prophecy, Peggy located the narrative and caught something about the Kefauver mess, the obscenity trial...

Closing in...

Hot needles...

Red stop sign...

She knew her mind played host to many guests—hundreds—the ones who waited for her outside—her legion. But when she tried really hard, she could find herself among her inner crowd, cut the others out and know only what she should know.

As shocking as it seemed, Lucy was betraying her. She had somehow regained dominion over her prophecy-cunt and was now exposing Peggy to her devils—the E Queens—the ones who had pursued her all her life.

The two chronics by the door appeared oblivious. The old woman maintained her intense scrutiny at an awkward angle into the corner of the ceiling. The younger woman side-longed her with a knowing parrot-like appraisal, her tongue lolling lasciviously around her month, trying, and failing to contain an endless river of drool onto the sodden napkin tied about her neck. Peggy knew only that her name was Jeanette and that even if she had understood what she'd seen, she could never relate it. Just like she could never relate how the orderlies used her mouth.

Mercifully, the feature wound up with a few words from Hugh Hefner—who she never even met, let alone knew, who said something about her being 'an enduring icon...'and how he had no idea where she was now.

Lucy concluded the segment.

*'So, the mystery endures. Whatever did happen...'* She smiled engagingly. *'... to Peggy Deveroux?'*

They were onto her now.

If she stayed here, she would be engulfed, and the prophecy of the Seven Apostles would remain untold. It was only when she rose to leave the room that she noticed a chubby hippie-type with frizzy dirty-blonde hair sitting by the window, wearing a knowing smirk. If Peggy had a knife, she would put her fucking eyes out. She envisioned her hands around the woman's throat, choking every sputtering breath out of her. But the chemicals they obliterated her with had rendered her a big, useless jelly-baby. All she could do was quicken her pace out of the room. The woman was a patient and a familiar presence, but Peggy did not know her. She could only hope the obscurity remained mutual.

### Sunday May 26th

Normally she arose from a slumber worse than death, but not this morning. She had lain awake the entire night and watched the shadows from the trees outside slash her ceiling as relentlessly as she would like to slash that woman's face. For the first time in years, she stood at the head of the bed and peered out of the window. Her faceless legion was gone. She was alone now. Alone and defenceless.

The shadows faded, and Zombie Boulevard stretched and yawned. For once, Peggy rose before morning checks. She needed to find out who that woman was. She needed to sound her out.

*'I've only got a little face. A little face... It's only little. I've only got a little face...'*

What annoyed Peggy wasn't so much the endless repetition of Maud Pafko's inane mantra, but the fact that her face was, if anything, too big for her sparrow-like skull. During daytime hours, the woman shuffled around the Boulevard to announce it to all present as if for the first time. Her twittering was as innocuous as the faint smell of disinfectant as it rose from the floor like a continuous loop of music, so low as to not be music, more like a barely heard rumour.

*'Only a little face…'*

On this morning, Maud seemed to find the outside of Peggy's dormitory door particularly appealing. Peggy had to elbow her aside to get out.

She recalled seeing the frizzy-haired hippy in the art room a few days earlier, so began her search there. Sure enough, there she was, mauve smock, beaded bracelets, and sandals; her tied-back frizz, visible above the easel she stood behind in the corner. The wheelchair-bound Jeanette had been positioned next to her, seemingly enthralled by the artist's industry. Only the old chronic was missing from last night's Peggy Exposé posse.

Peggy approached the couple. An effective opener escaped her, but she found her mouth saying, 'Good morning.'

Neither woman answered. Neither woman took their eyes off the canvas.

It was only when the hippy said, 'You eatin' that?' did Peggy realise she was holding a plate of buttered toast and a beaker of milk; handed to her as she wandered absently through the canteen.

Until last night's encounter in the television room, Peggy had little to no previous recollection of the woman. But now, since she had inadvertently demanded her attention, memories came flooding back. *Those damn meds.* She even remembered her name: Arlene. She was always on the hunt for food, and any going begging had only minutes to exist.

'No.' Peggy offered. 'Do you want it?'

'Put it on the table.'

Milk and toast reminded Peggy of Larry, her third husband, the last man she hid behind. She felt she had a special talent for seeing through people but finding nothing lurked behind most of them was a curse. *The last man she hid behind*? He was transparent to a fault. How can you hide behind a fucking window?

Arlene's masterpiece was a fair attempt at Mickey Mouse with a revolver to his head and swastikas for eyes... in watercolours.

Arlene took a mouthful of Peggy's breakfast. She spluttered from the corner of her mouth and gestured to the picture. 'Wanna buy it?'

*Žiemelis.* That was her name; *Arlene Žiemelis.* Sarah Crank told her. Not only did Arlene claim to have been a member of Charles Manson's band of murderous hippies, but she also claimed that she *was* Charles Manson and had escaped jail by transporting himself into her body. The skewed irony of escaping jail, via the body of someone who is now similarly incarcerated, escaped Arlene as completely as ol' Charlie supposedly had from San Quentin.

Arlene had a big mouth and had been quite vocal about her intention to leave the hospital as soon as the mood took her. In fact, when she was first admitted all but five weeks ago, she made like George Raft in *Each Dawn I Die*. *'Just visiting, boys. Just visiting...'*

But now she asked Peggy, 'Are you in hiding?'

Peggy's mouth said, 'No' a long time before her mind did.

'Peggy Deveroux, huh?'

'It's a regular name.'

'Yeah,' Arlene scoffed. '*In fuckin' France*! So, you're famous. Kinda? Sorta? You an actress?'

The question jangled. This time, Peggy managed to ambush her tongue.

Arlene continued to daub thick swathes of red paint onto her pallet, 'How did *you* end up *here*?'

'Same ways as you did, probably,' Peggy countered.

'Via Transcendental teleportation? I doubt that. Speaking of which, I'm outta here. Like soon. But this time I gotta do it the old-fashioned way. Ley lines cross straight through here and

269

it's fuckin' with my powers. Gotta take this actual body with me. Come with. If you're on the run, you're a sitting duck here.'

'You're getting out? How?'

'This place has more holes than the Albert Hall, but when push comes to shove, a suck-job in the right direction'll get ya in an' outta most places.'

Peggy glanced at an orderly mopping the hallway floor. She looked at Jeanette, absorbed with Arlene's painting, oblivious to the statement. 'I don't think so.'

'Don't underestimate the power of a fall guy. Comes in handy if things go to shit.' Arlene continued to daub. 'Well, there's a 'Play and Shake' day trip into town next week. I'm going.' Arlene winked. 'Maybe you should too.'

Maud Pafko appeared and hovered between them.

'I've only got a little face...'

Arlene told her, 'Scram!'

The 'Play and Shake' was a bi-monthly therapeutic outing for the ward. It was felt by 'the powers' that a stage adaptation of an obscure L. Frank Baum tale and a milkshake might encourage some of Patton State's residents along the yellow brick road to the Oz of sanity.

*'Suck jobs...'*

She thought of poor Jeanette. Putting it in the mouth conjured hideous memories for Peggy. A bunch of kids dragged her behind a schoolhouse once and made her do it. From then on she held firm to the notion that no man would trespass against her in that way again. She liked lovin' it up as much as the next gal. But no, not that. All her marriages had failed and if the truth be known, 'suck-jobs', or the lack thereof, were the culprit.

The list for interested parties hung in the hallway. *Next Saturday*. She added her name to the list. Maud watched Peggy as she scribbled.

*'I've only got a little face...'*

As the prospect of freedom loomed, Peggy thought it prudent to get to know her fellow escapee. Arlene could be found every morning in the art room, engaged in a series of increasingly bizarre, and often obscene, paintings. A few of the more savoury works were quickly removed by the orderlies. These removals would elicit Arlene's shouting after the confiscator, 'Don't let the nurses catch ya jerkin' off over it! They'll have yer fuckin' balls!'

The years had roughened Peggy around the edges, but next to Arlene, she was positively refined. Arlene was the best part of twenty years younger than Peggy, but, with the two-extra stones she had on board, looked older.

It took zero to zilch to get Arlene talking (and talking) candidly of her iron-clad belief that she was bound for greatness; a great actress, or a great painter, or a great writer… But it was clear that what she really wanted was to be famous and damn the means by which that desirous state of salvation would come to pass. She talked in a Louisianian gutter-splutter; the words tumbling over themselves, of how her acting genius and total character immersion were the things that got her sent to the laughing academy in the first place. Said she played the Bruno Antony part in an all-girl high school production of Strangers on a Train, and almost strangled her co-star. 'Ah absolutely channelled that mutha fucka! Thought I did a fuckin' great job, but they said it wuz a mental breakdown and sent me off to Longleaf and diagnosed me with a Borderline-Personality-Disorder. But then I knew,' she testified. '… what I was destined to be. So, when I got the fuck outta there, I went straight t'Hollywood. Show me an actor or actress that wasn't a fuckup in real life. I was born for it! But those Hollywood Jew queers couldn't see the real deal when it wuz right there in front ah them. After five years, a million auditions and a serious acid burnout, I wound up in Mendocino to get myself cleaned up. Started selling my paintin's and met Charlie who wuz passing through Casper. He liked my stuff, so I went with him back to where they were livin', on Spahn Ranch. For a coupla years there it wuz paradise—lotsa fuckin' and lotsa drugs. I kept on paintin' and wrote a whole buncha

271

screenplays, which we'd put on for everone. I'd direct and get everone t'act. They were sweet kids, for the most part. We had movie stars and all kindsa people visitin'. We were gonna make a movie—a real movie. Film it right there at Spahn. We were on the brink of everthin'. Then the whole place got raided over that Tate/LaBianca bullshit. Blamed Charlie for the whole fuckin' thing. Made him out to be some kinda Devil on earth. Bullshit! That Bugliosi prick made the whole thing up. If I didn't know better, I'd say he had that Helter Skelter book already writ and wuz just lookin' for a name to stick all over it. Did everthin' I could t'git Charlie and the rest out jail. I was protestin' with the rest of 'em outside the courthouse during the trials, but some a them girls, turned out to be real little bitches. A couple months before, I was their mother hen, but as soon as them news cameras turned up, suddenly they didn't even know me! And then the books started comin' out and not one mentioned me. Not one! That little Squeaky Fromme bitch took over the whole fuckin' operation. You see her now, on TV 'n' whut not, and she don't even mention me!'

At first, Peggy wondered how much of this Arlene related to her therapists, but soon understood that characters of Arlene Žiemelis' stripe related everything to everybody. She was one of those people who lived her life inside-out and was oblivious to the reality of not being the focus of everyone else's attention; of her every utterance not being met with rapt withal. Very 'Beverly Hills', thought Peggy. A completely reversed psych-mirror-image of herself.

Before the week was out, Peggy had Arlene's entire history. The newest chapters told of how she was transferred from the women's facility in Alabama with the help of her young boyfriend, Carter Haines. Haines was some half-assed country singer from Austin who had heard about her from somewhere and thought she might be able to help him get in touch with Charles Manson. Their correspondence quickly took a pornographic turn and pretty soon they were talking marriage—fifteen-year age gap notwithstanding. His family had clout, being the owners of an old fertiliser business, and some of his uncles were high ups in the Klan. So, he got them to

272

use that clout to convince the 'powers' of Arlene's deteriorating mental state and have her moved here; closer to where he was now living down in the Baja, Mexico… with the sole intention of springing her.

Occasionally, but not often, Arlene would turn the talk around and grill Peggy for her story. Inevitably, Peggy remained guarded and attempted to deflect dangerous enquiries with gossip from around the ward. Arlene was a hustler par excellence, and Peggy knew that her diversions raised Arlene's antenna. Peggy had more success throwing Arlene off track with quotes from the movies and her uncanny mimicry of their favourite actresses. Arlene was one hell of a mimic, too. On the day before their great escape, they spent the day, before a small and appreciative audience, reciting entire scenes from *Gone with the Wind*.

At Friday's session, Peggy resolved to give them more. Not much, but… more. She felt she was about to sign off yet another closing chapter of her life and wanted it to sound like one.

The subjects of tapes and oranges were quickly cleared from the table and Niedermeier, once again, circumnavigated the devastation of Peggy Deveroux's broken mind.

'Why do you think God is insane?'

'His vanity.'

'His vanity…' Niedermeier scribbled. 'Can you elaborate?'

Peggy let the revelations arrange themselves within her.

'He wanted to see hiself, and when he did, he realised the enormity of his vanity and destroyed it all.'

The doctor employed his poker face, but Peggy thought she detected a flicker of incomprehension. Of course, something could go wrong tomorrow, but her faith—her unshakeable belief that her world was about to change—told her otherwise. On what she believed would be her last and final session, she gave it up. Today she would give Niedermeier some truth.

'Before all of this—the universe—the galaxies—all of creation… God wanted to see himself. So, he made a universe of light. But when he saw it all, he realised the enormity of his vanity. He saw his face, and it was so beautiful it made him

273

insane, and he destroyed it all and cast himself into the void.
He exploded all the suns and left them as they are now—burnt-
out, smouldering hulks in a cold and ever-expanding darkness.
But one world survived. Us. That little ball of blue hope that we
would one day call Earth. Whatever the moon used to be,
protected us. Took the brunt of the explosion and left us to
evolve and grow until we could find him again and bring him
back. Back to us. Back to sanity...'

Niedermeier scribbled and recorded. Recorded and
scribbled... Peggy watched as he immortalised her revelations
and wondered for how long they might remain in a filing
cabinet before being discovered by someone who may one day
be enlightened by them. Maybe even after the apocalypse.

For the last time, the session ended. She got up, thanked the
doctor, and asked him, as always, to thank his wife for the
flowers.

# .44 OUT

## Saturday June 1st

She had vague ideas of going to her brother Billy's, but
hitchhiking from San Bernardino to Lawndale without
being recaptured was ambitious at best. Besides, he'd be
just about as pleased to see her as she would be to see him—
which was not at all. She came all the way out from Florida to
live with him in '78. Big mistake. He was nothing but an angry,
degenerate gambler now and took out all his shit on her. She
told him she'd kill him if she ever saw him again, and she knew
she would. She still had no clue as to what she would do when
she found herself outside, believing freedom and the grace of
God would send inspiration. But on the morning of Saturday,
the 1st of June 1985, the bus trundled through the wire
perimeter gates en route into town.

For the first time in nineteen months, Peggy saw the outside
of the hospital as it receded into a cloud of highway dust. The
innocuous buildings reminded her of the chalets around the

grand hotels of the Miami coast, where old money would frolic, entertain, and pleasure itself to Hell.

Not a quarter of an hour later their bus pulled into Court Street, Arlene leaned across her and pointed out a tall floppy-haired young man in denim leaning against a Vietnam-era Ford in the Wells Fargo car park across the road from the old Fox Theatre.

'Our chauffeur.'

The highlight of the day's itinerary was an 'Our Lady of Guadalupe Church's' matinee production of The Patchwork Girl of Oz. Followed by malts all round at the Hi-De Hop.

The performers were teenagers, Latino and predominately female. For this afternoon's audience, L. Frank Baum's oeuvre, beyond the tale of his fabled Wizard of Oz, was uncharted territory. A plump schoolgirl in a red velvet dress narrated between the scenes like a Greek chorus of one, telling the tale of a hapless animated doll called Scraps, who goes in search of ingredients to reverse a spell which has turned her creators to stone.

The production transported Peggy back to a period completely obliterated by the years between them, to those long intense sessions at the Herbert Berghof acting school in the 50s where she would be urged to locate horrors and ecstasies buried within, in her quest to be the next Ann Sheridan. The show seemed to have a similar effect on Arlene, who offered a running commentary of her own thespian genius back in drama school, until she was shushed by one of 'bull-dyke' Alice's guard-come-chaperones.

The girl in red concluded the first act with a final line about how the head of a patchwork girl was the most curious part of her, and how a good servant's head must be properly constructed. Arlene had to shake her from her transported state even after the curtains drew and the lights came up for the intermission.

*'... a good servant's head must be properly constructed.'*

A bunch of them got up and made for the restroom, Arlene and Bettie among them. Once in the corridor, eight of them broke away from the group and took a detour through the fire doors and out onto an overcast main street. Arlene hung back and watched the five of them run down to the main strip. Arlene grabbed Bettie's arm, dragging her in the opposite direction, with Maud Pafko trailing behind. They hid around the corner and watched as Alice and a couple of her goons came out of the exit and chased the five down. 'You fuckin' bitches! Come back here, right now!'

Arlene smirked and whispered, 'C'mon.'

The women double-backed around the building and made their way through a rubbish-strewn alley until they came to an entrance in a high brick wall leading into the yard of the Woolworth's next door. They cut across the yard, took a left and crossed Main Street, where the boy Arlene had pointed out earlier was now sitting in his car and gunning the engine. Arlene told Maud, 'Scram!', jumped in beside her driver and told Peggy to get in back.

'Carter, Peggy. Peggy, Carter.'

The car pulled away past the theatre, up Main Street and out on to the Highway, leaving Maud forlorn, confused, and twittering about her *little face* in the parking lot. Carter kept his eyes on the road but tipped an imaginary Stetson. The stereo was low, but Arlene shouted anyway.

'He's from Texas; Austin, to be precise. Mah young cowboy!' Her eyes devoured him as she spoke. Her hand gripped his thigh. 'Wrote t'me when I was in that fuckin' lady jail in 'Bama and somewhere between fate, destiny and the US Mail, love hit.'

Carter's steely grey eyes clocked Peggy in the rear-view. 'Where y'frum darlin?'

Peggy's mouth got the drop on her again. 'Tennessee.'

Carter chuckled. 'Just the way you say it; couldn't be anywhere else.'

Arlene said, 'She's an actress. Like me.'

'Actress, huh?'

'She does a mean Joan Crawford. Peggy, do ya Joanie.'

Carter came to Peggy's rescue. 'Awww,, don't put her on the spot...'

Arlene turned around in her seat and said to Peggy, 'Dontcha you think he looks like Captain America? You *seen* Easy Rider, right?'

'Easy Rider, no.'

'I'll be *damned* if he don't look like Peter Fonda outta that movie.'

Carter smiled long clean teeth and addressed Peggy's reflection in the rear-view. 'So, where you goin, actress?' He didn't wait for an answer. 'Cos, see, we're going over the border...'

Carter glanced at Arlene for some kind of authorisation. Peggy detected a nod. Carter continued, '... we got ourselves a promised land down there and Lord knows you're more than welcome.'

Arlene joined in. 'You know about growin' vegetables and shit. You can help us with that.' She petitioned Carter. 'She can help us with that, right?'

'With the farm? Hell yeah.'


They drove to the coast, where Carter said he had a friend with a yacht waiting for them in Dana Point. The plan was to sail down the coast and into Mexico that way. They waited for two hours but the friend and vessel failed to materialise. They drove for four hours and crashed with a couple of Carter's homosexual friends in San Ysidro, just a few miles from the border. The apartment was small and a veritable shrine to Godzilla. The walls were festooned with unopened blister packs of toys and framed movie posters of Japan's most famous movie star.

The boys were amiable enough; more a reflection of each other than a couple. Whether it was a mutual fascination for the big Jap lizard that brought them together or the ability of one of them to imbue the other with this unlikely obsession was unclear. But they made tea, small talk and didn't ask questions. The only gnat in the ice cream was Arlene's telling all present that Peggy was an ex-Playboy centre fold. The boys seemed genuinely fascinated, but to Peggy's relief, were unfamiliar with the name Peggy Deveroux.

That night Peggy lay in the fold-out cot with the sound of Arlene and her young man in the next room. In the dim glow of the 'Destroy All Monsters' table lamp, Peggy drifted into a listless sleep as the sounds of fornication started up for a third time...

In the morning Carter had rear-ended the Ford backing out of the driveway into the side of a passing Chrysler. The Zilla-fags, as Arlene quietly referred to them, had left for work, and the absconding trio had now found themselves locked out of the apartment.

As the women shopped nervously for big hats and snacks in a nearby Winn Dixie, the Ford got towed and Carter marched off down the street. Forty minutes later, he returned in his new purchase; a Volkswagen Camper van and their escape continued. Money did not seem to be an issue for Carter Haines.

No sooner had they set off for the border, Arlene announced, 'You know my daddy had a whole stack of your magazines. Used to keep 'em in the bottom of the dresser.'

Peggy stared at Arlene and wished she would shut up. Carter's attention was on the road. 'Hold on, darlin', here's the border.'

At Tijuana Border Control, Carter presented his passport with a fifty-dollar bill neatly folded between its pages. The officer nodded in recognition and glanced briefly at the two women with him; saw that were undeniably white, and undeniably of age, and waved them though without incident.

Jammed between Carter's luggage and a guitar case Peggy stared intensely through the window and could no more see where America became Mexico, any more than she could see where, when, and how the 'Queen of the Pin-ups' became an overweight sixty-two-year-old acute psychotic. The Volkswagen churned up hot grit as it smuggled its cargo of crazy.

# .45 TAKE ME TO YOUR DADDY'S FARM

## 1987
### Sunday May 10th

The mid-morning sun shone hard into the cemetery dirt. A hundred yards from the Son of Man Temple, Carter Haines was led naked to the grave by his new favourite, Martha.

He held his arms out and tilted his head back, offering his face to the burning sky. The young woman fondled the prophet's penis, masturbating him expertly and quickly, bringing him to orgasm. With a violent grunt, he brushed Martha aside, staggered forward and caught the issue in his palm. He sunk to his knees and plunged his spunk-filled fist into the hot earth.

He was known now as the prophet Mr. Kite, and the three hundred and seven members of his congregation stood transfixed from where they gathered at the cemetery fence.

The prophet screamed, 'Arise! Arise!' then slumped sideways to the ground.

An immense cold silence seemed to slide down the Sierra de la Laguna Mountains and engulf the scene. Then the earth where Kite had plunged his fist shifted. The crowd gasped. Martha beckoned help, which arrived in the form of two shrouded young women with rusty spades. They chugged at the hump of dirt around where the earth continued to move. Martha, with long dark hair and a soulful face, joked, 'Be careful! We don't want to kill the dead.'

The Prophet Kite lay seemingly exhausted and oblivious to the point of losing control of his bowels. A brief arc of orange urine sprayed up and hit the dirt—quickly vaporised by the searing heat. The women stepped back away from the grave as panicky gossip emanated from the crowd. The ground collapsed some more, and a head appeared at the women's

279

feet, caked in dirt, and screamed like a newborn. An immediate schism occurred as some of the onlookers stepped over the low wooden fence to approach the epiphany. The rest, at first, stood frozen with rapture and fear—then recoiled as a shaking wreck of a man was dragged from death's womb and back into their living world. Some panicked and fled the scene. By now, the grave was surrounded as the emaciated shrouded form— lousy with filth—cowered before the enthralled spectators. His trembling hands reached up to the cloudless sky and croaked with a voice like it came from the depths of a distant cave. 'Dios ayúdame!'

Kite, assisted by a few members of his flock, unsteadily found his feet. Martha draped a gown about him as he stumbled towards the risen man.

'Brother.'

The prophet and his miracle froze in each other's gaze. Kite bade the man approach, and as they hugged, the congregation exploded in cries of jubilation.

As prophesied by Mr. Kite, the Mansonite Church's first miracle had come to pass. The two men hugged each other and walked arm in arm to the open doors of the temple as the crowd followed in stunned, respectful silence. As the congregation approached the building, a frightened few scurried out, carrying hastily packed rucksacks and cases. They ran for their vehicles parked haphazardly around the site.

Martha, concerned by this partial exodus, exclaimed, 'Mr. Kite, they're leaving!'

Kite stopped to see. The following congregation stopped with him. People-carriers and pickup trucks sped off in every direction and disappeared into fugs of churning dust.

Kite smiled great teeth. 'Let them be. They'll carry the good news.'

Mr. Muñoz had said something very strange to her as they concluded their business. Strange, insofar as this was the third time she'd heard it. Or, at least, something very similar.

'Did you find the bookstore?'

'Bookstore?'

'Si, on Calle Rangel?'

From behind her heavy Polaroids, she searched for the man's pip-like eyes set deep in his desert-battered face. No clue as to what the man referred to was forthcoming. She knew that store and knew it well. Why would she have needed to look for it?

'I was looking for a *bookshop*?'

'You no remember? Yesterday you ask where to buy eh… good books.'

She only ever came into Todos Santos when necessity dictated. Yesterday was not one of those occasions.

'You sure it was me, Mr. Muñoz?'

He adjusted the cap on his head along with the recollection inside it. 'I think so. Maybe… too much sun, eh? He coughed a laugh. 'Too much sun…'

She took her hat from the counter and made for the door. 'You can never have enough of *that*, Mr. Muñoz.'

She struck something of an innocuous figure as she negotiated the town's narrow dusty streets with her purposeful stride, large straw hat, oversized sunglasses, billowing shirt and loose slacks—but everyone knew she was a Mansonite bride from out there, from the Son of Man commune. They knew her only by her middle name—Mae— Sister Mae, and that's the way Peggy liked it.

The land up at the Rancho Pineda was so fertile that the commune produced more than it could eat. At Peggy's instigation, they sold the excess to the markets in town— which is where she found herself that Sunday morning when she first got wind of the *good news*.

With The Walrus, she off-loaded the delivery of strawberries to Mr. Muñoz at his corner store and zipped the damp bills safely into her leather fanny pack. As she exited his store, she pulled her hat tight over her head. For a moment, she stood on the sidewalk and scanned the street. The sensation of being followed had never left her—including the notion that she stalked herself. On more than one occasion, she saw herself duck into an alley. Sometimes she would see herself turn a corner, freeze on sight of herself, then disappear back behind

281

it. Peggy knew she was still ill and accepted these hallucinations as a consequence of her condition. But now, as ominously suggested by Muñoz's belief that he'd spoken to her recently, others appeared to be sharing her condition.

She slammed and bolted the back of the pickup as The Walrus, her sullen young chauffeur, whose real name was Pedro, turned the ignition and blew thick hot smoke.

As they pulled out from the market service road onto Ocampo, they were nearly hit by a speeding purple Suzuki jeep that Peggy instantly recognised from the ranch. The Walrus broke and stalled, causing them both to slam onto the dash. He quickly composed himself and re-started the engine. The truck lurched into reverse to avoid another speeding car, seemingly in hot pursuit of the first. The second car had carried on, but the Suzuki screeched to a halt at the entrance of the market halfway down the street.

Peggy, having collapsed into the foot-well, unlatched the door and tumbled gracelessly onto the sidewalk. By now, The Walrus had come to her aid, and as he helped her to her feet, she could see Brian Hawtry leap from the Suzuki and run into the market, calling frantically for his wife, Sarah.

Brian was already living at the commune when she first arrived with Arlene two years ago. He, with his wife and four kids, had been among the longest staying residents. Like most of the Mansonite sycophants, the entire Hawtry clan believed the holy light shone out of the *now called* Prophet Kite; but their function beyond sycophancy was 1: something of a mystery and 2: of no interest to Peggy, whatsoever.

What *was* interesting was the sight of Brian, having now located his beloved and brood in the crowded market, and frog-marching them to their car.

The Walrus said, 'Senior Hawtry, he's leaving?'

Peggy swiped her straw hat from the ground and beat it clean against her chunky legs.

'Idiot nearly damn well killed us! Whut's put a cracker up his ass...'

Hawtry's kids were loaded in the car, but Sarah stamped feet and protested.

'Brian! What the hell has gotten into you?!'

'Just get in the car, Sarah. Now!'

One of Mr. Muñoz's young sons appeared from the market and tried to snatch the basket of fruit from the dithering Sarah. 'Usted no ha pagado! Usted no ha pagado!'

Brian flipped a few bills from his pocket at the young grocer who chased them as they blew off down the street.

Peggy pushed The Walrus in the direction of the ruckus. 'Pedro, (She refused to use the commune's silly Beatles designations) Ve a ver lo que está pasando.'

*Pedro* did as he was told and approached the noisy couple around which a crowd was starting to form. Peggy heard Pedro say, 'Que esta mal?' but couldn't make out Hawtry's reply. Whatever it was, was hurried and to the point. Sarah finally climbed into the car, which took off at speed and out of town.

Pedro returned, flustered and earnest. Peggy could see that some of the people's eyes followed his progress back to her. This tuned her into the wavelength of scrutiny and unrelenting heat on her shoulders. She put her hat on and climbed back into the pickup. Pedro got in bedside her and gunned the engine.

'Well, what did he say?'

'Diablos trabajo.'

'The Devil's work?'

'Si. At the ranch, Senior Kite is doing Devil's work.'

Thirty minutes later, as their truck approached the ranch, along its mile-long dirt track, she could see that the fields had been abandoned. Something of significance had taken place. From the entrance of the temple, they could see the area outside was crowded. She bade Pedro ignore the commotion and take her back up to the big house on the hill where she lived alone.

Peggy tended to avoid the intrigues and petty power-plays of the commune. Her only concern was personal invisibility, organising the farm and ensuring all were fed, but very little occurred within the Mansonite Church without her knowledge.

As always, the latest chapter and verse was delivered by Arlene herself—the would-be priestess who found herself being side-lined yet again. It happened at Spahn Ranch twenty years ago, where she claimed to be a member of the Manson family, and now, here we go again, right here at the Ranchero Pineda. And, as always, Peggy knew Arlene would be paying yet another of her unannounced visits, waiting for her in the house with the latest instalment of the life and side-lined times of Arlene Žiemelis.

The truck pulled up, and Peggy got out. 'Pedro, get Eleanor t'take a look at that exhaust. I'd give it a week t'live.'

The young man nodded a 'si' and drove back to the workshops, east of the temple.

Peggy wandered into the kitchen and set the kettle on the stove. Normally, she always knew when Arlene was in the vicinity by the infantile shuffle of her feet as she dragged them along the floor. Why the idiot woman refused to walk properly was another of life's phenomena that vexed Peggy. She guessed it was this habit that caused Arlene's alleged troublesome back and not the other way around.

As the gurgling of the boiled water subsided, Peggy could hear a voice from a distant room. She stepped out into the hallway. It was *her own* voice drifting down the huge ornate stairway.

'Sonofabitch...'

She took careful double steps up to the balcony and crept along to the bedroom from where her voice was coming from. So Arlene had found her precious tapes and was playing them loud. Peggy expected to find Arlene naked. She liked to wander around naked, for some reason. Peggy couldn't understand why. The woman had a body like a gunny sack of doughnuts. She expected to find her sitting on the bed propped up with big cushions, surrounded by cassette tapes and playing Peggy's little Sony.

The door was ajar. But Arlene was neither naked on the bed nor messing with her tapes. She was standing in front of the full-length wardrobe mirror wearing one of Peggy's homemade shawls and impersonating her distinctive heavy Tennessee drawl—with uncanny accuracy.

This stopped Peggy in her tracks. She watched and listened.

'Haa, m'name is Peggy Deveroux and ahm so glad to meetchu...' Arlene caught sight of Peggy in the mirror and yelped.

'What in the blue fuck are you doin', Arlene?'

The surprise stopped Arlene dead. She was slacked-jawed for but a second before she escaped into another persona.

'Nuthin' dear, Ah... it's been so lowng since you were outta the house ah thought perhaps you had gowne for a drive or sumthin'. Y'know, I was thinkin', it's ever so lowng since we had a tawk, y'know, a real tawk about t'future and everythang. Jane, ah didn't want you t'be worried 'bout the house. Even if ah do havtah sell it, we'll still be together.'

Peggy knew the piece. It was Joanie Crawford's dialogue from Whatever Happened to Baby Jane?

Peggy moved to the window and peered out at the distant compound where the image of the temple shimmered in the heat. She delivered Bette Davis' response.

'Blanche, you're not gonna sell this house. Daddy bought this house, an' he bought it fer me! You don't think ah remember that, do ya?'

Peggy turned to Arlene, awaiting the next line. For a moment, silence reigned... then both women collapsed into uncontrollable laughter. Arlene managed to splutter, 'You *know* we both belong back in that fuckin' nut house. I am I right?!'

Peggy quickly returned from the land of Blanche and Baby Jane and, with Mr. Muñoz's strange question in mind, considered asking Arlene if she had been parading her 'Peggy act' in town yesterday. Instinct suggested otherwise. 'What's going on? Down there?' Peggy asked. 'I saw a couple of the congregation high tailin' it through town.'

Arlene joined Peggy at the window and looked out. 'The first prophecy has come to pass...'

'Oh, and which one wuz that now?'

'Carter raised a dead man right outta that cemetery. In fronta everbody. I saw it fer m'self.'

'A dead man...'

285

'A dead man right outta his grave. An old grave. Baby, you could see that ground ain't been touched in a coon's age.'

'Whad he look like?'

'Pretty fucked up… covered in shit. I think he wuz a soldier. Had bitsa uniform hangin' offa him an everthing.'

'So where is the new Lazarus?'

'He's down there now, at the Temple with Carter, talkin' to the papers.'

Now *this*, Peggy had to see.

# 46. INTERVIEW WITH THE DEAD

I t was late in the afternoon when Peggy entered the Son of Man Temple with Arlene and found the entire remaining population sitting on the marbled floor around the unholy triumvirate of the Prophet Kite, the risen man and Martha—all sat in a row along the apron of the stage. A cloud of marijuana and incense smoke hung over the room like Japanese monster movie smog.

Kite wore a white leather rhinestone encrusted suit like some star-spangled country singer. The risen man sat beside him in a green velvet robe, drinking hot soup. Martha sat cross-legged and wore no panties. Only Arlene appeared to be aware of this vaginal apparition. The image of Carter's long dick entering it seized Arlene's imagination and churned her guts. A new rage ascended, and she knew it would have its day.

Close by, the free-lancer, Echo Hernandez, sat among the flock, fiddling with her cassette deck. She had her long black hair tied back in a bun and wore dungarees. Her countenance declared seriousness. Her swarthiness suggested native blood. She stood up, said her name, and announced that she was from the Enquirer. Peggy, sitting next to Arlene, relaxed on hearing this. She hissed in Arlene's ear, 'This was all the media attention a resurrection could generate? The fuckin' Enquirer?!'

Hernandez cut straight to it and addressed the prophet. 'What right do you have to bring a man back from the dead?'

Kite smiled those great teeth. 'What right do we have to question a prophecy? Miracles are way beyond our tiny yearnin's.'

Hernandez watched the wheels of the cassette in her recorder roll as she answered. 'But to have someone face death more than once is kind of obscene, right? Death is the thing that we all fear the most and now this man will have to face it again— just to fulfil a prophecy? I mean, resurrection is kind of murder in reverse, right? A few might want to die, but no one asks to live.'

'You know what a prophecy is, sweetheart? A fulfilment of a message from... what you might refer to as God... from above, or the other side, or maybe even...' Kite beat his chest with a clenched fist, '... from right here. Nothin'—*and I mean nothin'*— has the right to obstruct *the word*! Not a man's...' He gestured expansively to the crowd of predominantly females at his feet, '... nor a women's pain...' A collective swoon rippled among them. Kite smiled. He never failed to get a kick out of the effect he had on his sheep. '... should stand in the way of a truth that will lift us from outta this air-conditioned, superficial, deposit now and pay later, love-resistant nightmare!'

Hernandez, attempting a coup in plain sight, aimed the next question at the risen man—the real star of this show—who gazed sullenly into the middle distance. '¿Qué piensas?'

The risen man's red eyes penetrated from out under his prominent brow like tiny lights at the end of a tunnel. It took a beat for him to realise she was talking to him, before he said, 'Solo, he conocido oscuridad por tanto tiempo. Y ahora hay luz.'

She looked at Kite for a sign that *he* understood this. His expression betrayed nothing.

She put it to him 'You speak Spanish, right?'

Kite kind of sneered and looked at his miracle in a conciliatory, appeasing manner. The risen man sipped at his cup. Remembering that taking the theological line always leads into a cul-de-sac of grandiloquent horse shit, Hernandez changed tack, played ball, and re-aimed the next question back at the risen man. 'You speak English?'

The risen man glanced at his resurrector and said 'Si. Some.'

'Those graves out there. Mexican soldiers. Can you tell us anything about that war? About... those times? The 1840s? 'Do you remember what it's like to be dead?'

The risen man seemed to have lost interest in the interview, continued to sip soup and stare into what the audience assumed was the void of his recent death. Kite snorted and kind of laughed. No one else responded. He looked at Arlene. She got it. '*I know what it's like to be dead.*' Beatles lyric.

Hernandez asked the resurrected man again. 'Do you remember your name?'

Kite interceded and half sang 'Look up the number.'

This got laughs.

Hernandez threw Kite a look more of sympathy than annoyance, and asked the risen man again, '*Do you*? Know your name?'

The lights at the end of the dead man's tunnel fixed her solemn gaze. His voice sounded like it came from somewhere far away, raw, guttural; like his throat was built for something else—for a machine of some kind. 'El pasado está tan muerto como yo. Ahora solo veo el futuro.'

Hernandez translated aloud. 'The past is as dead as I was?'

She wanted the congregation to know what was being said. Their response would colour the tone of the article that was already forming in her head.

'*I see only the future now?*' Hernandez looked around at the trance-like expressions around her. 'Then tell us about the future.'

The risen man glanced tellingly at Kite, who continued to gaze proudly at his miracle. The voice ground and dragged itself into language. His indecipherable monologue held the room. Few understood the words, but all were transfixed by their sound, by the knowing that whatever they were hearing had echoed across the ages to find them here and now on the brink of the rapture.

Hernandez let the last word die on the risen man's tongue for all to hear and repeated what he had said as best she could.

'There will be a new Babel....' She announced, attempting to mimic the rhythms of the risen man. 'A new attempt to thwart the natural order of things. To enter heaven without death, find God and bring him to account for having abandoned us...'

She looked around at the seated flock. They seemed to ignore what she had just translated and appeared to be transfixed by the sound alone, in its original tongue, of the risen man. It was as if what he *said* was of no significance. It was the *sound*—the *fact* of his speaking—was all.

Peggy studied the wan ghost that was the risen man as Hernandez reiterated this. She knew those words had come from her prophesies. *Her* Prophesies of the Seven Apostles. She caught Arlene's eye, who seemed to understand the accusatory glance and looked away.

The Prophet was on fire that night. It was only when Haines was overcome by his Mr. Kite persona that Peggy could see what had so consumed Arlene. If you saw him at all around the ranch, he kind of blended in. If you didn't know he owned the place, his floppy, overgrown boy demeanour would do nothing to make you think otherwise. On the rare daylight hours you saw him, he was always in jeans, a suede jacket or waistcoat, and kept his long dirty-blonde hair tied back in a ponytail. In the right kind of light, he could have been a girl. But now, as he prowled the stage like a caged lion, he had every last one of these sonsobitches' undivided attention. He stood like a superhero conqueror—like Glen Campbell or somebody, on the precipice of some impossibly won triumph, in which he was about to lead the universe into an era of unimaginable enlightenment.

The last time Peggy bore witness to one of his sermons was when she first arrived at the ranch nearly two years ago. Then, Haines would deliver his 'good word' as he walked among his congregation while they were engaged in their chores. He'd talk softly, as if coaxing a calf from its mother's womb. The people would down tools and be transported from their

289

endeavours as he described how the paradise they now enjoyed would one day be shared by all of mankind. They'd follow him as he spoke, and climb with him, up to a favourite spot overlooking the distant temple and surrounding car park. There he would bid everyone sit with him as he finished his sermon, which usually concluded with a Beatles-like lyric. Something like 'Love is the word. Love is the number...'

He'd let this nonsense float on the warm Bajaian air, and his flock would drift back to their dorms with it as if it were oxygen gold.

Tonight, the tone was light-years away from the almost lilting delivery of yesteryear and was now a blitzkrieg of theological science-fiction. The Prophet Kite stood and waited until absolute and total silence reigned. And only then... he would begin...

'The rape of the unknown has given us everything,' he declared. 'Nature does not give up its secrets willingly. They must be taken. Taken... and made to *yield* to our will.'

The prophet allowed this to be absorbed, then continued.

'The Jews knew this. The Jews knew this back two thousand years, when they nailed their own to the cross. And the Jews knew this when they financed Adolf Hitler's rise and fall in order to secure their holy land—their place in the sun—the base from which they will one day launch their *own* final solution.

If!

We!

Let them!'

Peggy looked around the room, expecting at least a ripple of dissent. But there was none. An unsettling tone of normality ensued, and she realised Haines' infantile Charles Manson obsession had deformed into something truly apocalyptic—if only on account of its unquestioned acceptance by this crowd's rapt withal. Peggy, remembering Arlene beside her, glanced at her perspiring profile. The Prophet's quasi-Nazi-isms appeared to escape her, still transfixed as she was on the apparent epiphany between Martha's legs.

'... *if* we let them!' the Prophet repeated. 'But that cannot, and will not, happen. And do you know *how* that cannot and will not happen?'

Murmurs from the crowd. The Prophet got louder.

'Do you know *why*... that cannot happen?'

Someone shouted, 'We'll do it first!'

Kite said, 'Louder, brother.'

Twenty people shouted, 'We'll do it first!'

Kite reiterated. 'We will do it first! We will do it from this temple. We will do it from this land. We will do it in the desert. We will do it in *every* city in *every* country around the globe! We will... ha ha...' He roared now, '... *do it in the road*!'

This got laughs.

'We are on the precipice of Helter Skelter!' The revolution of mind, body and soul as prophesied... by God's man on earth—Charles Milles Manson!'

Kite jumped from the stage and walked among his disciples.

'And YOU are its heralds; its golden legions; its shining, glorious excellence... and for that you will see a light that makes God's stars look like the Devil's black... black heart.'

One of the girls at Kite's feet groped his groin and was quickly joined by another. Kite pulled their heads into his hips and allowed them to unfasten his white leathers and release his already erect penis. Everyone around Peggy began to molest each other as if they'd suddenly lost their minds. Arlene flung her T-shirt off and made her way towards Martha, who began to masturbate as she watched Kite fucking one of his girls in the mouth. Mr. Kite was in full flow now, reaching the climax of his sermon. Literally in all senses. The women began to undress, seduced by the sweltering atmosphere.

Kite's sermons always concluded in a mass orgy, so Peggy got up and left as the prophet tore off his jacket and was immediately set upon by a group of women who threw themselves on their knees before him. Peggy glanced back before she exited the hall and was surprised by the sight of the Hernandez girl allowing herself to be fondled by Polythene Pam and her young son. Over at the apron of the stage, Arlene

291

had buried her face between the legs of her replacement, Martha, who appeared to be trying to get away from her.

From halfway up the hill, back to the big old house, Peggy could still hear the noise from the temple. Mr. Kite roared again. *'You are the sons and daughters of the Son of Man! You are the mothers and fathers of a new light!'*

The spectacle of Kite's incendiary performance took Peggy, despite herself, back to New Year's Eve, '58, the night on which she was truly born. The night she consigned her second husband, Arnie, the idiot-child she'd been married to for little more than a month, to the out-tray. She wanted to go dancing. He wanted to see the New Year in, drinking and fucking. She offered a compromise. She'd let him do his thing, then they'd go out. It didn't take long for him to finish up, but then he said he was tired. She hit him with a lamp, and he kicked her in the stomach. She stormed out into a sweltering Key West night. She cried hot tears and wandered aimlessly for what seemed like a lifetime.

Young couples walked arm in arm in their party clothes, meandering from one noisy joint to another. Queers were kissing openly. She had known queers in New York; one even wanted to marry her, but they were never blatant. Not like here. She stopped and stood at the end of an alley and watched a man on his knees sucking on his boyfriend's thing. The notion that they were damned anyway occurred to her, and that they may as well take whatever fragments of paradise they could, right here on earth. As the one on his knees gulped hard, a crucifix of gold smoke appeared suddenly before her, floating a few feet in front of her face. The crucifix passed by her and moved to the corner of the block. She followed it and watched it continue across White Street, where it faded at the doors of a small church. She didn't recall entering the place, only that she suddenly found herself standing at the back of a crowded hall where a rowdy service was in full effect. The heat in the room was unbearable. Sweat pasted the preacher's shirt to his lithe torso and his voice reached over the crowd like a giant hand and plunged itself deep into Peggy's chest. Her heart burst, and in that moment, she died and came back to a life that seemed to illuminate every dark recess of her entire existence... She had seen nothing but light ever since.

# 47. AVALON CALLING!

The Son of Man Temple was almost complete when Peggy arrived with Carter and Arlene at the Ranchero Pineda back in the spring of '85. The alarming fibre-glass-clad construction stood to the north of the thousand-acre ranch—backdropped by a churning shallow river and a spectacular wall of distant mountains.

They found the ranch haphazardly tended to by founder members of the commune as the construction crews vacated the site. The surrounding terrain was a land of whiplash-inducing tangents, of mountainous deserts filled with volcanic rocks, narrow canyons, and towering cacti. And ten miles west, green coastal strips: slender palms with pristine 'make a wish' beaches.

With great pride, Carter, as he was still known then, showed them around the ranch, telling them how the temple was a converted sugar mill which had been commandeered by General Pineda and used as a secret armoury during the Mexican/American war. When it went back to being a plain old sugar mill afterwards, someone decided to adopt the hapless General's name—being, as he was, a symbol of rebellion against the Yankee imperialist.

The main temple was a large extension of the old mill, encased with yellow panels and periscope-like spires at all four corners. Oval windows of green glass punctuated the convolutions of the structure. It was, in its surreal and childish fashion, set against the epic drama of its Olympian back-drop, quite beautiful.

An inevitable hierarchy established itself behind Carter Haines' declaration of himself as a prophet in the fall of '86. His priests and priestesses were little more than groupies who had descended en mass from over the border. Favoured disciples

found themselves bestowed with Beatles-inspired monikers—
Pauline Cooke, a supply teacher from shitsville, Arkansas, was
now known as Polythene Pam. They called her son Maxwell.
Natasha Stoan, from some war-torn East European hellhole,
was Prudence. Mr. Mustard was a dentist from Akron, Ohio.
Eleanor (Peggy never caught her real name) was a lesbian auto
mechanic who knew even more about fixing cars than she did.
There was a Doctor Robert somewhere around, so she was
told. On the off chance that he was a real doctor, Peggy had
been meaning to seek him out on account of her bad hip acting
up again. She used to get stuck in digging and planting with the
rest of them—the younger ones—but that hip of hers had
other ideas. So, with little more than a few secretarial
qualifications to her name, Peggy brought a little order to the
place. Soon, with the triumvirate of Carter's enabling, Arlene's
fervent promotion of the Son of Man temple and Peggy's admin
efforts, the Ranchero Pineda, for a little while at least, all but
flourished.

But these days, Mr. Kite had pretty much retreated to his
private quarters beneath the temple and Arlene had been
demoted from Sexy Sadie and back to plain old Arlene. Some
old girlfriend from Kite's Austin hometown had appeared and
was now the new Sexy Sadie. This class of '75 beauty queen,
and (so it was whispered) ex porn star, quickly established
herself, alongside Martha, as Kite's right-hand girl, and it was
via this divine vessel, that Kite would issue his commands and
wishes from his underground lair to the rest of the commune,
much to the submerged anger of lesser disciples.

Kite emerged only on the mornings of Wednesday and
Sunday, if only to remind all that he was still present and still
in charge. His sermons rarely veered from the subjects of
Charles Manson, the Beatles, and how the coloureds had to be
wiped out with the Jews to help them do it. It was an old record
and Mr. Kite played it often, along with the Rock-and-Roll
records he studied like biblical chapters. Endless
interpretations of the Talmud and Beatles lyrics became a self-
perpetuating gospel. Occasionally, he would lead a 'Family Jam'
in which the entire congregation would play loud electric

guitars which would rattle the windows of the temple—
howling feedback and Morse-code-like bleeps punching holes
in the tranquillity of the heavy desert air.

How Kite utilised the rest of his time could only be guessed at.
But whatever it was, rarely included Arlene anymore.

### Monday May 11th

The morning after the orgy, Arlene let herself into the big
house and made coffee. Peggy, long-since liberated from the
asylum's regimes and now an early riser, was startled as she
entered the kitchen at 05:30, to find Arlene, naked as usual,
with her leather-slippered feet up on the table and reading one
of Peggy's movie magazines.

'Getchur feet off the table, Arlene.'

Arlene stayed as she was and held up the cover for Peggy to
see. It had some young actor who Peggy didn't much care for.
Arlene said, 'I'd fuck this kid so hard and fast he'd think he wuz
surrounded.'

The idea of Arlene Žiemelis moving at any kind of speed
struck Peggy as funny. A wry smile escaped her. Arlene knew
she was in.

'Whatcha make of all that? Yesterday's big miracle.'

'Miracle?' Peggy snorted. 'Whut? The prophet finally git onya
agin?'

The prophet: that's how Peggy always referred to Carter
Haines now and everyone knew it wasn't out of deference.

'The *resurrection*, smart bitch! And very fuckn' funny. Hardy
fuckn' har.'

'I don't make nuthin' of it. I wasn't there, remember? But it
musta been some kinda trick, and anyone with half a mind
would know it.'

Arlene flung the magazine on the table and took her feet off it.

'Sure as hell spooked somathem idiots, though. Brian
Hawtry's bin with the Mansonites even afore I wuz. But when
they dragged that guy out the ground, he shit hiself and took
off. I mean, if Carter was lookin' to git a re-sponse, I guess
that's exactly whut he got.'

295

Peggy remembered the fleeing Brian, rounding up his family at the market yesterday, and wondered what new and less dramatic stars Brian and his brood would be hitching their wagon to next.

'Well, for all o' Brian's alleged brains, seems he's just as dumb as the next rube. I mean, ya gotta ask yerself; what makes a man of Brian's obvious gifts so ready to throw his lot in with a clear-cut charlatan like our prophet in the first place? It's like ah always said, there's somthin' about people that just compels 'em to stupid doin's, don't matter how many degrees and diplomas they got.'

'Well, belief transcends intelligence,' Arlene proclaimed. 'Faith is stronger'n all the facts in the whole universe. Love is— '

Peggy could feel a sermon coming on. She would have to head it off at the pass. 'Is the word they use to try tah make sex respectable!'

This had the desired effect and stopped Arlene in her stride.

'Whut movie's that from?'

'*Is* it from a movie?'

'Yeah't is.'

'Well, it's true, ain't it? How you *sell* a thing's more important than the *thing*.'

Peggy poured coffee and got around to wondering what Arlene's ulterior motive was; for coming up here at what for her is an ungodly hour. Arlene up before the sun was all the storm warning that Peggy needed to know that something was coming.

'What's on y'mind, Arlene?'

'These prophecies o'yours, the Comin' O' the 'Seven Gods; what would happen to 'em if you died?'

'It's Seven Apostles. It's the prophecy, not "the comin' of".'

'Apostles then.'

Peggy sipped on her hot black coffee, eyed her bare-ass naked visitor over the rim of the steel mug and said, 'You thinkin' o tryin' tah kill me, Arlene?'

'Don't you start tryin' be a fuckn' idiot now. I'm serious. What is the point of a prophecy if no-one hears it? You thought a that?'

Peggy sipped on. She really hadn't. So immersed was she in the industry of delivering the words intact from the untried super-loins of Lucy Hartman and onto her tapes, that *how* they would become the last testament for the new era had never occurred. Arlene sensed she had made an inroad, so brought it home.

'We could get her down here, Lucy Hartman. I know people who might be able to arrange it.'

'Fer whut?'

'Fer whut?! If someone tol' me I was the vessel through which Seven Gods... sorry... *apostles*—wuz making their gospel known, I'd wanna know about it. *She's on TV*, Sister Mae! She could get this thing out across the country... across the world. Think about it.'

'Y'don't havtah think about it to know it'd probably freak her out. Yeah, we're all God-fearin' 'till *He* actually appears before us, then we think we're lookin'at the Devil hiself. Believe me; that's what got me put away in the first place.' Besides, we don't *need* Hartman in person. The words come outta her to me whether she likes it or not.'

'But the publicity, Sister Mae...'Arlene beseeched, 'She's on TV! If Jesus Christ hiself was here today, you think he'd be walking 'round in the desert talkin' to idiots?! No! He would nhut! He'd be on the TV reachin' round the *world*!'

'Yeah, reachin' *idiots* 'round the world.'

'What if I get *him* onside? Carter.' Arlene recalibrated. 'Hell. Somewhere between Manson's teachin's and yours, we could have a fuckn' super faith! Can you imagine?!'

'Yeah, about that...' Peggy remembered those familiar elements, as translated by Hernandez, from the risen man's words last night and re-iterated. *'There will be a new Babel. A new attempt to thwart the natural order of things. To enter heaven without death, find God and bring him to account for having abandoned us...* Sounded familiar, don't you think?'

Arlene shrugged, non-committal. 'All that says to me is if a dead man is saying it too, it means you're on to sumthin.'

Arlene had been memorising the prophesies as told to her during their marathon midnight dialogues and, unbeknown to Deveroux, was testing them on some of Kite's flock. To her astonishment, everyone who heard them seemed to respond with vigour. Kite had been touting his Son of Man spiel for four years now and, Arlene believed, his listeners were growing bored with his repeat tirades. Peggy Deveroux's prophesies of the Seven Apostles might just be what the world was really waiting for.

But there was a problem.

Until recently, Mr. Kite's current number one fuck-piece, Martha (A Canadian stripper by the name of Samantha Quaddle) had been an attendee of Arlene's secret sermons, but since her elevation, no longer attended. With the new elements in Mr. Kite's recent sermons, Arlene realised that Martha had been a spy and had been feeding him from Arlene and Peggy's trough. If the truth be known, it was this treachery that had won Martha's exalted standing in the court of the prophet Mr. Kite. Clearly, if he was now using them in his sermons, the prophet saw the value in these new elements. The power of the two doctrines combined might create a super faith and ignite the Helter Skelter that Mr. Kite had for so long been working towards.

Arlene descended the thirteen concrete steps behind the pulpit and into the corridor that led to Mr. Kite's underground lair. Inevitably, Arlene had to go through Martha to get to Kite these days. Last night, at the orgy, Arlene had spent most of the night with her face buried between Martha's impossibly long legs. But now a thoughts of stab wounds to Martha's muscled stomach titillated Arlene's enraged desires.

She followed the dimly lit tunnel and rang the bell. Martha, wearing only an open black see though nightie, opened the door of the prophet's inner sanctum where Arlene could see him on the bed watching a wall of TVs whilst soundlessly strumming a guitar. The explosion of mirrored reflections around the room made her giddy for a moment. Once she had re-orientated herself, she sat at the edge of bed and waited for Carter to dismiss Martha. She did as she was told, in a sweep of pert tits and narrow hips, but Arlene knew she'd be out in the corridor—ear to the door. Carter put the guitar aside and smiled engagingly at the nervous Arlene. 'Did we have a party or whut, last night!'

Arlene was relieved to find she was dealing with the Carter Haines of old.

'It was that.' Arlene agreed. 'Worthy of Nero hiself.'

'Those old Caesars ain't got nuthin' on us.' Carter looked at Arlene like he used to. 'What can I do y'for, Arlene?'

Arlene was slightly put out that the 'Sexy Sadie' designation was still absent from his reference to her, but she was still confident that he could be turned around, in time. 'The Pin-up has got some interestin' ideas... Scripture ideas. Suma the new stuff in your sermon last night? Sounded like it'd blend right in...'

'Blend right in?' Carter interrupted.

Arlene steeled herself and locked the prophet's gaze. 'It's time for some new blood. A fresh shot in th'arm. The resurrection was all well an' good, but it freaked more people out than it did galvanise.' Arlene waited for the prophet to baulk—baulk big or baulk small, but the Carter of old held fast.

'Any idea how many left a'cos of it?' Arlene asked.

'We don't havtah worry none about that,' Carter replied, smoothly. 'Once that Enquirer story gets out, this place will have twice... *three times* the congregation. The Pin-up's gonna have her hands full keepin' everyone fed.'

'But we need to be ready when they come,' Arlene pressed. 'The Pin-up has a whole 'nuther branch that could be used to make the Son of Man gospels even stronger. I heard it last night—summa the things you said—it's like they were straight outta the Pin-up's visions. I think she might be some kinda apostle. I'm sure of it—her being here is no accident. We need to recognize it and bring her in. Her prophesies, I mean. Between these visions o' hers and Charlie's teachin's, we could have us a *super faith*.'

Arlene fixed the prophet's gaze, hoping she had reeled him in. Something on the TV distracted him and killed the moment. 'Why don't we go see her together...' Arlene continued;

competing now with some English comedy sketch dubbed into Spanish, '... Just hear what she's got.'

On one of the screens, a chubby comedian was getting chased around in fast motion by a line of girls in various states of undress. Carter laughed. 'Check this shit out...' and turned the sound up with the remote, seemingly oblivious to everything Arlene had just said. His eyes were black saucers. She realised the prophet was in the throes of a gargantuan drug comedown and she would have to choose a better time to raise her game.

Arlene passed Martha in the corridor on the way out. They exchanged curt nods, and Arlene wondered if the girl even remembered last night's drug-induced cunnilingus. Martha's nightie swished open, and her flat stomach reminded Arlene that another visit to the clinic was way past due.

# 48. UP!

Arlene drove all night. But when she got to Mexicali, she couldn't sleep. She left the motel and went on the prowl. She picked up a couple of back-packing kids at the nearest bar, got 'em loaded on tequila and cocaine and fucked the two of 'em all night.

Her appointment was at 11am. She figured they'd do tests of some kind—blood tests. She was worried the yayo might be detectable and that they'd cancel the operation. The clinic's reputation was impeccable; if the glossy pamphlets they gave out were anything to go by. But this was still the wrong side of the border; here it was safe to exterminate normality.

A nurse told her to get undressed and put on a blue gown. Doctor Dorin Manjarrez had warm hands and prodded and kneaded her flabby gut. He said reassuring things that she'd heard before, along the lines of liposuction being a routine procedure and that by the end of the day she would be a stone lighter.

They didn't knock her out. Just gave her a local and started sucking and cutting. They didn't ask her about any medications she might be taking, so she didn't mention any. She stayed the night, slept like the dead, and then they set her loose in the morning.

At the reception counter, as she made another appointment for the following month, she began to hallucinate. Or so she thought...

Peggy Deveroux; a young 1950s, 'couldn't be any older than thirty', Peggy Deveroux entered the reception hall and told the receptionist that she was here for her 10am. The receptionist smiled, seemed to know her and told her that Dr Alverez will be with her shortly.

Arlene shuffled stiffly across the room—her gut hurt like fucking hell—to a chair by the window and sat down and stared at the apparition of the woman who stood ass-perfect across the room. She wore a white linen dress and her hair hung in a thick wave of black gloss, like the hood of the Oldsmobile Arlene once stole from her daddy.

She thought it was a combination of the anaesthetic they had given her, along with what she already had on board from the previous night, that was causing this epiphany. Arlene was used to visions, drug-borne and otherwise—but the woman who stood waiting at the desk was Peggy Deveroux herself, having walked through a time warp. Dr Alverez appeared from a corridor and led the apparition away. Arlene only realised her mouth was hanging open when she sensed the receptionist staring at her. The desperate need to know who the woman was propelled her across the room.

'Who is that? The woman with Dr Alverez?'

The receptionist was taken aback but offered the party line. 'Miss Hudson, you know we can't tell you that.'

'Wah the fuck hell not?! Ahm a gonna wait out there and aska m'self if you don't. So whas the difference?'

The receptionist glanced towards the corridor and hissed, 'How would you feel, Miss Hudson, if we gave out confidential information about you?'

'Ahd feel just fine. Thank you for asking. Hell, ah jus want her name, is all.' There was a momentary standoff. 'Do ah wait here an ask her m'self or whut?'

The receptionist had a name tag that said Gloria. Her wire-framed spectacles bleached out her eyes. This young but somewhat worn-out white girl suggested 'on the run' status or marriage on the wrong side of the border. 'I will not give out patient's names. Now please Miss Hudson, we will see you next month.'

Just then, a big man in a tan suit sauntered in from outside. Gloria smiled big, with not a little gasp of relief. 'Mr. Jalisco, how are you today?'

Arlene gave him the old up and down and realised he had inadvertently become Gloria's cavalry.

Arlene smiled at the two of them lopsidedly. 'Y'gave *his* name up fast enough.'

Gloria ignored her, safe in the zone of the big man's regard. He glanced quizzically at the two women and then announced the time of his appointment.

Gloria asked him to take a seat, and Arlene backed off. 'See ya on the 20th…'

'Yes, Miss Hudson. We will see you then.'

Arlene peered out the back of her pickup truck facing the clinic's entrance. It was like one of her many trips had crossed over from some lysergic-drenched dreamscape and into reality. She just had to see that woman again. Ideas that she couldn't get a handle on were already scrambling all over her fevered brain. She couldn't wait to tell Sister Mae about it. Damn! If only she were here. She needs to see this for herself.

Four hours later and the realisation that the woman was probably staying overnight descended, along with an arid evening. The cocaine she had tucked under the dash would keep her going—and it had for the last couple of hours, but that clear head she needed… she needed it now. She wound down the window and called to a kid with a basket of bread, crossing Bénito Juárez. He came over and sold her some. She wasn't hungry now but come morning she would be. She appraised the fuck possibilities—the kid couldn't have been older than thirteen—old enough. But the last thing she needed now was a molestation felony. Or any kind of felony, for that

302

matter. No. Save it for the ranch. She got out and walked round
the building. It was new and featureless—nothing more than a
giant concrete shoebox with large square windows—some of
which were dimly lit. Arlene studied them all, but nothing
presented itself. Suddenly aware that her lone presence in the
near-empty car park might attract a uniform, Arlene went back
to the truck.

Her drug intake had diminished considerably in the last year.
Carter's mass-medicating of the commune with LSD was his
way of maintaining control. But Arlene had decided she needed
to take pains to escape it. Her fantasy of a new regime was
barely half-formed, but the way things were going at the
Ranchero Pineda, it was clear that it was time for a new
religion.

Kite's big resurrection had backfired. Half his congregation
freaked out and abandoned him. He was fucking this thing all
up, and it was down to crusader Arlene to save the day. And for
that, she needed that clear head. Flashbacks were part and
parcel of psychedelics, and there wasn't a darn thing she could
do about that. But she had to ease off... for now.

Despite her effort to stay awake, Arlene fell asleep on the
backseat and woke up in a sweat. The clock in the dash said
06:04—unlikely her quarry would have been discharged
before now. But how long was she gonna have to wait? She
could be staying another night for all she knew. Maybe a week!
And what would she say if she did see her? For reasons that,
for now, were obscure to her, Arlene figured she would hang
back before making herself known. First things first: who is
that woman?

The car park was all but empty and Arlene wondered if the
staff leaving last night would have taken any particular notice
of her 'Square-body' Chevrolet parked smack bang and centre.
She chomped on the hard bread and eyed the windows of the
clinic in the unbearable morning light. The place opened at
nine. Would she... could she... risk another confrontation with
that fucking receptionist? Maybe 'Gloria' would be less
guarded outside of office hours—if Arlene could, perhaps,
intercept her before she arrived—question her then. The

possibility rolled around her head some. Hell! She might not even be working today. Too many fucking variables! Damn! She needed a sheepdog of the mind to round up all those scattergun thoughts sometimes.

And what was the likelihood of the Deveroux look-a-like living locally? Zero to none. The accent was north of the border, but that didn't exactly narrow it down any. People came in from all over the world to have surgeries here in Mexicali—it was cheap, and it was anonymous.

Arlene must have fallen asleep again, because when she woke up at 10:05 she could see the receptionist through the brown tinted glass, sitting at her desk from clear across the car park.

It was time for the gentle art of force.

She got out, scanned the area. Late morning traffic was already clogging Bénito Juárez. A few cars had parked nearby but there were no pedestrians in sight. She crouched and reached up into the compartment above the back driver-side wheel-well and pulled out the Walther.

Arlene limped heavily across the car park and could see that Gloria had spotted her approach. There was no one else in the waiting area. Perfect. She shouldered the heavy glass doors into the clinic's reception area. She had her hand in her embroidered hold-all clutching the gun. She would lay it on the counter where Gloria could see it and calmly demand the name and phone number of Dr Alvarez's 10am of yesterday.

Annoyingly, Gloria was suddenly preoccupied with something on her computer screen. Arlene was about to pull the gun out when, without looking up, Gloria said, 'That woman you asked about. I'll give you her details for a hundred bucks.'

Arlene looked furtively around the room. Was this a setup? 'Well, you've changed your tune some.'

Gloria looked up with those blank lenses. 'Two bucks ten an hour does that. You want it, or not?'

Arlene's grip on the concealed gun relaxed. 'A hundred bucks? What do I get for that?'

'I already said. Her details. Name, phone number and address. Bear in mind, I can only guarantee the number. Our patients tend to be loose with their biographies, right, *Miss Hudson*?'

Arlene, still expecting some kind of trick, said, 'For the record, I've got a gun in this bag. Unerstan?'

Cucumber cool, Gloria said, 'You must really want that number.'

Arlene shuffled around in her bag. Found her purse and pulled out five Andys. 'Make it quick.'

Gloria took the notes, slipped them under the appointment book and handed Arlene a note pad and biro. She squinted at the glowing green text on her monitor and said, 'Write this down...'

Gloria spilled. Arlene wrote. Arlene read. 'Erika Xtravaganza? What's her real name?'

Gloria looked at Arlene with that white-out lens-stare. She whispered, 'No-one gives their real name, *Miss Hudson*. I told you, I can't guarantee the name or address, but I can the phone number. She's a regular. She's back in a couple of months.'

'She's already gone?'

'F'raid so.'

'How...?' Arlene interrupted herself. 'Forget it. Coupla months, when?'

Gloria scrolled down screen. 'September, four.'

'Scrap my August appointment, will ya? Can you book me in fer the third?'

Arlene ordered coffee at the nearest Dennys. While she waited, she looked at the torn-out piece of paper she had written on. The address was in Queens, in New York. She toyed with the idea of flying up there herself—using the phony passports Carter got for her and Peggy, in their Baby Jane names. She'd yet to test-fly hers—in the name of Blanche Hudson, so she had no idea if it was good enough to get her in and out of international airports. But she had never been to New York before. Wouldn't know her way around. Didn't know nobody up there.

But she did have a number and whole lot of ideas.

She would call her... call this... *Erika Xtravaganza*. But for what? And why? Notions were hitting her all over. She could hardly make head nor tail of what they were saying. First, she would get her story straight as soon as she could decipher what it was. But she knew it was big. Somehow, she knew she was on the precipice of her whole reason for being put down here on this Earth. Her guts were never wrong.

Arlene came back to the ranch talking a lot of silly ass shit. Peggy was out pruning the roses when she saw her—dressed for once, in a blue tracksuit—entering the house looking for her. Realising the house was empty, Arlene came back out onto the porch, searching the open terrain with her squinty pig eyes. Peggy shouted across the field. 'Put the kettle on. I'm coming in!'

She told Peggy she'd gone up to Mexicali, to some clinic, to get her gut drained—citing her bum leg for why she couldn't lose the weight the honest way. But on the drive back, she said she'd seen a message emblazoned in last night's sky, and it was this...

'The next Testament will be a movie.'

Peggy poured coffee and gazed through the window, annoyed at having been dragged in from her garden.

Arlene sat at the head of the table and seemed to be struggling to control things trying to escape her. 'Th'only reason the old and new testaments were books wuz cos that's all they had in them days. If they wuz wrote now, they would be movies! If they had cameras back then, there wouldn't be all ah this confusion and misinterpretation.'

'The camera cannot lie, huh?'

'S'right.'

Peggy gave Arlene her coffee, then sat at the opposite end of the long table. 'You heard of a little thing called editing?'

'I'll edit the fuckin' thing myself. With you—of course.'

Arlene sipped loud and looked at Peggy, who was still looking towards the window. Arlene said, 'You need to get behind this, Sister Mae. A lot of stuff along mah road hasn't always made a lotta sense. But this... You need to get behind this. God sent me to you. Us. Here. Right now. This ain't no accident. This is how it wuz meant tah go down.'

A lot of *silly ass shit*. Arlene was certainly full of that. But maybe she was right. Peggy had dutifully recorded the prophesies back when she lived in Santa Monica. They took them from her when they put her away. She wrote them again in the hospital—recorded them all again when she got here. Anything could happen. They could get lost or taken again. Somewhere, somehow, the prophesies must be presented to the world.

*A word unread is a word unwritten.*

But how could Peggy trust her? The woman was, at best, a buffoon. And at worst? Peggy suspected she had not yet seen the worst of Arlene Žiemelis. She looked at the old hippy who was watching her eagerly at the other end of the table, holding her mug in front of her like a bargain basement chalice. If the Good Book told Peggy anything, it was this: Jesus' disciples were as dumb as a sack of horse pucky, with a traitor among them to boot. That was all the friends our mad creator could spare his only son. Peggy had only the new gods to rely on now—the apostles in waiting who marshalled their messages through the television. Surely, they would give her someone better than Arlene to help spread the new gospels. Peggy's verdict was final, but she knew Arlene would ignore it before it even left her lips.

'No, Arlene. Best you leave them prophesies be. When the apostles are ready, they'll tell us. In their own way.'

# 49. DOWN

Neon Budweiser signs in the two dirty windows on either side of the door stuttered and fizzed. You could almost see the stink of half a century's worth of stale beer rise from the hardwood floor. The air was heavy. One of those afternoons where time has stood still and feels like nothing will ever happen again. But they will have driven an eight-hour round trip for this meet at the Oasis, so something better happen!

To the left of the bar, two men, cowboys, in sneakers, and a thin middle-aged woman with no arms played English darts. The woman's jeans defied gravity as they hung off her bony hips. The sleeves of her T-shirt lay forlornly over the cul-de-sac of her shoulders. One of the men loaded the plastic tube she held between her lips with a dart and—THUNK—she completed a spittle-dashed 180.

Carter, Arlene, and The Walrus sat hunched over beers at the counter where, via the big mirror over the bar, they had a panoramic view of the door behind them and the courtyard and highway beyond it, but Arlene couldn't take her eyes off the armless dart player. Arlene's so called 'mental problems' were a matter of opinion as far as she was concerned, but looking at that half-woman spitting her darts? Arlene would take a mental fuck-up over an *actual* one any day of the week. She wondered at the men with her... shit-kickers, Arlene thought.

Kin?

Carers?

Perverts?

A cluster of shacks five miles before Loreto on the east coast was a good enough place as any for a drug pick up. The Oasis wasn't isolated enough to stand out to casual scrutiny, nor surrounded by a population large enough to threaten a risky quota of snoopers.

Carter wouldn't normally accompany The Walrus and Arlene on these errands, but The Walrus told him his man 'Six'—a Vagos M.C prospect—had news that Carter might want to hear directly. Being off duty from the spiritual enlightenment business, Carter had dispensed with his usual Star-Spangled Mr. Kite attire and was in his 'Clark Kent's'—leather waistcoat and dirty denim. Only his orange tinted Elvis shades betrayed any allusions to religious superstardom.

Xander, the grizzly old Mexican ex-wrestler who owned the place, came out from his rooms behind the bar, scratched his belly through his vest and said, 'He's gonna be early.'

The words had hardly left his lips when Six's motorbike rolled and roared onto the forecourt.

Six came inside, and the group took their beers and followed him into Xander's back room. The Walrus and Six hugged big and addressed each other as brother. They all sat in overstuffed armchairs around the low table. Xander made himself scarce and went outside with a stepladder to replace bulbs on the roadside sign. Arlene didn't hold with all that 'brother' shit. She'd known bikers in Frisco and filed every one of them as 'would fold under questioning.' Six was desert-fried to the point of molasses, but his leathers were clean enough to suggest honest criminality. Undercover cops get carried away; go method and come on like a failed Mad Max audition. Knowing this made Arlene relax.

Six lifted the thermos out of his satchel and put it on the table. 'The Acid's gonna be late; a week. I offer this by way of appeasement.'

The Walrus threw an anxious glance at Carter. Carter sighed, unscrewed the lid and looked inside.

'Pills...'

Six scratched his beard. 'The future. Shit's gonna change the world. Ecstasy: the kids in Austin are necking these things like M&M's. Trust me bro, these'll keep the flock flocking back.'

'The future can wait.' Carter was unimpressed. 'A week you say—the Acid?'

'Round about.'

'What's the holdup?'

'The same old. Contraband of dubious transit. It marches to the beat of its own drum. Now, the Yayo? Readily available and in plentiful supply.'

Carter took his shades off and put them on the table. 'I'm into maintaining control. Difficult to control a flock that all think *they're* gods.'

Carter screwed the lid back and told The Walrus to take the thermos out to the pickup. 'You too, Arlene.'

These off-hand dismissals were becoming a regular occurrence of late. Arlene wasn't in a getting dismissed kind of a mood, but she went all the same. She lingered behind the bar long enough to hear Carter say, 'So, what news from our men in the north?'

THUNK!

A dart hit the board and jolted Arlene out of her surveillance. She stole a cold beer and stepped out into the heart stopping heat. The freezing beer was salvation in her mouth.

The Walrus reached up under the wheel arch and secured the thermos somewhere within the vehicle. Arlene guzzled the entire bottle and threw it across the highway.

The Walrus came and stood beside her. Together they gazed across desolate terrain. The heavens wobbled blue jelly. She looked at The Walrus' scuffed boots next to hers. 'What's the goin' rate for a knock-off these days?'

'A knock-off?'

'A. Sassination.'

Crashed cars and crushed armadillos littered Highway 1 as they headed south.

Carter drove.

What was the special information Six had for Carter? The mystery was eating into Arlene like acid—and not the kind they'd drove fruitlessly all the way up here for. Casual conversation with the Prophet seemed to be a thing of the past these days. An unsolicited enquiry as to what went down with Six at the Oasis was libel to send him into the kind of psychotic rage that would render some of the fits she'd witnessed at Patton mere hissies.

She was brutally aware that her failure to get a response from Charles Manson to her endless letters had severely damaged her standing in the court of Mr. Kite. Carter felt that any kind of acknowledgement from the great man would be just the blessing their Mansonite Church needed to take them into the next phase: The re-ignition of Helter Skelter.

Carter had retreated into himself, and Arlene knew she was losing her grip on the Queendom. They hadn't fucked for seventeen weeks. She had overheard him on the phone to yet another old girlfriend from home, talking about her coming down to join the commune: a visit that, she was sure, would usurp her once and for all from her throne.

Nobody said anything until a piss-stop in Ligüí. The men urinated with impunity into the landscape. Arlene squatted behind the truck. Behind them, the Gulf of California sparkled like a universe of diamonds.

Carter zipped up and watched Arlene's stream of urine roll to the edge of the road. 'Anyone know if San Quentin has a helipad?'

Arlene turned and realised Carter had been watching her. Self-consciousness in his presence was an unwelcome novelty. 'Think they've got a baseball field. If they needed to, they'd probably use that,' Arlene offered.

Carter paced back and forth across the highway, weighing up some internal conundrum. Finally, he deemed his accomplices worthy of his revelation. 'They're moving him south.'

'Who?', asked the Walrus.

'The Son of Man.'

Arlene buttoned her jeans. 'How south?'

'Not south enough. Probably to the new prison they're building in Corcoran.'

'By copter?'

'Well, *that's* what we need to find out. If they are—forget it. But if they're not... if by road... we could spring him.'

The Walrus and Arlene's mutual regard betrayed their astonishment.

Carter continued, 'Let 'em get him as close to Corcoran as possible...'

Arlene interrupted, 'If that *is* where they're moving him.'

'Right, or wherever, and we can take him out of that convoy... *take him out*! We could have a boat on the coast and get him into Mexico that way. Remember Arlene? Same way we were gonna get you out of Cali.'

'Only that boat didn't show. Remember?'

'Yeah, well for the Son of Man, we'll make sure that's boat's there.'

Carter stood, hands on hips, looking up the highway as if he could already see Corcoran and his fantasy unfolding somewhere at the end of it.

Arlene ruptured the moment. 'You even know when they're moving him, or how? And how do we know he even wants to be taken?' Carter turned to face her. 'Well, that's where *you* were s'possed to come in! He ain't answered none of your letters. Hell, I bet he don't even know who the fuck you are.'

'Believe what you will,' Arlene countered feebly. 'He probly ain't allowed letters. You thoughta that?'

'Ain't allowed letters…' Carter almost spat the words. He took another look up that endless highway, attempting to re-energise his dream. 'We're gonna do this.' He turned and treated them to the fervent glare he reserved for the climax of his apocalyptic sermons. 'We're gonna do this! It's comin' down.'

Arlene lay alone on Carter's bed. She mimicked the contours of the dusty concrete arches that formed the ceiling by running her tongue along the split in the inside of her mouth, where his slap had ripped it on her teeth.

The week had started beautifully. On their return from Lereto, she and Carter had test-piloted the pills they got from Six. The experience was beyond anything Arlene had ever known— even better than when she first came to the commune. Maybe as good as that acid she first took in '65 Haight-Ashbury.

In the mirrored doors of Carter's walk-in wardrobe, she had watched his powerful thighs as he gripped her legs up over his shoulders. Unable to climax, he had fucked her for what seemed like days. Her own ability to complete was all out of whack, but her failure to orgasm was more than made up for by the indescribable pleasure of her lost-in-sex delirium.

Even his voice vibrated deep, dark honey and chilled her to the core. All her senses were amplified and reverberated harmoniously. Arlene imagined that if there is a heaven, it was surely this. If not, then she was blissfully grateful to have experienced this in life.

They lay together in the sweet aftermath, and she received his private sermon to her. The sheer incomprehensible gorgeousness of existence was the dominant subject in his drug-drenched testament. But then a darker tone ensued. The subject of busting out Manson returned, along with the real and imagined difficulties of performing it. Due, it seemed, to Arlene's inability to contact Manson for information. She said, 'Do we need him... really?'

Carter leapt from the bed and into the persona of Mr. Kite. 'Resurrection comes in all kindsa forms. Releasin' the Son of Man from the crypt of the correctional system is a clear statement. People will know! With us, nothing is impossible. Unnerstand?'

'S'posin' he don't wanna *be* freed?'

'Y'think Jesus thought to knock afore he rolled away the stone? Thought t'ask Lazerous if he *wanted* to be bought back?'

Carter's testament became a tirade until he'd worked himself up to a terrifying frenzy—culminating in a hard slap to Arlene's face as she tried to pacify him.

It wasn't the first time she had suffered the sharp end of the Prophet's frustrations. In fact, it was the seventh. But, in the spiraling fuzzy warmth of a not unpleasant comedown, she was irremovably fixed on it being the last.

The intricacies of rescuing Charles Manson from the clutches of an army of federal marshals were irrelevant. Arlene knew Carter Haines' mad plan would never come to pass because Arlene Žiemelis' cooler head and colder heart would prevail first.

# 50. SCHISM

## 1988

### Saturday August 20th

The house was big.
Big enough to lose a family in... or herself.
If only.
Its 18th century whiteboard colonial charm defied its storm-whipped roof, which rendered the north end of the attic unusable. It was suitably gloomy and fulfilled some deep-seated sense of drama she immersed herself in; dramatics that would have her turn around and just catch sight of one of her faceless doubles leaving a room or lurking in the extremes of her own field of vision. The direct approach was not an option when encountering one of her other selves. Sometimes she heard breathing at her shoulder, her own breathing. These short rasps, slightly out of synch with her own, created the effect of a short echo. When she closed her eyes to sleep, she felt she was drifting into the cavernous mouth of a giant. She was now on familiar terms with her stalking ghosts—the legion that waited outside at night. Preferable, perhaps, to the multitude of personalities which haunted her when pumped full of Patton State's mysterious drugs.

*'Just me and my shadow...'*

This evening, she sipped coffee in the kitchen and stared out of the window and into a dark purple hue which hung across the plains.
The air swelled.
She had the spirit.
It was almost the hour of six.
She felt it in her lower back and barren hips.
It was time for the next instalment.

314

*'But when it's twelve a clock, we climb the stair, we never knock 'cos nobody's there...'*

The Walrus had helped her erect the telegraph poles and cable to the temple where Carter had the big mast installed. Lucy Hartman' vaginal communications continued to be beamed right into Peggy's room, courtesy of CBS North America.

In her room, behind the headboard in a recess in the wall, was where she kept them—her new tapes. The spines of the cases were named and numbered in her terse but florid hand. She had filled fifteen of them now. All identical grey TDK C90 cassettes. Only five Gospels of the Seven Apostles were complete. Tonight, she would begin the first tape of gospel six.

So far, these testaments told of how, in the late 22nd century, man would be able to move from the earth to heaven and hell at will. This ability came at a price and would ruin the earth until it was uninhabitable. Ore, millions of times stronger than earthly steel, would be mined from other dimensions and used to build a land above the poisoned earth. Eventually, the entire planet would become multi-storied, and humanity would be lost in its darkness. The fifth received gospel told how humans would be cursed with mutilated genitalia and thus the beginning of human extinction. Satan, wearing a woman's face, would create an artificial race capable of conception. But the real reason for this new race would become known: an army created to invade heaven and kill God. But God had given us a second son who might raise his own warriors—with the help of the Seven Apostles and prevent this ultimate parricide and save all of creation. But along with the rest of humanity, this second son was also lost in the darkness. A barren woman would be tasked with the mission to find him and reveal unto him his purpose.

Gospel six would reveal how.

Peggy wondered if, somehow, *she* could be the barren woman who would save God and the world. So now every waking moment was fraught with the screaming white fear that something would happen to her; that her pursuers would finally track her down before she could complete the

315

Prophesies. With only two gospels to go, all things would be revealed. She had been thwarted twice before. This could be her final chance.

She sat propped up by pillows on the bed with the box between her legs, but as soon as she opened it; she saw that the ninth tape was missing. Her ever-present double slid quickly past her into the bathroom. Peggy leapt from the bed, grabbing the hunting knife from the bed-side table, 'Cunting bitch!' and chased her. She tore the shower curtain away. As always, the other Peggy was gone.

*'Just me and my shadow...'*

With this revelation, sanity made a feeble appeal. The double was the produce of her unstable mind. Perhaps the missing tape was also. She tipped the box out on the bed.

No.

The ninth tape; part three of the fourth gospel; *had* been stolen!

She took the shotgun from under the bed, ran down the hill, across the cemetery and into the temple. She stalked the long over-lit corridors, looking for Arlene's dorm. A door opened and Mr. Mustard almost walked face first into the end of her gun. 'What the f...'

'Shut up! Arlene's apartment: Where is it?'

Mustard's mouth gaped like a hooked sprat for a moment, his eyes fixed on the barrels which were almost in his mouth. 'End of the hallway... forty...'

She headed for it before he spluttered, '... three.'

She came to the door and was about to kick it open when she heard a voice from inside. The voice was her own... reciting the prophesies. Peggy knew she had guessed the right Judas. She kicked the door. Her sneaker'd foot bounced off. She cocked the gun and aimed it at the lock. The door opened and the face of a nervous young man peered out and recoiled on sight of the gun.

Peggy shouldered her way into the room. Arlene stood in the far corner, surrounded by at least fifteen of the commune's residents who were sitting facing her on the floor. Peggy was shocked to see that Arlene had cut and dyed her hair in the style she used to have it during her modelling years. The tape, on a hidden deck, played on.

*'They were lost. Lost to the dark lands...'*

All eyes were on her when Peggy raised the gun, aimed it at Arlene and yelled, 'Shut that tape off or I'll blow your face right out the back of your damn head!'

Arlene's hands went up.

Peggy's eyes darted this way and that, looking for the source of the sound. Arlene pulled a Derringer seemingly from out of nowhere and regained the drop. 'Put it down, Sister Mae.'

Peggy pulled the butt tighter into her shoulder—her resolve turned to iron. 'Shut it off, Arlene.'

Arlene reached for the tape deck on a small table behind her and stopped it.

'Now, hand it over!' Peggy commanded.

Everyone on the floor stayed there, not daring to breathe as the two women faced-off and set to kill each other.

Arlene lowered her voice, but the gun remained levelled at Peggy. 'Sister Mae. Hold on now. I'll give it to you. But just... put it down...'

'Tape!'

Peggy felt a cold spot on the side of her neck. The shared tension of the seated congregation ramped up a notch with the appearance of the prophet Kite, who had slipped into the room behind her, wearing just a jockstrap and cowboy boots.

'Okay ladies, how 'bout we dispense with the gunplay?'

He pressed his automatic harder into her nape, accelerating his point. Peggy would not be moved. 'Her first!'

Jovially Kite said 'How 'bout it, Arlene?'

The absurdity of these two old gals in a showdown tickled him. 'Well, we're in the right country for a standoff, right?'

Kite's quip relaxed the room a notch. Recklessly, he kicked Peggy's shotgun up out of her hands, yanked her hair back with his left hand, and chinned her with his gun butt with his right. He stood over Peggy, who was out cold. He yelled, 'Arlene!'

Arlene's gun disappeared back to wherever it came from—concealed somewhere within her taffeta robes.

Kite shoved the nearest girl on the floor with his booted foot. 'Go fetch me that shotgun.'

She did. He shook out the shells and addressed the room. 'Does someone mind telling me what in the blue fuck is goin' on here?' Everyone looked at Arlene. She absorbed the scrutiny and turned it into resolve. 'We're discussing scripture.'

'Yeah, what part?'

'We were just getting started...'

'Horse shit! There ain't a dang thing that goes on within these walls that I ain't privy to. You're a Judas, Arlene—plain and simple. Consider yourself, and the 'Queen of the Pin-ups' here, cast out!'

# 51. CUT

**M**exicali's main drag was a choking hot smorgasbord of heavy traffic, both vehicular and human.

Peggy was double-parked outside the surgery on Bénito Juárez as sheets of sweat cascaded off her due to the late afternoon heat. Gratitude at the sight of Arlene was not a usual occurrence for Peggy, but grateful she was as the short dumpy woman in a billowing paisley shirt emerged from the glass swing-doors of Dr. Adrián Manjarrez Cortez's clinic, limping at surprising speed across its manicured lawn. The last thing they needed now was a run-in with some cop.

Arlene's face was mummified beneath fresh bandages, but she still managed to manoeuvre a Marlborough between them as the van coughed and spluttered and joined the rush hour chaos.

Peggy had to ask. 'So whatcha have done?'

'My nose. An' a bit o' chin.' Arlene exhaled slow and said, 'Why d'ya chicken out?'

'Ah nevah agreed to it in th'first place, Claude.'

'Claude?'

Peggy took off her heavy sunglasses and handed them to Arlene. 'Put these on.'

With difficulty, Arlene wiggled the glasses onto her face. Peggy flipped the passenger sun shield mirror down. 'Claude Rains—The Invisible Man.'

Arlene's attempt at laughter was rendered a wheezing choke. The sound caused both women to laugh hard.

Arlene had broached the subject of evasive surgery almost as soon as Peggy regained consciousness in the van after Kite knocked her out. According to Arlene, Mexicali was something of a plastic surgery mecca on account of quality and price. Peggy said she would think about it. She did, and that was as far as it went. Subjecting herself to a stranger's blade conjured up the nightmarish rumours that spread around the wards of the asylums that once held her. She was not chicken. Big hats, sunglasses, a phony passport, and driver's licence offered all the security she felt she needed, thank you very much.

They stopped off for groceries before returning to their hide out—an El Vado Motor Court. They chose it at random and had now been here for three days since being banished from the Mansonite Church. It was pleasant enough—freshly painted in white and orange, with multi-coloured bunting and lights which hung at zigzags over the expanse of the car park. It was a bit too near the border for Peggy's liking, but Arlene told her, 'There ain't no place better to lie low than in plain sight. 'Sides, all eyes are on that border. S'long as you ain't comin' or goin', no one gives a fuck whut goes on either side.'

But then, they had to be *somewhere*. Peggy, taking Arlene's theory to its furthest possible conclusion, considered the possibility of going back to San Bernardino and renting a place right next to the hospital from which they'd escaped. But it was an idea that would remain a fantasy until she figured how to get her tapes back. In their hurried expulsion from the commune, along with the fact of Peggy's semi-consciousness due to Kite's sucker-punch, the tapes were, God willing, still in her room in the recess behind the headboard.

Whilst putting away the groceries, Arlene told her, 'Don't worry—we're going back and gettin' them tapes.'

Arlene had an uncanny knack for guessing what was on Peggy's mind, an ability which seemed more pronounced every day. Then again, maybe it was due to the fact Peggy could think of little else.

'And what about Carter?'

'Don't you worry about Mr. Kite. Prophets have a way of being crucified on the beam of their own celebrity. It's part of the deal.'

'What did you *really* make of that resurrection?'

'What about it?'

'How'd he do it?'

'Who cares? Point is it backfired. Half the flock freaked out and left.'

'And now us with 'em.'

'I tole ya, we're goin' back. We're gonna git them tapes and… Sister Mae! Git away from the window!'

Peggy had a habit of haunting windows. She wanted to see all traffic—*vehicular and human* that came and went. It was something she had done since she could remember. Peggy remained where she was, peering between the closed curtains into the blinding light.

'And then what? You got any more young studs with remote farms stashed away?'

Arlene closed the cupboard and jammed the crumpled bags in the trash. 'One day at a time, sweet Jesus. Inspiration will present itself when it will. Who knows? Maybe your prophesies will tell us.'

Arlene's answers unnerved Peggy; the '*I know something that you don't*' tone was at once reassuring and irksome. The stark reality of the unfinished testaments haunted her as persistently as she haunted windows.

'We need to get to a TV—where we can get Showtime Tonight…'

'Sister Mae…' Arlene always referred to her as such, never with her own name. '… the prophesies *will* soon be complete, and all will come to pass. I got ideas, see.'

320

It had taken them two days to make the drive up from Todos Santos to Mexicali. They had been escorted off the commune by a couple of Kite's shotgun-wielding lady ministers. They let them take the old camper van and told them to fuck off. Arlene had stashed two Gs in the Jockey Box—having anticipated just such an ignoble eviction. She dropped a handful of those pills she took and did all the driving. Peggy slept for most of it. Nursing what she feared was a broken skull, but even in her semi-concussed state, she realised that their shared predicament had obliged them to join forces.

During the brief interims of consciousness, the women talked movies; the actors they loved and the actresses they wished they had been. Peggy told of her time at Herbert Berghof, of her triumphs and the actors she worked with who went on to successes that remained forever lost to her. She stopped short of that last audition with RKO at the Roosevelt—an event which seemed to 'full stop' the dreams of her previous life and herald in the one she had been in ever since.

Arlene apologised about the tapes; for snooping and borrowing. She explained how she overheard Peggy recording them in her room one night and understood, for the first time, the meaning of rapture. Sometimes, like Peggy, she was forced to confront her illness; doubt her sanity. But she memorised what she heard and recited it to a few of the least enamoured of Kite's flock. 'Man, them rubes were goin' fer it, Sister Mae.'

Their response galvanised Arlene's newfound belief that the Prophesies of the Seven Apostles could be the truth the world has been waiting for. Over coffee and pancakes at a roadside diner in San Felipe, Arlene put it to her that 'A gospel unheard is a gospel unwritten. Receiving the Word was only the beginning. Have you even thought about how you're gonna spread it?'

She had. 'I figured the final testament would tell how to reveal it. But...' Peggy paused while Arlene lit a cigarette. 'Remember what happened to Apostle Paul?'

Arlene did not and said so.

The waitress refreshed their coffees. Peggy waited for her to move on before continuing. '*He* had to make a decision. The

Roman's woulda suppressed the gospel of John if Paul told it like it was—how Pilate made the decision to crucify our Lord...'

'What's this about a pilot now?'

'Pontius Pilate—the prefect of Judea. The original gospel told how Pilate and the Roman's wanted Jesus dead, which made them the bad guys. Well, they couldn't have that. So, if Paul wanted the story to survive, he had a little bit of editing to do. So, they came up with that cockamamie story, 'bout how Pilate let the Jews decide his fate—and we all know how that panned out. Everbody's been bustin' on them Jews ever since. So, in a way, it's all Paul's fault. Change the facts to have *most* of the truth be known or have the whole thing cut down and no one'll hear any of it. I want the *whole* truth to be told.'

Arlene promised Peggy that she wouldn't let the Roman's or any other motherfuckers mess with the Next Testament, as they now referred to it. The Next Testament would remain pure.

Arlene's face was still healing behind her bandages a couple of days after her latest visit to the clinic when she announced they should think about heading back to the Ranchero Pineda. With the surgery and motel bills, they were down their last $600. She was dyeing her greying hair in the sink—careful to keep the surgical dressing dry with a towel tied around her head. Like a one note Pollock, splashes of blue stained the general area.

Peggy was happy to let nature take its course with what was once her own crowning glory—a course that was taking it through battleship grey and into a cul-de-sac of silvery white. Her once famous bangs were no more. Her high forehead, now lined and weather-beaten, had been emancipated from the chains of her youth.

She put it to Arlene that she should at least wait until her surgery healed. Arlene wouldn't entertain it. 'The longer we leave it, Sister Mae, the more chance someone's gonna find them tapes. And whut then? Can you remember all that stuff? Remember—we don't want the *gist*—we want the authentic word, right? Live and direct from the holy vessel that is Lucy Hartman.'

Peggy realised she was standing at the window again. She moved away, boiled the kettle and made coffee neither of them wanted. She sensed Arlene standing watching her from the bathroom door; her wet blue hair, damp bandages across her nose, and an ever-present cigarette dangling from her sulky bottom lip.

Peggy said, 'You know, you look like some Wizard of Oz character that didn't make the cut.'

Then, from out of nowhere, Arlene came back with this. 'I didn't tell ya; at the clinic I met a fan o'yours. This woman was, like, your double—y'know, when you were young? She came down all the way from New York to have some work. We got talking an... ah... turns out she's a big fan. Says a lot of people are. She had your hair style an everthing. Even the clothes. She looked like she stepped right outta one o' them old magazines o yours.'

Red stop sign.

Hot needles.

Why hadn't Arlene mentioned this before? Surely an occurrence like that would have been more newsworthy than reiterating her 'chicken' taunt when she picked her up from the clinic. 'You're making a point, *Sexy Sadie*...' She knew that reference would annoy her. 'What is it?'

Arlene stubbed the cigarette out on the wall, where it stuck briefly before joining the others on the floor. 'Just sayin.' She disappeared into the bathroom to rinse and shouted back. 'They're all wondering what happened to ya. Whatever happened to Peggy Deveroux...'

Peggy grabbed a bread knife from the drawer, charged into the bathroom, put the blade to Arlene's bandaged face and screamed, 'What did you tell her?!'

'Nuthin! Fuck!'

'I will cut you open. What did you tell her?!'

Arlene held Peggy's manic stare with one of her own. The splattered blue dye everywhere offered a litany of Rorschach possibilities. Arlene let a minute of silence reign, then softly said, 'Mae. Sister Mae. Put it down. Go on...'

Whatever devil had so suddenly taken charge vacated Peggy just as quickly. She wandered vacantly back to the window and seemed to address the world outside when she said, 'I thank you for helping me with the Prophesies, Arlene, but I swear I will cut you down if you talk about me, to *anyone*.'

They went out to see *Peggy Sue Got Married* at Cinepolis. The one where a worldly-wise Kathleen Turner goes back in time and tells a teenage Nic Cage to get out his wang. Later that night, with their conflict seemingly forgotten, they discussed the movie while Peggy showered. Arlene waxed lyrical about how she'd like to go back in time and fuck all the guys she should have done when she had the chance. While they were on the subject of ancient history, Arlene swung the chitty chat around to Peggy's modelling days, about how she got into it in the first place. They had covered this ground before, but there was always another nugget to be gleaned from repeat hearings. Some microscopic minutiae that might one day scream volumes. Arlene knew better that anyone; that the devil is in the detail. Peggy stepped out of the shower stall, drying her hair. As they spoke, Arlene noticed for the first time the small, jagged scar in the back of Peggy's right calf.

Sometime in the early hours, Arlene got up and snapped a Polaroid of Peggy's bare legs as she slept on her face. Arlene would make one final visit to Dr. Adrián Manjarrez Cortez before they headed back to the ranch.

# 52. STAR AGE BLUES

The final rays of a brutal sun were barely screaming over the mountains when the camper stopped in the desert half a mile away from the north-east perimeter of the ranch. The women made the rest of the way on foot. Climbing the ten-foot barbed-wire fence was not an option.

They'd brought the spade from the van and dug. They were getting nowhere fast. Twenty minutes had hardly made a groove in the hard soil. Peggy grunted, 'To hell with this!' and took the spade and hit the fence where it was nail-gunned to wooden posts. By the time the fence tore away enough of a gap, allowing room for entry, the day had screamed its last.

In the distance, the mood-lights around the temple were yet to come on. They approached the big house as the newborn night offered its dark cloak. They entered through the back door, stood in the hallway, and listened. Nothing but a creak as a gentle breeze worried the hinges of a distant door. They slunk along the hallway to the bottom of the stairs. Their long shadows threw that one-note Pollock again—in black.

They climbed the staircase and went to Peggy's room. Peggy pulled up the headboard and reached deep into the recess. Arlene went straight to the bathroom, removed the bandages, and studied her healing nose in the mirror. It was still bruised and swollen, so a verdict would have to wait. She went back out into the bedroom and this time she did the window haunting. Seeing a dim halo of light from around the area surrounding the temple, Arlene said, 'Not a whole lotta shakin' going on. The place looks deserted.'

Peggy extracted the tin from the wall and tipped the tapes out on the bed. 'They're all here.'

Arlene rummaged in her bag and tossed her the one she'd stolen. 'They are *now*.'

Peggy put the tape in the tin with the others. 'Try the TV.'

Arlene pushed the big button. The tube began to warm. From out of the on-screen electro-chaos, sound and vision emerged. 'We've missed tonight's show.' Peggy said. 'The next instalment of salvation will have to wait till tomorrow.'

Arlene messed with the aerial and made things worse. 'The lord our saviour will be back after these important messages...'

Peggy put the tin in her rucksack. Arlene put the aerial on the floor, which partially did the trick. 'You got any more guns here, Sister Mae?'

'No. You're not thinking of going down there?'

325

'Got a confession to make—I called Carter's private line when we were up in Mexicali—y'know, for yuks, and your little Chihuahua picked up.'

She was talking about her boy-about-the-house and chauffeur, Pedro—AKA the Walrus. Peggy was not oblivious to the son-like deference the young man displayed—just as Arlene would not allow her to remain oblivious to what she would do with him in the sack, given half a chance.

'Said Carter's gone; taken a powder.'

'And you believe it?

'Damn *right* I do. Followed ya round like a pup, that one—'

'Carter wouldn't just leave. This, the church, the ranch... it makes no sense.'

Arlene quoted the prophesies. 'The Final Testament—tape three, side two, minute four—*And when God saw the kingdom he had made and saw the enormity of his vanity; he rendered his universal paradise a dark void of burning suns.* Maybe Kite had a similar epiphany. Or maybe his mama called him home t'finish school an' be the rodeo clown he always shoulda been.'

They took the shortcut across the graveyard, holding their oil lamps in one hand and kitchen knives in the other. The silhouette of the temple towers loomed ominously ahead. All signs of life were non-existent. Peggy's stomach rolled as her fevered psych created the belief that they were about to come upon the scene of a mass suicide.

The entrance to the temple flashed erratically as mosquitoes hit the bug light above it in fits of blue sparks. Arlene led the way across the hall to the pulpit—a piece of hot-rod Gothic art made from impossibly polished walnut and chrome bike parts. Behind it was the stairwell down to the dorms and Carter's private quarters.

Arlene stage-whispered, 'Welcome to the Führer bunker...' Ten steps of a spiral staircase led down into a narrow stone corridor that stretched out and died in the void. The corridor threatened collapse. It promised rats.

Their descent into dank, dead air was as if into a vat of icy water—all but wet. Their feeble lamps suffocated in the dark and were barely able to create an areola of light more than a few inches around them. Their slow progress, past the dorms and into the void, concluded with a heavy wooden door. Behind it, a low rumble. A man's voice could be heard intoning over and over, *'Number nine. Number nine...'* Arlene put her ear to the door and held Peggy's gaze and gasped, 'The Beatles...'

Arlene nudged with her shoulder and the door swung slowly open. The room was a giant carousel of mirrors. It took a moment for her perception to calibrate and make sense of the space around her. On a red velvet Chesterfield sofa, Pedro the Walrus sat playing a bass guitar with his foot up against an amplifier. The room was every inch the armoury it was built to be. Around the mirrored room were shelves of guitars, firearms, and ammo. One way or another, Carter was preparing for a noisy revolution.

Pedro hardly had the chance to put the bass aside when Arlene galloped across the room and dropped ass-first into his lap. The two kissed passionately. Clearly, nefarious intrigue had transpired between them, and Peggy realised Pedro had always been Arlene's spy.

*Number nine... number nine...*

He seemed oblivious to Arlene's swollen face. His eyes were huge black saucers. Arlene said, 'Are you loaded?' and cackled delightedly. Peggy moved to the stereo and turned it down. Her meagre recollection of the fab four differed wildly from the unhinged mantra that shook the room. The notion that this is how *She Loves You* sounds when you're off your meds did not escape her. She got frank... 'So, where's the prophet?'

The boy's mouth hung open. Arlene seized the zeitgeist. 'It's *you* now, Sister Mae.'

Peggy saw the shotgun—the one Carter kicked out of her hands before knocking her unconscious—leaning against the amplifier that Pedro had his foot on. Daddy had one just like it. She cocked it, checked it, saw it was empty and snapped it back. The hippie and her spic stooge continued to suck face.

327

Peggy aimed the gun at the turned-off TV screen and said, 'I'm just a messenger. I ain't got no inerest in leadin' the sheep.'

Arlene pushed away Pedro's insistent face. 'Whadya think of inviting Lucy Hartman down here?'

'Again, with this. For whut?'

'For direct and un-obscured access to the testament, is whut. This thing's takin' too long. We need to step it up a gear, y'know what I mean...'

'And how do you propose to do that?'

'Leave that to me. I got ideas... unggggh!'

Pedro jammed his hand between Arlene's legs and began to rub hard. She hitched up her oversized shirt, flicked the belt catch on her slacks and gasped, 'Wait a minute baby...' She thumbed them down, revealing pale legs. Pedro tore off his shirt and plunged his face between her bruised thighs. Her right leg flipped up and around his head, pulling his face in tight. Peggy saw the fresh dressing on her calf but paid it no mind. His fingers edged desperately between his jaw and her pubis and managed to pull the gusset of her dirty orange panties aside. Her bad leg flopped aside, affording better access.

Peggy took the shotgun and retreated to the door. Without shells, the gun was just a threat. But usually, a threat was enough. She made a mental note of Mr. Kite's stockade-like inner sanctum and supposed the proximity of his rotting corpse added an aphrodisiacal dimension for the unlikely duo's fuck fest.

Arlene whined like a motor with a worn gear assembly, interrupted herself and moaned, 'Sister Mae... ughh... you need to get summa this...'

Peggy had already left the room when the worn gear assembly accelerated. The noise reverberated down the corridor like an animal being slowly eviscerated as Peggy ascended the staircase up behind the pulpit.

Across the darkened hall, a group of people were gathered around the arched entrance. Her squinted effort to identify them bore zero fruit. The hall amplified her voice to a Wagnerian degree. 'Who the hell are you? Whadya want?'

328

The group shuffled nervously as Arlene's distant screech fuelled its hellish ambience. Peggy reassured them. '*Don't* relax. It *is* what it sounds like.'

There were about eight of them, and of no discernible gender. One stepped forward. A male voice announced, 'We're here to follow the Prophet Kite.' Another said, 'We've read of the miracle.'

The issuer of the announcement moved down the aisle towards her. The others followed. With their cagoules and hooded sweaters, they appeared like a team of lost mountain climbers.

They surrounded the pulpit from where Peggy seemed to absorb some provisional authority, their faces hopeful, beatific. She drummed chipped nails against polished walnut and returned their eager regard. 'Read? Read whut?'

One of the two women—with a face too young for the grey hair that surrounded it—answered 'The National Enquirer.'

Peggy contained a sneer and intercepted it with a timeshare huckster's grin. She would play with these fools. 'Mr. Kite's work here is done. He has embraced the Holy Spirit and paved the way for the ascension. And it begins now... with *you*.'

Peggy retired back to the big house. She continued to receive the fragments of the prophesies and once again manage the farm—a task made easier now as new arrivals continued to appear in the wake of the Enquirer's *'Pineda Ranch Resurrection'* story. Carter had prophesied that news of the miracle would spread. And it did. Peggy put the flock to work, and within two months, the newly named Next Testament Temple was once again virtually self-sufficient.

If Arlene and Pedro had done Carter in, where had they disposed of the body? The graveyard was the obvious contender—perhaps the very plot at which the Prophet Kite had performed his first and only miracle. And speaking of which—what had befallen the risen soldier? Nothing had been seen or heard of him since the Enquirer interview.

But it was Arlene's transformation from New-Age buffoon to Boadicea-esque alpha-bitch that was the real miracle of

Ranchero Pinada. Within weeks, she had filled the messiah-shaped hole left by the celebrated Mr. Kite; her interest in the tenets of the Mansonite Church diminishing exponentially as her star within the compound rose

# 53. CORONATION

## Wednesday September 28th

You would think a morning like this would be too bright for surprises. But no. Two cops, one black, one white, ambled as if from nowhere as Peggy was about to start working the tamarind patch at the back of the house. She hadn't seen nor heard any approaching car, so if the idea was to catch her unawares, she considered herself caught.

The white one said 'Morning, miss. I'm federal agent Hubbard. This here's agent D'Oyley.'

Hubbard offered his hand. Peggy speared her shovel into the dirt, wiped her palm on her apron, and shook it—relieved to find it dry and cool. Both men were preppy and clean. Black suits, white shirts, black ties. The black one, D'Oyley, with his big sunglasses looked like Ray Charles. This made Peggy re-access Hubbard who, with his tortoiseshells, looked like Dave Brubeck. Hubbard undid the one button on his jacket, put his hands on his hips and admired the house.

'Quite a place you got here.'

If they were here to arrest her, she figured they would have done just that. Before the questions. She leaned on the standing shovel.

'How can I help you boys?'

D'Oyley stepped in. 'We just want to ask you a few questions...'

'Y'wouldn't be here if y'didn't, right?'

Hubbard asked, 'When's the last time you saw Carter Haines?'

Peggy kept D'Oyley in her peripheral vision as he looked around the yard in front of the house while she answered Hubbard's question.

330

'*Carter Haines*...' She said it like she had to think about who he meant. 'Coupla months ago, maybe. I don't have a whole lot to do with the goings on down there. I just stay out the way. Mind the farm...'

D'Oyley cut back in. 'Is that your function?'

'My function?'

'Mind the farm?'

She sucked through her teeth. The scent of Azaleas gladdened whatever part of the brain it is that flowers gladden. 'Pretty much.'

Hubbard took the reins again. It appeared to her that they shared a single persona, which seemed to hop between the two bodies, just as her own inner legions fought over the one.

'People are saying he just up and left. What do you think?'

'Ah don't have no opinion about it. I wasn't here when he left, and he was still gone when I got back.'

'Got back? From where?'

'North.'

'For?'

'Agent Hubbard, is it?'

'Hubbard. Yes, m'am.'

'It's kinda embarrassing. I had some work done in Mexicali.' She lifted her chin and waved around the general area of her throat. 'See.'

Agent D'Oyley came over and lowered his sunglasses and squinted at the directed area. 'Uh huh... Looks like a good job.'

'It was that...'

His eyes were small and mean—like a couple of weevil holes in a post. The 'fits all sizes' cop persona leapt out of him and back into Hubbard. 'So, you came back, and Haines was already gone?'

'S'right.'

Round one. No clear winner. Hubbard started round two. 'I'm sorry to ask, m'am, but can I trouble you for some identification?'

'Got a driving license somewhere around. Any good?'

'Driving license'll be fine.'

She went inside the house, to the kitchen where her shoulder bag hung on the door. She watched the agents through the window, kick stones and converse, while she retrieved the phony driving license that Arlene had gotten for her from Carter, via his biker-gang connections. Had they spoken to anyone else at the commune, or was she the first on their list? The agents were waiting on the porch when she came outside. Both had removed their jackets, but their ties remained straight and unloosened. She handed the license to Hubbard, who, without even looking at it, handed it to D'Oyley, who sat on the bench by the door, placed it on his knee and copied the license number into a small notebook. The document had never been put to the test. She watched him carefully, waiting for something to raise flags—give her away.

Finally, he stood and handed it back. 'Thank you, Miss Hudson.'

*Hudson*: Arlene's little Whatever Happened to Baby Jane joke. They were sisters now. Arlene was Blanche, Peggy was Jane.

Hubbard flung his jacket over his shoulder, gazed in the direction of the temple compound, and lowered his voice conspiratorially. 'Obviously, Mr. Haines still owns this place. Course, if he don't show soon, the Haines clan will, and claim it. The family are money'd up and are very keen to locate the prodigal son. Reckon anyone with information to that end would be rightly rewarded.'

The statement hung in the air a beat. It suddenly occurred to her that they might not even be real cops; that they were as phony as that license. 'I tole ya, I don't know nuthin' 'bout where he went.'

Finally, that single personality split into two and one said, 'Thank you for your time, m'am,' and wandered off down the hill to the temple.

Peggy shouted after them. 'Whut parta Texas you boys frum?'
The other shouted back. 'Austin, m'am!'

She turned to go inside, but the sight of a buzzard not thirty feet away, at the edge of the cornfield, stopped her in her tracks. It was stretching the guts out of another beast of ambiguous identity. Beyond this display of natural savagery, a woman stood in the middle of the field.

The redhead's visage shimmered in the heat. Peggy knew she wasn't really there because the woman looked exactly as she did when she went with her to that RKO meet and greet back in '57. Peggy had forgotten all about her. Why was she seeing her now? The redhead's voice seemed to echo in the distance and Peggy knew, somehow, that something had happened to her on that very night. Peggy strained to decipher the words, but they were worlds away. She would pay it no more mind. Her own death, like everyone else's, would one day answer all her questions. She turned and went back into the house, leaving the ghost of the redhead who she last saw fingering discordantly at that big piano at the Roosevelt Hotel—that flame of hair spiralling down over her pale cheek as she played her own death waltz.

The squeal of noisy electric guitars and drums violated the warm night. Black vinyl curled, folded, and shrivelled in on itself as the fire devoured Carter Haines' record collection. Arlene had decided to emphasise the changing of the guard with a ceremony. How this differed from the rest of her increasingly regular desert parties was impossible to tell. Membership of the commune had swelled now to a hundred and thirty, with new arrivals bringing minds, bodies, souls and money to the Next Testament Temple almost every day.

Peggy had decided to leave it until the evening before venturing out to see the results of Hubbard and D'Oyley's visit that morning. Once again, she needed to see Arlene and, if it's not too late, get their story straight. She half expected to find the place abandoned yet again, and Arlene and her flock arrested. But clearly the Federal Agent's visit had left the commune unaffected.

Peggy stared into the epicentre of the blaze and succumbed to its hypnotic glow. Some of the congregation crowded around the towering bonfire, sharing her trance. Most of the others, men, women and children, danced with the same fit-like rhythms as the flames that consigned Mr. Kite's earthly effects to the heavens. It was clear that all were under the influence of some drug or another. Peggy guessed that where Carter attracted followers with a persuasive doctrine and irresistible charisma, Arlene controlled her flock with the mind-altering pharmaceuticals that Pedro procured from the local biker gangs who effectively policed the Baja Peninsula.

It was only now that Peggy was irrefutably convinced that Haines was dead. She knew as well as Arlene that if he returned and found what had happened to his precious collection that he, to borrow from his own vernacular, would kick Arlene's fuck hole until she haemorrhaged her lungs.

Directly opposite her on the other side of the bonfire Peggy could just make out another of her doubles, emptying a box of records onto the blaze. People cheered. The fire roared. The acrid fumes of the burning vinyl loaded her nostrils and began to have a hallucinatory effect. This double was naked and considerably fatter than her actual self. The heady effect of the fumes had her ignore the vision at first until she noticed the larger, floppy breasts sported nipples small and mean. Peggy thought of Agent D'Oyley's 'weevil hole' eyes. The woman limped to a nearby steamer trunk and bent over to grab another handful of albums to hand out to her adoring crowd. The clear sight of heavy scarring on the vision's right calf jolted Peggy out of her trance and she knew right then that this was no hallucinatory double—it was Arlene!

Peggy had not seen the self-appointed priestess since she removed the surgical bandages after their return to the ranch. Then, her face was still a swollen mess of bruises. Now her hair was jet-black and fashioned in the style of Peggy's modelling days. But now Arlene's *face* was different. The slightly bulbous nose was neater and pert—the woman's chin was... well... now she had one. So, *this* is what she herself would look like if she put on any more pounds.

Arlene's grotesque parody grabbed a cigar from the mouth of one of her young suitors and began to shimmy around. Peggy pushed her way through the crowd to get around to the other side of the fire. Finally, she managed to get behind where Arlene was dancing with a young man who was gripping her dimpled ass. Peggy stood behind her quarry who was oblivious to impending death. She braced herself to push Arlene squarely in the shoulders—already envisioning her own screaming face, as worn by Arlene, blistering, and popping as the flames peeled it away. Peggy stepped forward and her foot hit something on the ground...

Arlene's bag; a Cheyenne-style embroidered holdall.

Arlene continued leaping around and whooping it up.

A reprieve.

Peggy scooped up the bag and took it to the nearby temple.

The main hall was deserted. In the incandescent glow of nearby candlelight, Peggy tipped the bag up and emptied it out on a bench. Pill vials, cigarettes, a roll of dollar bills, pesos, a hip flask, and an embroidered purse—a suburb of the bag it lived in. Peggy took out the driving license.

LICENCIA DE AUTOMOVILISTA – PEGGY MAE DEVEROUX

Arlene's adjusted physog smiled convincingly from the photograph—a surreal violation. So much for Sister Blanche Hudson...

Peggy's first instinct was to go back out there and do what she originally intended—throw the woman to the flames—let Hell do the rest. And then it became clear. Something fell into place, like a distant gear hitting the right cog. The machine hard-wired to Peggy's mind began to turn.

She went back outside and dropped the bag where she found it. The crowd continued to yelp and prance around the roaring pyre. Bare feet slapping and whipping up desert dust. Arlene, with her stolen identity, screamed in orgasm as she sat astride some anonymous young man.

Peggy took the shortcut back across the graveyard with the noise of Arlene's coronation fading into the night. Somewhere vultures screamed. Snakes wrested jackrabbits. The blue moon's dead eye lighted the way.

335

# 54. VENT

## Friday October 7th

I t would be gone midnight by the time she finished tending
the garden behind the house. Tonight, the Bajaian moon
was so bright that she could leave the floodlights off. A wall
of towering cacti obscured the distant fence, and it was on
nights like these that she was truly transported to a better
world.

Fig trees, dates, and tamarind flourished. And those oranges!
Put the ones they deprived her of back at Patton to shame. The
soil here really was kissed by something wondrous. It was
inconceivable that all things were not the product of a once
benevolent consciousness. The Prophesies held that the
Earth's survival was due to the protection from an exploding
sun afforded by the moon—once a thriving paradise. In 2167,
the seven angel prophets—the new apostles—will find our
self-exiled creator and appeal for his love once more. It would
be gardens like Peggy's that would entice him home.

Usually, you could hear coyotes howling ten miles away. But
tonight, all that could be heard was the low growl of trucks as
they rolled into the compound like impending danger.

Had the Haines clan finally come to reclaim the Promised
Land which she had called home for these three years?

She was not privy to what deal, if any, Arlene had managed to
strike with whoever now owned the Ranchero Pineda—or
what story she had concocted to explain Carter's
disappearance. Was it possible that she had somehow
managed to legally acquire this paradise? It would not be
unrealistic to assume, given Arlene's Machiavellian zeal, that
she had done just that.

It had been a couple of weeks since the police had questioned
her, and since Arlene proclaimed herself High Priestess of her
pack of lunatics. But recent and sustained activity around the
temple issued fresh storm-warnings. Newcomers continued to
join Arlene's circus. The temple walls were surrounded by a

refugee camp of Winnebagos and caravans. The tents of those who had walked or hitchhiked stretched out into the wilderness—a primary-coloured shanty town.

This activity continued all over the next day. The same trucks seemed to be coming and going and could only be shuttling from town. She had to investigate. See what the hell was going on. It was just after six in the evening when she grabbed the keys from where they hung in the kitchen and took the Ford flatbed truck.

It was a mile of dirt track from the compound to the highway; another eight to town. Traffic on the 19 betrayed nothing of what had befallen Todos Santos, but by the time Peggy hit Hidalgo, the place was grid locked. Some kind of carnival was taking place. The truck growled and crawled as far as Centenario before she had to pull over onto the sidewalk to escape the jam.

The usually sedate town had been invaded. Packs of journalists and news photographers seem to prowl and pounce. Locals were conspicuous by their complete and total absence. A crowd of women in the centre of the plaza stood together and posed—many of them aping her style from her pin-up days.

*Hot needles...*

One in particular, from where Peggy sat, appeared to be her exact 1950s double. She seemed to be their leader and was being interviewed by a microphone-wielding woman—hideous in comparison, caked in rouge and super-power-dressed in a mauve pantsuit. Somehow, thirty years had just died.

The local chapter of the Vagos motorcycle gang had taken over the bandstand nearby—bemused and excited by this oasis of raven-haired beauties as they tottered in high-heels on the uneven flagstones. The gang's sleeveless leathers hung from the handlebars of their hogs—green and red insignia declaring outlaw status. Energised by the attention, Peggy's clones struck shapes and paraded before the cameras.

337

Rowdy crowds jostled her vehicle good naturedly, where it was stranded on the corner of the Delegacion building. Through the windshield, Peggy had a clear view of the theatre on the other side of the plaza. The facade was covered in giant posters—an Igor Krane shot of herself in knee-high lace-up boots, wielding a whip—across it, big cinematic letters...

RESURRECTION
THE RETURN OF PEGGY DEVEROUX!

A young padre outside seemed to be quarrelling with random passers-by—his long head quaking under the weight of his argument, objecting perhaps to the proximity of these racy images to the Iglesia de Nuestra Señora del Pilar church on the south of the plaza. The Teatro-Cine, it seemed, was the centre around which all this lunacy was spinning. Her distant youth had returned and splintered into hundreds of identikit facsimiles—posing and vamping as hordes of lenses hungrily devoured them. In front of the church, a film crew had set up and panned their camera across the square.

Peggy sunk in her seat and pulled her straw hat down over her eyes. Madness was everywhere—her madness—spilled out onto the streets of Todos Santos. Her doubles—her shadows—had vacated her addled mind and joined the throng who drank and sang at the blazing sun.

She knew Arlene had ignored her refusal to be involved with the Next Testament movie, as proven by the trucks of film equipment that had been making regular deliveries to the ranch for the last six months. Some of the flock could be seen wandering around the ranch with cameras, shooting what looked like nothing in particular. She had to chase a few of them out of her garden. She knew the project had gone ahead, but had no idea that Arlene was already launching it out into the world.

Peggy had lived under stones for thirty years. Marriages, bible schools, insane asylums... all the suns in the cosmos could not make her forget how she lived in the shadows; a darkness she shared with her inner crowd. And now this; torn from bladder

338

to throat—publicly dissected. This carnival had turned her inside out. She was so close to sanity she could feel its hot breath behind her ear. She was exposed now in the most humiliating and obscene way. A chill of clarity wiggled down her spine, into her desolate hips, and back up into her heaving chest.

One thing was now irrefutably clear.

This time, she *really would* have to kill Arlene.

### Saturday October 8th

Peggy's senses returned when she found herself driving south on the 19, back to Todos Santos at nearly 5am the following morning. The truck was sounding funny. She got out to see what the fuss was all about and saw Arlene, broken, twisted, and jammed into the grill. She tried to pull her out but could not un-jam the fat traitorous bitch.

Options.

The sun was about to rise. She could hide out and maybe spend the night in one of the abandoned houses by the beach. But it was busy. Too many people. Men's voices—a whoopin' and a hollerin' somewhere between where she stood on the highway and the sea. Time was a wastin'. She remembered the wrecked cars up on drums a hundred yards back.

She walked back the way she had driven and saw a naked man limping down the highway. Was this the man that Arlene's girls had on the ground before she ran her down? It was a fair bet. She ducked down into bushland and let him pass, dragging a lame leg behind him. Yeah, it was him alright. He would soon find the truck, and Arlene's corpse, and see that justice had been done.

When he finally disappeared from view, hobbling south towards the town, she started north. She came to the second of the wrecks and climbed up into it—a half-crushed VW Beetle Campervan, not unlike the one that Carter had first brought her and Arlene down here three years ago. It had been rear-ended—concertinaed up to the back wheels. Splats of tar-like black blood coated the dash. She got on the floor, lay between

339

the benches, on a bed of windshield fragments, and stared up at the splintered interior. She had a bag of tomatoes. She had a flask of water. And she had her tapes. The heat became unbearable, so she removed her sweat suit and lay deathly still in her underwear. She flittered in a no-man's-land of dreams and half-sleep. The highway became busy for a while and woke her in fits and starts.

The sun rightly came up, and, finally, she slept deeply. She awoke a couple of hours later and decided to wait for it to go down again before making another move.

Options.

Go back to the house.

Re-group.

Re-think.

She'd made a pretty good job of wiping her prints from the truck. They'd have to be pathological about it to find any.

If insanity taught her anything, it taught her that it knew no time. She knew the sender of those sex-death threats she received all those years ago in New York never stopped chasing her. He could appear any time and as anyone. He would sometimes be her husbands, her landladies, her friends, her family. She could never tell. Trying to kill him always got her into trouble—got her put away.

Time died, and the sun died with it. The cold returned. Arlene the doppelgänger was dead. Peggy put her clothes back on and figured that the show at the Teatro-cine must surely be cancelled now.

She took her hat out of her bag and put it on. As predicted, it took her just a little over twenty minutes to walk to the outskirts of town. The crowds were gone, and the serenity of earlier days had returned. The square was an expanse of desolation. Broken glass, wood, and two overturned cars. She would head for Mr. Muñoz's market. He had always been very gracious, and her dealings with him had always been cordial. There was no reason, at all, that he would not be willing to give her a lift back to the ranch. As she passed the square, the few people she saw seemed to be wandering towards the theatre. Something was happening. The posters that flanked the entrance still hung in their frames. The Return of Peggy Deveroux now had 'Memorial Screening' plastered across them.

They were going ahead with the show.

# 55. THE NEXT TESTAMENT!

Her arms and legs were tied back with ropes to the legs of a padded stool. Her eyes were wide open, her scream nullified with a gimp-ball in her mouth, strap-tied around her head.

It was one of a series of monochrome blow-ups that hung over the entrance to the main hall of the Teatro-Cine. Marco gazed up at the huge slab. With an index finger hung over his cigarette he dragged slow and received some unidentified pang, beamed in, long distance. Her expression was cartoonish. A put-on. Somehow, you could see she knew it. As helpless as she was supposed to be, *she* was the one who was in total control, and the viewer, the dupe, the dope, the rube. The silky black panties between her open white thighs appeared impregnable—a veil of darkness concealing a spring-loaded boxing glove.

Pow!

He wandered into the main hall, which was starting to fill with people now. Into the purgatory of Erika Xtravaganza's dream. Rows of mannequins in silk and lace flanked the long walls—mass produced compliance arranged in onanistic repetition. He wondered how long it had been since these scanty creations, self-made, according to the plaques that accompanied them, hung on her. He toyed with the possibilities of what she might have been doing on the day she wore them last; what the world shook with when she packed them away for the final time—cosmonaut dogs and beatnik paranoia. Never could she have envisioned this destiny and where they would wind up all these years later.

The projectors, set to loop endlessly, clattered on the balconies. Beams of light jostled and switched, soaring overhead, across the hall, hitting their screens opposite—quasars of a pornographic Aphrodite calling through space and time. Effigies of glamour and cheesecake betrayed nothing of the woman's descent into madness. But the bondage and fetish-wear, in anonymous apartments and makeshift dungeons, declared nothing less. The bondage shots found her draped in a white-hot dread of restraint, compelling her to run and hide into the arms of lunacy.

Once again, Bonnie and her inexplicable decision to leave him occurred. Could there have been a reason beyond his belief that she was the phony he always expected her to be? How did she open her 'Dear John'?

*I'm going to do us both a favour...*

Had she been threatened in some way? Was she protecting *him*? This possibility had never occurred before. Only now, among these displays, did the fourth wall collapse and suggest... alternatives.

Battle-ragged film crews, descending from a collective comedown, continued to flood into the hall. Blood and mud-splattered t-shirts, torn pants... like a bunch of war correspondents who had been handed thousand-dollar cameras to track and kill a Pulitzer.

Marco checked the program. The Q&A would not be happening now. Not with its star, at least. He looked over at the star-spangled autograph table that would now not be occupied.

An over-reverbed minor chord wobbled out of the speakers. The gels above the stage turned blue. The diminishing light drew the crowd closer. The hall was still only half full now. The slaughter at the Pineda Ranch had upstaged Deveroux's resurrection and stolen her posthumous thunder.

The sideburns and corduroy guy Marco had seen opening Xtravaganza's Leroy Street club took the stage; said simply, 'Erika Xtravaganza', then scuttled off.

She looked shaken as she emerged from between the curtains. Her comportment of when he first saw her in New York on Friday compared to now was as distant as the miles they had both traversed. She wore a black velvet pencil dress. A matching pill box hat pinned to her tied up hair. The blue lights gave her a deathly pallor, and the concept of Deveroux's ghost appearing now to address the room escaped no one. She coughed politely into a gloved knuckle and absorbed the room with those hydrogen-blue sloe eyes. The noise notched down to near silence. She spoke softly into the mic. Momentary feedback squalled like a baby demon running for cover.

'Peggy Mae Deveroux was no ordinary woman. She was a dark angel with a presence that reached across the decades and bewitched us with an almost supernatural power that will continue to bedazzle us beyond the pale reason of her untimely death. But more than this; she was a trailblazer. A visionary who transcended her own arena and found ways of utilising her uncanny and seductive powers in ways unimaginable to most of us. Our friendship was brief and not without its conflicts, but very few profound experiences are happy ones. So, I relish every torturous exchange we had. She was a deeply religious woman. So much so that she believed that her ultimate mission was to find God. Whether or not you believe in such things, it would be easy to accept that God—as she believed—has abandoned us. She believed the second coming would return to help us find him. She had visions that there would be a Third Testament. But it would not be another book—not a tome of words that could be misinterpreted, edited, crossed out... or lost. She believed the next testament would be a movie. She often said that if the Old and New Testaments had been movies, then interpretation and distortion might not have happened. Naive? Perhaps. Optimistic? The case could be made. Visionary?' Xtravaganza scanned the room meaningfully. 'Absolutely.'

Ripples of discontent ruffled the ragged crowd. An anchor-man in a pith helmet behind Marco spoke for many when he muttered, 'What the hell has this got to do with tits and ass?'

Xtravaganza heard it, but then, she had heard it all before.

'The film you are about to see is a rough-cut of the movie she was working on before her tragic death last night. The Prophesies of the Seven Apostles as received from what she believed were from the heavens themselves.'

Xtravaganza stood away from the mic and, with an expansive sweep of her arm, directed the room's attention to the big screen behind her.

'Behold... Peggy Deveroux's Next Testament!'

The extinguished lights plunged the room into total darkness. The main projector in the back of the theatre powered up. Sound and vision hit the screen as Xtravaganza disappeared between the curtains below.

A title card appeared with the title in a jumpy typeface. The opening shot was of the old woman, Deveroux herself, as seen through the approaching windshield of a car, standing in the middle of a lost highway, halting the driver to stop with one hand and holding a movie camera in the other—a trailer-trash Libertas turned maverick film director. A nonsensical series of Noir-ish images flickered and hopped as Deveroux narrated in that thick, almost drunken, Tennessee drawl—smiling young boys and girls working the fields of Ranchero Pineda. Deveroux atop a hill, reading scripture to her adoring flock. Naked men and women dancing around a huge pyre... Marco recognised some of the dialogue from the tapes he listened to with Hernandez in her car. The preoccupation with genital deformations...

From the blackest recesses of the balcony, Sister Mae—the real Peggy Deveroux—watched Arlene's celluloid interpretation of the Prophesy of the Seven Apostles. She could see now. Arlene's film adaptation of her stolen visions played out for all to see. This would have been the opening volley of her deliverance of the prophesies to a wanting world. But Arlene's attempt to avoid misinterpretation had already failed. The

Word, as received from Lucy Hartman, and via herself, could not be translated. To give the Word a physical form was to distort it before it hit the page; before the light hit the celluloid of Arlene's cameras. That thing in her peripheral vision disappeared as soon as she looked at it. She realised now that it was an impossible dream. Like the good book. Everyone who read it brought their own malformed desires and came to their own private hell... heaven... salvation; then made the fatal mistake of inflicting it on others as The Truth. It was not a collective thing. It could not be shared. We were our own prophets, messiahs, Gods... Left to wander the wilderness of our desolate mindscapes.

After fifteen mind-warping minutes, the film faded into a credit-less void. There was some mocking laughter. The room bristled indignantly. Someone shouted, 'What in the *actual fuck*!'

Before the mood escalated into disorder, blinding lights hit the stage as a troupe of Deveroux look-a-likes went into a burlesque performance of perfect skin, mesh-hose and giant feathers, all to the pounding tattoo 'n' twang of some old Surf instrumental.

Marco assumed that Xtravaganza had anticipated the crowd's reaction and now offered this 'tits and ass' show by way of recompense. The movie reminded Marco of the trippy 'Mardi gras' sequence at the end of Easy Rider and wondered if Borg had drunk the whiskey that he spiked with the acid he'd found at Deveroux's lair. Why the hell had Xtravaganza agreed to show the film? Deveroux was dead now. Any agreement they had was null and void. No?

As the burlesque show played out below, Sister Mae's glory years screamed across the decades. The Xtravaganza woman who introduced the film must have been the one Arlene spoke about. The super-fan, intent to be her missionary, but this intolerable facsimile could not be anything but one of her inner selves; the ones that spilled out of her at night. According to the prophesies, they would not come to the Earth until the year 2160. Their appearance now would ruin everything. Sister Mae's madness would ruin everything. She regarded the room

345

below her, the multitude of her inner selves that came to her but did not speak, had now spilled out here, but were contained within these walls. When they came to her, they came under God's moonlit night. But now, along with the totems of her distant past, they were trapped.

She knew now.

How to be sane.

How to return.

How to send the multitudes of her tumultuous mind back to the perdition from which they came.

The projectors were heavy and hot to touch. She gripped a tripod and wrestled the first of them over the balustrade. It crashed down onto the polished wooden floor and exploded so spectacularly that she knew she would not need to upset the rest. Hot glass sprayed the room. The lingerie-clad mannequins immediately erupted in flames. An exhilarating tempest of blood-curdling screams rose up with the fire. She made for the stairs and fought her way through the crowds as they scattered away from the spiralling inferno.

Marco backed away from the soaring heat as the crowd surged towards the main entrance, creating a bottleneck of heaving terror. Having entered by the exits at the back of the building, he raced for the nearest one. He didn't see the woman, head hung low, as she barged into him, jolting him off course. 'Hey!' She ignored him and stomped with chunky legs towards the emergency doors. A lightning-bolt of pain shot down his right side and dropped him to his knees. Then he saw a pool of crimson expanding around him—flames and warped skylights in its reflection.

# 56. REWARD

'Get me the number for Patton State Hospital in San Bernardino… or put me through, please?'

Strauss necked the receiver during the long-distance kerfuffle. Portland, at the other side of the room, seemed to be searching himself. 'Where the fuck is my badge?'

Strauss called across to him. 'Bill, can you call Reynder and...'
A voice came on the line, interrupting his request. *'Putting you through now, sir.'*

Strauss told the hospital receptionist who he was and who he wanted to speak to. It took nearly three minutes for this to happen. The man introduced himself as Managing Director, Carlo Madden.

'Good evening, Mr. Madden. Apologies for the late hour. This is Agent Strauss of the City of Austin Police Department. I'm working a case down in the Baja and need confirmation as to the current status of one of your patients. To put it bluntly: escapee. If we run a name by you, how quickly can we get an answer?'

'Can I ask what this is about?'

Strauss detected exasperation in the director's tone. 'It's about a case that requires an urgent response, Director.'

'With all due respect, how do I know you're a genuine police officer?'

'Strauss sucked it up. 'We may have picked up one of your escapees. We need to confirm their identity.'

'Any and all escapees would have been reported to San Bernardino PD, as and when,' the director said quickly, 'So you would need to speak to them as to any progress.'

'My case concerns two murdered police officers. To cut to it, Mr. Madden, we have fingerprints of one of your patients who may, or may not, be involved. Now, how do you suppose that's possible?'

'Agent Strauss; can I suggest you may have answered your own question?'

'My question to *you* is can you confirm the incarceration status of an Arlene Žiemelis? Is she there or not?!'

'Again, Agent Strauss, this is something you will need to run past San Bernardino PD. I'm sorry I can't be of more help.'

Strauss noticed something had drawn Portland to the window.

'Well, I thank you for your tremendous help, *Mr. Madden*,' Strauss said dryly. 'We'll be sure to catch up with you again, in person, *real* soon.'

Strauss slammed down the phone. 'Prick!'

Portland tuned away from the window and said, 'There's a fire at the theatre.'

Leonard Borg's mind was blown.

At first, he thought that his meds were either failing or working spectacularly. The palm trees, the sea, the sky; even the grains of sand around him swelled with beatific significance. The hilarity of chance—of the molecular accident of this moment in space-time—claimed his free-falling mind. He tasted the metal in his mouth and knew Mascini had put something in the whiskey. He stumbled along the beach back to town. To hell with the honourable way. He would kill the kid—squeeze the life from out of him—then put his trusty old Ruger to his own head blow his brains out, right here on this impossible beach. He fast-forwarded to a scene of his corpse spread-eagled on the sand—surrendering to a sky that wobbled and harmonised into a chord he could ride out into eternity.

He welcomed it.

He wanted it.

And then he saw the oily black columns of smoke pirouetting up from the roof of the theatre and into the pulsating blue...

All understandable notions of direction were warped. Geography was now a dark art. But somehow, he made it to the back of the theatre.

Hernandez's orange car was parked nearby.

Mascini was here.

The back entrances were hung with loose chains and were unlocked. A half-assed deterrent. He shouldered the door open and found himself in a blue-illuminated corridor. Beyond it, he could hear yelling and screams. His spine shuddered pure ecstasy.

Peggy Deveroux barged through the exit door into a blue corridor where she saw that red stop sign.

The one she always saw when she sensed danger.

Red-hot needles.

Before her.

The man.

Waiting for her in the grand concourse of Grand Central Station on a cold December morning in 1957. The one she always knew would come for her.

Borg saw her. A short dumpy old woman, her eyes sad and defeated, froze on sight of him. Something like a flash gun went off in the back of his mind.

She was alive!

Had her raped corpse come for him now?

His mind spluttered and choked as his lungs did likewise. The grey-haired woman in the magenta sweat suit before him stared from a place somewhere between reproach and despair, then morphed into her 8th Street, 1957 self.

The cacophony of that Manhattan Street melted and there she was, young and smiling, in whore's apparel—garter belt, nylon stockings, brassier... She began to dance. Out of proportion to the svelte upper body, her hips sashayed like a puppet as she cavorted around the lounge area of a small anonymous apartment to the abrasive mantra of clattering projectors. As she bounced around, she held a stuffed clown toy and Borg imagined himself as a cartoon too. A big bad wolf, a monkey man. King fucking Kong.

The blaze consumed the hall behind her and created a hellish backdrop as she morphed again, now into a celluloid Salome. Her breasts were those of a teenager, functional, polite mounds that made the faultless orbs of that derriere all the more obscene. Tits of a girl, ass of a fuck goddess. A combination that had sent men to confession, and more... to hell. Bluto Borg was blowing her house down, fighting with her huge headed bulldog in its doghouse, taking delivery of ACME rocket skates, lifting the entire shack above his head, and dropping it down over them, trapping her. She squealed as he chased her around and around in a big bouncy red house...

Bluto Borg saw himself fucking her with a cock bigger than himself, giant pink, endlessly pumping into her as she squealed in comic alarm. Her belly grew until it crushed them both

349

against the walls and ceiling of a red, yellow, and blue cartoon kitchen...

Disney spunk flooded the room like a tsunami as Borg pulled his giant pink cock from her swollen belly, trembling with immediate pregnancy. A baby Peggy popped from between her open legs, all big fluttering eyes and bald, and into the end of Borg's red jelly helmet. And then another, and another, and another until Borg too, swelled with pregnancy and baby Borgs squeezed from his ass; hundreds of them until the room bounced with the rhythm of baby Borgs and Peggys—all fucking happily... De beaux rêves, mon amour...

The big bald man seemed to freeze before her—consumed by some internalised horror. The muscles in his face sagged. A sick prank? She pulled the knife from her bag and prodded the space between them. He groaned and wheezed as air escaped him. His mean little eyes followed her as she moved tentatively past him. Expecting a sudden lunge, she put the blade to his eye, but he remained frozen. She had seen her fair share of fits and seizures in her time, but this somehow stood outside the natural order of things. The skin was smooth and perspiring. She could see him now at the platform turnstile of Grand Central Station, in his camel coat and Derby hat, his eyes telescopic and inescapable. She remembered the accident... screams... commotion on 8th Street...

She could hear the same screams and commotion now. The building around them; a hurricane of swirling, flaming, roaring hell.

Up on the balcony, the last working projector ray-gunned its monochrome Peggy Deveroux dream onto the roiling dense black smoke. In quick succession, the last of the mannequins folded in on themselves, surrendering to the flames. The surging crowd had crashed through the doors of the main entrance and out into the square in a riot of spluttering vomit.

Left alone in the inferno, Marco dragged himself up from the thick puddle of his own gore and dragged himself up onto trembling legs. Through the smoke, he could almost make out the green exit sign to the back of the building. He threw himself through the emergency doors and saw Borg convulsing like a jammed frame of a stop-motion movie monster.

*You'll turn into a pillar of salt...*

Marco charged headlong into the stricken man. The force propelled them both through the exit doors and into the alleyway. He could hear voices—recognisable—Strauss and Portland shouting for help. The smell of murder. Wet cardboard, stale food. And the metallic taste of blood in the air clogged his failing mind as he faded into credit-less black.

## Sunday October 9th

A minute past midnight: The 19 joined Highway 1 like an old boyfriend. A reunion that promised all a them 'lovin' it up' good times and none of the bad. Higher ground loomed up in front of the orange car as it sped north, over the speed limit. Arrest held no fear for her now. They would only send her to where she wanted to go. She had destroyed the ghost legions that came out of her, so now she knew she was sane. She doubted it for a moment—when she opened the glove compartment and found the old cassettes that they arrested her with in Santa Monica back in 1982. But whatever benevolent power had given her this car was the same as the one who had now returned her original prophesies.
 No. She was sane now and fixed on proving it.
 She had found the Opel with the keys still in it down a side road near the theatre. With the fiery revelation in the rear-view, she knew now what must be done. It would take a day to drive back to San Bernardino if she only stopped for gas. The hospital had all the tests, the gizmos, the ways to find out what goes on in people's brains. They would take one look in hers and... hell, they'll probably let her out that same day.
 A mile north out of La Paz, with the town's few streetlights twinkling behind her, she saw him.

The hitcher stood at the side of the road. He wore a brown leather jacket, oil-stained jeans and had his long greasy hair tied back. But she knew who he was. He was the old soldier Mr. Kite had brought back from the dead. She stopped and let him in. As she drove into the aurora of the new day, the risen man stared sullenly at the shadowy hillsides.

Sister Mae broke the silence. 'Can I ask you something? Do you know if the Walrus killed Mr. Kite?'

'No, yo lo hice.'

'What? You?! Why?'

'Obtuve mi gran recompense…', the risen man muttered vacantly. '… y él me la quitó.'

'You earned your big reward, and he took it away?'

# 57. BACK TO THE WORLD

## 1989
## Tuesday May 23rd

**D**ale waddled into the canteen. His ruddy face heavy with epiphany. 'You will *not* believe what I've just found in Kappor's locker.'

Marco didn't look up from the new James Ellroy he was reading when he said, 'Do tell.'

Dale snatched the book from Marco's fingers and flung it on the table. 'Follow me, won't you? This has to be seen.'

Marco's cool appraisal of the fat man who stood over him did nothing to betray the sensual desire to do him serious physical harm. Clutching hot coffee in his own tin cup, Marco followed Dale outside—the air sweet with cotton candy—and along the boardwalk to the shower annex just beyond the dodgems of Astroland. The derelict and forlorn spike of the Parachute Jump, Brooklyn's Eiffel Tower, beckoned ahead, looking over them, as always, like some benevolent totem to an age when the world was a simpler place and dug this kind of shit.

This wan afternoon rendered Coney Island a shadow of its former glory. Many of the attractions were in a serious state of disrepair and covered with grey tarpaulin, which flapped in sympathy to the gathering winds off the Atlantic.

Dale worked the dodgems and was born for this line of work. His was a world of mindless toys and novelties that spun round noisily again and again, a land of hysterical laughter; and not without an air of the sinister, as encapsulated in the hardboard facades of giant clowns and movie monsters. If they ever made a movie about 'Killer Clown' John Wayne Gacy, Marco thought, Dale would be their man. Marco found it impossible to understand how anyone could derive any kind of joy from being thrown up in the air or around and around in these demented rides, but then he'd look at Dale—a product of these 'nothing' times—and it was as clear as a blue Kentucky moon.

Dale fumbled with his keys as they reached the annex, almost dropping them in his excitement. The door swung open. He hit the switch, flooding the locker room with anodyne light, fumbled again with the keys and unlocked 226. 'Check it out.'

Marco hesitated. 'What are you doing in people's lockers, Dale?'

'Security. We have to. Every six months.'

Marco placed his cup on top and saw the locker was empty but for a vinyl duffle-bag at the bottom. He threw Dale a quick glance, who licked his lips in quick anticipation; living the moment of discovery again through Marco, who squatted and loosened the drawstrings of the bag.

It was heavy.

Bills?

He peered into it carefully before reaching inside.

Magazines…

He knew right away where this was going, the glossy texture, the weight, the weight of a secret. He looked up at Dale.

'Percussion manuals, right?'

'Percussion manuals?'

'Jerk-off rags, fool.'

Dale trembled like the big fat jolly idiot that he was. 'You ain't seen nothing yet. Check it out…'

Marco, bored with this game already, slid a wedge from the bag. He stood up and regarded the cover of Man 2 Man—a well-oiled fruitcake shaving his chest. Now *that* he didn't expect. Marco flicked through the well-thumbed pages—this was the shit—24 carat San Fran; full-on hard-core 'sunk to the kidneys' fag rags.

Dale chuckled, 'The Hindu's a fuckin' fruit. Are they even allowed to be fruits?'

Marco glanced at the open door. 'Who else has seen these?'

'No one.'

'I'd keep this under your hat if I were you. You don't know these are hi Dale would not be denied his revelation and grabbed the magazines from Marco, quickly stuffing them back in the bag. 'These are the only other keys.' He slammed the locker shut, fumbled again and locked it—his discovery safe from parade-pisser Marco.

'I'm serious; don't be telling anyone about this.'

Dale's jaw dropped like he had a Twinkie slapped out of it. 'Fuck you! All that pious "let's all achieve dharma" bullshit. Just 'cos he's worked here forever, he thinks he's fuckin' royalty, the guy... the Pope of Stillwell Avenue! Fuckin' faggot hypnocrite...'

'Hypocrite.'

'Right!'

'Popes are Catholic, no?' Marco offered.

'Whatever.'

Marco took his cup from off the locker, made for the door and didn't look back when he said, 'If this gets around, I will throw you in the sea.'

With a pre-recorded hiss and a screech, Diesel Dennis pulled into the station. With long strides up the platform, Marco up sided the latches on the carriage doors, liberating a noisy crowd of infant passengers who ran out and into the waiting arms of their parents and guardians. A family of Cagoules— three of them all matching yellow—daddy, mummy and baby Cagoule interrupted his marshalling of two confused sisters back the right way up the platform. Daddy Cagoule spoke.

'I think my son has had a bit of an accident...'

Marco peered into the dark cabin of the front train with pursed lips. 'Don't worry. I'll take care of it.'

Diesel Dennis was a six-minute figure-of-eight train ride for kids; a locomotive with a face which grimaced dementedly as it trundled around and around a miniature plywood village. It was Marco's job to escort the kids into the little carriages behind Dennis, lock them in, hit the switch, send the train round twice and get them all off, ready for the next group. Dennis himself was only big enough for one kid and so most of them wanted to ride in the carriages in back with everyone else. But every parent, anxious to project their fucked-up-ness on their progeny, wanted their little darling to be the one in the front, whether they wanted to or not.

Every other trip and Dennis would get about halfway around when the kid 'driving' would suddenly realise they were alone in a dark cabin to a destination unknown. Then the screaming would start. Marco would hit the switch and go lurching over the fibre-glass mountains and cellophane lakes to rescue the kid who had by now pissed themselves with fear. This happened on Marco's very first day. He went to see the supervisor, Mr. Kluge.

'What do I do?'

Kluge told him, 'You mop it up, Einstein. The mops are in the fuse box cupboard.'

Marco had developed a thick skin in terms of what bullshit he was prepared to put up with whilst playing regular working stiff, but playing piss-boy to a bunch of knicker-wetters was a bridge too far. He ignored the puddle in Dennis' dark cabin and allowed the next kid on the next ride to sit in it, and then the next... and the next. After four or five kids, all the piss had been soaked up.

That was four weeks ago, and despite one kid in every ten letting go, Marco had managed to avoid reaching for the mop. Now, Diesel Dennis stunk like fucking hell. In a high wind, he was convinced the stench engulfed the whole resort and couldn't believe he still hadn't been rumbled. The next batch of infant suckers invaded the platform, and Marco ushered a cute little Korean girl into Diesel Dennis's cabin of piss.

Tonight's movie was at 9pm. Finally. His shift over. He had an hour to get to Soho. He dragged the tarpaulin from under the platform and shook away the puddles of rain trapped within. He stamped it flat and dragged it over Dennis and his pals. He jogged to the annex to get his bag from his locker and saw that 226 was still safely locked. The notion of breaking it open and disposing of Kapoor's bag of shame presented itself, but he let it go.

Kapoor had been off work for a week with an ailment that Kluge was 'not at liberty to discuss'. In light of today's expose,

Marco wondered if Kapoor had AIDS. If the papers and TV are to be believed, all the fruits have got it, and unless everyone miraculously stopped fucking, everyone else will have it too, eventually. Marco hoped whatever it was would keep Kapoor away for as long as possible.

Dale was right though; Kapoor was Coney Island royalty. According to all who worked here, he'd worked the resort since the late 60s. Back then, he must have been as much of a novelty as some of the attractions themselves when most of the neighbourhood's experience of Asian Indians was Peter Sellers. In Marco's near month of working at the resort, Kapoor was the first one to make the effort to say hello to him. Short, but with the remnants of a previously impressive physique now running to fat, he'd greet Marco every morning in his own tongue "Kemchu" and receive the reply 'Saruche,' which was as far as Marco's mastery of Hindi went. Beyond that, he knew only that he lived out on Rockaway somewhere and that he was married with a couple of grown-up kids. But a closet fruit? It would be—Marco had to admit—a revelation. There was nothing outwardly faggy about Kapoor, but then, his faith would be a factor. He was a Hindu, but *how* Hindu? Dale and the rest of the fools that worked the resort would be compelled—if by nothing more than their own idiocy—to do something about Kapoor.

Part of him welcomed this inevitability. He'd be hard-put to imagine anything more satisfying than having an excuse to bitch-slap Dale's stupid, fat face.

Scorsese's latest was showing on a rerun at the Forum. God's whack-job protesters of last year were long gone now, leaving the blasphemers to see the movie and go to Hell in peace.

Afterwards, he did a detour on the way home and stopped for a cigarette across the road from the Brevoort. He drew hard, and he drew strength from both monstrosities—the tube of tobacco he was killing himself with, and the brutal panorama of glass and concrete that towered over him. Mark Twain had lived in a hotel here before they built this monolith... and Buddy Holly moved in.

Satan, disguised as the angel that leads Willem Dafoe's Jesus Christ from the cross to his last temptation, came to him now in the form of Bonnie Rachanski. His own brush with crucifixion exploded into surgically sharp relief. He had sat there in that near empty movie house and remembered how it was *her* face he saw on that Mexican ranch as he hovered before the great void. Unlike the stab wound that had punctured his right kidney, the terrors of Todos Santos were yet to be exorcised.

### Wednesday May 24th

It was nearly midday. Diesel Dennis had had an unusually busy, but so far piss-free, morning. Marco had barely hit the start button to send the ride round when the next crowd was already forming at the gate. Marco watched Dennis trundle around until his attention was taken with the sight of a couple of girls in shades leaning against the pier's balustrade, smoking as a photographer unpacked from an aluminium case. Both were wearing pedal pushers that looked like they'd been sprayed on—one a leopard skin design, the other glossy black—her legs looked like they were made of liquorice. One was a blonde. Hair curled into a Monroe do and punctuated with a black rose. The other girl had hers black and piled high—an Empire-State—Ronettes carry on. This visage took him back to that madness in Todos Santos—to the Peggy Deveroux look-a-likes who seemed to parade right out of 1952. His idle gaze across the bay, towards the misty rumour of Breezy Point, was interrupted with a shout. 'Kemchu!'

Marco turned to see Kapoor, a portrait of rude health, crossing the boardwalk and heading for the annex. Marco yelled back, 'Saruche.'

Kapoor entered the annex and Marco saw Dale and a couple of his goons from the concessions stand slip in behind him.

Marco grabbed the CLOSED sign from out under the platform and hung it on the gate. Most of the kids lining up were too young to read but understood that this was not good. They looked up and read mom and dad's expressions, which

358

confirmed it. Marco waited for the train to pull into the station, unlatched the doors quick-fast and ushered everyone off the ride. He reached down behind the box office and pulled the power. He vaulted the low fence and told the people who were still waiting, 'Sorry folks—back in ten minutes.'

By the time he reached the annex and entered, Dale was on the floor clutching his nuts as Hot Dog and Cotton Candy slammed Kapoor up against the lockers. Marco hindered a fist meant for Kapoor's head, twisted it down and found himself on top of Hot Dog with his knee in his chest. He followed through with a couple of quick digs at his man's mouth. Hot Dog deflected the third blow, brought his knee up hard into Marco's back and sent him sprawling face first onto the floor. Hot Dog was back on his feet and attempted a few clumsy stomps.

Marco caught his foot, twisted it, but the shoe came off in his hand. He threw it at his assailant's face, which bounced off with a klunk. The foot came down fast again, and Marco found himself gripping it within its sweaty sock. Somehow, he manoeuvred Hot Dog's ankle under his own right armpit and brought his left fist up into his balls. Hot Dog collapsed to his knees beside him; his groans upstaged by a bowel-loosening screech from across the room. From where he lay, Marco kicked Hot Dog out of the way and saw Kapoor had Cotton Candy in an arm-lock, his powerful left forearm around his man's throat, forcing his arm up his back and sinking his teeth into the back of his neck. Candy screeched again, 'DON'T DON'T DON'T...' Kapoor swept Candy's feet from under him and slammed him into the concrete floor. Dale was nowhere to be seen.

5.52pm: Just before the end of his shift, Marco heard the Tannoy squawking that he was to go see Kluge in the mobile cabin he was still using as an office.

'Did you know Kappor was a fag, Mascini?'

'I can't say the notion ever presented itself.'

Kluge moved around his desk, sat down, and scratched his chest through an opening between the buttons of his stone washed shirt. 'So, it's true?'

359

'Kapoor's being a fag or me knowing about it?' Marco fixed Kluge's gaze and said, 'Shall we cut to the chase?'

Kluge pulled open a drawer, took out a brown folded envelope and placed it on the desk. 'Your week-in-hand and the two days you just did.'

'What about Kapoor?'

Kluge's head tilted slightly, trying to find the correct angle to regard him.

'Those boys out there...' Kluge scratched an ear. '... I think he'll be going of his own accord.'

Immediately, Dale appeared in Marco's mind's eye, clearing the rail at the end of the pier. He glanced through the warped Perspex window at a mesh of shadows on gravel outside. Somewhere above them, one of the Cyclone's trains trundled over rickety tracks. Riders screamed.

# 58. EPILOGUE

**JOURNAL: JUNE 1st, 1989**

I found her. In what's left of the Deuce. A video tape in a 42$^{nd}$ Street porno parlour.

'The Last Temptation of Christine'
(A Fourth Reich Production, Culver City, Los Angeles)

The lurid colour photo on the sleeve had her dressed in a latex habit and getting serviced by a couple of priests. I thought it was Deveroux or Extravanganza. She had the hair. The black-as-night Deveroux bangs. But it was Bonnie Rachanski. No question.

Summary: Profound experiences are rarely happy ones. I got drugged and blown by a guy. I nearly got crucified. I got kangarooed for murder. I carried a foot in a bag. I got stabbed. And Echo. . . Echo Hernandez. A damsel died on my watch. This cannot stand. I spent three weeks in a Mexican hospital and came back to the world. I embraced the straight life. It was not for me. Deveroux's hooks remain dug in, and there's nothing I can do about it. I dream now. Well . . . nightmares really. About the bugs. Drowning in a bathtub of bugs. With Deveroux and Hernandez standing there and watching me drown . . .

What if I hadn't seen that package on the bed that night? Blown myself into the next world and missed my own sequel. My movie is missing its love interest. . .

 She had come to me in the moment of certain death. . .

He never did find out who stabbed him in Todos Santos. Or why. He figured she must have been one of the women from the ranch trying to make good on their earlier attempt. But while he recovered in that Mexican hospital, Agent Strauss had told him that the woman they scraped off the front of that truck, and who tried to kill him up at the ranch, was not Peggy Deveroux. She was some old hippy method actor who escaped from a mental asylum and had herself cut to look like her—right down to the scar on her leg that had so convinced Leonard Borg of her identity. Strauss told him Borg had gone screaming bat-shit crazy and that they'd put him in a San Bernardino mental hospital. He felt guilty about putting so much of that acid in the whiskey he'd given him. But, hey; being a dyed-in-the-wool lapsed Catholic, guilt could go fuck itself.

## Monday June 5th

Years ago, a girl on the subway, obviously stoned, asked him, what year is this?'

He told her, 'Year zero!' But it really was now.

Mecca called him.

Hollywood.

The coming week would be a series of financial reckonings. That still sealed $20,000 he never trusted? He would have to trust it now. For one, the rent was due. Kuzma will be down there in his store, noon sharp. First Monday of the month. Marco would tell him today.

'I'm leaving town and I need storage space.'

'Coney Island, not work out?'

'I got canned. But thanks for the opportunity.'

'Too Mickey Mouse to work on the ding dings, huh?'

Kuzma came up to look at the apartment. He walked into the lounge, making an internal assessment of how many cubic feet Marco's earthy possessions might require. 'You wanna sell anything? The jukebox?'

The concept of letting any of his possessions go was a painful one but abandoning the totems of an existence that had already expelled him was essential. It would also mean he might not have to pack everything up. 'Give me a number and I will ponder.'

Marco handed over the wad of bills that would cover the final month. 'The jukebox won't include the records though, okay?'

The sign over the forecourt said, 'FOREIGN AUTOS OUR SPECIALITY'. He went in and told them about the Tatra 603 and that no; he didn't know what was wrong with it beyond six years of neglect. They came around with a trailer truck the following afternoon and took it away. Told him they would call him next week and let him know what a revival would entail.

362

Bonnie Rachanski still came to me in jerk-
off dreams. I remember her like a series of
outtakes. Her light fails me now, and she
remains unceremoniously edited, like a logo
they didn't get clearance for. Somewhere
over the rainbow I will make my director's
cut.

A week later, he got the car back. New battery, brake pads,
filters, tyres and a complete oil transfusion. The list was long
and beyond the reach of his attention as the guy read it all out.
It cost $2,010.56 + tax. The car lived. That's all that mattered.
  Kuzma told him, 'You will be facing the sun on much of the
trip. It's on the driver's side all day. If that piece of shit car
don't die on you, you'll make it in a week.'
  Marco drove the resurrected Tatra up through Delancey
Street, across town, under the Holland Tunnel and began to
devour the 2800-mile journey to the Promised Land.

She had come to me in the depths of chemical
dementia. She had come to me in my moment of
certain death. Now I will go to her.
I stabbed it, steered and pointed the car
west, towards Mecca. Hollywood. And if I
can't find her? Find out where DeNiro lives
and give him two in the head.


THE END
If you liked this type movie you can get more of this type film
from
IGOR KRANE

## ACKNOWLEDGEMENTS

To **Lux** and **Ivy** of **The Cramps** for that wonderful evening back in '85 and for alerting me to the storm warning that was to be… **Bettie Mae Page**.

(Photo by The Exotic Adrian Street)

Thanks to Cormac McCarthy, Don DeLillo and James Ellroy for the continued inspiration. Also… Mike 'Fats' Dalton for being the first to read this book, Judi Moore for her early notes; 'Southside' Jimmy Price and Shirley Jones for spotting those 11th hour schoolboy errors. And, especially, **Karen Lynch** for the major grammar overhaul.
And for much of the research material…

**The Real Bettie Page** by Richard Foster
**Bettie Page: The Lost Years** by Tori Rodriquez
**The Bettie Pages** magazines by Greg Theakston
**Bettie Page: The Life of a Pin-Up Legend**
by Karen Essex and James L. Swanson
**Eric Stanton and the History of Bizarre Underground**
by Richard Perez
**The Art of Eric Stanton for the Man Who Knows His Place**
by Eric Stanton and Eric Kroll
**Bettie Page Reveals All** by Mark Mori
**Howard Hughes – The Untold Story** by Peter Harry Brown
**Helter Skelter** by Curt Gentry and Vincent Bugliosi
**Charles Manson in His Own Words** as told to Nuel Emmons
And… **The Bible**.

## ABOUT THE AUTHOR

Adrian David Stranik is a musician from South West London.
His father was a wrestler.
His mother was not.
He lived in Milton Keynes.
He spent a lot of time in America's Deep South.
He now lives in Bedford, England.
Monomania, Mon Amour is his first novel.
He doesn't own any animals.

(Photo by Ben Chamberlin)

Printed in Great Britain
by Amazon

81050826R00214